CASA
Clara

Also by Kate McCabe

Hotel Las Flores

The Beach Bar

The Book Club

Forever Friends

Published by Poolbeg

CASA Clara

KATE McCABE

POOLBEG

Published 2011
by Poolbeg Press Ltd
123 Grange Hill, Baldoyle
Dublin 13, Ireland
E-mail: poolbeg@poolbeg.com
www.poolbeg.com

1

A catalogue record for this book is available from the British Library.

ISBN 978-1-84223-456-3

Typeset by Patricia Hope in Sabon 11.5/15.5
Printed by CPI Cox & Wyman, UK

www.poolbeg.com

Note on the Author

Kate McCabe is married with two children and lives in Howth in County Dublin. She is a former journalist and recently began writing fiction full time. Her first novel *Hotel Las Flores* was published by Poolbeg Press in 2005 and became an Irish bestseller, as did her following novels *The Beach Bar*, *The Book Club* and *Forever Friends*. Kate's hobbies include reading, music, travelling and walking along the beach in Howth while she thinks up plots for her stories.

Acknowledgements

I would like to thank the following:

My family: Gavin, Caroline and Maura for their enduring encouragement and support.

Marc Patton for invaluable assistance with computer problems.

The wonderful team at Poolbeg Press: Paula, Niamh, Sarah, Lisa, David and staff.

My eagle-eyed editor, Gaye Shortland.

My best friends, the booksellers.

And you, dear reader, for being smart enough to buy this book.

Hope you enjoy!

This book is for Pat Foley and Deirdre Morrissey
who have been with me from the very start.
With love and affection.

Fuengirola

Chapter 1

Every morning when Emma Frazer threw open her window at Casa Clara she was greeted with a scene that warmed her heart. Directly below her was a little cobbled courtyard with a fountain that splashed water from the gaping mouths of four bronze horses. And all around was a vista of flowers: pink and yellow roses, trailing purple wisteria, flaming blood-red geraniums spilling from their brown terracotta pots and pushing their bright heads to the sun. If she lifted her eyes a little higher, she could catch a glimpse of the sea beyond the pines, the morning mist rising like a pall of smoke towards the sky. It was a scene that never failed to uplift her and fill her with energy for the tasks that lay ahead.

Mornings were the best time but the evenings had their magic too. Then the air was cool and heavy with the intoxicating scent of the flowers, and the lights from the lanterns danced and sparkled off the water in the fountain. This was a peaceful time when Emma liked to sit and reflect on the day that had passed. And often she thought too of the transformation that had taken place in her life since she first arrived at Casa Clara four short months before.

Sometimes when she looked back she shivered at the terrible risk she had taken and how it could all have ended in disaster. There were times when she thought she must have been crazy – to pack a single bag and leave everything behind with no clear idea of where she might end up or what she might do. But she had no choice. She felt her life was being squeezed out of her. She had to escape. And in the end, she had found the Casa and everything had turned out fine.

The existence she had at Casa Clara was so different to what she had left behind. She thought of Dublin with its grey skies and rain-swept streets. She thought of her workplace with its mind-numbing boredom that was slowly driving her to distraction. But none of these things had been responsible. What had forced her to flee was the sense that a knot was tightening around her and the certain knowledge that unless she went, she would end up doing something she would regret for the rest of her life.

Casa Clara was a small hotel at the edge of the sea in Fuengirola, a thriving holiday town in southern Spain. It had once been a fine mansion with sturdy walls and gates and beautiful trees to provide shade from the unforgiving sun. It had been the home of a wealthy wine merchant but after he died the house gradually fell into decline until a local man, Miguel Ramos, had seen its potential and bought it for a song.

Miguel borrowed money from the bank and renovated the old house. He called it Casa Clara, in honour of his mother who he adored. He installed new plumbing. He hired landscape gardeners to replant the grounds which had become wild and overgrown with the passage of time. Out of the mansion's vast rooms, he constructed eighteen cosy bedrooms with en-suite bathrooms. He turned the former mansion into a successful business and then, a few years later, he suddenly died and left it all to his glamorous young widow, Concepta Alvarez.

* * *

Emma had first set eyes on Señora Alvarez late one evening in the previous April when she'd turned up at the reception desk with a single bag and nowhere to stay. She had earlier arrived at Malaga airport on a flight from Dublin, hailed a taxi and asked the driver to take her to a hotel in Fuengirola. And that was when she'd encountered her first setback. The young taxi-driver took her to several large tourist hotels only to find they were fully booked. Emma began to get nervous. She knew absolutely no one in Fuengirola, or the whole of Spain for that matter. She began to have terrible visions of ending up sleeping on a park bench or under a boat on the beach.

But the taxi-driver had come to her rescue.

"There is one last place we can try. It is small hotel, a bit old-fashioned. But it is right on the beach."

"What is it called?"

"Casa Clara, *Señorita*!"

He took her straight to the Casa. A glamorous creature with flashing eyes and coal-black hair sat behind the reception desk and checked the computer before announcing that they had received a last-minute cancellation and a room had become available. Emma thanked her lucky stars and gave the taxi-driver a generous tip. After she had signed the register and paid her deposit, Paco, an old man who seemed to double as concierge and general factotum led her up the narrow, winding stairs and along a corridor before pausing to lift a heavy bunch of keys from the chain fastened to his thick leather belt. He opened the door and showed her into the most charming little room that Emma had ever set eyes on.

The walls were bare whitewashed stone. At one end was a comfortable wooden bed covered in crisp white sheets. Beside it, a heavy chest of drawers stood with a vase of fresh flowers on top. In another corner, a large mahogany wardrobe sat beside a writing desk and chair. Paco pushed open another door to reveal a small bathroom with shower, bidet and toilet. Emma was overcome with relief.

She tipped Paco and the old man beamed with pleasure. She waited till he was gone then walked quickly to the window and flung it open. She was on a balcony looking down into the courtyard – her first sight of the scene that she would grow to love. The light was fading and a new moon was riding high in the sky but she could see the fountain and smell the heady scent of the flowers. She turned back and looked once more around the little room. It was perfect. It was snug and cosy and clean. But most of all, it was safe. She sat down on the bed and silently thanked God for directing her here.

After she had unpacked and had a shower, Emma began to feel hungry. She had been so relieved to find a room that she had forgotten to ask about meals. So she went downstairs again and inquired at reception where she was told that the hotel only served breakfast. Feeling slightly disappointed, Emma set off to explore the town. She had been here once before with a group of school friends to celebrate the end of their exams and she had pleasant memories of long, sunny days and star-filled nights, and the scent of orange blossom on the air. She strolled along the sea front past the fish restaurants and pavement cafés till at last she came to the Castillo. Now that it was evening, the old Moorish castle was lit with lamps. It looked majestic where it perched at the edge of the ocean, guarding the town. Emma climbed the winding path beside the walls till at last she stood, breathless, looking down at the dark, heaving ocean.

As she watched the lights of the ships passing on their way to Malaga, she thought of what the future might hold as the days unfolded. She would have to find work of course and somewhere permanent to stay. The small amount of money she had brought wouldn't last forever. But all that could wait till tomorrow. This evening she would relax and enjoy her first day of freedom.

At last she turned away and headed back to the town. Soon she was in a maze of narrow little streets that were bustling with life and filled with the aroma of cooking. She had eaten practically nothing all day and now she was ravenous. She came to a restaurant in a pretty little square and found a table outside.

She sat down and ordered a dish of prawns and rice and a half carafe of chilled white wine with a basket of crunchy bread. Above her, the sky was a bright canopy of stars. She could feel a cool breeze waft up from the sea. A wonderful feeling of contentment began to steal over her. No one would find her here. For the first time in months, she felt truly happy.

* * *

She woke early next morning to find the sunlight pouring in through her bedroom window. She glanced at her watch. It was almost eight o'clock. She had slept for seven hours and now she felt rested and full of energy. She would celebrate her first morning in Fuengirola by taking a swim in the sea. She wondered if there was a gate from Casa Clara down to the beach.

She pulled her swimsuit out of her bag and put it on, then quickly slipped into a pair of baggy pants and a cotton top. She took a towel from the bathroom and made her way down to the reception desk. But when she got there, she found it was deserted. She rang the bell but no one came. After waiting for a few minutes, she wandered out into the courtyard and found Paco and a young man setting up tables for breakfast.

"I want to go for a swim," she explained in her halting Spanish. "Is there a gate that will take me to the beach?"

"*Sí, sí,*" Paco replied and spoke rapidly to his young companion who stopped what he was doing and gestured for Emma to follow him. He led her past the fountain and down to the end of the garden where he showed her how to open the gate by tapping in a security code.

"What is your name?" she asked as she scribbled the numbers on a piece of paper so she would remember them.

"Tomàs."

Emma smiled. *"Muchas gracias, Tomàs."*

The young man blushed. *"De nada, Señorita."*

She skipped lightly onto the beach. It was deserted. She got undressed and stepped carefully into the water. It felt wonderful to be in the sea, to feel the cold, clean water envelop her. She felt so alive, so invigorated. She swam for twenty minutes, occasionally lying on her back and gazing up at the bright sun as it climbed higher in the morning sky. Then she got out and dried herself.

On her way back to the Casa, she saw that a buffet had been set up in the courtyard on a long trestle table. On it were urns of coffee and fresh rolls and plates of cheese, ham, boiled eggs and fruit. Emma sat down at a table near the fountain and had breakfast under a tree. Above her, she could hear the birds singing in the branches and the lazy hum of the bees as they foraged among the flowers. It was so tranquil, so peaceful. So different to what she had left behind.

She thought of the things she had to do. First of all, she had to get a job. She had no idea what she might do, but she was prepared to work at anything that would provide her with an income. And she would also visit some estate agents and see if she could rent a small apartment. If she was going to remain in Fuengirola, she would need a permanent base. By now, the courtyard was filling up as more people turned up for breakfast. But, as she drank her coffee, she became aware that an air of confusion appeared to have overtaken the staff. They seemed disorganised, rushing about as if no one was in charge. It was odd; last night when she arrived everything had been so orderly. She wondered what had happened to disturb the calm.

On her way back to her room, she met Paco again as he was carrying suitcases down the stairs to the hall. The old man had a glum look on his face as he stopped to let her pass.

"Is everything all right, Paco?" she asked.

He slowly shook his grey head. "Señora Lopez is no more."

"Who is Señora Lopez?"

"She is the lady works the reception."

"Was she the lady who checked me in last night?"

"No, that was Señora Alvarez. She is the owner. Señora Lopez works reception and now she is gone."

A terrible thought struck Emma. "Do you mean she is dead?"

"*No, no. Resignada.*" He waved his arms. "This morning she leaves. She says she can take no more of the pressure. Now we have no one in charge. Everything is confusion."

So that was the cause of the panic Emma thought, as she continued up the stairs to her room. The receptionist had resigned. Well, she hoped they would have the problem sorted out when she returned this evening. She preferred Casa Clara as it had been when she first arrived – a haven of peace and tranquillity.

She set off for the town and spent the day checking out employment possibilities. But this was when she suffered her second setback. Several of the souvenir shops had notices for staff but they wanted people with fluent Spanish and Emma knew that her grasp of the language was certainly not good enough. She sought advice at a little restaurant where she ate lunch and the kindly waiter explained that many bars and restaurants hadn't opened yet. Until the tourist season got fully under way, her chances of restaurant work were not promising.

She inquired at a few bars and got the same response. So it was with a heavy heart that she made her way back to Casa Clara that evening. And here she found another cause for concern. The situation had got worse since she had left that morning. Now the place was in utter disarray. Suitcases were piled in the hall, new arrivals stood patently waiting to register, but the staff seemed totally disorganised. She found the glamorous owner, Señora Alvarez, sitting at the reception desk looking very cross as she tried to cope with the myriad demands of running the little hotel.

Emma went up to her room, got undressed and took a shower. She could see that in a small place like this, every person would count. It just took one employee to be sick or fail to turn up for work and the smooth running of the operation would be thrown into confusion. And the receptionist played a key role in the whole business. She could understand why Señora Alvarez was looking so cross. And then a strange thought entered her head. She could do the job herself!

She shook her head. She was allowing her imagination to run away with her. But why not? She was desperate for work and prepared to roll up her sleeves and tackle anything. And here was a job staring her in the face. She tried to think of the tasks the receptionist would have to perform: answering the phone, taking bookings, making out bills and probably one or two other small chores. She could easily do it. She had some Spanish but, what was equally important, she could speak English and most of the guests appeared to be British tourists.

She had nothing to lose by asking. The worst that could happen was for Señora Alvarez to say no. But if she said yes, then Emma would have a job and an income and might even be able to live here at Casa Clara where after just twenty-four hours, she was already beginning to feel at home. There was only one way to find out. She would go right now and speak to the proprietor.

She quickly dressed in a sober skirt and blouse, brushed her long dark hair and put on a little lip-gloss. She examined herself in the mirror. She looked the image of respectability. Summoning all her courage, she went back down the stairs again to the reception desk.

Señora Alvarez was on the phone and Emma could see that the strain had already got to her. She was tense and irritable and small beads of perspiration stood out on her dark forehead. At last, the conversation ended. She put down the phone and looked up at Emma.

"*Sí, Señorita?*" she asked, quite curtly. "Your room is to your satisfaction?"

"Oh yes," Emma replied. "I'm very pleased."

"So what can I do for you?"

Emma took a deep breath.

"I understand you have a problem."

Señora Alvarez stared. "Problem? No. We are under a little pressure that is all. But everything is in order."

"I understand you need a receptionist," Emma pressed on, putting on her most winning smile. "I'd like to apply."

Señora Alvarez looked surprised. "*You* want the job?"

"Why not? I'm looking for work. We might be able to help each other."

"Have you any experience?"

"No. But I think I could pick it up quite quickly. And I know I would be good."

Señora Alvarez considered for a moment. She looked Emma over and then her mood seemed to change. She quickly summoned the startled cleaning girl and instructed her to take her place behind the desk. Then she indicated for Emma to follow her to a small office where they both sat down.

Emma composed herself and took a good look at Señora Alvarez. She was about thirty-two with a shapely figure, ample bosom and a handsome face. She had jet-black hair and dark, flashing Spanish eyes. And she was clearly fond of jewellery. Her fingers and wrists were cluttered with rings and bracelets and a heavy gold chain adorned her slender neck.

"This is not an easy job," Señora Alvarez began. "You must always have the calm head."

Just like you, Emma thought mischievously but kept the thought to herself.

"Let me explain your duties," the proprietor went on.

For the next fifteen minutes, she outlined the responsibilities of the receptionist. In addition to taking the bookings, greeting the guests and keeping the register and the accounts, Emma would be expected to oversee the entire staff. She would be in charge of the cooking, cleaning, housekeeping and gardening staff. In fact, she would be responsible for the smooth running of the entire operation, although Señora Alvarez retained the official title of manager.

"So, do you think you could do this job?"

"*Sí*," Emma said, without a moment's hesitation.

"There would have to be a period of probation, of course. Shall we say one month?"

"One month seems reasonable," Emma replied.

"And we must also get you a permit to work. But we can arrange that."

"Thank you."

"Now as for your salary," Señora Alvarez continued with a serious look in her eye.

Ten minutes later they both stood up again and shook hands.

Emma was the new receptionist at Casa Clara. Her salary was to be €250 a week and Señora Alvarez had agreed that she could live in at the hotel. The Señora had a smile of relief on her handsome face. Emma could barely contain her joy.

* * *

She started her new job the following morning, determined to be a success. Her working day began at eight o'clock and didn't finish till nine or ten in the evening. She was supposed to have every Saturday off but when the first Saturday came along she was compelled to work because of pressure of business. After a fortnight, she began to understand why her predecessor, Señora Lopez, had left in a hurry. But she loved the work and there were many compensations. Señora Alvarez left her alone and didn't interfere. The staff were loyal, cheerful and hardworking and clearly delighted that someone was in charge once again. Very quickly Emma settled down and began to run Casa Clara efficiently. Señora Alvarez, who lived in a large house on the edge of the town, led a busy social life and she couldn't be bothered with the hundred little details that demanded attention. She was happy to let someone else run the place while she partied with her society friends.

This arrangement suited Emma perfectly. She soon discovered she had a talent for managing people and getting the best out of them. Even though she worked hard, she got enormous satisfaction from her job. She had practically no outlays and most of her salary went straight into her bank account.

Gradually her Spanish began to improve till she could converse quite easily with everyone. Her probation period ended and she was kept on. She even persuaded Señora Alvarez to employ a young assistant called Cristina, an eager twenty-year-old from Seville who was keen to learn the hotel business. And this allowed Emma more free time. She could enjoy the beautiful weather, the lovely food and the tranquillity of the garden and the courtyard where she loved to sit and relax in the evening when her shift was finished. It was bliss.

Time moved quickly and before she knew, four months had passed. Coming to Fuengirola had worked out far better than she had dared to hope. She had not only found peace but also fulfilment. She loved being here and her life had changed out of all recognition.

But a cloud was gathering over Emma's happy life. This morning when she threw open her window, the scene that lay before her failed to work its usual magic. Last night, she had received a message that brought bad news. Emma had a foreboding that her tranquil existence was about to come to a sudden end.

Dublin

Chapter 2

All her life Emma had lived in the shadow of her sister Trish. Even now at the age of twenty-six, she went in awe of her. Trish was three years older but those years represented an enormous gulf of experience and confidence. She had always been the leader and ever since she was a child, Emma had looked up to her older sister. Trish was the one who made all the big decisions. She was the one with the successful career and the glamorous lifestyle. Trish had always been the dominant sibling and Emma the one who followed quietly in her wake. And like many similar situations, it had all started out very innocently.

From the time she was very small, Emma had been aware that there was something different about their family. The most obvious thing was that they had no father. Everybody else seemed to have fathers and what was more, they had lots of brothers and sisters whereas she had only her mother and Trish. She wasn't quite sure what to make of all this. Big families with plenty of children seemed to have more fun. It would be very hard to be lonely in a home like that and, in those early days of childhood, Emma was often lonely.

But any time she voiced these thoughts to her mother, Mrs Frazer shooed them away with a smile and a cuddle.

"Aren't we a cosy little club, just the three of us? Like three bugs in a rug, all warm together. You mark my words, Emma, if this house was coming down with bawling children all demanding attention, you would change your tune pretty fast."

Her mother worked as a secretary for a solicitor in Dublin called Mr Carter and, until they were old enough to look after themselves, they were cared for by Aunt Mollie who was her mother's unmarried sister. This was another odd thing because most of the mothers that Emma knew stayed at home to look after their families. But Mrs Frazer made a virtue out of the fact that she went out to work. She called it her *profession* and the way she said it carried a clear implication that those mothers who didn't have a profession were somehow inferior and that was why they stayed at home "*chained to the kitchen sink*".

But the thing that really confused Emma was that she had no father. By now, she had enough knowledge to realise that there must have been a father at some stage. But she had absolutely no memory of him. He was never mentioned around the house and whenever the girls asked questions about him their mother would get uncomfortable and try to shut them up by saying he had died when they were babies. When this response only provoked further questions, Mrs Frazer would get quite irritable and snap, "What's the big deal about it? Lots of children have no fathers. Some children are orphans and don't even have mothers. Now I've said enough and I'm saying no more."

And that was usually sufficient to bring the conversation to a close.

There wasn't even a photograph of their father. Even though their little parlour was crammed with photographs of other people like their grandparents, there was none of their father. It was as if he had never existed. Emma tried asking Aunt Mollie about him but her aunt, who was a kind-hearted woman, was no help at all. It was as if she had taken a vow of silence. Her habitual response was that a good mother was worth half a dozen fathers and Emma should be grateful for what she had. This only deepened the mystery further.

Trish claimed to remember him. She said he was a tall man with dark hair and glasses who smelled of tobacco.

"What did he die of?" Emma wanted to know, eager for any scrap of information she could find.

"He got a disease."

"What sort of disease?"

Trish thought for a moment. "I think it was called bronchitis."

This was a big word and sounded very serious.

"What does it do to you?"

"It kills you, of course. That's why he's dead."

But Emma could never be sure if her sister was simply making this up to appear important. Trish liked to give the impression that she knew things that other people didn't. It was one of the tricks she used to maintain her superiority. She enjoyed the power it gave her over others and the feeling of respect that it instilled. As a result, Emma came to rely heavily on her sister from early childhood. Trish was the one who led the way; she was the one Emma went to for advice and guidance and protection. Over the years, she came to rely on her too much but by the time she discovered this, it was already too late.

* * *

One of Emma's earliest memories was her first day at school. She was five years old and keen to join the big world. But she was also frightened to be leaving the safety of Aunt Mollie and scared of the new people she was going to meet and the new situations she would encounter. Mrs Frazer had dressed her in a new skirt and blazer and bought a shiny schoolbag which contained an apple, a sandwich wrapped in a plastic bag, a jotter and a pencil case with an eraser, pencil and a pencil-sharpener.

The schoolbag was almost as big as Emma herself and sat on her back like a small suitcase. But she felt quite proud as Trish held her hand and led her through the big iron gates and into the scary new world of school.

Her mother, aunt and sister had tried to prepare her by telling her stories about how exciting school was going to be and all the wonderful things she would learn and the friends she would make. But the moment she got to the door of her new classroom, the pent-up fear overcame her. She started to cry; big fat, salty tears running down her cheeks at the terrifying thought that Trish was leaving her and now she was going to be all alone.

However, the teacher, Miss Brady, had dealt with hundreds of new girls and was well used to this sort of thing. She brought Emma into the class and told the other girls to stand up and say together, "Good morning, Emma" before placing her in the front row beside a plump girl called Annie Murphy who cuddled her and told her not to worry, she would take care of her. Eventually, Emma began to enjoy the fuss they were making of her and soon settled down.

Her school years passed by with scarcely a ripple. She got all the usual infections that seemed to pass through the school like a wave from time to time. But she never got into trouble or caused her mother a moment's worry. Emma was solid and reliable. She made steady progress at reading and writing. She was careful not to draw attention to herself and seemed content to remain in the background.

The school reports came regularly with the same handwritten remarks: *Emma is an attentive student who should do well.* The reports never said she was brilliant or outstanding or even very good. She was clearly destined to be a model student who would never cause any concern but was unlikely to set the world on fire.

Trish was very different. She was the bright sister. She was the one who was clever and could understand things quickly and easily. Everyone who knew her said she was sure to do well and end up in a big job some day. For someone so young, she was extremely disciplined. Each afternoon when she came home from school she sat down at the kitchen table and finished her homework before she even had a cup of tea. She always had her head stuck in a book and seemed to have a photographic memory. Trish only had to be told something once to remember it whereas Emma's mind seemed to be filled with distractions which caused her to forget things and mix everything up and give the wrong answer when asked a question.

And then a change occurred. The sisters had always regarded boys with horror. In their eyes, boys were dirty and rough. They used bad language and played stupid games. Why any self-respecting girl could find them remotely interesting was beyond their comprehension. But around the age of eleven, Trish began to keep company with a group of girls who gathered together in the schoolyard where they would whisper and giggle in a small conspiratorial group and, horror of horrors, they talked about boys. But what was even worse, they froze Emma out and, any time she approached, they frowned menacingly to let her know she wasn't welcome.

This was a hard blow for her to take. She loved Trish and found this sudden change of attitude confusing and hurtful. Trish was her sister, after all, why was she rejecting her like this? Why did she have to take up with these other girls? Why couldn't they remain as they had always been, close friends and allies? At the very least, why couldn't Trish include her in her group instead of treating her like an outcast?

She finally picked up the courage to ask.

"Because you're still a baby," Trish said angrily.

"No. I'm not. I'll soon be nine."

"Age has got nothing to do with it. You haven't grown up yet.

And what's more, I don't want you following me around like a little lapdog. You can't be trusted."

This remark stung Emma.

"Why can't you trust me? You're my sister and you're supposed to be my best friend."

"Well, you'll just have to find some new friends."

"Why can't *you* be my friend?"

"Oh for God's sake!" Trish exploded. "We're talking about things you wouldn't understand. Can't you see that you're just embarrassing me?"

Emma took her rejection very hard, particularly the suggestion that she couldn't be trusted. But worse was to come. At the end of the school year, Trish departed for St Benedict's secondary school and Emma found herself entirely alone. The person she had relied on to look after her was gone. Now she was forced to take her sister's advice and seek out new friends. But it wasn't easy.

Emma wasn't the type of girl who made friends quickly. She was shy and she lacked Trish's self-confidence. She wasn't good at sports and she wasn't witty or bold. She didn't have her sister's leadership qualities. Besides, by now most of the girls at school had already made their friendships and were forming little cliques like the one that Trish had belonged to. Emma found it impossible to break in and for the next few years she was left to drift along on her own in a state of permanent unhappiness.

Meanwhile, other important developments were taking place. After much pleading, Trish had finally persuaded their mother to allow her to go to the local disco. This was held each Saturday evening in the parish hall. From bits of gossip she had picked up at school, Emma had learnt that the disco was a great place to meet boys.

Going to the disco seemed the height of sophistication. It was *so* grown up. Each Saturday afternoon she would watch as Trish got ready for the dance. Trish would sit at the dressing-table in the bedroom they shared and comb her hair and pout her lips at the mirror. Then she would take out the secret bag of make-up she kept hidden in her drawer and apply a thin layer of eyeliner and lipstick. Emma watched this ritual with envy. She would have given anything to be allowed to go to the disco like her sister.

Then about seven o'clock, Trish's friends would call and they would all gather in the downstairs front room and lock the door to keep Emma out. Inside, she could hear them whispering and giggling. It was just like the school playground all over again.

It wasn't very long before Trish had a boyfriend. She was now fourteen and wore a bra and was beginning to look more and more like a woman. The boyfriend's name was Kevin Finnegan but she called him Kev. He was seventeen and worked as an apprentice car mechanic. But even more exciting – he rode a motorbike!

Emma had never set eyes on a creature as exotic as Kevin Finnegan. He was tall and thin with long black hair and a silver chain with skull and crossbones which he wore around his neck. He dressed in denim jeans and a black motorcycle jacket and goggles. And he had a little wispy moustache which told Emma he was more than a mere boy. Kevin Finnegan was a man! And to top it all, he smoked cigarettes which Mrs Frazer had warned them about so much that it appeared not only dangerous but positively *cool*.

He called for Trish on Sunday afternoons and took her riding on his bike out to the Bull Island. Emma used to wonder what they got up to on these trips. No doubt they kissed. But did they do anything else? Did she let him touch her? Did she touch him? And what did it feel like? Was it exciting?

Trish never said. Any time Emma got up the courage to ask, her sister would abruptly end the conversation, saying it was personal matter and she didn't wish to discuss it. It was her old trick of withholding information. But it was also evidence that she still didn't trust Emma and this upset her. If Trish was a proper sister, she would share this information and then Emma would know what to expect when her turn came to have a boyfriend of her own.

But if the girls thought Kevin Finnegan was wonderful, this view wasn't shared by Mrs Frazer. She was horrified at this development and did her best to discourage it. She said he was far too old for Trish and was distracting her from her schoolwork. And besides, he wasn't the sort of boy she should be associating with. She felt her daughter could do much better. She shouldn't be throwing herself away on someone who was only a car mechanic and not even a fully-fledged one at that.

However, Mrs Frazer was smart enough not to ban him altogether for fear that Trish would simply go on seeing him behind her back. But she was only allowed to see him once a week and whenever he called Mrs Frazer was icy cold with him. She kept him waiting at the front door and never invited him into the house. Her disapproval couldn't have been more obvious.

One Sunday night as they were getting ready for bed, Trish said: "Can you keep a secret?"

Emma couldn't believe her ears. At last, Trish was going to trust her with something. A secret! Maybe she was finally going to tell what happened on these mysterious trips to the Bull Island. She sat up straight and tried to look serious.

"Of course you can trust me. I won't tell a soul."

"If you ever breathe a word of this to anyone, I'll kill you. And I'm not joking either."

She gave Emma a menacing look that only intrigued her further.

"Go on, you can tell me."

"Kev and me are getting engaged."

Emma was stunned. She had no idea it was anything as important as this. Getting engaged meant they were planning to get married. This was really grown-up stuff.

"*Engaged?*"

"Yes. He asked me today."

"When's it going to happen?"

"On my 16th birthday. He's saving up for an engagement ring. What do you think of that?"

Emma struggled to take in this exciting news. It was incredible. It was like something out of a romance story.

"I think it's wonderful." She jumped out of bed and hugged her sister. "Oh Trish, I'm so happy for you. Honest I am. That's the most brilliant thing I've ever heard."

Trish seemed suitably pleased with Emma's reaction.

"You know Mum doesn't like him. That's why you must keep it a secret. If she ever got wind of it, she'd have a fit."

"I'll tell no one. Honest. When are you going to get married?"

"That will have to wait till I'm older. But I don't mind. He loves me, Emma. That's the important thing."

Emma gazed at her sister with admiring eyes.

"You're so lucky to get someone like him. He's so handsome."

"Yes, I suppose I am," Trish said. "But remember that I'm trusting you. Don't let me down."

* * *

After that, the two girls began to grow closer. Trish would share little pieces of information with Emma who was delighted that she was now being brought into her sister's confidence. It was like it used to be when they were small before Trish met her new friends and grew away from her.

"What's it like to be kissed?" she asked.

Trish shrugged. "It's all right, I suppose."

"Is it like the films? Does it make you feel dizzy?"

"Sometimes – it depends on the boy. Kev is a fantastic kisser but some of them haven't a clue."

Now that they were finally venturing onto forbidden ground,

Emma wondered if she should go further and ask what else they did on their motorbike trips. But Trish wasn't about to confide anything more. She seemed to sense that they had strayed far enough. She quickly brought the conversation to a close.

"You'll find out soon enough when you get a boy of your own."

"When will that be?" Emma asked morosely. "Mum won't even let me go to the disco."

"Why don't you just tell her you're going and let her try to stop you?"

"Oh God, I couldn't do that!"

"Why not? You'll have to stand on your own feet sometime. You can't allow Mum to rule your life forever."

It was obvious that Trish and Kev were in love. He was always buying her little presents which she would show off to Emma. On Valentine's Day, he gave her a locket and chain with a photo of them both inside. Emma thought it was so romantic. But Trish had to hide it in her cosmetic bag and only wore it when she was away from the house where her mother couldn't see it.

Then, one evening as she was studying in the bedroom, Emma was surprised to hear raised voices coming from the kitchen. She stopped to listen as the voices grew louder. It was mainly her mother's voice and she seemed very angry.

Emma sensed at once it was something to do with Kevin Finnegan. There had been increasing arguments over him in recent months. Maybe their mother had found out about the engagement?

"In the name of God," she heard her mother shout, "did I not raise you to have some respect for yourself? Did I not bring you up to be decent? And now you've gone and made a tramp of yourself!"

Emma quietly opened the door so she could hear more.

"I never liked him from the moment I set eyes on him. I knew he was up to no good. But I never thought my own daughter would turn out no better than a slut! Now what are we going to do?"

The shouting turned to screams and then Emma heard footsteps come running up the stairs. The door opened and Trish was in the room. She looked distraught. Her eyes were red from weeping. She flung herself down on the bed and began to sob uncontrollably.

Emma went to her at once and tried to comfort her.

"What's happening?" she asked. "Why is Mum so angry?"

Trish looked at her with tear-stained eyes.

"I'm going to kill myself," she said.

"Why? What's the matter?"

"Oh Emma, I'm pregnant!"

Emma could barely believe what she was hearing.

"Pregnant? Is it Kev's?"

"Of course."

"But that's good news. Now you can marry him."

Trish looked at her through her teary eyes.

"First I'd have to find him. He's done a runner."

* * *

For the next few days, Mrs Frazer went about with a martyred look on her face as if she was the one who was going to have the baby. She didn't go to work and spent hours on the phone talking in hushed tones. The following Saturday, she packed two suitcases and Trish and her caught a flight to Manchester. Emma was sent off to stay with Aunt Mollie. When they came back on Tuesday, Trish looked pale. She was put to bed and stayed there till the weekend.

Mrs Frazer sat down with Emma at the kitchen table. She told her that nobody must ever know what had happened. If word got out about Trish's pregnancy, her reputation would be ruined and no decent man would ever look at her.

Kevin Finnegan's name was not allowed to be spoken in the house. But news eventually filtered back that he had gone to London and was working in a garage on the Edgware Road.

The baby was never mentioned again.

Chapter 3

The time came for Emma to transfer to secondary school. She had been looking forward to this with increasing confidence. She had outgrown the tight little world of primary school and was anxious for new experiences. Trish had already been at St Benedict's for three years and was the undisputed leader of a whole new network of friends. But this time it didn't matter so much because Emma began to make friends of her own.

Her closest friend was a small, freckle-faced girl called Jackie Flynn who sat beside her in class. She was blonde and plump and lived on a road near Emma's house. Both her parents went out to work and the two girls fell into the habit of going to Emma's house after school to do their homework.

The first time Emma visited the Flynn home, she was amazed. It was a large detached bungalow several times bigger than the Frazer house and filled with expensive furniture. Emma had never seen anything like it. Jackie had her own bedroom where the girls went to study after they had first called into the kitchen for a snack.

This was a bright, airy room furnished with lots of fancy appliances including a fridge which was almost as big as a wardrobe. It was here that Mrs Flynn left the snacks she prepared before she went to work each morning. The fridge was always stocked with food: hams and cooked chickens, sausages, fruit and vegetables and usually a bottle or two of wine left to chill.

Emma was very impressed by the grandeur of the place and the conspicuous wealth. It made her own house look very small and shabby by comparison. She reckoned the Flynns must be extremely well-to-do.

"What do your parents work at?" she asked.

"Well, my dad's a company director."

"And your mum? What does she do?"

"She's a sales rep in a jewellery shop in Grafton Street."

Jackie tossed out the phrases as if they were nothing special but to Emma they sounded magical and mysterious.

"What exactly is a company director?" she wanted to know.

"He has his own business," Jackie said. "They make parts for computers. What does your dad do?"

"My dad is dead," Emma said. "He got bronchitis and it killed him."

"That's awful," Jackie said. "Do you miss him?"

"I don't remember him. We were only babies."

"It must be terrible to have no dad," Jackie said, sadly. "I don't know what I'd do if my dad died. It doesn't bear thinking about."

Emma had never considered her life like this before. She had never known her father so she had no memories him. But now she began to see that he might have made a difference to their lives. They might have had more money for one thing and a bigger house. She might have had her own bedroom like Jackie. This was what she envied most. She would have given anything to have a bedroom like Jackie's with its comfortable single bed and writing desk and dressing-table, instead of having to share the cramped room at home with Trish.

Meanwhile, secondary school was turning out to be every bit as exciting as Emma had hoped. She was making new friends and instead of the narrow curriculum of reading, writing and arithmetic, she was now studying a whole range of new subjects: French, Classical Studies, Science, History, Home Economics. And rather than having the same teacher all the time, she now had a different teacher for each subject.

Her favourite teacher was Tim Devlin and he took them for English. Mr Devlin came from Northern Ireland. He was one of only a handful of male teachers at the school and was also the youngest. He was in his early twenties and fresh out of university. He was tall and fit with broad shoulders and jet-black hair. By now, Emma was fifteen and she was immediately taken by him.

She thought Mr Devlin was the most handsome man she had ever seen. Everything about him seemed perfect – his Northern accent, the way he looked, the way he walked, even down to the way he always kept his fingernails neatly trimmed. And he had a completely different style to the other teachers. He didn't talk down to his pupils. He wasn't stiff or formal. He didn't insist on petty rules and regulations. On warm days, he would take off his jacket and hang it on the back of a chair and teach the class in his shirtsleeves. He shared little jokes with them and never patronised them or made snide remarks.

As a result, he was very popular with the girls and his class became the highlight of Emma's school day. Mr Devlin was very passionate about his subject and his brown eyes would shine with intensity. He put a lot of energy into his work unlike some teachers who gave the impression that they couldn't wait for the bell to ring so that they could go off home for the day.

For the first time, Emma began to find English exciting. She hung on every word that Mr Devlin spoke because she desperately wanted to please him. If he mentioned a poet or a writer, she would hurry away to look them up on the computer in the school library. When he corrected her essays, she studied the comments he made in his neat handwriting in the margin of the page and made sure to follow them. Very quickly, she became the best girl in the class at English and earned much praise from Mr Devlin. This gladdened her heart.

Mr Devlin's favourite poet was WB Yeats. He said he was the greatest poet of the twentieth century. He was fond of quoting from "The Lake Isle of Innisfree". Emma thought it was beautiful the way he read the poem with his lilting Northern voice. She would close her eyes and see the small cabin and the bean rows and the beehive as if they were right there before her very eyes.

One afternoon, Mr Devlin asked her to stay behind after the class was finished. He pulled out a chair for her beside his desk and invited her to sit down.

"I've been observing your work," he said with a smile. "And I'm very pleased. I think you've made tremendous progress."

These encouraging words were like music to her ears.

"You seem to have a natural aptitude for English."

Emma blushed with pleasure. "Thank you, sir," she replied. "I enjoy it very much."

"Well, it certainly shows. I was thinking. You should consider taking English at Honours Level when the time comes to do your Leaving Cert. I know it's a few years away but you can't start too soon."

Emma looked into his deep brown eyes and felt her heart soar. Right now, she was prepared to do anything the teacher asked to gain his approval.

"What should I do?" she asked.

"You should read as widely as possible. You like reading, don't you?"

"Oh yes, sir," she replied.

"I could make out a list of reading material for you if you like, writers you might enjoy. Reading will broaden your interests. If you find a poet or an author you enjoy, you could go on to read more of their work. It will develop your critical taste and extend your vocabulary. You're quite a stylish writer as it is but there's always room for improvement." He smiled again. "And remember, Emma, if there's anything you're not sure about, don't be afraid to ask me."

She left the classroom as if she was floating on a cloud. Mr Devlin had said she had a natural aptitude for English and had commended her writing skills. He had singled her out from all the other girls in the class. She could barely contain her joy as she went off to her next class, determined to do everything she could to gain the teacher's praise.

About a week later, Mr Devlin presented her with a list of books to read. She took it away to the library and borrowed as many as she could. Now, she spent her evenings immersed in reading. Some of the books he had recommended were heart-breaking love stories like *Tess of the D'Urbervilles* and *The Return of the Native,* two novels by Thomas Hardy, a writer she had never heard of before. She eagerly devoured them, lingering over every word.

However, her new-found interest didn't go unnoticed. Other students began to comment and one day she got into an argument with some girls who teased her about being the teacher's pet. But by now, Emma had grown in confidence. She was taller than most of the girls in her class and well able to defend herself. She decided to meet the challenge head on.

"You're calling me the teacher's pet because you're jealous," she said to the ringleader, a skinny, pasty-faced girl called Tracey Dunne.

"Jealous? What's there to be jealous about?" the girl sneered while the others watched with glee to see how the argument would develop.

"Well, I don't hear Mr Devlin congratulating you. You can't even read the poems properly. Yesterday you said nine bean pods instead of nine bean *rows*. There's a big difference. Or maybe you didn't know that?"

The others sniggered and Tracey Dunne began to look uncomfortable.

"It's plain to see what you're doing," she retorted. "You're licking up to him. You're trying to kiss his ass."

"How charming," Emma said with heavy disdain. "That sounds like something you might get up to. Maybe that's what has you upset?"

The others laughed openly now.

"You're just a stupid swot," Tracey said in a feeble parting shot.

"Oh really?" Emma replied. "Just because I want to pass my exams and get a decent job when I leave school, that makes me a swot, does it? Maybe I should follow your example and end up on the dole?"

By now Tracey was totally routed. She slunk away to a chorus of hoots and jeers and the subject of Emma and Mr Devlin was never raised again. At least, not to her face.

But later, when she was alone with Jackie, her friend said: "You know, Tracey did have a point, didn't she? He is very fond of you."

"Don't you start," Emma said, giving her a warning glance. "I've had enough on that subject for one day."

"It's nothing to be ashamed about. I think he's very dishy. All the girls do."

"I don't know what you're talking about," Emma said, dismissively. "I just happen to like English, that's all."

"Oh, c'mon," Jackie replied, putting her arm across her shoulder. "It's got nothing to do with English. Why don't you be honest? You fancy him, don't you?"

Jackie's remark came as a great surprise. Despite everything that had happened over the past few months, despite all those wonderful feelings she had experienced in the presence of her teacher and the warm glow she got from his praise, it had never crossed Emma's mind that something else could be involved.

But now that Jackie had said it, she began to turn the idea over in her head. Was she developing a crush on Mr Devlin? Was that what these beautiful feelings were all about? They had crept up on her unawares until suddenly he had become the centre of her life. Now she thought about him all the time. He was the only one she cared about. He was her ideal man. And if others could see it, maybe it was true?

The idea made her tremble with excitement. But something warned her that it was dangerous. What should she do? He was her teacher so she could hardly stop seeing him the way she could with some boy she had met. Besides she enjoyed feeling the way she did. It was a good feeling. Why should she stop?

She wondered if he had the same feeling for her? Was that why he had been paying her so much attention, giving her extra lessons, having cups of coffee together? Emma studied her reflection in the dressing-table mirror. A handsome young woman stared back. She was growing fast. She was about five feet seven inches tall with long dark hair and bright hazel eyes. Already she had developed a firm bust. There was no doubt she was attractive. Was it possible that Mr Devlin fancied her too?

She felt herself grow giddy at the very thought. It was so daring and exciting that she couldn't keep it to herself. She had to talk to someone about it. And the only person she could trust was Jackie. So, the first opportunity she got, she raised the subject again when they were alone in Jackie's bedroom after school.

"Why did you say I fancied Mr Devlin?"

Jackie studied her carefully before replying. "Did it upset you?"

"No, I'm just interested, that's all."

"It's the way you look at him. I can see it in your eyes."

"But he's a good-looking man. You don't deny that?"

"No, but you're always trying to please him. If he asked you to jump out the window, you'd probably do it."

"That doesn't mean I fancy him."

"But you do it constantly. He just has to mention some writer and off you run to the library."

"And what's so bad about that?"

Jackie shrugged. "Nothing, I suppose. But I don't see you doing it for any other teacher."

"Do you think I'm his pet?"

"Oh, definitely," Jackie replied. "You're his favourite. Look at the way he always asks you to clean the blackboard and read from the poetry book. And he always gives your essays top marks. And he gave you a list of books to read, didn't he?"

Emma felt her heart brim with joy.

"Jackie, I'm going to tell you something that you must never reveal to another living person. Do you promise?"

"Sure."

"I *do* fancy him. I think about him all the time. I think I might be falling in love."

Jackie was so excited that she clapped her hands. "In love?"

Emma nodded.

"Oh my God, I think that's so cool. I've never known anybody fall in love with a teacher before."

Now Emma began to look at Mr Devlin in a completely different light and her imagination was on fire. She began to construct elaborate fantasies about him. She convinced herself that he was in love with her but couldn't declare it in case he lost his job. She thought how terrible it must be for him to see her every day and not be able to tell her how he felt. If only there was some way of letting him know that his love was being returned.

She thought of writing him a letter telling him. But what if it fell into the wrong hands? It could land them all in trouble. She considered the difference in their ages. He must be about twenty-three. She was fifteen. It wasn't such an enormous gap. In a few years' time, she would be legally entitled to marry. She would be only too happy to wait.

By now she was becoming completely infatuated with her teacher. She studied his every move, watching for a sign that he understood. She followed him around the school, hanging on each word. Her behaviour became so blatant that people couldn't fail to notice. But Emma didn't care. Her only concern was her love for him. She wanted to send him a signal that she was waiting. At one sign from him, she would pack her bag and they would run away together.

But this illusion couldn't last.

Eventually, the term holidays arrived. Emma spent much of the time at Jackie's house, listening to music and watching videos. But every night before she went to sleep, she made sure to read a couple of chapters of some novel that Mr Devlin had recommended. When the new term began she wanted to take up where they had left off. She wanted to be able to impress him. She wanted him to see that his love for her was recognised and returned.

Eventually the holidays came to an end. She couldn't wait to get back to school to see Mr Devlin again. She counted the minutes till her English class came around. But when it arrived, instead of Mr Devlin an elderly, grey-haired nun came in and sat down at his desk.

"I'm Sister Agnes," she said, as she introduced herself. "Mr Devlin has left the school. I'm going to be your English teacher for the new term."

Chapter 4

Emma was devastated. She thought her heart was broken and would never mend. Mr Devlin had vanished out of her life as suddenly as he had come into it. And he hadn't even told her he was going. It felt like a great big void had opened up. She wondered where he had gone and what had happened to make him leave so suddenly. She wondered if it had anything to do with her.

Perhaps the school authorities had got wind of their relationship and fired him? That was the sort of thing they would do to keep them apart. For several weeks, as she made her way to and from school, she half-expected to hear Mr Devlin call her name and turn to find him waiting for her. At the very least, he would surely write to tell her where he was. But as the time passed and nothing happened, he slowly began to fade from her mind. But she didn't forget him.

Other things were happening to claim her attention. The time arrived for Trish to take her Leaving Cert and when the results were announced it was revealed that she had secured five straight As and two Bs and had also come first in the country in Business Organisation. It was one of the best results in the history of the school.

There was great celebration. The teachers were delighted at her success because Trish's achievement gave a tremendous boost to the school's reputation. They could point to her as an example of the high academic standards that prevailed at St Benedict's. She got her photograph in the local paper and was presented with a medal by the headmistress who encouraged her to take a university degree.

But Trish surprised them all by deciding she didn't want to go to university. She wanted to get a job. She'd had enough of penny-pinching. Now she was eager to get out into the workforce and start earning money. By September came the news that she had secured a position as a clerical officer in a bank.

But, watching from the sidelines, Emma sensed that this was only the beginning. She knew that Trish would not be content to remain a bank clerk for long. Her sister was too ambitious. Very soon, Trish was attending seminars and weekend courses on different aspects of banking. She enrolled in evening classes to study Economics and Accountancy. She went around with her briefcase stuffed with books and notepads. Emma knew she had her sights set on higher goals. Eventually Trish's career at the bank began to take off. Her attendance at seminars and courses started to pay dividends and she was rewarded with several internal promotions.

By now, she had put the episode with Kevin Finnegan far behind her and had started to go out with men again. One man in particular seemed to have caught her attention. His name was David Smyth. He was twenty-five and worked as a negotiator in an estate agent's office. This was a business which was beginning to thrive with the boom in the property market. David drove a new Volkswagen Golf provided by the company and was always dressed impeccably in freshly laundered shirts and well-shined shoes when he called at the Frazer house. He was tall and dark and muscular and seemed to have a perpetual blue shadow on his cheeks even after he had shaved. Emma thought he was very good-looking.

One evening, while he waited for Trish to get ready, Mrs Frazer managed to ferret out the information that David's father was a partner in a major accountancy firm and had set up a trust fund for the children in the event of his death. Emma quickly came to the conclusion that David Smyth would be a very good catch indeed for her sister.

By now Trish had started to call him Smitty and it soon became obvious that he was captivated by her. But she treated him with cool reserve which bordered on disdain. Emma often wondered why he put up with it. When she mentioned this to her sister, Trish laughed.

"The trick is to keep them guessing. You mustn't let them get too confident or they begin to take you for granted. Besides, Smitty enjoys it."

"Enjoys it? But you practically bully him!"

"Bully is not the right word. I'm forceful, that's all. There's a difference. Smitty likes me to make the decisions."

By now Emma had also left school but with a much less flattering Leaving Certificate than her sister. Unlike Trish, Emma hadn't a clue what to do next. She considered a number of possible careers until Trish took a hand and suggested the Civil Service.

"It's a good solid job," she said. "The pay's okay. And there are big advantages. You'll never be out of work and you can look forward to a pension when you retire. You could do a lot worse, Emma."

Emma took her sister's advice. Like Trish before her she wanted to be out in the big world earning money and enjoying the freedom it brought. She sat the Clerical Officer exams and was successful. In due course she was appointed to the Department of Social and Family Affairs where she worked from nine to five, Monday to Friday, filling out forms and answering telephone queries from members of the public. It wasn't the exciting world of high finance but, for the time being, Emma was satisfied.

Eventually Trish was made assistant manager of a branch in Stillorgan which was a big step forward. Everyone congratulated her. But Trish was only getting into her stride and a year later she was promoted to be manager of her own branch in Swords.

This was a major achievement and was to be a turning point in her career. The appointment caused a great stir. At twenty-four, Trish was the youngest manager of a bank in the entire country and one of the very few women. A reporter came out from the *Irish Independent* to interview her. The reporter wrote that Trish personified a new breed of successful young women. She had managed to break through the glass ceiling and was blazing a trail for other women to follow.

The interview was followed up by other newspapers. Whenever they needed someone to comment on the subject of women in business, they came to Trish who was always available with a snappy quote. Now her photograph was appearing regularly in the papers. She was interviewed on radio and television. She was asked to give talks on empowerment and assertiveness.

Her employers were quick to realise what a publicity coup had landed in their laps. Trish's appointment allowed the bank to appear forward-looking and progressive and did no harm when it came to the lucrative business of attracting female clients. She was encouraged to develop this side of her activities as much as possible. To allow her more time, she was given an assistant – another young woman called Eva Doherty. Before long, Trish had moulded Eva into shape and soon had her jumping through hoops to do her bidding.

It appeared that Trish could do nothing wrong. Everything she touched had turned to gold. She had a wonderful career and a handsome partner. And she was still only twenty-five. It seemed the right time to move on to the next step in her career. She announced that she was going to get married.

* * *

Trish's wedding plans proceeded smoothly. The wedding dress was quickly decided on along with the bridesmaids' and the reception and the honeymoon and all the myriad details that surrounded the great event. Then came the question of who would give the bride away since her father was dead. Trish caused a stir when she announced that she would walk down the aisle alone. She was an adult, she said, and nobody's property. She didn't need anyone to give her away.

But in the middle of all the wedding planning, Trish also found time to locate somewhere to live. After weeks of investigation, she settled for a large four-bedroomed house that was under construction in Malahide. Through connections in the property business, Smitty was able to secure a reduction in the purchase price and Trish arranged a cheap mortgage in their joint names from her bank.

Afterwards, everyone said it was a fairy-tale wedding. And just as she had calculated, Trish's solo walk down the aisle caused gasps of admiration. People said how brave she was and how sad it made them feel that Mr Frazer wasn't there to see his beautiful daughter get married. Outside the church, they were besieged by photographers and reporters. With a keen eye for publicity Trish had made sure to alert them well in advance.

The reception went off like clockwork and the assembled guests ate a delicious meal of roast Wicklow lamb and lobster and drank champagne before settling down to witty speeches from the best man, Smitty and finally, Trish herself. Afterwards they danced to the lively music of the Tartar Kings, an up-and-coming young Dublin band which was being hotly tipped for stardom.

At 3 a.m. the newly married couple left for their hotel and an early-morning flight to Las Vegas to begin their three-week honeymoon. The wedding had been an awesome tour-de-force. Emma was left wondering what her talented sister was going to do for her next trick.

Chapter 5

Emma had maintained her long friendship with Jackie Flynn who now worked as a secretary in a busy newspaper office and they spent most of their spare time together along with a group of friends. It was through Jackie that she came to meet Alan Casey one Friday evening in Mulligan's pub in Poolbeg Street. Alan was the paper's crime reporter. He was tall and handsome with blue eyes and blond hair. He was also extremely good company. The first thing he said after they were introduced was: "What do you call a gangster with a machine gun?"

Emma had a vague idea that she had heard this joke before but she went along with it just to keep him happy.

"Tell us," she said.

"Sir," Alan Casey replied and the company roared with laughter. This only encouraged him to tell more jokes and so the evening progressed with Alan keeping everyone entertained with witty stories about the interesting characters he came across in the course of his work.

Emma was drawn to him at once. He certainly had style and

personality. At closing time, as the girls were preparing to leave, he put his hand on her shoulder.

"Where are you guys off to?" he asked.

Emma explained that they were heading for Nirvana, a new dance club that had just opened on Dawson Street.

"I'll come with you," he said and immediately took out his mobile phone and began organising taxis.

At the club, he insisted on ordering champagne.

"You don't have to do that," Emma said, quickly. "They rip you off in here. Beers are fine."

"It's okay," Alan said, brushing her objections aside. "I'll put it on my expenses. I'll say I was entertaining The Dwarf."

"The Dwarf?" Emma asked. "Is this another of your jokes?"

"No, he's a real person. He's one of my criminal contacts. He supplies most of the cocaine on the south side. He's got a taste for high living."

"I'm sure he can afford it," she said, "with the ill-gotten gains he's making."

The girls got up to dance and each time they came back, Alan had ordered another bottle of champagne. Emma shuddered to think what the bill was going to cost. But Alan didn't seem to mind.

"If I don't spend my expenses, the News Editor thinks I'm not doing my job properly," he explained with an odd kind of logic that Emma couldn't quite understand. But by this stage, she was too inebriated to care.

By four in the morning the others had left and only Alan and Emma remained.

"I suppose I'd better get you home," he said at last, taking out his mobile and ringing for a taxi once more. But he didn't take her home. Instead they ended up in his apartment in Ringsend. By now, Emma was exhausted from the champagne and the dancing and just wanted to go to sleep.

"What do you call a bag-snatcher in a suit?" Alan asked as he slipped off her jacket.

"Tell me," Emma said, feeling a wall of tiredness hit her.

"The defendant," he replied and fell down beside her on the bed.

* * *

Alan rang the following afternoon as she was stepping out of a long, luxurious bath.

"How are you?"

"I'm wasted," she replied with a groan. "I feel like I spent the night being tossed around inside a washing machine."

"Ho, ho, ho – that's very funny! I like a woman with a good sense of humour. Do you feel like going out tonight?"

"I don't think I'd be able for it, Alan. I was planning on having an early night."

"Oh c'mon," he coaxed. "There's a new comedy club opening in Camden Street. I've got free tickets."

"Would you mind if I took a rain check?"

"I'd like you to come. I really enjoyed myself last night. I promise to get you home at a reasonable hour."

"There won't be any champagne at it, will there?"

"Not unless you insist."

"Okay," she said. "But I'm leaving at the stroke of midnight. And I don't care if The Dwarf himself turns up and brings Snow White along with him."

"Ho, ho, ho," Alan Casey said. "I like it. I really do. I'll pick you up at nine o'clock. Where do you live?"

After that, they began to meet several times a week and, before long, she was seeing him all the time. Good-natured Jackie didn't seem to mind that their little group of friends had lost a prominent member. She was pleased that Emma had found a regular man.

"He's a nice guy, isn't he?" she said as they had lunch together one day at a hamburger joint near her office.

"For a journalist, he's very nice," Emma replied.

"Now don't go talking like that," Jackie scolded. "They're *all* very nice. At least they are to me. They're always polite and respectful. Not like that shower in the last place I worked who regarded me as their personal slave cum doormat. One of them even asked me one time to pick up his laundry from the dry cleaner's and check they had pressed his shirts properly before I paid. Can you imagine the cheek of him?"

"I'm only joking, Jackie."

"It's just an image they have. They like to pretend that they're hard-bitten hacks. But when you get to know them, they're really very pleasant."

"You'll be telling me next that some of your best friends are journalists," Emma replied and they burst out laughing.

"Well, I know one thing for sure," Jackie continued. "Alan's very fond of you. He's always pumping me for information. He's very subtle, of course. It's a skill journalists use to get people to tell them things. But I know what he's up to."

"What sort of information?" Emma asked, now that her curiosity was aroused.

"What you were like at school. What your family are like, what's your favourite food, stuff like that."

"Really?" Emma said, with a smile. "Maybe he's planning to write an article about me?"

"The only articles he's got on his mind are articles of clothing," Jackie replied with a lascivious grin.

Later, Emma thought about what her friend had said. If Alan Casey was asking these types of questions, it sounded like he was getting serious. This led her to consider where the relationship might be heading. She had been going out with him for three months which was the longest period she had ever gone out with any man. And this told her that something must be working between them. Usually if a man didn't inspire her, Emma gently dropped him after a couple of dates.

But, once again, her sister intervened to help her make up her mind. Trish's bank was launching a new product aimed specially at women. It had the rather uninspiring name of *Ladysave* and the idea was that regular savers would earn discounts at hairdressing salons and clothing boutiques. Trish had been asked to take charge of the publicity. She decided to organise a launch party and invited Emma. When Alan rang to ask what she was doing that evening, she told him and he said he would come with her and afterwards they would have a meal together.

When they turned up, they found the place packed with financial journalists and writers from the women's pages. Alan headed straight for the bar where he immediately made himself at home with a large gin and tonic. In no time at all, he was entertaining the assembled reporters with the exploits of the latest criminal celebrity – a gangster called The Barrister who was a former legal student, reputed to know more about criminal law than the police who were trying to convict him.

He was in the middle of telling a joke when Emma felt a tug at her sleeve. She turned to find Trish beside her, dressed in a smart business suit with spotless white blouse, and an armful of information literature.

"So you were able to make it," she said.

"Yes. Thanks for inviting me."

"And I see you've already found the movers and shakers."

She smiled at the assembled press corps who nodded appreciatively. Most of them already knew Trish by now.

"Can I introduce you to someone?" Emma said, drawing Alan away from the bar where he was topping up his drink.

"This is Alan Casey. He's the Crime Correspondent with *The News*. Alan, this is my sister, Trish."

Alan immediately planted a wet kiss on Trish's cheek, smudging her carefully applied make-up.

There was silence from the assembled crowd as they waited for Trish's response.

She gave Alan a withering look. "Well, if everyone is suitably refreshed, I think we'll proceed with the presentation."

After the party broke up, Alan and Emma went to a little restaurant on the quays and had a quiet dinner. It was after ten o'clock when she finally got home and found her mother had gone to bed. She had a shower and made a cup of hot chocolate and was just settling down to catch the television news when her phone rang. It was Trish.

"I tried calling you earlier, she said. "I want to talk to you."

"I was out to dinner," Emma explained.

"That creature you brought to the launch this evening."

"Alan?"

"Yes – Alan. Where on earth did you pick him up?"

"He's my boyfriend."

Trish gave a weary sigh.

"I have to tell you, Emma, the guy's a tiresome boor. He's loud-mouthed and has no manners. He kept interrupting the presentation with his stupid jokes. And he drinks far too much. He must have gone through half a bottle of gin at the reception. I checked with the barman afterwards."

"All the journos are heavy drinkers," Emma said. "You know what they're like."

"He's got no dress sense. That suit he had on – it was like something one of his criminal friends loaned him for the evening."

"That's just an image thing," Emma said, stung into defending Alan. "He's a very nice person really."

"I hate to say this to you," Trish continued, "but you're letting yourself down. I hope this relationship isn't serious?"

"I've been seeing him for three months."

"Do yourself a favour," Trish said. "Get rid of him."

* * *

After that, the pressure became relentless. Trish wasted no opportunity to denigrate Alan Casey. Every chance she got, she pointed out his shortcomings and ran him down. He was shallow, coarse, adolescent and halfway to being an alcoholic. He was unreliable. Getting involved with him would be a disaster and was bound to end in tears. Emma tried to defend him but her heart wasn't in it. Before long, she began to believe her sister's propaganda.

Besides, other doubts were now beginning to surface. She was much too young for a serious relationship. She needed to see more of life. She was attractive and who knew what other exciting men were out there? Why opt for the first handsome man who came along?

One evening a few weeks later when they were having a quiet drink together, she broke off the relationship. She tried to do it gently but she knew that Alan was hurt even though he tried to laugh it away with a joke.

"I won't forget you," she said, trying to make it easier. "But you'll soon find someone else."

"You're right," he said with a grin. "I probably will. But she won't be anything like you, Emma."

When she told Trish a few days later, her sister sounded relieved.

"That's the most sensible thing you've ever done," she said. "Believe me, you'll never regret it."

Chapter 6

A few months after the break-up with Alan Casey, Jackie surprised Emma by announcing that she was moving out of her parents' home and renting a flat of her own in the centre of town.

"I'm a big girl now," she said. "I can't be tied to their apron strings forever. And having my own flat will give me greater freedom. I'll be able to have parties and I'll have somewhere to bring any nice man I might meet."

Within weeks, she was telling everyone who would listen about the benefits of independent living.

"I go to bed whenever I like, get up when I please, eat when it suits me. It's brilliant. I'm just sorry I didn't do it sooner."

In no time, several friends had followed her example till suddenly Emma was the only one in their group who was still living at home. She liked it well enough. Following Trish's marriage, she had finally got her wish and now had the bedroom all to herself. And her mother didn't charge her any rent although Emma insisted on making a contribution to the household budget. But something else had happened to make her wonder if she should follow Jackie and get a place of her own.

After years of working as a secretary to raise the family, Mrs Frazer had finally retired. Everyone had expected her to keep busy with local clubs and committees but she surprised them by sinking into a swamp of lethargy. She rarely left the house and took to spending her days in the front parlour doing crossword puzzles and watching soap operas on television while she drank endless cups of tea.

Now, whenever she came home, Emma found her mother was always there. She began to feel that she had no privacy. Even though she rarely interfered, Mrs Frazer was aware of all her movements. She knew when she stayed out late at night. She intercepted her phone calls. She knew where she went and who she was with. It was as if Emma was still a child and she began to see it as an affront to her maturity.

But she did nothing about it till a chance conversation spurred her into action. She was spending a Saturday afternoon with Smitty and Trish who had invited her to lunch. Trish had invested her redoubtable energy and resources on turning her new house into a showcase and now it sparkled with stunning furniture and shining modern appliances.

The spacious living room was dominated by an imposing settee and several comfortable armchairs and a massive television where Smitty liked to watch the sports channels. Fabulous drapes hung from the windows. Little tables held vases of imitation flowers. There were fashionable prints on the walls and cosy rugs on the polished pine floors. Each room was furnished with immaculate taste so that the house resembled a shrine to modern living. Each time she visited, Emma had the impression that she was stepping into the pages of a lifestyle magazine.

"How is Mum?" Trish asked as she poured Emma a glass of wine and led her into the gleaming kitchen with its views over the immaculate lawn.

"She's fine," Emma replied. "She was watching a repeat of *Coronation Street* when I left."

"Does she never do anything interesting?" Trish inquired as she began to prepare a salad for lunch. "I was sure she'd get involved in the parish council. I know they were looking for new members."

Emma shrugged. "She rarely moves out of the house except to go shopping."

"I'm beginning to get worried about her," Trish confessed. "She was always such an active woman but since she retired she seems to have gone to seed. I must have invited her for dinner a dozen times but she refuses to come. Smitty even volunteered to drive her over."

"You know Mum well enough by now. She doesn't like fuss."

"It's got nothing to do with fuss," Trish replied. "The truth is she's becoming eccentric. How do you stick it? You must be driven demented."

"What can I do? If she doesn't want to go out, I can't force her."

"But you're getting older, Emma. Have you never thought of moving out? It might be the trigger to get Mum up off her ass and doing things."

"As a matter of fact, I *have* thought about it."

"Well then, do something about it! And don't let Mum stop you. She's well able to fend for herself."

At that moment, Smitty came lumbering in from the living room.

"I was just telling Emma she should get a place of her own," Trish remarked and Smitty, who loved any conversation to do with property, immediately nodded his head in agreement.

"Only thing to do," he said, his eyes lighting up. "Best piece of advice I could give any young person like you. Owning your own place is a very wise investment."

"But I wasn't thinking of *buying*." Emma said quickly,

anxious to clear up any misunderstanding. "I thought I might rent an apartment."

"Are you crazy? Nobody rents any more. Nobody with any sense, that is."

"But I could never afford to buy," Emma protested.

"Nonsense. It's not difficult." He suddenly threw his arms wide to embrace the room. "How much do you think this house is worth?"

"I haven't the foggiest idea."

"Would €750,000 surprise you?"

Emma found herself gasping. It sounded like an enormous sum of money. "That's three quarters of *a million*."

"Put that way, it sounds more, doesn't it?" Smitty said with a self-satisfied grin. "But that's what a house up the street got last week at auction. And do you know what we paid for it?"

Emma shook her head.

"Five hundred thousand. That means we have made a profit of €250,000 in less than two years. Now tell me where else you would get a return like that on an investment?"

Trish joined in. This was a subject they both enjoyed talking about.

"And that doesn't take account of the fact that we've had first-class accommodation during all that time," she added. "Smitty is right, Emma. Paying rent is a fool's game if you can afford to buy."

Emma blinked. Her head couldn't cope with these sorts of statistics. "I'd never be able to afford it," she said, again.

"Well, let's see." Smitty ran a hand along his handsome jaw. "What sort of property did you have in mind?"

"All I need is a one-bed apartment."

"Any particular location?"

"Somewhere close to the city so I can get into work easily."

"And what about price?"

"I haven't got a clue. You tell me," Emma said, beginning to worry that she had found herself on a very slippery slope.

Smitty sniffed. "What sort of money are you earning?"

Emma told him, painfully aware that her meagre salary was probably a fraction of what Smitty and her sister were earning.

"Do you have any savings?"

"I have a few thousand euros in a demand account."

"That's good," Smitty said, slipping effortlessly into sales mode. "A track record of savings looks positive when you come to apply for a mortgage."

Meanwhile, he had got hold of a pen and paper and was busy doing calculations. Emma watched him in silence. After a few minutes, he glanced up with a serious look on his face.

"You could probably go as high as €200,000. Maybe €220,000 if Trish was able to get you a discounted rate from her bank for the first few years."

Emma glanced helplessly from one to the other.

"And what would I get for that?"

"You'd get a smart one-bed in a new development. Nice lounge, kitchen, bathroom. And close to the DART line which adds value to your property." He tapped the pen gently against his chin. "Would you like me to make some inquiries for you?"

"I don't suppose it would do any harm," Emma said, amazed that the whole thing appeared to be so painless.

* * *

As she left Trish's house, Emma's head was spinning. She wondered how she had allowed herself to be shanghaied into becoming a property owner when all she wanted to do was rent a flat. But she was also excited at the prospect of owning her own apartment. It would enable her to escape from under her mother's feet at last. She would be fully independent. She would be able to host little dinner parties for her friends. And if Smitty's forecast was right, she would be investing in something that would increase in value as time went by.

Fired up with enthusiasm, she suddenly took an interest in the property market, something she had completely ignored till now. That weekend she went out and bought all the papers and spent Sunday afternoon going through the property supplements to get an idea of prices.

On Monday after lunch, Smitty rang her at the office to say he had contacted some developers and had located three apartments that might suit her. He could pick her up after work and take her to view if she was still interested.

"Yes, please," she said, excitedly. "I can meet you at a quarter to six at the top of Grafton Street, if that's all right."

"Bingo," Smitty said.

He turned up right on time, wearing a smart business suit and tie and driving a brand-new Audi A4 that the company had given him as an upgrade. He looked so fresh and brimful of energy that he might have stepped out of the shower. Emma began to understand why Smitty's career, like Trish's, was on an upward curve.

"These properties are all on the south side," he explained once she was comfortably installed in the passenger seat with her seat belt securely fastened. "Two of them are in Booterstown and the other in Blackrock. They are all within walking distance of the train. If you want me to look on the north side, we can do that tomorrow."

"Let's see these ones first," Emma said.

The Booterstown apartments were situated in similar large blocks in gated complexes with landscaped gardens. But while they were new and attractive, they didn't excite her. The blocks were too big. Emma thought of all the other owners and tenants in the buildings living quiet, anonymous lives. What was missing was a sense of community. It was the sort of place where you might never get to know your next-door neighbour.

"Let's see the other one," she said as she climbed back into Smitty's car.

As soon as she stepped inside the Blackrock apartment, she

knew she had found the place she wanted. It was on the third floor of a small, cosy block of fifteen units. The rooms were bright and airy, the décor was tasteful and the apartment came with a range of appliances that included a built-in washing machine and tumble dryer. But what really caught her attention was the beautiful little balcony that opened from the bedroom and had wonderful views of the sea. Immediately, she could picture herself here on a balmy summer's evening with a glass of wine in her hand as she watched the moon rise over Dublin Bay.

She turned at once to her brother-in-law.

"This is it," she said. "This is the one I want."

He looked surprised, as if he had expected her to take more time to make up her mind.

"Are you sure?"

"Yes, I'm positive. How much are they asking?"

"€210,000. But I might be able to persuade them to shave a bit off as a favour to me."

"Can I afford it?"

"Comfortably. You'll have legal costs of course but you're still well within your price range. I'll talk to Trish this evening about a mortgage and let you know exactly what your repayments will be."

"And then what do I have to do?"

"Just leave all that with me," Smitty said confidently. "Let's take it one step at a time."

He rang the following morning to give her the figures. If she borrowed €200,000 on top of the money she had saved, she would have monthly repayments of around €1,300.

Emma's immediate reaction was shock.

"I didn't think it would be that much," she said, as she struggled to recover her breath. "It's an awful lot of money."

"It's not so bad," Smitty said, encouragingly.

"Maybe not for you but it's going to take most of my salary cheque."

"You should be able to afford it," he said, smoothly. "You might have to tighten your belt a little bit."

"More than a little bit," Emma said, getting cold feet at the prospect of paying back €1,300 every month. "Could you find something cheaper?"

"Not for what you want. This is a bargain, Emma. Go any cheaper and you'll be living in a shoebox."

"Let me think it over," she said, finally. "I'll get back to you."

"Okay," said Smitty, sounding disappointed as he put down the phone.

But Emma didn't care. She was beginning to get worried about what she was getting into. €1,300 was a massive chunk to come out of her pay cheque every month. She would be back to counting every penny she had to spend. What would happen to the cosy dinner parties she was planning? She'd be lucky if she was able to serve her guests beans on toast.

But around ten o'clock, when her mother had just gone to bed, she heard the phone ring. It was Trish and she sounded bright and cheerful.

"Smitty tells me you've found a place you like," she began.

"Yes. But it's far too expensive. I'd never be able to afford it on my salary."

"It's a bargain at the price. Do you realise it's worth much more?"

"But I'd be living on bread and cheese," Emma protested. "I don't think I'll go ahead with it."

There was silence for a moment.

"You're making a big mistake," Trish said.

"Maybe I am. But we've got to be realistic here. The repayments are just too much. I'm only a junior civil servant, remember."

"But your salary goes up every year, doesn't it? So, as a proportion of your income, the repayments will actually be falling. In a few years' time, they'll be negligible."

"And what will happen if I get behind?"

"Don't even think like that," Trish said, dismissively. "I've run a stress test on you. Your debt to capital ratio is well within the margin."

It just sounded like gobbledegook to Emma. She wondered if this was some spiel her sister had learnt at these courses she'd been attending.

Emma took a deep breath. It was time to be honest.

"The truth is, I'm scared, Trish. I've never borrowed that sort of money before. I'd have nightmares just thinking about it."

"Well, that's a pity. That apartment is a hot little property and it won't stay on the market forever. In a few years' time it will be worth twice what you pay for it now."

"Well, there you are. We don't always get what we want in this life."

Her sister paused. "There might be a way round this," she said at last. "What if I was to lend you some money?"

"*You* lend me some money?" Emma gasped.

"Yes. I'd hate to see you lose that place for the sake of a few grand."

"I couldn't allow it. It wouldn't feel right."

"Oh, don't be silly. People do it all the time. Smitty's parents gave us some money to pay for the deposit when we bought our place. And already we've paid off a big chunk of the mortgage. I can easily afford it."

"Are you sure?"

"Absolutely. I want to see you get your foot on the property ladder. You can pay me back somewhere down the road."

"It would certainly make a big difference," Emma conceded, still reeling from the shock of her sister's offer.

"Then just leave it with me," Trish said confidently as she put down the phone.

Suddenly, buying the apartment seemed not only feasible but

highly desirable. Trish offered to lend her €50,000 at zero interest which brought her repayments down to €950 a month. This was much more affordable.

"And remember, you'll also get tax relief on that," Trish added. "That will reduce it further."

"You're being very generous," Emma said, hugging her sister. "I wasn't expecting this."

"Oh, give over," Trish laughed. "You're my only sister. We have to look out for each other. I just want to make sure you have a roof over your head, that's all."

Emma thought of the dinky little terrace with its views over the sea. She thought of having coffee out there on a bright summer's morning with the sound of birdsong filling the air. It would be bliss. And now the dinner parties were back on the agenda. She would be able to practise her culinary skills.

She handed everything over to Trish and Smitty who got to work immediately with the paperwork. Within days, she had arranged a mortgage and signed the initial contract with the solicitor. Now she had to tell her mother. She wasn't sure how she was going to react to the news. Emma didn't want to hurt her feelings by making it appear she was deserting her.

But Mrs Frazer wasn't put out in the slightest.

"I suppose your sister put you up to this," she said.

"No, it was my idea."

"Well, you have to make your own way in the world sooner or later. I suppose it can't do any harm."

With Trish and Smitty handling everything, the purchase went ahead without a hitch. Emma became a mere spectator. One Friday afternoon, six weeks after she had first viewed the apartment, she went into the solicitor's office and completed the purchase. Half an hour later, she walked out again with a set of keys. Trish, who had come with her, insisted that they retire to a nearby pub and celebrate with glasses of champagne.

Now Emma was a homeowner, a woman of property. She felt

exhilarated at the prospect. She had her own little place at last and the freedom to do as she pleased.

But it wasn't long before she was brought crashing down to earth. In her haste to buy, there was one important thing she had overlooked. She had no furniture! The apartment came with fridge, washing machine and tumble-dryer. But where was she going to sit? What was she going to eat off? Where was she going to sleep? She could hardly stretch out in a blanket on the floor.

She explained her dilemma to her mother, who agreed that she could have the bed she had slept in since childhood. The next day, she hired a van and with Jackie's help, transported the bed to the new apartment. Then they drove across to the Liberties and spent the afternoon scouring second-hand furniture shops till they managed to salvage a dining table and four chairs, a settee and two armchairs, and an ancient coffee table – all for the grand total of € 500. Emma felt terribly disappointed. This dreary old furniture took the shine off the spanking new apartment. But it would have to do till she could afford something better.

However, when Trish came over the following day, she let out a shriek of horror at the sight.

"My God, you can't seriously propose to use this antique stuff," she wailed. "What will people think?"

"They can think whatever they like. It's all I can afford."

"No," her sister said, defiantly. "I'm not having people talking about you. You can borrow some of mine."

After some argument, it was finally agreed that Trish would lend her some furniture from her second living room which was rarely used and which she said she wouldn't miss.

Emma and Jackie spent the remainder of the weekend licking the apartment into shape. With the aid of several vases and the strategic positioning of some soft cushions, the place now looked much more presentable.

"Aren't you going to have a housewarming party?" Jackie asked when they were finished.

"Do you think I should? I hadn't thought about it," Emma admitted.

"Oh definitely, it's good luck. You don't have to invite everyone in Blackrock, just your close friends."

It was decided that she would give a small party the following weekend with wine and cheese and some canapés for people to nibble on. She invited some colleagues from work and several neighbours from the surrounding apartments. Mrs Frazer, who wasn't feeling well, said she didn't think she could manage a party but would come over the following week on her own to see Emma's apartment.

The evening went very well. People came bearing small household gifts, drank a couple of glasses of wine and stood around chatting for a few hours. She got to know the young couple who lived in the next apartment and worked in advertising and the middle-aged man from upstairs who brought a male friend and who Jackie insisted *had* to be gay. She said she could tell by the trendy clothes they wore. Gay men were very fashion-conscious.

Everyone admired the terrace and the view. By midnight, they had all gone home. Emma carried the glasses and plates into the kitchen and dumped them in the sink, then collected all the empty wine bottles and put them in a black plastic sack for recycling. By one o'clock, she was tucked up in bed. When she could afford it, she would buy bright new furniture and give a bigger party. But for the moment, she was happy. At last, she had achieved something in her life.

She owned her own home.

Chapter 7

But it didn't take long before another truth began to dawn. Emma had only been able to buy the apartment because of Trish's generosity. This gave her sister even greater control over her and now she realised that she was even deeper in her debt.

But at least the decision to purchase the apartment had worked out well. Eventually, she managed to buy new furniture and return the pieces that Trish had loaned her. She turned the apartment into a cosy little nest for herself and got to know all her neighbours including the gay man from upstairs who worked in publishing and turned out to be a fabulous friend.

On weekend mornings, she had breakfast on her terrace with its lovely views of the sea and on summer evenings she sat with a book and a glass of wine and watched as the golden sun sank over the bay. However, there was one problem that continued to cause her concern. Her mother's situation was continuing to deteriorate. Since moving out of the family home, Emma had kept in regular contact and visited her at weekends. But each time, she came away feeling unhappy. Her mother had changed her mind about Emma's move and now seemed to believe she had abandoned her. She began to grow cranky and constantly found things to complain about.

"What did I ever do to you?" she would ask.

"That's a silly question," Emma would reply.

"Didn't I always look after you? Even though I was a widow and had no money? Didn't I always do the best for you?"

"Of course you did."

"So why were you in such a hurry to get away? Was this house not good enough for you any more?"

Emma would repeat for the umpteenth time that the move had nothing to do with the house or her mother, even though this wasn't strictly true.

"I've already explained, Mum. I wanted my own little place. I couldn't expect you to look after me forever."

"You could have stayed here as long as you liked. You didn't have to leave. It wasn't as if you were getting married like your sister."

After every visit, Emma left feeling sad. Her mother's constant complaining made her feel guilty. And she noticed other things that began to worry her too. Mrs Frazer had started to neglect herself. For a woman who had once been so meticulous and insisted that the house should always shine like a new pin, she had grown slovenly. Dust began to pile up on the windowsills. Dishes lay unwashed in the sink. The bedclothes weren't changed. And her diet seemed to consist entirely of junk food and precooked meals, some of which lay in the fridge till they began to go stale.

One weekend in a fit of conscience, Emma went to her mother's house and cleaned it from top to bottom and then prepared a nourishing meal which she forced Mrs Frazer to eat at the dining table instead of sitting in her armchair in front of the television. But she knew that sooner or later some hard decisions would have to be made. Her mother's attitude wasn't likely to change.

It was at times such as these that she valued the friendship of people like Jackie. She talked to her every day, they had lunch several times a week and they continued their forays into Dublin's pubs and nightclubs in search of adventure. But now these outings were restricted to weekends. The cost of maintaining her apartment had put an end to partying every night. Besides, she was beginning to tire of the noisy club scene and the brittle, insubstantial people she met there.

With her lithe figure and dark good looks, Emma had no difficulty attracting boyfriends. But it was the quality of these admirers that was the problem. Since Trish had persuaded her to dump Alan Casey, she had taken up with a succession of men but none of them interested her and few lasted more than a couple of weeks.

The men she met seemed to fall into two camps. Some were arrogant and full of their own self-importance, boasting about their careers and their ambitions and how much they were earning. They seemed to regard themselves as God's Gift to Women and they bored her rigid. Others seemed to be in awe of her, as if they couldn't believe their good fortune in meeting such an attractive woman and terrified of doing or saying anything that might displease her. These men were the worst. She found them insipid and lacking in any trace of personality. They seemed quite happy to allow her to make all the decisions about where they should go and what they should do. They reminded her of Smitty and his relationship with Trish and she recalled her sister's remark about not allowing a man to become too confident.

But this wasn't what she wanted. Emma longed for a man with a bit of spirit, someone she could look up to. She wanted a man with independence and a mind of his own, someone she could admire and trust. However, as time went on, she found this increasingly difficult and sometimes she wondered if she was ever going to meet the man of her dreams.

* * *

It was in this gloomy mood that she came into work one morning to find the office in uproar. A notice had gone up on the bulletin board to say that the Human Resources department was undertaking a review of work practices and would be paying a visit the following week. Each member of staff would be given the opportunity of an interview to discuss any problems they were experiencing in their job. They would also be asked for their views on how the operation might be streamlined and improved.

After work Emma went straight home, sat down at the kitchen table and began to write out a list of problems with the job and suggestions for remedying them. By bedtime, she had filled ten foolscap pages with notes. The following morning when she came into work she made a beeline for her supervisor, Dolly O'Brien, and told her she wanted to put her name down for interview.

Her interview was scheduled for Monday afternoon at three. The morning dragged and by lunchtime she was itching to get up to the third floor to meet the people from Human Resources. At two fifty, Dolly O'Brien gave her the signal that it was time to go. Emma gathered her notes, straightened her blouse and set off. There was a small waiting room and a secretary who asked her to take a seat. She waited as the minutes ticked away and then at a minute past three the door opened and the previous interviewee came out. Emma rose, smoothed down her skirt and politely knocked on the door. She heard a male voice invite her to come in.

She entered the room. A dark-haired man was sitting behind a desk. His head was bent over some papers. He looked up and she felt her heart miss a beat. She stared in disbelief. The man sitting behind the desk was her old teacher, Tim Devlin.

Chapter 8

For a couple of seconds she stood there feeling dumbstruck. It was years since she had seen him but she recognised him at once. He had barely changed at all. His hair was still dark and shining and his brown eyes sparkled with the intensity she remembered from her schooldays. He was smartly dressed in a neat shirt and a pale blue tie and a matching handkerchief in the breast pocket of his jacket.

He smiled warmly, stood up and held out his hand. She grasped it firmly.

"Emma Frazer?"

"Yes," she replied.

"Please take a seat, Emma. My name is Tim Devlin."

"I know," she said, in a voice just above a whisper.

"You do? Has my fame spread through the department so quickly?" he laughed. "I only arrived this morning."

"We've met before," Emma said as she struggled to recover from the shock of seeing him again.

"Have we? Where was that?"

"You were my teacher."

Suddenly his face broke into a smile of recognition.

"Of course, you were at St Benedict's! You know, I thought there was something familiar about you. But you've changed, Emma. You've grown up."

"*You* haven't changed at all. I knew you at once."

"Oh, I don't know," he said modestly.

"You look exactly as I remember you," she protested.

"But I was only a young teacher fresh out of college. I wanted to inspire the world. I'm afraid I don't have that kind of energy any more."

"You certainly inspired me," she said. "WB Yeats. 'The Lake Isle of Innisfree.' I loved it when you read that poem."

He laughed. "You were my star pupil, Emma. Teaching you was a pleasure."

She felt a blush creep across her cheeks.

"Did you take Honours English like I suggested?" he asked.

"Yes, and I got a B grade, thanks to you."

"Congratulations! Do you still like reading?"

"Of course."

"Who is your favourite author?"

"Thomas Hardy. You introduced me to him, remember?"

"So I didn't waste my time, after all?"

"Oh, no, you were our favourite teacher. We were all heartbroken when you left. Why did you go so suddenly?"

"My contract ran out. I was only temporary. I was sorry to leave too. But permanent teaching jobs weren't so easy to come by back then. So I joined the Civil Service. That's how I'm here." He shook his head. "And now our paths have crossed again in the Department of Social Affairs, of all places. It really is a funny old world."

They both laughed and their eyes locked.

"It's wonderful to see you again," he said.

"You too."

"And you look so good."

"Thank you."

He glanced down at the papers on the desk before him.

"So you're a Clerical Officer in the Pensions section?"

"Yes."

"How do you like your job?"

"It's fine," Emma said. "But it can be quite boring. There are a lot of things that should be changed."

Tim Devlin nodded. "Well, that's what we're here to talk about."

For the next half hour Emma unburdened herself about the petty regulations, the old-fashioned work practices, the boring repetition of the tasks she had to perform.

"What would you change if you could?"

"I would give people more responsibility. I'd let them take more decisions. I'd trust them more."

"Not everybody likes responsibility," he said.

"But there are plenty who do. I know a lot of the work we do is routine. But with a little bit of imagination it could be made much more interesting."

Tim Devlin interjected something from time to time but mostly he let her speak. Talking to him like this had a wonderful soothing effect. But the half hour was gone too soon.

He eventually looked at his watch and put down his pen.

"I'm sorry to have to cut you short, Emma, but our time is up. Someone else is waiting. But I've listened carefully to what you've had to say. And I can give you an assurance that your views will be taken seriously."

He stood up and shook hands once more. His dark eyes seemed to fasten onto hers.

"It was lovely meeting you again. Will you promise to do something for me?"

"Sure."

"Keep up the reading."

"I don't need to promise. I do it anyway."

He held the door open and a minute later, Emma found herself back in the waiting room.

She returned to her desk feeling totally uplifted. It was amazing the effect Tim Devlin had on her. He had lost none of the magical charm she had known when he was her teacher. He still retained his easy manner and the ability to make her feel important and appreciated. She couldn't help but marvel at the way fate had conspired for their paths to cross once more.

Over the next few days she felt her mind drifting constantly to thoughts of Tim. He still looked as handsome as the first day she saw him. She couldn't help wondering if he was married. She had seen no wedding ring but that meant nothing. Many men didn't wear rings. But she knew that a man as good as Tim Devlin was unlikely to have remained single for long. She thought enviously of the lucky woman who had managed to get him for a husband.

Eventually, the Human Resources team completed their interviews and departed. Life in the Pensions section returned to its normal humdrum routine and Emma got on with her life. She visited her mother every weekend and made sure the house was kept clean and tidy and that Mrs Frazer was eating properly. She had a couple of dates with unsuitable men. But the sparkle seemed to have gone out of her life and now everything seemed flat and dull.

But one afternoon about six weeks later she was jolted out of her lethargy by an unexpected phone call. When she picked it up she heard the unmistakable Northern lilt of Tim Devlin's voice.

"I was wondering if you might be free for lunch some day?" he said.

Emma was completely taken aback.

"When?"

"Tomorrow?"

"Of course," she heard herself say.

When she put the phone down her hand was shaking like a leaf in a storm. Tim Devlin had arranged to meet her for lunch the following day at the Shelbourne Hotel. Emma had to pinch herself to make sure this was really happening.

*   *   *

The lunch had been arranged for one o'clock. As she hurried through the streets crowded with shoppers and tourists, she felt her heart begin to beat faster. She was dressed in a black pencil skirt with a plum-coloured jacket and a crisp white blouse. She had kept her jewellery to a minimum: a simple silver chain and small silver earrings. She'd wanted to look her best but not too obviously dressed up for the occasion. Her hair needed cutting and she cursed herself that she hadn't got it done at the weekend when she'd had time. But how was she to know that Tim Devlin would appear again out of the blue and invite her to lunch?

She had struggled to keep her soaring imagination under check up to now but as the appointed meeting drew near she realised that she couldn't wait to see Tim Devlin again and hear his voice.

He was waiting in the hotel lobby. And what a gorgeous figure he made! He was wearing a pale grey sports jacket with grey slacks and a pale blue shirt with a tie in a deeper shade of blue. In Emma's eyes, the clothes just served to emphasise his dark good looks. As she came through the doors and spotted him, she couldn't escape the thought that she had never seen a man who looked so perfect.

He saw her and his face lit up with pleasure.

"Emma," he said, coming forward and warmly grasping her hand. "It's so good to see you again."

His eyes sparkled as he spoke. In an instant, his glance had travelled over her, appraising her appearance. He seemed pleased with what he saw for his face immediately broke into a broad smile. Emma felt herself glow in the warmth of his approval.

"Have you been waiting long?" she managed to say.

"No, I only arrived a minute ago."

"I thought I might be late."

"Not at all, you're bang on time. I've already booked. Why don't we go in?"

He ushered her politely before him into the dining room where the waiter came forward and bowed before leading them to a table at the window. Outside, they could see the busy city pass by.

Emma let her gaze travel round the splendid room. She had been here once before for one of Trish's press receptions but had never eaten in the hotel. So she was quite impressed by the magnificent décor, the gleaming glasses and shining silver and the way the waiters swooped and glided around the table to make a fuss of them.

Tim leaned across and spoke softly to her.

"You look radiant," he whispered and she felt a thrill of pleasure tingle along her spine. She glanced up and found herself staring into his dark brown eyes. They were boring deep into hers.

"Thank you."

"You've grown into a very beautiful young woman, Emma."

She felt her cheeks burn scarlet. This praise was like a sweet symphony to her ears.

He reached out and gently stroked her hand. "You don't mind me saying that, do you?"

"Why should I? Every woman likes to be complimented."

"Well, I'm glad you see it that way because it's true. It's amazing the transformation that's come over you. You're easily the most beautiful woman in the room. Look around if you don't believe me."

Emma glanced once more at the tables dotted about. A number of thin, elegant, well-groomed ladies were dining with their partners. Their tanned complexions shone with vitality. They wore expensive jewellery and fine clothes. Much grander than anything she could hope to afford. And Tim was telling her that she looked more beautiful than any of them. She felt her heart warm at the compliment.

"What would you like to drink?" he asked.

"I'd better stick to water. I've got an afternoon of work ahead of me."

"Can't you risk a glass of wine?" He winked boyishly. "For old time's sake?"

She smiled in assent.

He smartly summoned a waiter and gave their order, then buried his head in the menu for a few moments.

"I think I'll have the lamb," he said at last. "What about you?"

But Emma's appetite had mysteriously disappeared. She could order anything and it wouldn't matter. It was enough just to sit here in these beautiful surroundings and gaze into the face of this handsome man.

"Lamb sounds fine," she managed to say.

The waiter returned with the wine and Tim gave their order for the food. She noticed how deferential the waiter was. It was amazing, she thought. Even the waiters can sense how special Tim is. Look at the way they show him respect. See how they look up to him.

He poured the wine and raised his glass.

"To us. To a happy future."

They clicked their glasses together and Emma sipped the wine. She felt a contented feeling spread over her.

"You know, I've been thinking about you a lot since our last meeting," he said.

"Really?"

"Yes. You brought me back to St Benedict's. I think that was the happiest period of my career."

"Why? Aren't you happy now?" she asked.

A pensive look came into his eyes.

"I enjoy my job well enough," he said. "But there's something missing. Sometimes I wish I could be more fulfilled."

"Perhaps you should go back to teaching?"

"That would be difficult. But, in any case, I realise that it's not the teaching in itself that I miss." He straightened his napkin. "It has to do with the environment I worked in then. It has to do with books, with poetry, with literature. I enjoyed teaching because I was imparting the love of words to eager, receptive young minds like yours. That is why I found the job so rewarding."

"So what would you really like to do?"

He swirled the wine in his glass. "Can't you guess?"

"No."

"I'd like to be a writer, a full-time writer, creating images and ideas and stories, surrounded by books, allowing my imagination to take flight. You can't believe the sheer pleasure of that, Emma, the immense, indescribable satisfaction. *That's* what I'd really like to do."

"Then you should go for it," she said.

He looked up and smiled but this time there was a hint of sadness in his eyes. "If only it was that simple," he sighed.

"What is preventing you?"

"We're not always in control of our own destinies, Emma. Sometimes we make decisions and later we realise we have taken a wrong turning and it's too late to go back."

"I don't think it's ever too late if it's something you really want."

He stared into space for a moment before replying. "Perhaps you're right," he said, at last. "But it takes enormous courage. And not all of us can be so brave."

Their meal arrived and the moment of intimacy between them passed. It was as if Tim had allowed her a glimpse into his soul and now he was drawing back.

"Did you ever finish your report?" she asked, changing the conversation.

"Almost," he said, holding up his fork as he chewed a piece of lamb. "We should have it finished in a week or so. I want to thank you, Emma. Your contribution was the best we received. It was the most frank and the most constructive. I'll send you a copy when it's finished."

"But will anything be done? That was the whole point of the exercise."

He shrugged his broad shoulders. "That will be for others to decide. We have set out a list of recommendations for improving the efficiency of the department. But it will be someone else's job to implement them. However, between you and me, they'd be crazy not to."

His mood changed again and he became jolly. He regaled her with funny stories that had her laughing out loud and occasionally caused heads to turn. By the time the dessert was served, Emma was wishing this lunch could go on forever. But eventually she saw him glance at his watch.

She suddenly realised how quickly the time had passed. It had been so relaxing and Tim had clearly enjoyed it too. What was going to happen next? Was it possible he might ask to see her again?

He summoned one of the waiters and paid the bill and she followed him out to the busy street. He stood awkwardly for a moment as if he too was sorry that their meeting had finally come to an end.

"Thanks for a lovely lunch," she said.

"It was my pleasure."

He fumbled with his briefcase and took out a book.

"I bought this for you. I think you'll enjoy it. It's something to bring back happy memories."

She looked at it. It was a collection of the poetry of WB Yeats. She felt a wave of emotion sweep over her.

"What a beautiful thought," she whispered.

He bent closer and placed his hands on her shoulders. She felt his warm lips gently brush her cheek.

"It's been wonderful seeing you again, Emma. I have enjoyed it immensely." He paused. "Perhaps we might have lunch another time?"

"Yes," she replied, quickly. "I'd like that very much."

They stood for a while longer as if they both wished to delay the moment when they must part. Then a hint of sadness came back into his face.

"Now, I've got to fly. I promised my wife I'd meet her in Grafton Street at three o'clock. I mustn't keep her waiting."

It was as if a thunderbolt had struck Emma. It was as if the ground had opened beneath her feet.

He kissed her once more then turned and began walking quickly away. She looked at the book he had given her. She opened the flyleaf and read the inscription: *For Emma with fond thoughts, from Tim.*

She watched his departing figure as he hurried along the busy pavement. *Of course* he had a wife. Why had she ever allowed herself to think otherwise? But it was little consolation. As she turned away from the hotel, she felt her heart flood with sadness and it was all she could do to stop herself from weeping.

Chapter 9

Meanwhile, Mrs Frazer was a continuing cause of concern. Her odd behaviour seemed to get worse. Now, she hardly ever left the house. She took to sitting in the front parlour for days on end, never leaving except to go to Mass on Sunday. And her appearance started to decline along with her physical condition. On several occasions, Emma had to persuade her to take a bath and insist that she come with her to the hairdresser's to get her hair styled.

Her diet now consisted almost entirely of tea and buttered bread. She lost weight and began to look frail and vulnerable and much older than her years. Emma wondered if the time had arrived to get her into a nursing home or at the very least see if Social Services could provide her with a home help. But she knew this would be a battle. Her mother had always been fiercely independent and was certain to resist any attempt to get assistance for her. Then she began to get sick.

It started with back pains. Emma noticed it one day when she was visiting and her mother got up to go to the bathroom. She winced as she lifted herself out of the chair.

"What is it, Mum?" Emma asked, suddenly alarmed.

"Just a little dart," she said. "It'll pass in a minute."

She rubbed her back with her arm as she hobbled out of the room.

"How long have you had these pains?" Emma asked when she returned.

"Now don't you fuss," her mother warned. "It's just a touch of arthritis. Everybody gets it at my age."

"Maybe you should go to the doctor and have it checked?"

At the mention of the doctor, Mrs Frazer bristled. She had a long-standing contempt for the medical profession who, she claimed, were only interested in making money and were sure to find something wrong with you even if you were as healthy as a trout. She was convinced that once she fell into their hands, she would never escape.

"What? And pay good money for some scoundrel to tell me what I know already."

"I don't see that it can do any harm," Emma insisted. "At least it will put your mind at ease."

"I'm not going. End of story," her mother said.

"They might be able to treat it."

"If I want something, I can get it from the chemist," Mrs Frazer announced with an air of finality that said the subject was closed and she would brook no further argument.

So instead of seeking medical attention, she relied on herbal remedies which she bought from the local supermarket. Before long, she had a collection of pills and tablets with exotic-sounding names like Oil of Wild Dandelion and Extract of Gorse Petals which the supermarket assistant had assured her were natural remedies and would help the body to heal itself. She took them religiously every morning with a cup of tea. And for a while, they seemed to work. She said she could feel them doing her good. Then one evening Emma turned up at her house to find her bent in agony over the kitchen sink.

She rushed to help her to a chair then knelt beside her on the floor.

"Where's the pain?"

Mrs Frazer pointed to her stomach. "I'll be fine," she said. "I just need to rest."

"How long has this been going on?"

"Just a week or two."

"I'm getting you to a doctor," Emma said.

Despite her mother's protests, she bundled her into her car and took her at once to the local GP who examined her with a stern face and asked why she hadn't come to see her earlier. The GP arranged for X-rays to be taken at Beaumont hospital. The results were not good. When the doctor studied them, she made an immediate appointment for Mrs Frazer to visit a specialist.

Emma took the day off work and went with her. Her mother was extremely nervous and irritable and the situation wasn't helped by the long queue of people waiting in the consulting rooms in Fitzwilliam Square. Emma tried to cheer her up.

"This doctor will soon sort you out. He's one of the top men in the country."

"With top prices to match, no doubt," Mrs Frazer snapped.

"Don't talk like that. You should have gone to the GP sooner instead of wasting your money with that herbal stuff."

"It wasn't wasted. And there's nothing wrong with me. Now, for the last time, will you stop fussing?"

Eventually, her turn came. Mrs Frazer gripped Emma's arm and insisted that she accompany her into the surgery.

The doctor was a friendly, middle-aged man. He immediately smiled at Mrs Frazer and tried to put her at ease. He read the letter from the GP and studied the X-ray results.

"Now just show me exactly where the pain is," he said and began gently probing Mrs Frazer's back and stomach while he asked questions and took notes.

When he was finished he took a deep breath and stared intently at her.

"I'm going to send you for more tests."

"I don't know what all the mystery is about," Mrs Frazer replied. "It's only arthritis."

But the doctor shook his head. "It's not. If it was arthritis, it would show up in your X-rays. And there are the stomach pains to be considered."

"So what is it?"

"I can't be certain till we get these tests carried out. In the meantime, I'm prescribing some medication to relieve the pain. My secretary will arrange an appointment for the tests and she'll call you again for another visit."

He had resumed his pleasant professional manner, trying to reassure her. "Try not to worry. We'll soon get to the bottom of this."

But Mrs Frazer was far from satisfied. Outside on the street, she became quite angry.

"What did I tell you? It's all a moneymaking racket. They pass you around from one to the other like a second-hand car. You heard him. He hasn't got a clue."

Once Emma got her safely home, she rang Trish.

"I'm worried about Mum," she began. "Her pains are getting worse. They've spread to her stomach. We've just been to see a senior consultant in Fitzwilliam Square."

"My God," Trish said. "What did he say is the matter with her?"

"He doesn't know."

"It's probably that junk food she's been eating. These guys have to do something to justify the outrageous fees they charge. Anyway, you'll have to handle this on your own. I'm going down to Waterford for a conference next week. I'm run off my feet. You've got no idea."

Thanks for nothing, Emma thought as she put down the

phone. She felt resentful that her sister hadn't been more helpful but at least Trish had been told.

The following week, Mrs Frazer went for the tests and a few days later she got a call from the doctor's secretary to say he wanted to see her again as soon as possible.

Emma accompanied her once more. This time, she detected a slight change in his attitude. He appeared much more solicitous and made sure that Mrs Frazer was sitting comfortably and had a cup of tea before telling her the diagnosis.

"There's no easy way to say this, Mrs Frazer."

"Say what?"

"I'm afraid the news isn't good."

"Why don't you just tell me?"

"You've got cancer of the liver. I'm going to admit you to hospital straight away."

* * *

For once, Trish was at a loss how to respond. Her usual can-do self-confidence seemed to desert her and she sounded devastated when Emma rang to tell her the news.

"Oh my God," she said. "I never suspected for one minute that it was something this bad. What are we going to do?"

"There's nothing we *can* do except wait. But I have to tell you that the consultant didn't sound very optimistic."

"Oh, poor Mum! When can we go to see her?"

"Whenever you like."

"What will I bring her? Does she need anything?"

"Bring her a book or some magazines. I think she's got everything else she requires."

"I'm useless at this sort of thing," Trish moaned. "Thank God you were around, Emma. I don't know how I would have handled this on my own."

But strangely, Mrs Frazer didn't seem particularly fazed by what had happened. She appeared to accept it as her fate. It just confirmed her suspicion of doctors. She had always said that once she fell into their hands, things would only get worse. When they went to visit her in hospital the following day, she actually seemed quite cheerful.

"It's like a hotel in here," she said, pointing to the television set above the bed. "I can watch my soaps and the staff couldn't be nicer. At least I'm getting something for all the taxes I've paid over the years."

Meanwhile, Smitty had been busy making inquiries. An old school friend who was a doctor was able to inform him that cancer of the liver was very serious. There was a strong possibility that it could be terminal. This sent Trish into a further tizzy. Now she began to blame herself for not looking after her mother better when she had the chance.

"I should have insisted that she come and live with us," she told Emma. "We've got loads of room. I could have kept an eye on her instead of leaving her alone like that. What sort of daughter am I?"

"Don't beat yourself up," Emma replied. "She wouldn't have wanted it. You know how independent she is. Even if you had persuaded her to come, she would have hated every minute of it."

"You're right," Trish agreed. "But I can't help feeling guilty. After all she did for us over the years, scraping and saving to make sure we were well looked after. She didn't get very much thanks, did she?"

"We did all we could. You can't force gratitude on people."

"You know, you're absolutely right," Trish conceded. "I never thought of it that way."

* * *

After more tests and further consultations, it was decided that Mrs Frazer would require surgery. Even this development didn't appear to bother her. She regarded it as inevitable. Now that she had fallen into the doctors' clutches they would do what they liked with her.

The day for the operation came around. The two sisters sat with her till it was time to go off to the theatre then settled down to await the outcome. By now, Trish had dropped everything she was doing to make time to be with her mother. It meant long hours of hanging around in the waiting room till eventually the doctor came to see them. Emma knew at once from the look on his face that things had not gone well. He drew them aside and shook his head.

"I'm afraid it didn't work," he said. "The cancer is too far gone."

Emma felt an empty sadness take hold of her.

"So what happens now?" Trish asked, anxiously clutching at straws.

"We'll have another consultation in the morning and decide what to do next."

"Could she have a transplant?" Trish persisted.

"That is one of the things we'll consider."

He looked from one to the other and shrugged.

"I'm sorry," he said and left them.

Emma now feared the worst. She had guessed for some time that her mother might not survive but, like Trish, she had tried desperately to keep hope alive. Now she had to face the truth and, despite being prepared, it was not easy. And little did she know that another shock lay just ahead.

"I need a drink," she said when the consultant had left. "Will you join me?"

Trish nodded and they went off to a nearby pub where they each had a gin and tonic.

"You realise she's not going to recover?" Emma said grimly when they were both seated.

"Yes," her sister said with a sigh. "I've figured that out."

"I've spoken to one of the consultants. You know that most

of them are afraid to tell you what time it is in case you sue? Well, this guy wasn't holding out much hope."

They sat in silence for a few minutes.

"Do you think she knows?" Trish asked, at last.

"Probably. She's not stupid. I'd say she has guessed by now."

Emma watched the tears well up in Trish's eyes.

"It's all so sad," she said. "She didn't have much of a life, did she, what with Dad leaving her and everything?"

Emma's mouth fell open. She sat forward and stared into her sister's face. "Leaving her? What are you talking about?"

Trish took out a handkerchief and began to blow her nose. "Didn't you know?" she asked.

"I thought he died. That's what we were always told."

"He didn't die. He ran off and left her when we were babies. With some floozy he had met."

Emma felt like she had just been kicked in the head. She reeled from the shock. "It can't be true!"

"It *is* true. Aunt Mollie told me. Did you never wonder why she never kept any photographs of him?"

"Of course I did."

"Well, that's the reason. He did a runner. He abandoned us."

"My God," Emma said, catching her breath, "I had no idea. She never said a word."

"She wanted to wipe out all memory of him."

"But he might still be alive."

Trish sniffed and wiped her eyes. "He might be. But it was a long time ago. I'd say the chances are he's dead by now."

Emma sat back, stunned by this shocking revelation. What else was there in the family history that she didn't know?

"Poor Mum," she said, at last. "She must have been destroyed. Can you imagine the shame and all the gossip behind her back?"

"And the betrayal and rejection she must have felt. It must have been terrible for her."

"Did you ever talk to her about it?"

"Oh God, no," Trish said. "Aunt Mollie swore me to secrecy. She only told me because I badgered it out of her. I had worked out there was something odd about Mum's story and the fact that there were no photographs."

Another thought struck Emma. "We could have brothers and sisters," she said.

"Half-brothers and sisters."

"But they could be out there. They could be anybody."

"I know," Trish said. "I've thought about that too."

"Those stories you used to tell me about him. You didn't remember our father at all, did you?"

Trish shook her head. "I just made that up to impress you. You were always easily impressed, Emma."

* * *

After the failed operation, Mrs Frazer's situation quickly deteriorated. She never really recovered and by the end of the week she had slipped into a coma. Everyone accepted that it was only a question of time before she succumbed.

It was very hard watching her die. They had been a close family, particularly when they were children growing up, a cosy little club, her mother had called them. She passed away in the night when neither of the sisters was there at the bedside. It was Trish who got the message from the hospital. As the eldest child, she had assumed the role of next of kin. She tried to put a brave face on things when she rang Emma to tell her.

"Awkward to the end, eh?" she said. "She decides to wait till our backs are turned before popping her clogs. That's typical of Mum, all right."

"She's better off," Emma said.

"Maybe but I still wish it hadn't happened."

Smitty immediately stepped in to take charge of the funeral arrangements. He said the sisters had enough to concern them, grieving for their dead mother. With his usual brisk efficiency, he dealt with the priest and the undertaker and the cemetery. He inserted death notices in the papers and arranged for the floral tributes. The sisters, who were worn out by the ordeal, were happy to leave everything in his capable hands.

But there was one final surprise waiting for Emma. Smitty made inquiries about Mrs Frazer's estate and came back with the startling information that she had more money than anyone had ever suspected. She had been saving for years and had over €100,000 squirreled away in a bank account. Her will stipulated that everything was to be divided equally between the sisters, including the house which Smitty said could now be quite valuable. The area was undergoing a renewal and was much sought after by young professionals. If they decided to sell, it was sure to fetch a good price.

Emma was pleased by the turnout for the funeral. Her mother had few friends and in her last years had become practically a recluse but the church was packed and that gave her quiet satisfaction. She knew that Mrs Frazer would have regarded it as an indication of her good standing in the community.

Many of the people who came to show solidarity were work colleagues, particularly people who knew Trish. But there was also a good attendance of old neighbours. And she was pleased to see Jackie and some of her own friends among the mourners. After the funeral service, Smitty had arranged a reception at a local hotel where food and drinks were served for the attendance. The sisters, in their severe black mourning clothes, welcomed those who turned up. People shook hands and said how sorry they were and how much they had admired their mother. Several had little anecdotes about the kind things she had done in her life. Everyone said she would be sadly missed.

Emma found it a weary ordeal standing in line making small talk with people she didn't know very well and many of whom she had never met before. She began to feel quite tired so when the crowd started to thin out, she seized the opportunity to slip away to a sofa in a quiet corner of the room. She sat down and her mind drifted into a reverie. She thought how her life had been turned upside down in the last few weeks. Only now was she beginning to appreciate the emotional toll it had taken on her. But she was no sooner seated than she was suddenly interrupted again.

"Excuse me," she heard a voice say. "I don't think you know me, but I used to work with your mother."

She looked up to see a figure in a black overcoat standing beside her.

"Oh," Emma said, sitting up straight.

The man held out his hand to introduce himself.

"My name is Colin Enright. I was terribly sorry to hear about her death."

Chapter 10

Emma took the outstretched hand and found herself staring up into a pair of penetratingly blue eyes. They belonged to a tall, handsome man of about thirty with thick, dark hair.

"Forgive me," she said, "I was daydreaming."

She attempted to get up from the sofa but Colin Enright quickly moved to restrain her.

"Please don't disturb yourself. You're probably tired. I'm sure this has been a very trying ordeal for you."

"Well, it *has* been a terrible shock," Emma conceded, repeating the mantra she had already used a dozen times today. "Until a few weeks ago, we had no idea that Mum was even ill."

"Death of a parent is never easy. Even when it is expected. I thought I would come along and extend my condolences."

"That's very kind," Emma said. "How well did you know her?"

"I'm not sure anybody knew your mother terribly well. She was a very private person. But I had great admiration for her. She was a wonderful woman."

Colin Enright explained that he had worked with Mrs Frazer when she was a secretary in Mr Carter's solicitor's office. Then he had been a young legal trainee. Now he was qualified and was a partner in a busy law firm. He chatted pleasantly with Emma in the polite tones that she assumed all solicitors learnt in law school.

"She was always patient and considerate, particularly towards younger staff like me. Mr Carter was very old-fashioned. He expected everything to be exact. But your mother had a lighter touch. I have very fond memories of her."

"Really?" Emma replied. Since her mother's death, she was discovering things about her that she had never even guessed.

"Oh, yes," he continued. "She used to keep him under tight control. We used to joke that she was the human face of the firm." He lowered his voice to speak in a confidential whisper. "She had her own way of dealing with him. Between you and me, I think he was afraid of her."

Emma smiled at the thought of her mother bullying the important lawyer. "Come to think about it, it does sound like Mum, all right," she said.

"Would you like me to get you another drink?" he asked, pointing to her empty glass.

Emma found that she was enjoying this conversation with Colin Enright. She felt at ease with him. He had helped to take her mind off her gloomy thoughts. And talking to him kept other mourners at bay. She had already shaken hands with so many people that her arm felt sore.

"If you don't mind," she said. "It's gin and tonic."

He took her glass and disappeared in the direction of the bar. A few minutes later he was back with two fresh glasses.

"Do you mind if I sit down?" he inquired.

"Of course not, I should have offered." She moved along the sofa to make room for him. "How did you learn about Mum's death?"

"I saw the notice in the newspaper."

"We should have alerted the firm," she said, suddenly feeling guilty that they had forgotten to tell her former employers.

"But she left us more than five years ago. And you had so much to do. Funerals can be a terrible time. You can't be expected to think of everything."

"How is Mr Carter?" Emma asked, wondering if he was here too and no one had welcomed him.

"He died a few years ago, a few months after he retired, in fact. Some people say that's what killed him although the official version was coronary heart disease. His son-in-law is running the firm now."

"I'm sorry to hear that. He was very kind to Mum. She always had a good word for him."

He paused and she found his blue eyes staring intently at her.

"This has been a very hard blow for you. If I can be of any assistance, anything whatever, don't hesitate to call."

He took a little business card from his pocket and handed it to her. They chatted for a while longer and then he looked at his watch and said he had better get back to the office. He solemnly shook hands and Emma watched as he made his way to Trish and shook her hand too before striding confidently from the room.

* * *

About ten days later, she was surprised to receive a phone call from Colin Enright at work. She had just spent the morning dealing with a knotty problem concerning the pension of a retired farmer in Co Clare and was taken aback to hear Colin's voice on the line. She didn't recall giving him her number. But then she remembered that solicitors were like detectives. They had ways of ferreting out information. He wanted to know if he could take her to dinner some evening.

"I thought it might help lift your spirits," he explained.

Emma was thrown into confusion. She had never expected to

hear from him again. She said the first thing that came into her head.

"Thank you. That's very thoughtful."

"So when would suit you?"

"I don't really know."

"How about tomorrow evening? Does eight o'clock sound okay?"

"I suppose so," she said.

"Would you like me to pick you up?"

"If it's not inconvenient."

"No, it's not inconvenient at all. Where will I call?"

She gave him her address.

"Till tomorrow at eight," he said. "I'm looking forward to seeing you again."

"Me too," Emma said and put down the phone.

The following evening she left the office early and hurried back to her apartment to prepare for her date. It was some time since she had been out to dinner with a man. She soaked in the tub for half an hour and thought about the evening ahead. She prayed that he wouldn't spend the time talking about work or golf or rugby. Even dinner with Tom Cruise would be a heavy price to pay for an ordeal like that. When the water began to cool, she got out of the bath and got dried then sat in front of the dressing-table and stared at herself in the mirror.

It was very intriguing. Neither Trish nor Emma looked at all like their mother. They were both dark with black hair and hazel eyes and high cheekbones whereas Mrs Frazer had been fair. She had always assumed that she had inherited her looks from her father. She wondered if there was a photograph of him in existence somewhere. Perhaps when she got time, she would conduct some research in the Registrar's office and see if she could come up with more information.

Now she needed to decide what to wear. Emma didn't possess a wardrobe like Trish who had racks of clothes which she was forever clearing out and giving away to charity shops. Occasionally she would offer something to her sister but the clothes rarely fitted. As a result, Emma's range, like her salary, was much more limited. In the end, she picked a little black dress that she had bought on a whim in the New Year sales and never worn.

It looked terrific with black high-heeled sandals and some silver jewellery. She had just finished dressing when she heard the buzzer announce Colin's arrival. She quickly sprayed a little perfume on her wrists, locked the apartment door and hurried downstairs to find him waiting for her.

But if she was expecting a sober lawyerly type, she was in for a surprise. She was struck by the transformation since their last meeting. He had discarded the formal business suit he had worn to the funeral and now he was dressed in a blue woollen jacket and dark slacks with a casual sports shirt. Even in the dim light of the hallway, she thought he looked quite fetching.

"You look lovely," he said, as she settled into the passenger seat of his smart black Hyundai Coupé.

"Thank you very much."

Emma felt pleased. At least things were getting off to a good start, she thought.

"You're looking quite smart too, Colin."

Their eyes met and they both laughed.

"I think we can agree that our partners are looking good tonight," he said. "Now let's go and get something to eat."

They drove to a fashionable bistro in Dalkey which Emma had seen positively reviewed in several of the Sunday papers. Colin had made a reservation, which was just as well as there was a queue of hopeful diners already waiting at the door. They were shown to a table near the back where they could observe the whole room and were given menus.

"What would you like to drink?" he inquired.

"What are you having?"

"I'll just have some wine. I'm driving, remember."

"Then I'll join you."

"You know, I think I'm really going to enjoy this evening," he said, opening the leather-bound menu.

They chose salads to start and then chicken for him and pork in a tarragon sauce for her. Emma decided to let him select the wine. It was a subject she knew very little about and she didn't want to spoil the evening by ordering an expensive bottle of rot-gut. He settled for a bottle of Burgundy which was very palatable indeed. And she was delighted to discover that for once the reviewers had been right about the restaurant. The food was superb.

"Have you been here before?" she asked.

"A few times. The food is good and the atmosphere is nice and relaxed. What about you?"

"I don't eat out very much," she confessed.

"Well, I can't say I blame you. The cost of dining out in Dublin has become outrageous. Do you like cooking?"

"Yes."

"So you know a thing or two about food?"

"I know what I like," Emma replied.

"Maybe I could persuade you to cook a meal for me sometime?" he suggested with a cheeky gleam in his eye.

"That will depend."

"On what?"

"How well you behave yourself."

"And if I pass the test?"

"We'll cross that bridge when we come to it."

"I'll hold you to that," he said, as he smiled and tipped the wine bottle to replenish their glasses.

The conversation moved on. Colin asked her what she did.

"I'm a civil servant."

"You might be just the person to talk to about my income tax."

"I'm afraid not. It's the wrong department. And anyway, I'm just a lowly clerical officer. I don't get to make any big decisions."

"That's a pity," he said, putting on a sad face. "Do you enjoy your job?"

"You want to know the truth?"

"Of course."

"I find it quite boring."

"Oh dear," he said with a grin. "I think we've wandered into a sensitive area. Why don't we talk about the weather instead?"

The evening passed very smoothly. Colin didn't once talk about sport and he steered well clear of conversation concerning legal matters. But he did entertain Emma with lively anecdotes about her mother that left her smiling.

"I remember one time an aggrieved client turned up at the office to query his bill. Your mother went over the bill with him item by item and actually found several things that we had forgotten to charge him for. So she demanded a cheque on the spot and told him he was lucky she didn't report him to *Stubbs Gazette*. He left the premises faster than a scalded cat and we never had any trouble from him again."

"She was a bad woman to cross," Emma agreed with a laugh.

"But an absolute dote if you managed to get into her good books."

They rounded off the meal with coffees. It was after midnight when he drove her home.

"Thank you for a lovely evening," she said, as he stopped the car outside the gates of her apartment block.

"The pleasure was all mine," he said gallantly.

There was an awkward moment while she wondered if he was going to kiss her goodnight. He hesitated and then quickly leaned over and pushed open her door.

"Maybe you would like to repeat this exercise another time?" he asked.

"Sure, why not?"

"Good. I'll be in touch."

He drew her close and his lips demurely brushed her cheek.
She stepped out of the car.

"Sleep well," he said, as he started the engine and waved
goodbye.

Chapter 11

But Colin didn't ring and, as the days passed, an odd thing began to happen. Emma found her mind drifting back to the dinner and wondering why he hadn't followed up on his suggestion that they go out together again. She had to admit that he was very handsome. And he had been the perfect dinner companion, polite, witty and charming. But why had he not called? Emma was discovering that she *wanted* to see him again.

This was an unusual emotion for her to feel and she wasn't sure that she liked it. Usually when it came to men, she was the person who called the shots. Now the roles had been reversed. She was waiting for the phone to ring and the longer she waited, the unhappier she became.

She told herself she must get the situation into perspective. It had only been one date after all. Perhaps Colin Enright had simply been polite and had no intention of ever calling her again. She had done the same thing herself on many occasions, promised to ring some poor guy because she hadn't the heart to tell him the brutal truth – that she didn't want to see him any more. Perhaps she was now being given a dose of her own medicine.

There was one way to find out. *She* could ring *him*! She could conjure up some excuse to phone him, maybe something to do with Mr Carter or her mother. It would give him an opportunity to move matters forward and it would also put her out of her misery. But her pride rebelled at the idea. And she knew how her sister Trish would react if she ever heard of such a thing. She would read her the Riot Act.

She made up her mind. The best thing was to forget all about him. Besides, something else was about to occur to take her thoughts off Colin Enright completely.

* * *

One evening after supper, as Emma was curled up on the settee with a cup of hot chocolate and a good novel, her phone rang and she heard Trish on the line.

"Hi," Trish said. "Not out clubbing tonight?"

"I've stopped going to clubs," Emma replied, a little more testily than she intended. If Trish was ringing to invite her to meet some interesting man at one of her dinner parties, she was going to tell her to take a hike.

But it was something else entirely.

"Are you free to have lunch with me tomorrow?" her sister asked. "There's something I want to discuss."

"Sure," Emma replied. Trish's lunches were usually a cut above the average since they were charged to her expense account which the bank gave her for entertaining clients.

"I'll see you in The Montebello," said Trish. "Do you know it? It's on the south quays near the Halfpenny Bridge. Nice little Italian place. You'll like it. Shall we say twelve thirty?"

"That sounds fine," Emma said, brightening up at the prospect of a decent meal that she didn't have to pay for.

"Okay then. That's fixed."

"What do you want to talk about?"

"It will wait till tomorrow," Trish said. "Be good."

The following morning she woke to see a weak sun hiding behind a bank of dull, grey clouds. It was threatening to be another uninspiring Dublin day. But at least it wasn't raining. She had a shower, quickly got dressed and drank a cup of coffee before heading down to the DART station, making sure to take her umbrella.

At midday she told her supervisor that she had an early lunch appointment and might be late back to the office but the good-natured Dolly O'Brien simply waved her away.

"Do something for me," she said as Emma reached for her coat.

"What?"

"Bring me back some nice dessert."

"I'll ask for a doggy-bag," Emma promised as she made her way out the door.

Trish was at the restaurant before her, wearing a white blouse, black shoes, smart grey business suit and a pair of reading glasses perched on the end of her nose. She was reading the menu.

"I didn't know your eyesight was going," Emma said as she slid into the seat opposite.

Trish glanced up. "It's not."

"So why are you wearing glasses?"

"They're a management accessory," she replied.

Emma stared. "A management accessory – am I missing something here?"

"The glass is plain. I wear them for effect. Studies have shown that people take you more seriously if you're wearing glasses."

"I don't believe it."

Her sister nodded. "It's true. There was an article about it in *Business and Finance* magazine last week."

"And does it work?"

"Oh yes. I've noticed a definite improvement in people's attention levels since I started wearing them."

She whipped off the glasses and slipped them into her handbag.

"So how are you today?" She beamed across the table, radiating goodwill like a spray gun.

"I couldn't be better," Emma replied, giddily shaking her head and waving her hands. "If I felt any better, I'd explode."

"Good," said Trish. "Now why don't we both have a nice glass of wine?"

The food was superb, a delicious minestrone soup followed by veal in Marsala wine for Emma and sole for Trish who said she was watching her diet. They chatted for a while before Trish finally got around to business.

"I was talking to the lawyers yesterday about Mum's will," she said. "All the paperwork has now been completed."

"Oh," Emma replied.

"There will be a small amount of inheritance tax to pay but the good news is the bulk of her estate will now be divided between us. We'll get the house and the money."

Emma hadn't forgotten about the will but it had not been in the forefront of her mind. However, Trish had obviously taken a different approach.

"The money is straightforward. We'll both get around €45,000 after the tax has been deducted. But the house is more problematic."

"How do you mean?"

"What are we going to do with it?"

"Sell it," Emma said. "Smitty said it would fetch a good price. He says the area is coming on."

But Trish shook her head. "I've thought about that. I'm not sure it's a good idea. There is talk out there of a recession coming. Smitty says that property could take a hammering. We could be putting the house on the market at the worst possible time. Besides, I have a sort of sentimental attachment to it."

"Really?" Emma asked. "You surprise me."

"Well, it was where we grew up."

"So what do you propose we do?"

Trish sniffed. "Do *you* want to live in it?"

"Not particularly. I'm very happy with my apartment."

"Neither do I."

"So?"

Trish rested her arms squarely on the table and stared into Emma's face. "I've got a proposition to put to you. I've discussed this with Smitty and he agrees it's the best plan of action."

Emma watched her sister warily. "What sort of proposition?"

"I could buy out your portion."

Emma sat back in her chair. Trish's proposal had taken her completely by surprise.

"I'm not sure I follow you," she said. "How would that work?"

Trish straightened her jacket and suddenly slipped into super-friendly mode like a bank manager attempting to sell a client a dodgy investment product.

"It's all very simple. First we agree a price. Smitty can do that. And just so you can see that everything is above board we will get several valuations."

"Then what happens?"

"Once we have settled on a value, I will give you half. Of course, I'll have to deduct the € 50,000 I loaned you to buy your apartment. But that means you'll have discharged the debt."

"Go on," Emma urged, mesmerised by her sister's soothing tones.

"You can use the balance how you like. But if I was you, I'd pay off some of your outstanding mortgage. However, we can talk about that later. The main thing is, what do you make of my proposal?"

"I don't know. If I understand you correctly, I'll be selling my share and you'll be buying it. You'll end up owning the house."

"That's it in a nutshell."

"So what are you going to do with it?"

"Let it. Smitty reckons we'll have no problem getting tenants. It's a good area and close to town. Of course, we'd have to spend some money refurbishing it. It has got a little bit shabby over the last few years."

"And if I don't agree?"

"We'll just have to sell it and split the money. Somebody else will be living in our old home. And we will probably get less than the house is worth. Are you sure that's what you want, Emma?"

"Somebody else will be living in it anyway, if you let it."

"Ah, but I will still own it."

"Let me have a think about this," Emma said.

Trish gave her a tight smile. "Would you care for a dessert?" she asked as the waiter came sailing into view.

"Yes, I would," Emma replied, suddenly remembering her promise to Dolly O'Brien. "But could I have it in a doggy bag, please?"

* * *

For some reason, Emma found herself in bad humour that evening. This latest episode was just another in a long line of similar incidents involving Trish that stretched far back into their childhood. But what was acceptable when they were children was no longer proper now that they were adults, and Trish's attitude was beginning to irritate her. Her sister had already persuaded her to join the Civil Service and got her to dump poor Alan Casey. Now she was taking charge of their mother's will and even telling her what she should do with the money she was going to receive. It made her feel stupid and incompetent and she didn't like it.

But she didn't have long to mull over the proposition. A few days later, she got a phone call from Smitty at work.

"About the house," he began.

"Yes?"

"I've had a good look over it and I've also got two independent valuations. They all agree that it's worth in the region of €500,000."

"That much?" Emma said in disbelief.

"It would be worth more only there is a recession on the way. I think Trish already mentioned this to you. Have you had a chance to think about her proposal?"

Emma quickly made some calculations in her head. If the house was worth €500,000 that would leave her sister paying her €200,000 after she had deducted the €50,000 she was owed. She could completely wipe out her mortgage. The removal of the monthly repayments would make a huge difference to her budget. She would have money to spend and she would still have the €45,000 her mother had left her. It was a no-brainer.

"Yes," she said. "I've decided to accept."

"Don't you want to see the independent valuations?"

"Oh come on, Smitty. You're my brother-in-law. I trust you."

"Thank you," he said. "That's a very wise decision. It makes sense all round. Would you like me to look after the paperwork?"

"If you don't mind."

"Not at all, Emma."

She put down the phone, feeling almost light-headed with excitement. Now she was going to be free of that damned mortgage which she had been dragging around like a ball and chain. She felt guilty about her earlier ill feeling towards her sister. Trish had been right, as she so often was.

Immediately, the phone rang again. Emma picked it up, still feeling slightly giddy after talking to Smitty.

"Hi," she trilled. "How can I help you?"

"You can come out with me this evening," a husky male voice answered.

Emma sat frozen to the spot. "Who is this?" she managed to ask.

"It's me, Colin. Look I'm sorry I haven't been in touch with you like I promised but I had to go over to London on urgent business. I've got two tickets for the Abbey Theatre tonight and I need a good-looking woman to come with me. Will you oblige?"

Chapter 12

The theatre? With Colin Enright? She couldn't imagine a better way to spend the evening but she quickly checked herself. Not a good idea to appear too eager. It might give him the wrong impression.

"I don't know if I'm free," she said.

"It's a very good show," Colin coaxed. "*Dancing at Lughnasa*. It's an all-star cast."

"But this invitation is rather sudden."

Whatever happened, she must maintain her poise. She mustn't let him get the idea that she had been sitting at the end of the phone waiting for him to call. She had to create the illusion that she was a busy young woman with loads of interesting demands on her time.

"I accept it's very short notice," Colin conceded. "But I've quite literally stepped off a plane. I'm ringing you from Dublin airport."

She thought of asking why he hadn't called sooner. He had plenty of time to ring her. But if she adopted that tone, he would realise she was upset.

"The problem is I've got other plans. Let me see if I can change them and I'll ring you back."

"Please say you'll come. I've really missed you," he said.

"I'll ring you back," Emma said quickly and put down the phone.

She sat for a few minutes lost in thought. This was what Trish would call a defining moment. Suddenly the tables had been turned and he was pleading with her for a date. It meant she had gained the high ground. But she had to handle this situation carefully if she wasn't to lose it again.

She waited for ten minutes then reached for the phone and rang him back.

"All right," she said in a warmer tone. "You can relax. I've managed to rearrange my schedule."

"That's brilliant." She could hear the relief in his voice. "We can go to the theatre and then have a bite of supper afterwards. What time will I call for you? Curtain's up at eight."

"How about a quarter past seven?"

"That will give us buckets of time."

"Okay. Quarter past seven it is."

"Thanks, Emma. Can't wait," said Colin as he put down the phone.

She sat at her desk with a satisfied grin. She was very pleased with her little performance. She had managed to turn things around quite neatly. It might teach him not to take her for granted. And then she almost jumped out of her seat with fright. Where was she going to get her hair done at such short notice?

Please God Dolly O'Brien doesn't land a load of files on my desk, she prayed as she spent the next half hour frantically phoning various salons trying to book an appointment. She was just about to give up when she managed to secure a slot for one o'clock at a place off Grafton Street which had just had a cancellation. She mumbled her everlasting gratitude to the snotty receptionist as she checked her watch. It was a quarter past twelve. Now she had to persuade Dolly to let her have some time off and she'd better come up with a very convincing reason.

She found her supervisor having coffee in the canteen. Emma pulled up a chair and sat down beside her.

"I'm terribly sorry," she began, "but I have to ask for the afternoon off. A bit of an emergency has just come up."

"What sort of emergency?" Dolly asked, taking a large bite out of a chocolate muffin.

"You know my old aunt?"

"Not personally. But I've heard you mention her."

"She used to be a missionary."

Dolly O'Brien brushed some crumbs from her mouth. "I didn't know that."

"It was several years ago. Well, now she has come down with Bubonic Plague."

Dolly choked and bits of muffin spattered all over the table. "Bubonic Plague? This is a joke, right?"

Emma solemnly shook her head.

"No. It's true, unfortunately."

"But I thought Bubonic Plague had died out hundreds of years ago?"

"Apparently it still flares up from time to time."

The supervisor stared at her. A frightened look had now entered her eyes.

"Is it bad?" she whispered.

"Bad enough. Her temperature is up at 102 degrees and she has boils on her arms as big as billiard balls."

"My God," Dolly O'Brien gasped. "Is it fatal?"

Emma nodded gravely. "Can be."

"Infectious?"

"Very."

The supervisor was now moving her chair away from Emma as fast as she could.

"Go," she said, waving her arms. "Do whatever you have to

do. Don't come back till you've been given the all-clear. The last thing we want is an outbreak of Bubonic Plague in the office."

"Thanks a bundle," Emma said, feeling guilty at the outrageous lies that had just popped out of her mouth. "You've been very understanding."

She spent much of the afternoon in the hairdressing salon having her hair cut and styled. For good measure, she opted for a manicure and a face massage. On her way down Grafton Street, she passed a store that had a sale on. What the hell, she thought, it's been ages since I've been to the theatre and I want to look my best. I might as well be hung for a sheep as a lamb. She spent another half hour trawling through the racks of clothes and emerged with a little red cocktail dress that would look superb with barely-black tights, red heels and a black sequinned evening bag she had bought the previous week. By five o'clock she was on the train for home.

Once inside the door of her apartment, she put U2 on the CD player, poured a glass of chilled white wine and filled up the bathtub. She lay back and gave a loud sigh. Why am I doing this, she thought as she luxuriated in the scented water and wriggled her toes above the foam.

Because I want to see Colin Enright's jaw drop the minute I step out to meet him. Because I want him to realise what a lucky man he is that I have condescended to go with him to the theatre tonight. I want him to learn that if he ever takes me for granted again, he'll live to regret it. That's why I'm doing it and he'd better bloody well appreciate it. Feeling justified and triumphant, she finished off the wine, pulled the plug and watched the water drain away.

By ten past seven, she was dressed. She sat at the dressing-table while she applied her make-up. She had managed to pick up a lipstick in exactly the same shade as the dress. She looked good. And she felt good. Colin Enright couldn't fail to be impressed tonight. She was feeling so exhilarated that she contemplated another glass of the wine that she had just put back in the fridge. Better not, she decided. She was putting on her coat when she heard the door buzzer sound.

One look from Colin told her all she needed to know.

"Wow," he said, letting out a low whistle of appreciation. "You look marvellous. You look like one of those catwalk models. No, on second thoughts, you look better," he added quickly.

He thrust a bouquet of red roses into her hands.

Emma wasn't expecting flowers.

"They're beautiful," she said. "What are they in aid of?"

"You. They're a peace offering for not ringing you sooner. Now, why don't you nip back inside and put them in some water? We've got loads of time."

Five minutes later, they were seated in Colin's car and emerging into the traffic at Merrion Gates. But Emma was in for another pleasant surprise when they walked into the foyer of the theatre at a quarter to eight. All around them, heads turned to stare at the handsome young couple who had just come in. From the corner of her eye, she could see people whispering and conferring. A few smiled and waved at Colin. Emma felt a warm glow of satisfaction. All her efforts had not been in vain. It felt good to be appreciated and admired. But her pleasure was short-lived. A few minutes later a voice came over the sound system to announce that the play was about to begin and the audience was asked to take their seats.

* * *

Later, as they ate supper in a cosy little restaurant on Wicklow Street, Colin leaned across to whisper.

"You caused a sensation tonight."

"Did I?" she responded, trying her best to look innocent.

"Don't pretend you didn't notice."

"I saw some people staring at us. But they do that all the time at the theatre."

"They weren't staring at us, Emma. They were staring at *you*. And no wonder. I told you earlier, you look absolutely stunning."

"Well, that's nice to know," she said with a smile and turned her attention once more to the menu.

"Did you enjoy the play?" he asked, as he poured the wine.

"Yes I did. I've been meaning to see it for some time."

"Are you a regular theatre-goer?"

"Not as regular as I would like. I live a pretty busy life, Colin."

"Well, perhaps we can change that. I have a client who works in the theatre. He sends me tickets quite often. Maybe you'd like to come again?"

She kept her head buried in the menu. "Maybe," she said, determined to keep him on a tight leash.

But Colin wasn't easily deflected. The food arrived and as they ate he kept up a constant stream of conversation.

"Your sister is that important woman in the bank, isn't she? I've seen her on television a few times."

At the mention of Trish, Emma felt herself bristle. Was she never going to escape from her sister? Now Colin Enright was talking about her.

"That's her all right."

"She seems to be very bright."

"Oh, she's certainly bright," Emma replied.

"You know it's remarkable the way banks have suddenly wakened up to the female market. It's not so long ago that a woman needed her husband's permission just to open an account."

"They *what*?" Emma asked, staring at him in amazement.

Colin seemed pleased to have got her attention at last.

"Oh, yes. Women have come a long way in recent decades, Emma. Your sister is a good example. Incidentally, are there only you and her?"

"Yes. We were an all-female household."

"What about your father?"

"I never knew him."

He raised an eyebrow.

"My parents separated when we were small," she said.

"And you never had any contact with him?"

"No. We assumed he was dead. That's what Mum told us. I never even saw a photograph of him."

Colin put down his knife and fork. "That explains why she never talked about him. But it must have been very hard for her. It must have been a struggle bringing up two children on her own."

"I suppose it brought us closer," Emma said.

This news seemed to have caught his interest. He kept firing questions at her.

"How did you find out?"

"Trish badgered my aunt and she told her. But she had sort of figured it out."

"But your mother never told you?"

Emma shook her head.

"Do you know anything about him at all?"

"I know his name was Peter."

"Were you ever tempted to find out more? He might still be alive, you know."

"It did cross my mind," Emma admitted. "But I didn't know where to start."

"It's not too difficult. You could begin with their marriage certificate. What was your mother's name?"

"Margaret Nolan."

"Margaret Nolan and Peter Frazer. Do you know when they got married? Once you have the marriage certificate, it will give your father's date of birth. That way you can trace his family."

"I could find out," Emma replied, her curiosity now aroused.

"You can also discover if he's still alive."

"Really?"

"Yes. Once we know who he was and when he was born, it should be fairly straightforward."

He made it all sound so simple. But something caused her to hesitate. Did she really want to do this? It could uncover long-buried secrets and who knew what she might find?

"Do you think it's a good idea?" she asked.

"That's your decision but I know if it was me, I'd want to find out more. I'd be quite happy to do it for you."

"You would?"

He smiled.

"Sure. I enjoy a bit of investigative work now and again. It makes a change from boring old title deeds and stuff like that."

* * *

On the drive back to her apartment, Colin opened up about his own background. His family had been in legal practice for generations. Both his father and his uncle had been solicitors and one of his grandfathers had been a High Court judge.

"He didn't hang anybody," Colin said with a grin. "Although I think he was tempted a few times."

"So you might say that the law is in your blood?"

"You could say that. I don't think I had any choice. My father used to read me articles from the Constitution instead of bedtime stories."

She laughed. "That's a joke, right?"

He grinned. "Sort of."

"And where does your family live?"

"My father and mother still live in the family home in Killiney, although they're getting on a bit. I've got a modest apartment in Dalkey."

"How modest?" she wanted to know. Now that he had opened up, she wanted to find out all about him.

"It's really just a small place: a couple of bedrooms, bathroom, living room, bit of a terrace. But I seem to spend less and less time there."

"Why is that?"

"Our firm has developed a lot of business in the UK. I've been put in charge of it. That's what took me to London."

"London sounds interesting. Bright lights, big city."

But he was shaking his head. "Not really," he said. "I prefer Dublin."

"Why?"

He looked at her and smiled. "Because you're here."

He pulled up outside her apartment block and switched off the engine before turning to her once more.

"You know, you really are very beautiful."

"Am I?"

"Yes. The most beautiful woman I've ever met."

He reached out and stroked her hair with his fingers. Next moment, she was in his arms and he was covering her mouth with passionate kisses.

Chapter 13

Now that the ice had been well and truly broken, Emma was keen to see Colin again. That weekend, they met for drinks in a little pub in Fleet Street before going off at his suggestion to a nightclub called Diablo. It was a mistake, as she soon found out.

First, they had to queue for twenty minutes and subject themselves to the scrutiny of a team of bouncers who looked like Sumo wrestlers in dress suits. That was bad enough. But inside, worse was to follow. The crowded room was hot and clammy and the bar charged outrageous prices for a couple of tepid beers. The dance floor resembled the main deck of the *Titanic* before the lifeboats were launched. It was a confused mass of heaving bodies and flashing strobe lights and was so noisy that it was impossible to hold a conversation without shouting at the top of your voice.

Emma wondered why she had agreed to come here. The time when she would have enjoyed this sort of thing had long passed. But Colin seemed to be quite at home. He was an energetic dancer, gyrating to the throbbing beat from the sound system.

She stuck it out till eventually she could take no more. She found a couple of seats in an alcove and collapsed in a heap while he went off to the bar to get fresh drinks.

Ten minutes later, she saw him fighting his way through the crowd with a couple of vodka and tonics clutched tightly to his chest.

"Having a good time?" he asked as he put the drinks down on the table.

"That might be a slight exaggeration."

"At least you're getting some exercise," he said with a grin.

Emma was too exhausted to argue. She grabbed the vodka and took a large gulp. It had taken Colin so long to get from the bar that the ice had melted but she was grateful nonetheless.

A wall of noise was continuing to boom out of the sound system. It felt as if someone was sticking knitting needles into her brain.

"Feel like dancing again?" he shouted above the din.

"I think I'll sit it out. Anyway, you don't need me. Nobody on the dance floor seems to have a partner."

"But it wouldn't be the same without you."

She looked at him. Was he trying to be sarcastic? Reluctantly, she dragged herself onto the floor once more. Beside her, a young man with a shaved head and an earring in his nose seemed to be having an epileptic fit. Several young women kept waving their arms and accidentally kicking her shins. She endured it another five minutes before returning to her seat to find that one of the waiters had removed her vodka while she was gone.

Colin followed.

"What's the matter?" he asked. "I was just getting into my stride."

"I think I'd be safer taking up ladies' rugby," she said as he plumped down on the seat beside her.

"I'm sorry. You're not enjoying this, are you?"

"That's an understatement. I've seen more civilised behaviour at a football riot."

"We'll go," he said.

"It's okay," Emma protested. "I don't want to spoil your fun. I'll sit here and watch. You go right ahead."

"No, we'll leave."

He took her hand and helped her to her feet. Ten minutes later, after fighting their way through the crowds, they found themselves back on the street.

"I really am sorry," Colin said.

Emma clapped her hands over her ears. "You don't have to shout any more."

He began again in a quieter tone. "I said I was sorry. I don't know what I was thinking of."

"You don't have to apologise."

He saw that she was limping. "You're hurt," he said.

"I'll be all right in the morning. What I need is a good night's rest. And after that racket, I'll probably have to wear earmuffs. I can still hear those drums pounding in my brain."

By the time they found his car, she was beginning to feel slightly better.

"Forgive me for being such a wet blanket," she said.

"It's fine. If you don't like clubs, you don't like clubs. I've no problem with that."

She reached out and gently took his hand.

"I think we've found something we can disagree on," she said.

* * *

After a couple of weeks of Colin's company, she decided it was time to let Jackie in on her secret. Sooner or later someone was going to spot them together and word would leak out. She didn't want Jackie to think she was hiding something from her. They agreed to meet for lunch at Mama Mia's Italian trattoria in Camden Street.

"Let's have a bottle of plonko," Jackie said, flopping into a seat and waving for the waiter. "Can we have some of your best jungle juice, please?" she asked.

The skinny waiter looked confused. "Jungle juice? I no understand."

"Vino," Jackie explained. "A bottle of vino – it's just a little joke."

The young man's face brightened. "Ah, of course, what would you like?"

"Red okay for you, Emma?"

Emma nodded.

"House red, please."

Jackie peeled off her coat and folded it neatly on the seat beside her.

"So what's been happening to you?" she asked.

Emma shrugged. "The usual. How is Liam?"

Liam was Jackie's new boyfriend. He was in advertising and they seemed to be getting along very nicely.

"He's fine," she said, pushing her blonde hair away from her freckled face. "You know what men are like. His idea of a good night is watching Arsenal on Sky Sports while he scoffs a Chinese takeaway and a six-pack of Heinos."

"Well, it certainly beats having your shins kicked all evening at a noisy nightclub," Emma replied, memories of the recent visit to Diablo still fresh in her mind.

At the mention of the nightclub, Jackie sat up straight. "I thought you'd given up clubbing?"

"So I have but I got persuaded."

"Really? And who did the persuading?"

"Just a guy I met."

The waiter brought the wine and poured, then took their orders.

"Spill the beans," Jackie demanded as soon as he left.

Emma took a sip of wine. "His name is Colin Enright. He's a solicitor. He used to work with Mum. I met him at the funeral."

"What does he look like?"

Emma realised she was enjoying this. "He's in his early thirties. About six foot tall, dark hair, blue eyes."

"He sounds cute," Jackie said. "Why have you been hiding him away?"

"I haven't been hiding him."

"Your mother's funeral was six weeks ago. Where has he been in the meantime?"

"He's been around. But I wanted to see if the relationship was going to develop before I said anything."

"And has it? Developed, I mean?"

"I'm not sure. He's a nice guy, very kind and considerate although he did drag me off to this God-awful club where I thought I was going to be trampled to death by drug-crazed Ecstasy fiends. Oh, and one other thing. He doesn't spend the whole time talking about his job."

"Well, that's a big plus. But you've been seeing him for six weeks. Surely you've reached some conclusions by now?"

"I enjoy his company," Emma mused. "He's witty and charming and very generous. But there's something missing. I still haven't made up my mind if he's right for me."

"Well, for God's sake don't take too long. He sounds like a prize and guys like that don't hang around forever. When am I going to meet him?"

"Maybe we could make up a foursome some evening?"

"I'll tell you what," Jackie said, suddenly having a bright idea. "Why don't you bring him over to my place some evening and we'll all have dinner together?"

Emma had already been thinking along similar lines. "No," she said. "I have a better suggestion. You come to *my* place. I promised to cook a meal for him. This way, I'll be able to kill two birds with one stone."

"And afterwards, I'll give you my honest opinion," Jackie

said, moving the wine bottle to safety while the waiter put down their steaming plates of pasta. "So when will it be?"

"This weekend," Emma said. "Let me get back to you."

* * *

As soon as she returned to the office, she rang Colin.

"What are you doing on Saturday night?" she inquired.

"Saturday night is a blank sheet. I was thinking of taking you back to Diablo, since you enjoyed it so much the last time. Only joking," he added quickly.

"Well, you're about to have an experience that few men have enjoyed before."

"My God, this is an unexpected treat. And we're not even engaged."

"Will you get serious and listen," Emma scolded. "I'm cooking dinner for you."

"Hey, that's brilliant. And afterwards can I have the experience?"

"That will be slightly difficult since there are two other people coming."

"Damn," he said. "There's always a snag, isn't there?"

"This is my best friend and her boyfriend. Their names are Jackie and Liam. I'll brief you about them later. Now do you think you could manage to get to my apartment for seven thirty?"

"Wild horses wouldn't stop me."

"And if you behave yourself, I might even cook for you again."

"Promise?"

"I promise," Emma said and put down the phone with a gentle smile.

Next she had to decide what to feed them. It would have to be something special. She had told Colin she was interested in cooking and now she would have to prove herself. Over the next few days, she spent her spare time designing menus and then discarding them because they were too complicated or too exotic or just not suitable. Strips of hake on a rocket salad might look impressive but it would only leave Colin and Liam feeling hungry and raiding the fridge in search of something more substantial.

Finally, she settled for a goat's cheese tartlet and salad as a starter to be followed by roast lamb with sautéed potatoes, broccoli and asparagus tips and they would finish the meal with a chocolate bombe. She could buy the tartlets and the bombe pre-prepared so the main work was going to lie in cooking the lamb and the vegetables. On Saturday morning, she got up at eight o'clock and spent a couple of hours cleaning the apartment from top to bottom. She dusted all the furniture and aired the rooms, made sure the pictures were straight, washed the windows and cleaned the bathroom. Her mother had been fond of saying that you could tell an awful lot about a person by the state of their bathroom and Emma didn't want to leave anything to chance. When she had finished, the bathroom was so clean her guests would be able to eat their food off the floor.

After a breakfast of scrambled eggs and toast, she set off for the shops. There was a new delicatessen in Blackrock village where she was able to buy the goat's cheese tartlets and the chocolate bombe. Then it was on to the supermarket where she picked up the vegetables and half a dozen bottles of wine. She knew very little about wine but a kind man helped her choose when she explained that she wanted a good wine that wasn't too expensive. She came away with three bottle of Italian Soave and three bottles of a red South African wine that was on special offer. Finally, she found herself at the butchery department.

For the past few days she had been trying to decide what size leg to order. But the butcher came to the rescue once she explained it was for a dinner party and at least two of the guests could be described as hearty eaters. She ended up with a seven pound leg that he assured her would feed the most ravenous appetites and still leave some meat to spare. On her way out of the shop, she stopped to buy some flowers.

By the time she returned to her apartment it was almost two o'clock. So far, everything had gone smoothly. She put several bottles of white wine in the fridge to chill and sat down at her laptop to check her emails. There were about half a dozen including a funny one from Jackie warning her not to burn the spuds. She quickly replied to them all, logged off and went into the kitchen to begin the main task of preparing the meal.

This involved rubbing the meat with a clove of garlic, covering it with sliced lemon and a sprig of rosemary, wrapping it in tinfoil and placing it in the oven at the recommended temperature. Then she began the job of chopping the vegetables. As she worked, Emma felt a cosy feeling steal over her. The secret of a good meal lay in the preparation and this was a labour of love. Two of the most important people in her life right now were coming to eat tonight. She wanted everything to be perfect.

When she had finished in the kitchen, she carefully set the table and spent a few minutes arranging the flowers in a vase and placing them in the centre. Then she stood back to admire her handiwork. The table would have done justice to a Michelin-starred restaurant. Let's hope the food is as good, she thought to herself as she returned to the kitchen.

By six o'clock, it was all in order. She could feel a little buzz of pride that she had achieved so much and everything looked so well. She poured a glass of wine, went into the bathroom and ran the hot water in the tub. She was just settling into the lathery suds when she heard her mobile phone give a loud buzz.

I don't believe it, she muttered as she climbed out of the bath and went dripping back into the living room. Some people have an impeccable sense of timing.

It was Colin.

"Hi," he said in his cheery voice. "How's it going?"

"Perfectly," Emma lied, as she watched the pool of water gather at her feet.

"I'm just ringing to say there's been a slight hiccough."

She felt her heart sink. Please don't say you've been sent to London on some urgent business, she prayed.

"I'm going to be slightly delayed. I just got a call from my mother. I have to drop in and see her on the way over."

"So what time will I expect you?"

"About eight o'clock. Is that all right?"

"No later," Emma warned. "Otherwise, I will not be a happy bunny."

"We could never allow that," he chirped and hung up.

"Men!" she growled through clenched teeth and went back once more to the bathroom.

Colin's delay meant she had to reset the lamb and the vegetables. But by half seven when the buzzer rang, she had managed to bathe and dress in a pretty little party dress and have everything prepared so that when the time came to eat, all she would have to do was serve the food.

She found Jackie and Liam in the hallway, each holding a gift.

"This is for you," Liam said, thrusting a bottle of wine into her hands.

Jackie handed over a box of dark rich Belgian chocolates. "It's just a small reward for all the hard work you've put in."

"Come in, come in," Emma said, holding the door wide. She ushered her guests into the living room and made sure they were seated comfortably.

"Now, what can I get you to drink?"

"Beer for me," Liam said, stretching his long legs and gazing round the apartment.

"Glass of wine, please," Jackie said.

Emma went off to the kitchen to pour the drinks.

"Where's Colin?" Jackie asked on her return.

"He's on his way. He had to go and see his parents. He should be here soon."

They sat chatting for a while till Liam had drained his beer and Emma got up to replenish it. By now, it was ten past eight and there was still no sign of Colin. Emma was beginning to get uneasy. She rang his mobile and got no reply so she left a message for him to ring urgently.

Back in the living room, Liam was beginning to show distinct signs of hunger. He had already demolished a bowl of nuts that Emma had set out and a bowl of olives. She put on a CD and sat down again, silently cursing Colin. He knew how important this dinner party was. Why couldn't he get here on time?

By nine o'clock, she could delay no longer. Liam had drunk four glasses of beer and was eyeing the basket of bread that Emma had placed on the dining table. Jackie was politely trying to make her third glass of wine last as long as possible. If they didn't start eating soon, the dinner would be ruined.

"Maybe something's happened to him?" Jackie ventured.

The same thought had already crossed Emma's mind. She rang him once more and again got diverted to the message minder.

She made up her mind. "We'll have to start without him."

"I don't mind waiting a while longer," Jackie said helpfully while Liam's eyes lit up at the prospect of getting fed.

"No," Emma said firmly. "If we don't eat now, the food will be overcooked."

"Well, can I help you with anything?" Jackie asked.

"No, just sit up to the table and I'll serve."

In quick succession, Liam demolished the cheese tartlet and devoured the lamb, potatoes and vegetables while making a major dent in a bottle of South African red. While she struggled to maintain a calm appearance, inwardly Emma was seething. All that work and Colin couldn't even bother to be here.

They were just settling into the chocolate bombe at a quarter past ten when the buzzer gave a loud squawk.

"It's me," she heard Colin announce through the intercom.

She buzzed him in without a word.

"Sorry I'm late," he said as he came bustling through the front door.

"So what happened?" she demanded.

"I had to take my mother to the hospital. She was complaining of stomach pains."

Everyone stared. Emma remembered her own mother's experience. This could be a serious development.

"Is she all right?" she asked, in a softer voice.

"She's fine," Colin announced with a light wave of his hand. "It was only indigestion. The doctor prescribed some tablets for her."

Emma struggled to contain the fury that overtook her. The dinner party on which she had spent so much effort had been ruined because Mrs Enright had indigestion. It was like something out of a sitcom.

She glared at Colin but he had quickly turned to the others and was introducing himself.

"Hi, I'm Colin Enright, pleased to meet you."

They shook hands and he glanced at the empty plates on the table.

"I'm starving. Is there anything left or have you guys scoffed the lot?"

Emma forced herself to bite her tongue but if there had been a carving knife handy, she might well have been tempted to murder him.

Chapter 14

For the remainder of the evening, Emma struggled to hold her
anger in check but once Jackie and Liam had left around one
o'clock, she rounded on Colin.

"Well?" she demanded. "Are you going to apologise?"

He looked at her with an innocent face. "Apologise for what?
Being late? I've already said I was sorry."

"For ruining my dinner party and turning the evening into a
disaster."

He tried to laugh. "You're exaggerating, Emma. The only one
who suffered was me. I got cold scraps of lamb while the rest of
you had a slap-up meal."

"Do you realise that I have been working since eight o'clock
this morning?"

"Yesterday morning," he interrupted, glancing at his watch.
"It's now Sunday."

"Don't be pedantic," she snapped. "I spent the entire day
preparing for that meal and you turn up almost three hours
late."

"I explained about my mother."

"Indigestion and you rush her to emergency? Is it any wonder the A and E departments are grinding to a halt?"

"How was I to know it was only indigestion?" he sniffed defensively. "It might have been serious."

"Why couldn't your father have taken her?"

"Because he's got an arthritic knee and can't drive."

"Then why didn't you *tell* me?"

"I *did* tell you," he said, indignantly.

"At seven o'clock. You promised to be here at eight. And then I hear no more and every time *I* ring *you*, I get diverted to your damned message minder."

"That was a mistake," he conceded. "I should have checked my messages. But I don't see what I was supposed to do about the rest of it."

"That's precisely the problem," Emma said, folding her arms. "You don't see. You think only about yourself. You didn't care that I had spent an entire day slaving in that kitchen. And what's more, you show your contempt for me in front of my friends."

"I think that's a bit much," he said, standing up and pulling on his jacket.

"Is it? I could go on," she said. "I'm only getting into my stride."

"I've heard enough. I'm leaving."

"That's the best thing you've done all evening," she said, marching to the door and flinging it open. "I think you know your own way out. Goodnight and goodbye."

She slammed the door so hard on his retreating back that it shivered on its hinges.

* * *

It took several days for her to calm down. She continued to be upset by Colin's behaviour and the casual manner in which he had treated her dinner party. But what hurt her most was that he had let her down in front of Jackie and Liam. This was to be an occasion for her to show him off and what her guests saw was a selfish man who couldn't even be bothered to ring to let her know what was going on. In Emma's eyes, it was unforgivable.

He rang on Monday morning but she refused to take his call. She was becoming expert at dealing with unwanted phone calls. At work, she used her colleague, Betty Carr, to filter them with instructions that she was not available for anyone called Enright. Her mobile was even easier because it showed the number of the incoming caller and she could simply ignore him.

On Tuesday he rang five times, twice in the morning and three times in the evening. By Wednesday, he was obviously growing desperate because he rang ten times and sent a total of fifteen text messages.

Jackie thought she was being a little hard on him.

"Give him a break," she advised when the two of them met for coffee. "The poor guy was obviously worried about his mother. He was probably distracted. You know what some old ladies can be like. Maybe she's a hypochondriac."

"It's his selfish attitude that bugs me," Emma replied. "All he had to do was ring and tell me what was going on. He has to learn that he can't behave like that. Not with me, at any rate."

"It wasn't the end of the world," her friend went on. "I enjoyed myself. And so did Liam. He said he hadn't eaten so well since he won a dinner for two at Rossini's restaurant in the staff Christmas raffle last year."

At this news, Emma perked up somewhat. "Did he really?"

"Yes. He thought the food was marvellous. You saw the way he demolished all before him."

"That was only because he was starving. And I don't blame him."

"No, it wasn't. Liam is actually quite a picky eater. If he doesn't like something, he won't touch it, no matter how hungry he is."

"Jackie, I know you too well. You're saying this to make me feel better."

"No, I'm not. It's true. Honest."

"Well, that's very flattering. It's good to know *somebody* enjoyed it."

"And you want to know something else?" Jackie continued. "I think Colin is a very attractive guy. He's got a nice, warm personality. I liked him."

Emma turned her full gaze on her friend. "You did?"

"Definitely. He's the best-looking man I've seen you with."

"But *they* can be the worst," Emma replied. "They get spoiled. They think the world owes them a living."

Nevertheless, Jackie's good opinion pleased her.

"Why don't you lighten up a little?" her friend urged.

"Because I don't want him to think he can walk all over me. He's got to learn manners. He needs to understand there are limits to my tolerance."

"Don't you think he's got the message by now?"

"Let's see," Emma replied.

But events were about to overtake her. The following morning at ten past eleven the phone on her desk rang. Her colleague, Betty Carr lifted it as they had arranged. She spoke for a moment before clamping her hand on the mouthpiece and turning to Emma.

"A man called Smyth?" she said.

"I'll take it," Emma replied, reaching for the phone and expecting to hear her brother-in-law with news about the sale of the house.

"Smitty," she began.

"It's not Smitty, it's me," Colin said. "And don't put the phone down. I've got information about your father."

She caught her breath. It had been several weeks since Colin had offered to find out about her father and in the meantime, it had slipped from her mind. But it occurred to her that this could simply be a trick to gain her attention.

"You'd better tell me," she said.

"Not on the phone. It's too sensitive."

This only served to intrigue her further.

"Why can't you tell me now?"

"Because some of this stuff is delicate and you're sitting in an open-plan office where everyone can hear. I think it would be better if we could meet somewhere."

By now he had got her full attention.

"Where do you suggest?"

"There's a little pub called Johnny's at the back of Mercer's Hospital. It's discreet. Why don't I see you there at one o'clock?"

"All right," she said, somewhat reluctantly. "But I'm warning you. If you're stringing me along, I'll walk straight out again."

* * *

He was waiting for her at a corner table and the room was practically empty. The moment she arrived, he stood up and swept her into his arms. Before she could stop him, he was smothering her in kisses.

"What are you trying to do to me?" he demanded. "You're driving me crazy. Why don't you take my calls?"

"I didn't come here to talk about us," she said, pushing him away and glancing around to make sure no one was listening.

"You don't know how much I've missed you, Emma. This isn't funny."

"It's not meant to be funny."

"So what's it all about? This sort of behaviour is like something kids would get up to in the school playground. We're supposed to be adults, for God's sake."

She stared at him with cold, angry eyes. "I am furious with you," she said.

"Then talk about it. Don't go into a sulk."

"You were very inconsiderate. I spent the whole day preparing that meal and you couldn't even bother to ring me."

"*Please,*" he begged. "I apologised."

"Did you? I don't remember."

"Well then, I'm apologising again. I'm sorry."

She frowned but her anger was abating. He seemed genuinely contrite. She pulled out a chair and sat down.

"Your apology is accepted. But there is something you've got to understand. If we are going to have a relationship you've got to show me proper respect. You can't take me for granted. I won't wear it."

"I'm genuinely sorry," he said, looking relieved. "It won't happen again. Now what can I get you to drink?"

She asked for sparkling water.

"What about food? Now that we're here, we might as well have lunch."

"I'll have a chicken sandwich," she said and he summoned a waiter and gave their order.

When the meal was served, he reached for a briefcase at his feet and drew out a sheaf of papers.

"I don't know how to tell you this," he began, lowering his voice. "It's not good news."

She steeled herself. "Go ahead."

"Your father is dead."

At these words, she lowered her eyes and stared at the floor. "How long?"

"Four years ago."

"What happened?" she asked, softly.

"He had a heart attack." He reached out and took her hand. "I'm sorry, Emma."

She struggled to put on a brave face. "My mother always said he was dead. I suppose in the back of my mind, I had got used to the idea. What else did you find out?"

"He was a stockbroker, quite a successful one by all accounts. He worked for a company called Simpson and Ogilvie. It was a big company and very highly regarded. I think they merged with another firm a few years ago."

"Was that where he met the woman he ran off with?"

He looked surprised. "You know about this already?"

"Yes. My sister mentioned it."

"That's where they met. Her name was Emily Parker. She worked as a secretary. There's more and it's not very pleasant."

"You better tell me everything," she said. "I'm ready for it."

"There was a scandal over money. Your father raided several clients' accounts before he left. It was only discovered weeks later. The company wanted to avoid any damaging publicity so they decided not to prosecute and repaid the customers themselves. But word eventually leaked out. I suppose some of the clients must have talked."

At this news, her face had gone ashen. "How much was involved?"

"About £60,000, but remember this was over twenty-five years ago. It was a lot of money then."

"Were you able to find out where they went?"

"They fled to Manchester. He worked in a succession of clerical jobs for a few years. Then a few years later when all the fuss had died down, they came back to Dublin. They settled in Glasnevin and he got a job as a taxi-driver."

"Did he marry this woman?"

"No. There was no divorce in those days."

"Did they have any children?"

"No. But she had two children from a previous marriage. He became a sort of stepfather to them."

"Is she still alive?"

Colin shook his head. "She died a year after your father."

She sat quite still while her mind battled with conflicting emotions. She was sorry to learn that her father was dead even if she had no memory of him. But it was worse to learn that he was a thief.

It was a sad story. She wondered if her father had found happiness with his new partner. But she couldn't forget that he had deserted them and left her mother to rear two young children on her own. Had she done the right thing by digging up the past? Would it have been better to have left it alone?

At last she gathered herself together.

"Thanks for your work, Colin. I'm very grateful. How much do I owe you?"

He waved his hand. "You owe me nothing. It only involved some phone calls and a few hours trawling through old newspaper files."

"You didn't mention my name?" she asked.

"No, Emma, I was very careful. Nobody knows about you." He put his arm around her shoulder and drew her close. "I'm sorry to be the bearer of bad news."

"You don't have to be sorry. I asked you to do it."

"So, how do you feel?"

"I feel mixed up."

He toyed with his glass. "You shouldn't feel bad. None of this is your fault."

"I know, but it doesn't make it easier."

They sat silent for a few minutes.

"Look," he said. "You've been through an awful lot recently. I've got an idea."

She looked up.

"You need a break," he continued. "Why don't you come away with me?"

Chapter 15

It turned out that Colin had a friend who had arranged to rent a holiday apartment in Tenerife but couldn't go because a family problem had arisen. He was prepared to let him have it for half price.

"It will only cost us a couple of hundred euros plus the air fares. What do you say?"

The proposal had come out of the blue but right now it sounded very attractive.

"How long is it for?"

"Just a week but it's what you need, Emma. It will do you good."

Outside it had started to rain and the big drops were now running down the windowpanes. She thought of the sun and the sea and nothing to do but relax and take it easy. And Colin was right. She could do with a break.

"There's one drawback," he said. "We have to decide soon."

"When is it?"

"Next week."

"Okay. I'll let you know by tomorrow."

Getting leave would not be a problem. Ever since the scare about her fictional aunt and Bubonic Plague, Dolly O'Brien had been treating her warily as if she was afraid that Emma might infect the entire office and they would all come down with fevers and lumps. She would be quite happy to see her out of the office for as long as she liked.

But there was something more important to consider. Going on holiday with Colin Enright would move their relationship up a gear. It was a statement that they were serious about each other. Was that what she wanted? Was she ready for it?

She didn't have long to think about it. The matter was brought to a head when she rang Trish to tell her what she had learned about their father. She listened in silence while Emma related the scandal about the stolen money.

"Who else knows about this?" she asked with concern in her voice.

"Just Colin."

"Colin who?"

"Colin Enright. He's the solicitor who did the research for me."

"Is he trustworthy? This isn't the sort of thing I would like to get out. Think of the damage it could do. I have a reputation to uphold. We both have," she added quickly.

"He's very discreet," Emma said. "I don't think you've got anything to worry about. And he *is* a solicitor. Aren't they bound by confidentiality?"

"How well do you know him?" Trish asked, beginning to get suspicious.

"Pretty well."

"Oh?"

Emma heard the note of surprise in her sister's voice.

"He came to Mum's funeral," she hastened to explain. "He

used to work with her in Mr Carter's office. You met him too."

"I met so many people," Trish replied. "I can't remember them all."

"He's in his early thirties, tall, dark."

"Have you been seeing him?"

"Yes," Emma admitted. "In fact, I'm thinking of going on holiday with him. He's got an offer of an apartment in Tenerife."

She could hear the sharp intake of breath.

"This is all very sudden. Are you sure it's a good idea?"

"What do you mean?" Emma demanded.

"You've only met him. What is he going to think of you? You can't go throwing yourself at the first man you meet."

Emma gasped. "He isn't the first. And I'm not throwing myself at him."

"Nevertheless, men have a strange attitude when it comes to matters like this. If they get something easy, they tend not to value it."

Emma thought this was rich coming from Trish who had been hell-bent on getting engaged to Kevin Finnegan at the ripe old age of fifteen.

"It's only a holiday. I haven't agreed to marry him."

"How many bedrooms does this apartment have?" her sister continued, choosing to ignore the barbed remark.

"How would I know? What does it matter?"

"God, you're so naïve," Trish said, tartly. "Does he expect you to sleep with him?"

Emma felt herself stiffen. "I find that question incredibly insensitive."

"This isn't about morality. It's about tactics."

"We haven't discussed the finer details of the sleeping arrangements," Emma snapped.

"Well, I suggest that you do," said Trish. "As for our father,

I think the best thing is to put him right out of our minds. He didn't care about us and I don't see why we should care about him. Besides, he sounds like a thorough scoundrel. The least said about him, the better."

* * *

But if Trish believed her warning would stop Emma going to Tenerife, it had the directly opposite effect. It just made her more determined not to have her sister dictating any more life decisions for her. And the next conversation convinced her.

"I think you should go," Jackie said when Emma told her. "A holiday in the sun sounds perfect. I wish Liam would whisk me away to somewhere exotic. I should be so lucky."

"You don't think it's a bit early in the relationship? I've only known him a few months."

"Not at all. Regard it as a fact-finding mission. Now you'll have a chance to know him better. You'll be in his company all the time. You'll get to know what he's really like."

This was a strong argument. If Colin and Emma could survive a week alone together then it would bode well for their future.

"What are you waiting for?" Jackie said. "Go for it. And if you need someone to carry your suitcase, you know who to ask."

Colin sounded relieved when she rang to tell him she would go.

"You're going to love this," he said. "Have you ever been to the Canaries before?"

"Never."

"It's magic. The sun shines all day long, the nights are balmy, the sky is filled with stars."

"You sound like a holiday brochure," Emma laughed, beginning to get excited. "So what do I do now?"

"Arrange the time off. Then pack your bag and your passport and leave the rest to me. I'll organise the flights."

As she had guessed, Dolly O'Brien was happy to give her the time off. So, while Colin was busy with the travel plans, Emma checked the weather forecast on the internet and discovered that the temperature in Tenerife was 22 degrees. She ticked off the things she would need: some light summer clothes, a couple of bikinis, evening wear, sun creams, a couple of decent books to read and a fashionable pair of sunglasses. She spent her lunch breaks darting around city-centre stores frantically stocking up.

Colleagues who had been to Tenerife told her how much they envied her and said the weather would be beautiful down there just now and the flowers would all be in bloom. It would be idyllic. They gave her tips on what to look out for and the names of restaurants to visit. She began to count the days till she was gone.

On Friday morning, Colin rang to say that everything was finalised. He had cleared his desk and put all his business on hold. His assistant, a young lawyer called Brian Arnold, was on hand to deal with any emergencies that might arise. They would have a trouble-free week in the sun without fear of interruption.

"How about a drink this evening?" he asked.

But after all the hurried shopping, Emma was feeling drained.

"I think I'll get an early night, Colin. I've still got some last-minute packing to do and I want to be fresh for this trip."

"I understand." He sounded disappointed. "I'll see you in the morning. I've been warned to get to the airport in plenty of time."

"So when will you pick me up?"

"Eight o'clock. Is that okay?"

"That's perfect. See you then."

She put down the phone and stared at the empty suitcase and the piles of dresses and tops, towels and sandals that somehow would have to be squeezed into it.

* * *

The following morning at five to eight, she heard the sound of Colin's car horn outside her window. She went out onto the terrace and waved down to him. She had been up since six thirty, getting showered and dressed and making last-minute preparations before treating herself to a light breakfast of croissant and coffee. She glanced around the apartment, making sure that all the switches were turned off and all the locks were secure and there were no dripping water taps. She had heard too many horror stories about people going away on holidays and returning to discover the house was flooded. When she was finally satisfied, she let herself out.

"Excited?" Colin asked as she settled into the passenger seat and slipped on her seat belt.

"I think that's a fair description of how I feel," she laughed.

He gave her a quick peck on the cheek. "You're going to remember this holiday," he said, confidently. "Trust me."

The airport was crowded. Obviously a lot of people had got the same idea and had decided to grab some sunshine. Colin used the automatic check-in service and they passed quickly through security where Emma was surprised at the thoroughness of the checks. She even had to take off her shoes and hop about in her bare feet. But, thankfully, the flight was on time according to the information board.

"We've got half an hour before boarding," Colin said when they finally arrived in the departure lounge. "What do you say to starting the holiday early and having an eye-opener?"

"What have you got in mind?"

"A nice cool gin and tonic unless you fancy a snipe of champagne."

"I think a G and T would be lovely. It will help calm me down. All this frantic activity is beginning to get to me."

"A very wise decision," Colin said and went off to the bar.

They had barely finished their drinks when the departure desk opened and people began to move forward. They waited till the queue had thinned out a little before boarding. Colin had managed to get them adjoining seats and gallantly offered Emma the one beside the window.

"This is the life," he said, attempting to stretch his legs. "You know, we should do it more often. A break is just the ticket to top up the batteries."

He leaned back and closed his eyes and before long they heard the roar of the engines and the plane was airborne.

The journey passed pleasantly. Emma had brought Irene Nemirovsky's *Suite Française* to read. Colin had a John Grisham novel he had picked up in the airport bookshop. In just over four hours, they heard the captain announce their approach to Reina Sofia airport. Emma eagerly strained to look from the little porthole window and suddenly the vast blue sea came into view and then the snow-capped peak of Mount Tiede. She felt a thrill of excitement. Ten minutes later, the plane was on the ground and they were taxiing along the runway.

From then on, everything went like clockwork. They quickly passed through Immigration and picked up their baggage from the carousel then made their way out into the blinding sunshine where they found a line of cabs waiting. A cheerful young man loaded their cases. Colin showed him the piece of paper where he had written down the address of their apartment block and they were off again, speeding along the motorway towards Los Cristianos.

Below them, the sea sparkled blue and white as the motorway skirted the coast. Here and there on the mountainside, the sun glinted off the roofs of the little whitewashed houses. Before long, they were pulling up outside their destination.

Their apartment block overlooked the beach. It was in a modern gated complex with gardens and swimming pool and Emma was delighted to see lemons growing from the trees along the avenue. Colin paid the taxi-driver and drew out a bunch of keys from his pocket. The first one opened the hall door. They entered the lift and travelled to the top floor where another key opened the door into the apartment. While Colin managed the cases, Emma hurried inside. She was taken aback by the sight that awaited her.

The apartment was huge, about twice the size of her place in Blackrock. It had two bedrooms, one of them en-suite, and a bright airy kitchen well stocked with appliances. There was also a comfortable lounge which gave access onto a large terrace. She wandered onto the terrace and immediately caught her breath.

"Colin, come quickly!"

He joined her. There was a little wrought-iron table, chairs and half a dozen terracotta pots teeming with flowering geraniums. But it was the vista that had caused her excitement. From where they stood, they could see the mountains and the sea.

She turned to Colin. "Isn't it magnificent?"

"Yes," he said. "It's beautiful."

"I love it already," she said.

He took her in his arms and kissed her.

"Welcome to Tenerife," he said.

They unpacked and made a quick trip to the nearby supermarket to stock up on essential supplies such as coffee, beer, fruit and toiletries. By now, the afternoon heat was becoming intense. Emma announced that she was going to spend the remainder of the afternoon relaxing on the sun bed and working on her tan. She changed into the bikini she had bought specially for the trip. She could see the look of admiration on Colin's face when she came out of the bedroom.

"You look ravishing," he said.

She smiled as she began to apply the sun block. Everyone had warned her to be careful with the sun, particularly for the first few days. There was no point getting burnt and spending the rest of the holiday in bed.

"I think I'll join you," he announced. "But first I'm going to pour us two cold drinks."

He went off to the kitchen and returned with a couple of glasses and the Grisham novel he was reading. Emma turned on a radio she had come across in the lounge. It was already tuned to an English language station that played easy-listening music. She stretched out on a sun bed. A light breeze cooled them from the heat. She closed her eyes and sighed. This is bliss, she thought as she fixed her sunglasses firmly on her nose and turned to face the sun.

It was Colin who stirred first.

"A rumbling in my stomach tells me it's time to think about dinner," he said, getting up and stretching his arms.

Emma glanced at her watch. It was half past six and the sun was dipping towards the ocean.

"Good Lord," she exclaimed. "I'd no idea it was this time."

"That's the whole idea," he smiled. "You're here to relax and unwind."

She gathered her belongings and went into the main bedroom. She went into the en-suite bathroom, stripped off her bikini and had a shower, feeling the hot water sting her reddening skin. Then she dried herself and applied a layer of after-sun lotion. Now what was she going to wear? The sun might have declined but it was still quite warm. She shouted to Colin in the next room.

"Do I have to get dressed up for this?"

"Not at all, just wear something casual."

She checked the clothes she had brought and opted for a little short skirt that showed off her long legs to good effect and a tight cotton vest top. She would bring a jacket as well in case it got chilly as the night wore on. Then she put on a layer of lip-gloss and glanced at her reflection in the mirror. Her face glowed with vitality and was perfectly framed by her mane of dark hair.

Colin looked smart in beige chinos and a black golf shirt.

"Do I look sufficiently casual?" she inquired.

"You look perfect," he replied, allowing his eyes to run over her. "I'd be proud to be seen anywhere with you."

"Do you say these things to every girl you meet?"

"Only the ones I'm really interested in," he smiled.

They wandered off through the busy streets of Los Cristianos. The siesta period was over and the shops and cafés were bustling again.

"Any idea what you want to eat?" he asked.

"I'm easy."

"One thing about Tenerife," he said. "We'll never starve. There's no shortage of restaurants."

Eventually, they halted at a tiny place down near the port. People were sitting at pavement tables, drinking wine.

"How about here?" Colin asked, glancing at the menu which was written on a blackboard in white chalk.

Emma agreed so they sat down. She took the opportunity to study their surroundings. Beside her was a trellis covered in creepers and bright flowers. Their heady scent mingled with the salt air of the sea. She felt a relaxing feeling steal over her.

She took his hand. "You were right," she said. "Tenerife is magic."

Colin grinned. "I said you'd remember this holiday. And so you will. It's only beginning."

The restaurant specialised in fish. Emma ordered calamari while Colin had sole. They chose a bottle of chilled white wine. They finished with brandies and small cups of coffee.

"What do you want to do tomorrow?" he asked.

Emma shrugged. She was feeling so relaxed that tomorrow seemed like a distant thought.

"I was thinking of hiring a car, maybe seeing some of the island," he said.

"Sounds good. Why don't we go in the afternoon and I can spend the morning sunbathing?"

"Okay," Colin agreed, signalling to the waiter for the bill.

They strolled back along the water's edge. By now the sun had set and the moon was a bright yellow globe in the night sky.

It felt so romantic. Back at the apartment, he suggested a nightcap on the terrace.

"This has been a lovely day," she said with a sigh as she stretched in her sun chair.

Below them, they could see the lights of ships far out on the ocean. Colin raised his glass and tipped it gently against hers.

"To us!" he said. "May we have many more nights like this."

Emma sighed. "To us!"

He finished his drink and put down the glass. He pulled her close and his warm lips pressed down on hers.

She closed her eyes and heard the gentle sighing of the sea.

He took her hand and led her back into the apartment. With his shoulder, he edged open the door of her room. He turned to her and smiled.

"Why use two beds?" he said. "It will only make more work for the cleaning staff."

Chapter 16

The remainder of the holiday passed in a blur. One day merged effortlessly into the next as they drifted along in contented idleness. Every morning they woke to see a huge sun hanging in a cloudless sky. They ate breakfast on the terrace and swam in the sea. It was as if they had been transported to a different world. Only emails from colleagues and friends and the occasional phone call reminded them of what they had left behind in Dublin: the wind and the rain and the dull monotony of cold, damp days.

The evenings were for dining. Colin had an uncanny knack of finding the best restaurants where the food was delicious and the atmosphere romantic. Not that it was too difficult. Emma soon discovered that even the simplest little bar was capable of surprising them with a tasty meal. Once, they took a taxi up into the mountains where they dined on a terrace that looked down on the lights twinkling right along the coast while they ate prawns in garlic and roast lamb with a salad of lettuce and endives and plump ripe tomatoes washed down with rich red Rioja wine.

The nights were given over to passionate lovemaking. By now, Emma was well ensconced in Colin Enright's bed. It was the perfect ending to the day, to be wrapped in her lover's arms while she listened to his heart beating wildly inside his breast and then, sated with pleasure, to drift gently off to sleep. But at last it was time to go home. The week was over and reality beckoned once more.

The evening before they were due to leave, they went to a restaurant down at the port that was reputed to be one of the best in Tenerife. By now, Emma had managed to acquire a rich golden tan and even Colin's pale torso had taken on something resembling a healthy glow. She wore a white calf-length muslin dress that served to emphasise her tan and a little pair of jewelled sandals that she had picked up at the local market. Colin dressed in a white jacket with charcoal slacks and an open-necked white shirt. She thought he looked very dashing.

She stood back to admire him. "You look like James Bond, the Sean Connery version."

"I don't know whether that's a compliment," he muttered. "I thought Pierce Brosnan was the better one."

"Sean Connery," she said, firmly.

"Are you sure?"

"Positive. And if I say you resemble him, take it as a compliment."

Colin had called in advance to book a table and it was waiting when they arrived just before nine o'clock.

"Why don't we order champagne?" he said. "Since it's our last night?"

Emma didn't think this was any cause for celebration. She was beginning to feel melancholy now that the holiday was finally coming to an end. She could have stayed here much longer. But she didn't want to disappoint him.

"Okay," she agreed.

They sipped the champagne while they studied the menu.

"I'm hungry," he announced. "I'm going to order a sirloin. What about you?"

"I'll have the chicken fillets in lemon sauce."

"Right." He snapped the leather-bound menu shut and summoned the waiter.

When he had given their order, he reached out and took her hand.

"You look sad."

"I feel sad," she confessed.

He gently lifted her chin till their eyes met. "It's not the end of the world, you know. We will have plenty more holidays together."

"They'll never be the same as this one."

"You're right. There's always a magic in the first time, isn't there? And then you spend the rest of your life trying to recapture it."

The meal was a great success. At half eleven they finally took their leave with much handshaking and farewells from the waiting staff who were delighted with Colin's generous tip. He suggested they have a last drink in a nearby bar they had grown fond of. But when they arrived, the cabaret act was in progress and a plump, middle-aged drag queen was making a bad job of impersonating Madonna. The place was packed and noisy. They had a quick drink and left for the sanctuary of their apartment.

Once inside the door, he began to make love to her, kissing her lips, unbuttoning her blouse, running his hands along her thighs. She felt her blood catch fire.

"How are we going to manage when we get home?" he asked, as he caressed her neck.

She didn't want to talk. She just wanted this lovemaking to continue.

"We'll think of something," she said, sliding her hands inside his shirt.

"You could always come and live with me."

She stopped at once and pulled herself away.

"What did you just say?"

"You could come and live at my place. Why not? I've got loads of room."

She closed her eyes and felt her mind go into a tailspin. The thought of living with Colin Enright had never occurred to her. But she could see at once that it would open up all sorts of problems.

He gave her a squeeze. "You don't have to decide right now," he said. "Think it over."

He pulled her closer and his warm lips pressed tenderly on hers.

* * *

They arrived back in Dublin to a wet, cold, windy afternoon. Colin picked up his Hyundai from the long-term car park and drove her home before continuing on to the office and promising to call later in the evening.

She was still feeling a little depressed because the holiday had come to an end so she did what she always did when she was low. She poured a glass of wine, ran a hot tub and soaked in it till the water got cold. As she relaxed in the scented water, she mulled over his proposal to move in with him.

It had caught her completely off guard but Jackie had been right: she had certainly got to know him much better during the holiday. And it had all been positive. He was caring and generous. He was polite. He was charming. The selfish streak she had identified earlier seemed to have disappeared.

As she thought it over she began to see that there were definite advantages to taking up his offer. Wouldn't it be pleasant to have him permanently about the place, to go to sleep with him every night and wake up with his head resting on the pillow beside her? Wouldn't it be nice to watch television with him, to sit on the terrace after Sunday brunch and read the newspapers, to do all the little things that couples did together?

And there were practical considerations. Living together would save money on lots of things from food to detergents. There was more than a grain of truth in the old saying that two people could live as cheaply as one. And once the sale of her share in her mother's house went through she'd be able to pay off her mortgage. She could rent out her own apartment and put the proceeds straight into her bank account. For the first time in her life, she would have money.

But there was a downside too. Since she had bought her apartment, Emma had grown used to her own company. She had her little routines and individual ways of doing things. She had no one to please but herself and she enjoyed the freedom it gave her. If she moved in with Colin, that carefree life would be compromised. They had got on famously together in Tenerife when they had been on holiday. But would it work so well now that they were back home in Dublin?

How could she be sure that they wouldn't get on each other's nerves? Would he leave the top off the toothpaste so that the sink got covered in goo? Would he use up all the hot water when she wanted to have a shower? Would he insist on invading her space till she wanted to scream? Moving in with someone wasn't always as simple as it appeared. It could destroy a romance quicker than anything.

There was one other very important point. Emma still wasn't entirely sure of her feelings for him. She hadn't experienced the instant certainty that she had always said she would feel when Mr Right came along. And if going away on holiday with someone was a big step, moving in to live with them was like a massive leap. It was a public statement of commitment. It was like placing an engagement notice in *The Irish Times* and Emma wasn't convinced that she was ready for that just yet.

As she debated these things in her head, she heard her mobile phone give a shrill ring.

"Speak of the devil, that will be him now," she muttered,

climbing out of the bath and wrapping herself in a towel as she went off to the kitchen to answer it.

But it wasn't Colin, it was Trish.

"Welcome home," she said in the cheery voice that Emma had come to suspect. "I've got good news."

"Yes?" Emma asked.

"The legal work on Mum's house is all wrapped up. Are you free to go into the solicitor's office on Monday and sign off on the deal?"

"What time?"

"Five o'clock."

"Sure. Five o'clock sounds fine."

"Good. There'll be two cheques for you, one for €45,000 from Mum's bequest to you and another for €200,000 for your share of the house."

"That's marvellous," she managed to say, feeling overwhelmed at the thought of all that cash.

"You'll be rich, Emma. What are you going to do with the money?"

"I'm taking your advice. I'm going to pay off my mortgage."

"Sensible woman. Now tell me, how did the holiday go?"

"It was brilliant. We didn't see a single cloud the whole time we were there. We had glorious sunshine all day long and the starriest nights you could imagine. It was magic." Just talking about it had already transported her back to Tenerife.

"I'm not talking about the weather. I'm talking about the sleeping arrangements. Did he try to seduce you?"

She found herself laughing at her sister's audacity. "What a thing to ask. Do I inquire about your sex life with Smitty?"

"That's different. We're married. I'm your only surviving relative and I feel responsible for you. I don't want you messing up your life."

"But I'm not a child. I'm an adult and well past the age of consent."

"Don't beat about the bush," Trish said, firmly. "Did he or didn't he?"

"As a matter of fact, he wants me to move in and live with him," Emma said.

Trish let out such a howl of protest that Emma thought the people in the adjoining apartment would hear.

"Now I know you're crazy. By rights I should have you committed before you do any more harm to yourself."

"What do you mean?" Emma replied.

"You want to move in and live with him?"

"I just said he had asked me. Nothing has been decided."

"So now he'll get *everything* for nothing: cooking, cleaning, companionship, counselling *and* sex. Why in God's name would he want to marry you?"

"Who said anything about marriage?"

"But that's the whole object of the exercise. Why do you think marriage was invented? To stop men like Colin Enright freeloading off naïve young women like you."

Emma felt herself cringe. Trish had this unerring ability to get on her nerves. "I thought marriage was about love and commitment."

"Yes. And he gets all the love and you get no commitment."

"I don't think that's true," Emma said, suddenly feeling the need to defend him. "You don't know Colin. You've never even met him, apart from shaking hands with him briefly at Mum's funeral."

"Well, maybe it's time that I did. I think I'll set up a dinner party some evening – just me and Smitty and you and Mr Enright. Then I can run the slide rule over him."

Emma sighed. Here was Trish eager to interfere in her life once again. She should really tell her to bog off and mind her own damned business. But she couldn't keep Colin hidden from her sister forever and a dinner party was as good a way of introducing him as any.

"All right, if that's what you want. But I don't want you

pestering him about his income and his job prospects and things like that. You can find out all you want to know by simply observing him."

"I'll see you on Monday at the solicitor's office," Trish said and Emma heard the line go dead.

*　*　*

The initial excitement of getting all this money hadn't worn off and Emma was still in high spirits when she met her sister as arranged to complete the legal work on their former home. Smitty was itching to get started on the renovations and had lined up a builder friend to rewire the house, put in new plumbing and decorate it from top to bottom. He was keen to launch his new career as a landlord and already had several people anxious to rent it.

Meanwhile, Emma had made arrangements to redeem the mortgage and had another meeting scheduled with the bank on Tuesday. After signing the necessary documents, Trish handed her the two cheques in an envelope and the solicitor shook hands with them both and wished them continuing success.

On the way out of the office, Trish said, casually: "Next Saturday night suit you?"

"What for?"

"The dinner party of course."

"Oh. Yes. I suppose so."

"Good. We'll have drinks at seven o'clock and dinner at eight. I'm really looking forward to meeting this guy. I'll give you my honest opinion, Emma."

Thanks a bundle, Emma thought to herself as she made her way towards the DART station and home.

But when she told Colin, he sounded quite keen.

"I've always wanted to have a look at Malahide. It's been years since I was out there. Did you know it's the richest town in Ireland?"

"No," Emma confessed.

"Well, it is. It's got the highest per capita income of anywhere in the state. There are more millionaires in Malahide than there are in Ballsbridge."

"Fancy that," she said.

* * *

Saturday night came around and Emma was apprehensive. She had been apprehensive since she got the invitation. What would happen if Trish decided she didn't approve of Colin? She would start harassing her to dump him. Well, if she did, her sister was in for a surprise. Emma was ready to tell her to back off and stop interfering in her life. The time had come to put Trish firmly in her place.

Colin arrived at her apartment at six o'clock with a bottle of vintage wine and a box of expensive chocolates for the hostess. For Emma he had an orchid. She was pleased to see that he had got his hair cut and put on a smart business suit.

"You could wear the orchid in your hair like a Spanish *señorita*," he said, kissing her full on the lips.

"Stop, you'll get yourself covered in lipstick," she said, pushing him away.

"I've been thinking about you all week. I want to carry you off to bed and ravish you."

"Maybe later," Emma said, disentangling herself and straightening her dress. "Right now we have to concentrate on this damned dinner party."

"You make it sound like an ordeal."

"I'm not a big fan of dinner parties," she said with a scowl. "Remember what happened the last time I gave one?"

Colin looked suitably reprimanded.

"What's your sister like?" he wanted to know as they settled into the car.

"She's the brainy one in the family," Emma said. "She'll

probably tell you herself but it's better to be prepared. She was one of the first female bank managers in Ireland and the youngest ever. Now she works in Corporate Affairs, whatever that means."

"I know about that. But what is she *really* like?"

"I find her quite domineering. She's older than me by three years and she thinks that gives her the right to interfere in my life at every turn."

"What about her husband?"

"He's in property."

"Development?"

"No, he's an auctioneer. Although, knowing Smitty, I wouldn't be surprised if he ended up in development. He is already launching himself as a landlord. They're both insanely ambitious."

"I wouldn't hold that against them," Colin said. "Ambition is what makes most people get out of bed in the morning."

They arrived on the outskirts of Malahide at twenty to seven. Colin suggested they go for a quick drink till seven o'clock but they couldn't find anywhere to park so they ended up driving around while he took a good look at how the town had changed since the last time he was there. At five to seven, they arrived at Trish's house.

It sat on a large plot of land overlooking the estuary. The gardens were immaculate: roses and flower beds dotted the lawns which looked as if they had been tended with nail clippers. Emma could see that Colin was very impressed. They pulled into the driveway and, right on cue, the door opened. Trish was standing in the hallway wearing a dazzling dress. Emma sneaked a glance at her own outfit and immediately felt in the shade.

"Emma, how are you, my dear?" She kissed her sister on both cheeks and turned to Colin. "So this is Mr Enright? I'm so pleased to meet you," she said, taking the bottle and the chocolates and grasping Colin's proffered hand with her free one. "Come in out of the cold. Go right into the living room. Smitty will get you a drink."

147

They followed her instructions and found the smiling Smitty standing in front of an open fire in a room that was carpeted, curtained and furnished better than any showhouse on a new estate. The introductions were made again. Smitty moved immediately to the drinks cabinet and poured. Trish was back in the room, having deposited the wine and the chocolates in the kitchen, from where Emma could smell something delicious cooking.

"How did you find the traffic?" Smitty wanted to know as he handed them their glasses.

"It found us," Colin replied, making a little joke. "On the outskirts of Portmarnock."

Smitty grinned all over his handsome face.

"No, it wasn't too bad," Colin continued. "Once I learned to give way to all the Porsches."

"Sit down, everybody," Trish insisted. "Make yourselves comfortable." She smiled at Emma and sat beside her on the couch. Colin glanced in her direction and smiled to let her know he felt quite at home.

"So you both had a nice holiday?" Trish asked.

"It was lovely," Colin replied. "Have you ever been to the Canaries?"

"Never," Trish replied. "But I have a friend who owns a place in Lanzarote. A villa," she added for emphasis.

"Well, we only had a modest penthouse," Colin went on. "But we had a marvellous time – beautiful weather, lovely food, nothing to do all day but relax and unwind."

Trish shot a quick glance towards her sister.

"We did a lot of swimming, sightseeing, that sort of thing," Emma said hastily, sensing that the conversation was drifting onto dangerous territory.

"And what did you do in the evening?"

"Dining out," Emma said quickly. "We had some delicious meals. And it's ridiculously cheap."

"I don't know how they do it, tell you the truth," Colin said. "They practically give the food away."

"And when we had finished eating it was usually time for bed," Emma said.

There was a silence as she quickly realised her mistake.

"I mean time to *sleep*. We were both exhausted after all the activity. I mean all the swimming . . . and sightseeing . . . and everything. Isn't that right, Colin?" She glanced at him for support.

"Exactly, it's the heat. It seems to drain all your energy."

They sat for a moment, fidgeting with their glasses. Emma could feel her sister's eyes boring into the back of her head. Across the room, she silently appealed to Colin for help.

"This is a beautiful house," he said, suddenly looking around the room. "Who was responsible for the decoration?"

"I was," Trish said, coolly.

"Well, I have to congratulate you. You have excellent taste."

Trish managed a weak smile. "Thank you," she said.

"Décor is a very tricky area," Colin went on in a confident tone. "Not everybody has the touch. And it's not just a question of money. You can spend oodles of cash and get it all wrong. It's more a question of judgment. And judgment is an extremely rare gift."

Trish seemed to thaw a little at the blatant flattery.

"Do you know about décor?" she asked.

"I studied it at college. I was planning to become an interior designer. But I have to confess, I wasn't up to it. I just didn't have the skill so I got out and opted for something less demanding. I studied law."

This time, Trish smiled at Colin's little joke.

"Honestly," he continued. "I've seen people spend a fortune on their homes. I've seen them hire the most expensive designers and the house ended up looking like something out of a Disney cartoon. But this room . . ." He let his eye travel admiringly around him. "This room is exquisite."

Trish was beaming now.

Colin turned his attention to Smitty who had said nothing so far.

"And if I'm not mistaken, you've made a very shrewd investment here. I was telling Emma on the way over that Malahide has more millionaires per square foot than Beverly Hills."

Everybody laughed.

"We were just lucky," Smitty said.

"Nonsense, there's no such a thing as luck in the property business. *You* know that. It's all down to making smart decisions." Colin glanced again in Trish's direction. "But where you were really lucky was getting married to a woman who was clever enough to become the one of the first female bank managers in Ireland." He put on his winning smile. "Now that was a real piece of luck."

Emma looked at her sister who was now purring contentedly like a cat that was getting its tummy tickled.

Trish drained her glass.

"Let's all have a refill," she said delightedly. "The dinner can wait for a few minutes. I'm enjoying this little chat."

Chapter 17

The evening was a roaring success by any yardstick. Colin continued to charm his hosts, telling them how shrewd they had been in buying their wonderful house in cash-rich Malahide. He made it sound like Monte Carlo. He told them they had been light-years ahead of the so-called property experts and said how much he envied their taste, judgment and business prowess. They sat mesmerised and delighted as compliments were sprayed around the room like machine-gun bullets.

When everyone finally moved into the dining room and Trish presented her beef Wellington with roast potatoes, glazed carrots and blue cheese and walnut salad, Colin went into raptures of delighted appreciation. Trish glowed with so much pride that Emma half-expected her to burst into flames. Colin had her in his spell as surely as a snake charmer and his cobra.

On the way home in the car, Emma said: "I didn't know you studied interior design."

"I didn't," he smiled mischievously. "I just made that up to impress them."

"Really?" she said.

"I was invited to dinner so they could run me up the flagpole and see who saluted. Well, I think I passed the test," he said with a smile. "Don't you?"

* * *

Emma didn't have long to wait to hear Trish's verdict. The following morning at nine o'clock, she was wakened by the loud ringing of the phone beside her bed. Sunday was the one morning when she looked forward to a lie-in but that prospect was shattered as she pressed the phone to her ear and heard her sister's booming tones. She was so excited, it sounded as if she was right there in the room.

"This is the one," she announced with absolute conviction in her voice. "I don't know how you did it but Colin Enright is a prize catch. There can't be many of them left. He's the man you have to marry."

"*What?*" Emma spluttered, sitting bolt upright in bed.

"I was tremendously impressed with him. He has impeccable manners and excellent judgment besides being quite dishy to look at. You heard what he said about the décor in the living room. And he loved my beef Wellington. He said he hadn't tasted anything like it since he had lunch in the Savoy Grill in London."

"I'm so glad you liked him," Emma managed to say.

"Yes, I did. And I'm never wrong about these things. Smitty agrees with me. By the way, do you know how much he earns?"

"I'm afraid we haven't got round to discussing his income," Emma said tartly.

"Well, that's the first thing we have to discover. There are ways of finding out. He's a lawyer so he can't be stuck for bob or two. Those guys are made of money. Try to be diplomatic."

"Don't you think you're going a bit fast? No one has said anything about marriage."

"For God's sake, Emma, why else are you going out with him?"

"Because I enjoy his company. But I haven't made my mind up about any long-term commitment."

"How long does it take? You've been away on holiday with him. I had him summed up within five minutes of meeting him."

"I'd prefer to wait and see how things develop."

"Nonsense, you've got to grab him with both hands. Don't hang about. Think of the competition out there. While you're dithering, some scheming little seductress might nip in and steal him from right under your nose."

"You're talking about him as if he was a piece of furniture. Don't you think he might have his own views on the subject of marriage?"

"Rubbish! Men don't know what they want. It's up to you to convince him that you're the most desirable creature in God's universe and his life would be a misery without you. For Heaven's sake, Emma, do I have to come over there and woo him for you?"

The call ended with a sharp click as Trish put down the phone. Emma sank back on the bed and let out a loud groan. It was only half past nine and already Trish had ruined her day.

* * *

A couple of evenings later, Colin once more raised the question of moving in together. He had met her after work and they had gone for a drink in a quiet little bar in Blackrock. In the meantime, Emma had been giving the matter more thought. She had already discussed it with Jackie over lunch in the Blue Moon café.

"It seems such a big move to make and it sort of scares me," she confessed. "What if he turns out to be a slob who leaves his dirty underwear lying all over the bathroom?"

"Well, if he was a slob you would have picked up some sense of it when you were on holiday together," Jackie said reasonably, as she bit into her wholegrain sandwich with chicken, lettuce and mayonnaise.

153

"Sometimes these traits don't manifest themselves till later."

"Then you must house-train him like you would a dog. And remember, *you* might have personal habits that *he* will disapprove of. What do you do with your toenail clippings as a matter of interest?"

"What a disgusting question," Emma said, wrinkling her nose.

"I'm only using it as an example," Jackie went on. "This is a learning curve. That's one of the benefits of living together. You get to spot these things before it's too late."

"I'm still not convinced. Moving into his apartment puts too much power in his hands."

"Then invite him to move in with you."

"Oh, no," Emma said quickly. "I might not be able to get him out again."

"Well then, here's what you should do. Offer to move in with him on a part-time basis. It can be a trial run for the real thing." She smiled triumphantly and her freckled face gleamed in the light. "That way, you get the best of both worlds."

But Emma was still unsure.

"So what do you say?" Colin asked now, startling her as he put down two gin and tonics on their table. He settled on the seat beside her in a cosy corner of the bar. "Are you going to move in with me?"

"I'm still considering it," she said.

"What is there to consider?" he cajoled. "Think of the money we will save."

"If I move in with you, what guarantee will I have that we won't end up screaming at each other?"

"That won't happen," he said, gently caressing her hand. "We're adults, Emma. I'm sure if we have issues we'll be able to talk them through."

"If I agree to this, I want you to know that I'm not going to become your housekeeper."

"Of course not," he rushed to assure her. "There'll be no

154

question of that. My washing goes to the laundry once a week. And most of the time I eat out so you wouldn't have any cooking to do."

"Well, I might cook occasionally. You *did* mention saving money. And anyway, I enjoy cooking."

"I wouldn't object if you cooked dinner from time to time. I could even help you. You could show me what to do."

"And I would expect you to turn up on time unlike the last occasion when I cooked for you," she said pointedly, reminding him once more of the disastrous dinner party.

"Certainly. I told you that would never happen again."

"I won't go around cleaning up after you. And you're not to leave dirty laundry lying all over the place."

"Oh, no, certainly not. I'm actually quite clean. You've seen my place. I'm very tidy."

"We could draw up a roster of chores," she said.

"Or we could get a cleaning lady to come in."

"No," Emma said. "Cleaning ladies never do the job as well as you do it yourself."

"Well then we'll have a roster. I think that's a very good idea."

"And one final thing," she said, putting on a stern face. "I'm not about to become your sex slave."

"God forbid."

"I won't be there for sexual gratification any time you start feeling randy. That's not what this is about."

"Of course not, but there will be some sex, won't there?"

"By mutual agreement," she said, firmly.

It was decided that Emma would begin by moving in for weekends to see how it worked out. If everything went smoothly, she could extend the amount of time she stayed. This meant that she still had her own place to escape to if she felt she needed time and space.

Colin readily agreed. Emma had come to the conclusion that

he was lonely and welcomed the opportunity for close human contact. Over the next few days, she collected the things she wanted to bring with her. In the end, the items filled several huge cardboard boxes. The following Saturday morning, he came over in his car and they loaded it all onto the back seat.

"Have you ever done this before?" she wanted to know, as they drove the short distance to his apartment.

"Never," Colin said. "I shared several grotty flats with some guys when I was a student. But never with a woman."

"Are you looking forward to it?"

"Of course! Why do you think I asked you? Mind you, I wouldn't do this with just any woman. You're very special to me, Emma. You do appreciate that?" He took his hand off the steering wheel to give hers a little squeeze.

"Well, one thing's for sure," she said. "We're about to find out if we're suited to each other."

He left the car in the communal car park and they went up in the lift.

She had been in his apartment several times already and it was much bigger than the small place he casually referred to. It was almost as big as the apartment they had shared in Tenerife. It had a large living room, a good big kitchen and two bedrooms with en-suite bathrooms. It had been another of Emma's conditions that she should have her own room. While she was quite content to share his bed at night, she wanted her own privacy too.

They carried the boxes into her room and she began to unpack. It took her half an hour to store her clothes in the wardrobe and arrange her books on the shelf above the bed while a little table beside the window provided the perfect desk for her laptop. It even had a telephone plug so she could hook into the internet.

When she had finished unpacking, Colin suggested they go out to a restaurant for lunch to celebrate her arrival.

"I've got a better idea," she said.

"Yes?"

"We'll cook in."

"Are you sure?"

"Absolutely."

"Okay," he agreed. "But we'll have to get provisions."

"Where is the nearest supermarket?"

"I don't use the supermarket. I told you I never cook. If I want anything, I just nip down to the convenience store."

"You do *what*?" she asked in disbelief.

"Go to the convenience store."

"Well, that's a very expensive way to do your shopping," she said. "The supermarket is always cheaper. Now, the first thing is to make a list. Let's check the kitchen."

It yielded precious little by way of foodstuffs. There were a couple of tins of baked beans, a jar of coffee, a frozen pizza, a container of salt and a packet of jam tarts that were long past their sell-by date.

"I'm starting to believe you about never cooking at home," she sniffed as she closed the cupboard doors.

She sat down at the kitchen table, got a notebook and pen and began to write down the items they required. By the time she had finished, the list ran to three pages.

"Do you think we'll really need all this?" he said, peering at the paper.

"These aren't luxuries, Colin, they're basic necessities. Toilet rolls? Detergent? Bread? Milk? I don't know how you can live without them."

"I'm beginning to enjoy this," he said.

"We're only starting," Emma replied tartly.

They drove to a supermarket in Dun Laoghaire and she spent forty-five minutes pushing a large trolley up and down the aisles, while she meticulously ticked off the items they required. Colin trooped along in her wake, his eyes wide with wonder like a

157

child in a toy store. When they got to the checkout desk, the bill
came to over €200. He handed over his credit card and happily
pushed the trolley out to the car park.

"I'm amazed that you've never done this before," she said.

"It just never occurred to me."

"Well, it's going to become a regular experience. You can't go
throwing money away on convenience foods. And another thing,
we have to establish a budget. I have to pay my share."

"But it's my apartment," he protested.

"And I'm helping to eat the food. So I insist."

"Okay," he conceded. "This sounds like fun."

When they had finally unloaded the car and stored all the
food away, Colin uncorked a bottle of wine and poured two
glasses. Emma went into the kitchen and began to prepare the
lunch.

"Have you *ever* cooked before?" she wanted to know.

"I made baked beans one time."

"That's not cooking."

"I boiled an egg a few times. But it was like a cricket ball by
the time I was finished."

She gave him a scornful look. "I mean proper cooking!"

"No," he confessed.

"Well, watch me and learn. I'm going to prepare a chicken
stirfry. It's very easy."

She found a chopping board and began slicing up the fillets of
chicken and the piece of chorizo sausage she had bought earlier.
She poured oil into a large heavy pan and put the chicken and
sausage in to brown while she chopped some onions, garlic,
tomatoes and a large red pepper.

Then she added the vegetables to the pan and stirred them
into the chicken and sausage, saying, "You see, you can put in
anything you like. It's very nutritious. It's also cheap. And it is
very simple to make. Even you could do it."

He watched fascinated as she continued to buzz about the

cooker adding salt and pepper, herbs and lemon juice to the pan and putting some boil-in-the-bag rice on to cook. Soon the kitchen was filled with an appetising aroma.

"Aren't you supposed to time it?" he inquired.

"Ideally, but usually I go by instinct. If you taste the food from time to time, you'll know when it is ready. The rice should take about ten minutes."

She got out the lettuce she had bought, washed it under the tap and began slicing and chopping. She added tomatoes, slices of red onion and cucumber and some grated parmesan cheese. Finally she drizzled the salad with oil and vinegar. Ten minutes later the whole thing was ready.

It was a mild afternoon, so they decided to eat on the terrace. Colin had already laid the table. He helped her carry the steaming plates of food outside. He poured more wine and plunged his fork into the stirfry.

She waited for his response.

Slowly his face broke into a smile of satisfaction. "Umhhhhh. It's delicious." He smacked his fingers to his lips. "Mouth-watering perfection."

"I'm glad you like it."

"Like it? It's marvellous. This is the best food I've tasted in ages."

"It's not rocket-science. Even you could do it, Colin. Now eat up before it gets cold. We're not in Tenerife any more."

When they had finished eating, they lingered on the terrace, staring across the rooftops at Dublin Bay and the Hill of Howth in the distance.

"I'm so glad you've come to live with me," he said. "You make the place feel, well . . . kind of homely."

"That's exactly how it should feel. It *is* your home."

"I know. But until now, I never thought of it that way. I've always just used it as a sort of base."

"Well, maybe that's about to change," she said.

"You think you'll stay?" Colin asked, his face brightening.

"That depends. Let's just take it a day at a time and see how it works out."

"I'll take that as a yes," he said.

Chapter 18

One Saturday evening after she had shown him how to make spaghetti bolognese, they sat at the dining table drinking wine and she asked him about his childhood.

"I was the youngest," he said. "The last throw of the dice, you might say. By the time I came along my brothers were all away at boarding school and I only saw them at holidays. So I felt more like an only child."

"No sisters?" Emma inquired.

He shook his head.

"Only boys. It was quite a lonely existence. I would have liked company. I even used to invent imaginary friends. And of course, I was spoiled. My parents gave me everything I wanted. I think it made me quite selfish."

"And how are your parents now?"

"They're getting old. And their health isn't great. Dad has arthritis and Mum is getting a bit doddery. Early Alzheimer's, I suspect."

"I'm so sorry," Emma said, squeezing his hand, feeling a little guilty as she remembered her antagonism to his taking his mother to the hospital the night of the dinner party.

Gradually, she extended her stay at Colin's apartment till she was spending most of her time there, only going back to her own place for a couple of nights a week. The experiment had turned out well. They didn't get in each other's hair as she had feared and they never argued and rarely even had a disagreement.

She was also surprised to discover a marked change in her sister's attitude. By now, Trish's opposition to Emma moving in with Colin had given way to active encouragement. She took a full-time interest in promoting the relationship and was convinced that the fastest way to persuade Colin to propose marriage was to show him how good life could be with a permanent female companion and soul mate.

"You've got to be nice to him," she told Emma. "That's your role. Men need women to bolster their self-confidence. Despite all the outward bravado, they're very vulnerable creatures at heart."

"How do you mean?"

"You must compliment him from time to time. Tell him how good he looks, admire his dress sense, laugh at his jokes. And for God's sake, don't complain. If he does something to upset you, just put it out of your mind. Men can't stand women who are always complaining."

"Are you saying I should just let him walk all over me?"

"Of course not. But you mustn't be hypercritical. You've got to remember they see themselves differently to us."

"Don't you believe in equality of the sexes?" Emma asked.

"Certainly not," her sister replied. "Women are obviously superior. That's why you have the responsibility of protecting him from himself. Once Colin has come to rely on you, you can gradually introduce a little discipline. But try to do it subtly."

"I give up," Emma said.

Before long, Trish had taken to ringing Colin at his office for little chats. Emma got to hear about this development one evening when she was having dinner with him at a restaurant in town. They had just ordered coffees when he made his announcement.

"Your sister gave me a tip for the stock market last week, did I tell you?"

"I don't think so."

"Well, she did and already the shares have doubled in value. She's really clued in, isn't she?" he said, casually.

"She's very smart, if that's what you mean," Emma replied.

"She's definitely going places. I don't think she'll stay long at the bank. I've a funny feeling she'll move on to something bigger."

"How come you were talking to her?"

"Oh, she keeps in touch. Ever since the dinner party she's got into the habit of giving me a call now and again."

"How often is now and again?"

"A couple of times a week."

"That's nice," Emma said. "What do you talk about?"

"She keeps me up to speed on developments in the financial world. It's very helpful. A lot of my clients are in finance. And, of course we talk about you."

"Indeed?"

"Oh yes. Trish cares a lot about you, Emma. As your older sister she feels responsible for you, particularly now that your mother is dead. She just likes to know that you're happy."

"And what do you tell her?"

He laughed and gave the waiter his credit card.

"I tell her you're as happy as a pig in slurry."

Emma found this new development unsettling. She wasn't sure how she should react. It occurred to her that there were now three of them in this relationship and that was one too many. But at the same time, she didn't want to risk a full-scale row with her sister by complaining too much. Trish would be sure to argue that she was only trying to be helpful.

But it also forced her to look hard at the relationship. Where exactly was it going? It was now over a year since she had met Colin and for the past few months they had been living together for most of the week. It was nice to have a regular man in her life. But was she really in love with him? Emma wasn't sure. It occurred to her that some magic ingredient was missing. She compared her relationship with Colin to the way she had felt about Tim Devlin and found it sadly lacking. Tim had swept her off her feet but with Colin she just muddled along.

However, Trish seemed determined that marriage was the answer. She was convinced that once Colin Enright put a ring on Emma's finger, they would both live happily ever after. Emma didn't agree. It might have worked with Smitty but there was no guarantee that it would work with Colin. And in Emma's mind, a loveless marriage would be far worse than what they had now.

But Trish wasn't prepared to wait. It wasn't long before she began to apply pressure. One morning, she rang Emma at work just as she was about to take her coffee break.

"I was talking to Colin yesterday," she began.

"Again?"

"I get the impression of a man who is at a crossroads in his life. What happens in the near future will decide whether he settles down or becomes a confirmed bachelor. He has reached a sort of turning point."

"Really?" Emma said, barely able to conceal her irritation.

"Yes and it calls for tact and diplomacy on your part. You've got to persuade him to take the marriage route. I'll give you all the advice and assistance I can but, in the end, *you* have got to convince him. I can't do it for you."

Emma was tempted to ask why not, since her sister seemed to be doing everything else.

"I've noticed that when men get to a certain age," Trish continued, "they grow content with single life and often they don't get married till much later in their lives, if at all. But then they can afford to hang about. It's different with women. *We* have a much shorter shelf life."

Emma gritted her teeth. "What if he doesn't want to get married? I can hardly take a shotgun to him, can I?"

"There are ways of doing things. You don't need me to spell it out for you."

"Are you suggesting I should get pregnant?" Emma asked sweetly.

"Good Lord, no!" Trish said. "I would regard that as a last desperate measure. We're a long way from that point yet. But you could make it clear to him that you're not prepared to continue in this present set-up indefinitely."

"That *is* taking a shotgun to him, now isn't it?"

"Not at all, it's simply setting out the realities of the situation. I warned you at the start that if he got used to the idea of having everything for nothing, it might be difficult to shift him."

By now Emma's blood pressure was approaching boiling point.

"You're leaving someone out of the equation," she snapped.

"Who?"

"Me! You're assuming *I* want to get married. What if I was to tell you that I'm quite content with things as they are?"

There was a shocked pause.

"You couldn't be."

"I am. You've never once paused to consider my views on the subject."

"Now, Emma . . ." Trish was speaking in the soft, reasonable voice that you would use with a lunatic. "You're not thinking straight. Of course you want to get married. But if you continue in the present set-up much longer, you'll be throwing away all your trump cards. And God forbid, if he ever decides to end the relationship, you'll be practically unmarriageable."

"You're not hearing me," Emma said, ignoring the last remark.

"Of course I'm hearing you. I'll give you full marks for

finding Colin Enright. He's an excellent prospect. But now you've got to go in for the kill. You don't want some other little trollop nipping in and snaring him, now do you? How would you ever live with that?"

Emma's temper finally snapped.

"Why must you have this constant emphasis on marriage? It's no guarantee that I'll be happy. I'm not even sure that I love him."

"What's love got to do with it, for heaven's sake?" Trish snapped back. "The main thing is to get that ring on your finger."

"But when I get married I want it to be to someone I love. Someone I want to share the rest of my life with. You make it sound like it was just a financial transaction, like Smitty selling a house to someone. And I'm just not certain that Colin is the man I want."

She could hear her sister taking a deep breath.

"Your mind is muddled," she said at last. "You're under pressure. I'm going to end this conversation right now. But we'll return to it. You're not going to allow Colin Enright to slip through your fingers if I have anything to do with it."

Emma let out a loud groan. "Do we have to?" she wailed.

"Yes, we do. I have a responsibility to stop you making a mess of your life. And I'm determined to carry it out."

Chapter 19

By now, Emma was starting to feel that her life was heading for a crisis. It wasn't just Trish and her constant interference. There was also her job. It had turned out to be all the things that her sister had said when she had encouraged her to take the Civil Service exams. It was secure, it was steady, the working conditions were fine and she never had to worry about being laid off. But there was one factor that no one had thought of: it was boring Emma senseless.

Despite the visit by Tim Devlin and the people from Human Resources, none of their recommendations had been implemented. None of the work practices had changed and Emma felt wasted. She longed for challenges and excitement. She longed for fulfilment. The thought of spending the rest of her working life in the same dull environment filled her with dread.

But it was the situation between herself and Colin Enright that weighed heaviest on her mind. She resented the idea that he was now conspiring with Trish. She decided the time had come to confront him about it.

The next time they were alone together, she raised the subject.

"Trish tells me you were talking about me again."

He laughed.

"What's the big deal? We talk all the time and naturally your name crops up."

"Well, I'm not pleased. I don't like the idea of you and Trish discussing me behind my back."

"That's not the way it is, Emma. Your sister is your only living relative and naturally she is concerned for your welfare."

"You don't know her as well as I do," Emma said.

"Why? What's there to know?"

"You realise what she's trying to do, don't you?"

"She's trying to make sure you're happy."

She stared at him. Was he really so ignorant about what was going on?

"She's trying to get us married, you fool!"

Now it was Colin's turn to stare.

"Really? So that is what it is all about?"

"Yes. She's determined. She won't rest till we are man and wife."

He looked at her and a smile slowly came over his face. "You know something, Emma? That may not be such a bad idea."

She felt a panic grip her. This wasn't what she'd intended. The conversation had suddenly taken a very dangerous turn.

"Being married can bring a focus to your life," he continued. "And I have to settle down some time. I'm not getting any younger. What do you think?"

She turned away. "I don't know what to think."

"Just say yes. I'm asking you to marry me."

Suddenly she felt frightened.

"Let's change the subject," she said. "We'll talk about this another time."

"No," he insisted. "We'll talk now. I'm waiting for your answer."

She forced herself to look at him. She felt her lip tremble.

"I can't," she said. "I need more time."

"How much longer do you need, for God's sake? We've known each other for over a year. You either love me or you don't."

"I'm not ready," she said.

He lowered his eyes. "I'm sorry to hear you say that. I thought you would be happy."

He looked hurt, as if she had humiliated him. She reached out and took his hand.

"You know me well enough by now, Colin. I can't be rushed into things."

But he pushed her hand away, got up and left the room. A few minutes later she heard his car drive away.

So now they had had a row. Emma felt the tears well in her eyes. Trish's plan had worked and now Colin had proposed to her. But for Emma the outcome was bitter. She knew she should feel pleased by his offer. He was a handsome man and he had many fine points. Trish was right. Lots of women would be delighted to have him for a husband. But the spark was missing. Maybe in time it would appear but right now it wasn't there. There was no point pretending to be in love when she wasn't.

She would have to stand firm. Trish would be furious when she found out. But Emma was not about to be railroaded into marriage just because her sister thought it was a good idea. Trish already had too much control over her life. On this point she could not bend, no matter how much pressure was brought to bear.

She went into her bedroom, got undressed and slipped under the duvet. Later, she heard Colin return and go to bed. She lay awake staring at the ceiling. Their relationship had reached a defining point. It was a long time before she fell asleep.

The following morning, she rose before eight o'clock to find that Colin had got up before her. He was dressed and ready for work and was drinking a cup of coffee in the kitchen.

"Good morning," she said. "How did you sleep?"

He grunted a reply with a sullen look on his face.

"Would you like me to make you some breakfast?" she asked.

"No, thank you."

"I didn't mean to hurt your feelings last night," she said.

He shrugged and said nothing. He finished his coffee and left the cup in the sink.

"I'd better be going," he said, brusquely. "I've got a busy day."

He was gone from the apartment before she could say any more.

No goodbye kiss and barely any conversation, she thought. He's taking it badly. He's not used to rejection and it's hitting him hard. Well, I just hope he snaps out of it quickly because I don't enjoy long silences.

She wasn't going in to work that day so she went into her room, switched on her laptop and spent some time checking her emails. But Colin's attitude continued to distract her. She could feel resentment growing like a bitter weed. What right had he to be sullen with her just because she hadn't jumped for joy at his proposal of marriage? What arrogance, as if she should be grateful that he had condescended to consider her. She was in this frame of mind when, shortly after eleven o'clock, she heard her phone ring.

It was Trish.

"I heard the news," she said, breathlessly. "Congratulations."

"What news is that?" Emma said stiffly.

"You got him to propose. Well done. I knew if you persevered he would see sense in the end."

Emma bit her lip. Trish could only have heard the information from Colin. Was there nothing that he didn't share with her sister?

"I haven't accepted," she said bluntly.

"I know and I think that's a clever little touch. Get him excited and then keep him in suspense for a while. Full marks for tactics. But it has its dangers. Don't keep him dangling too long for God's sake."

"You don't understand," Emma said. "This has got nothing to do with tactics. I'm not getting married, Trish."

She heard a sharp intake of breath at the other end of the line.

"*What?* Are you off your head? After all these months of plotting and scheming, you're turning him down? What on earth are you thinking about?"

"I didn't say I'd turned him down. I've just asked for more time to consider."

"But what is there to consider, for God's sake?"

"Lots of things. I need time to reflect. This is the biggest decision I will take in my entire life and I want to get it absolutely right."

"Well, a period of reflection is tactically appropriate." Trish sounded slightly mollified. "After all, you don't want to create the impression that you're gagging to get married. But I wouldn't wait too long, if I was you."

"I'll wait as long as it takes."

She could hear her sister sighing on the phone as if she was dealing with a difficult child.

"He might change his mind," said Trish.

"Then the waiting will have been justified. It will prove that he wasn't totally committed."

"But Emma, don't you see? As long as he's single there is still danger. You don't seem to realise how fierce the competition is. Colin is an excellent catch. He's quite handsome and he has a nice home and a good income. He earns a hundred and twenty thou."

"How do you know that?" Emma asked sharply.

"I made it my business to find out."

"You mean, you asked him?"

"What's wrong with that? He was quite happy to tell me. And I also had it confirmed independently."

Emma struggled to control her anger. The nerve of Trish! To actually ask him what he earned! It was becoming more like a

171

business transaction every day. Where was the romance in all this?

"I feel very excited," Trish continued. "Once it's official, we'll sit down and work out all the fine details. Are you thinking of a big wedding? I've got good contacts in the media so we can make sure it gets loads of coverage. Have you thought about your honeymoon yet?"

"No," Emma said, firmly.

"I tell you what, why don't you and I have a little lunch? What about Friday? It will be a celebration and we'll talk things over. I know a marvellous wedding planner we could rope in."

Emma had heard enough. "I think that might be a little premature. As soon as I've made up my mind, I'll let you know. And Colin, of course. I think I should keep him in the picture too, don't you?"

Chapter 20

She finished the call with her head in a whirl. Already the pressure was becoming unbearable and she knew it would only get worse. Trish had planned this engagement like a military campaign and she wasn't about to let it fail at the last ditch. She would keep on and on until finally she had worn Emma down.

Suddenly she felt helpless, as if events were moving out of control. She was caught up in a relentless tide that was going to sweep her to the altar rails and straight into the arms of Colin Enright whether she wanted it or not. Another thought came flashing into her mind. If this was Tim Devlin who had asked her to marry him, would she have hesitated for a single moment? She already knew the answer.

She needed to get out of the house, to go for a walk and get some fresh air. She changed into runners and track-suit bottoms and set off at a steady pace for Dalkey Harbour. The day was warm but thankfully there was a cooling breeze blowing in from the sea. As she walked she turned over the events of the last few days.

It was all too much. She needed to get away, to escape to some place where she could think clearly without this relentless pressure. Tenerife immediately came to mind. It would be ideal. She would have peace and quiet. She could mull things over and come to some decisions without having Trish constantly badgering her. She could ring Dolly O'Brien and ask for some leave.

The thought immediately cheered her up. She returned to the village and bought some fresh bread in the bakery. When she got back to the apartment it was after one o'clock. She rang her supervisor only be told that she had gone to lunch so she made a cup of tea and sat down once more at her laptop and began to check flights to Tenerife. But immediately, she came up against a problem. The next direct flight wasn't till Saturday.

She could travel out of Manchester or London but there were no flights till tomorrow. She was checking connecting flights from Dublin when her phone rang. It was Trish back again.

"Sorry to bother you but I've been thinking. What we need is a meeting, you and me and Colin. I have a feeling that he may not have pitched his proposal properly. I know how clumsy men can be. If we can all sit down and talk about this rationally . . ."

"I can't," Emma blurted out. "I'm going away."

"You're what?"

The disbelief in Trish's voice was audible.

"I'm going to Tenerife for a while. I need a break. I need to get away so I can have peace to think."

"Are you crazy?" Trish said. "You can't do that. You've just got him hooked and now you propose to take yourself off. If you walk out on Colin Enright, you might never get him back. He'll think you're off your head and he'd be better off without you. And to tell you the truth, I wouldn't blame him."

Emma felt like screaming. "Don't tell me what to do, Trish!"

"I'm simply offering friendly advice. You're making a big

mistake. As your sister, I would be failing in my duty if I didn't try to stop you."

"You don't have to feel responsible. I'm an adult and I know exactly what I'm doing."

"Listen to me. I'm about to tell you some home truths and they may hurt. Colin Enright is the best prospect you're likely to find. You're twenty-six and you're not getting any younger. You're an average-looking woman with an average job. Colin is handsome, charming and a successful lawyer. Any woman would regard him as a prize. And time is not on your side. If you blow this opportunity, you might never get another."

"Thanks," Emma said caustically. "You do wonders for my morale."

"I know what's wrong. You're not well."

"I'm perfectly well."

"You're ill and I'm coming out there right now."

"Don't waste your time," Emma said. "You won't stop me."

"We'll see about that. You're not going to mess up this wonderful opportunity if I have anything to do with it."

There was a click and the phone went dead. Emma felt her head begin to throb. She stared at the phone for a moment and then she made up her mind. She was not going to sit around waiting for her sister to subject her to another brainwashing session. Immediately she swung into action. She got back onto the laptop. There was no time now to book connecting flights to Tenerife. She would go somewhere else. She searched for flights to Malaga and found one that was leaving at 5 p.m. She had no time to lose.

She paid for the flight and printed off her boarding pass. Then she went into the bedroom and quickly began to pack. The phone rang again. This time it was Colin. He sounded panicked.

"Trish has just been speaking to me. She said you were leaving."

"I'm taking a break. I need time to think."

175

"You can't go," he said, firmly.

Emma closed her eyes tightly. Here it was again. Somebody else was telling her what she could and couldn't do. She tried to keep her voice calm.

"Excuse me, Colin. But I think I can do as I please."

"I forbid it," he said.

"You *what*?" she screamed.

"You're distressed. I can hear it in your voice. You're not thinking straight. You need to calm down."

She took a deep breath and counted to ten.

"I'll pretend I didn't hear those last remarks, Colin. But get this clear in your head. You have no rights over me. I am free woman and I can do as I please. Now, I have a flight to catch. And, if you don't mind, I must go. You're holding me up."

"I'm warning you," he said. "If you go, it's over between us. You needn't come looking for me back."

She gasped. The arrogance of him!

"I'll bear that in mind, Colin. Goodbye."

She terminated the call. Her hand was shaking. The conversation had convinced her and now she was angry. But she willed herself to remain calm. Trish was probably on her way right now and she knew her sister's formidable energy. She must be gone before she arrived.

She finished packing then sat down at the computer once more and transferred €3000 from her bank account to her credit card. Then she ordered a cab. Now she had only one more task to perform. She rang Dolly O'Brien at work.

"I need a favour," she said.

"Yes?"

"Something has come up. I need some time off."

"We're short-staffed, Emma. Several people have gone sick."

"This is an emergency. I'm going through a crisis right now. I can't go into details but I really must have time off work."

"We have provision for compassionate leave." A guarded

note had now crept into Dolly O'Brien's voice. "How much time would you need?"

"Three months?"

"I don't think that would be possible."

"Could I take it as unpaid leave?"

"Not at such short notice. You would have to make an application and await a decision."

"But I haven't time for that. I must have it right now."

"If you're ill, you could get a sick certificate. That would cover you for a while."

"No," Emma said. "I'm not sick."

"Then, I'm sorry. It's not possible."

"I'm going to take it anyway," she said.

She heard the quick intake of breath.

"Emma, if you do that I will have to put you on a disciplinary charge."

"So be it," she said and switched off the phone.

She checked that she had her passport, boarding pass and money.

Five minutes later, she was in a cab on her way to the airport.

Casa Clara

Chapter 21

One evening about a week after she arrived at Casa Clara, when the excitement had died down and she felt safe, Emma went into the old town and found an internet café. In her haste to leave Dublin, she had forgotten to take her laptop and now she regretted it. She could have used the computer at the Casa but for security reasons decided not to.

She found a string of email messages waiting for her but three in particular were urgent. They were from Trish, Colin and Jackie. They sounded frantic with worry and for the first time she began to realise the enormity of what she had done. She had effectively disappeared and naturally people were concerned. Reading these emails, she began to feel guilty.

She thought of ringing Trish and Jackie to tell them she was all right but she didn't trust the phone. Phone calls could be traced and she didn't want anyone to know where she was, not even Jackie who was her best friend. Her big fear was that they would come here and try to get her to go back.

She sat down and typed a reply to Trish but she was careful

not to divulge too much information. She simply said she was safe and not to worry. She was happy where she was and now had the time and space to reflect on her situation. When the time was right she would contact her again. She knew that Trish would quickly pass this information to Colin.

She sent a more intimate message to Jackie telling her exactly what had happened: how she was being pressurised into marriage by her sister and felt trapped and had to escape. But she didn't tell Jackie where she was. She trusted her friend but she knew that she would be the first person Trish would go to looking for information. And Jackie couldn't tell what she didn't know.

After she had despatched the messages, she decided to send a similar one to Dolly O'Brien. In it, she apologised for the suddenness of her departure and for the disruption it had caused. She repeated that she had reached a crisis in her life and needed time to sort herself out. When she was finished, she felt better. She found a seat outside the café, sat down and ordered a coffee.

They would never find her here. Even if they managed to track her flight to Malaga airport, all they would know was that she had gone to southern Spain. And she might have moved on. She could be anywhere. The only danger was if she ran across someone from Dublin who recognised her. Word could get back that way. But that was a long shot and for the time being her secret was safe at Casa Clara.

By now, Emma had fallen head-over-heels in love with the Casa. Everything about the little hotel enchanted her: the staff and the peaceful surroundings, the gardens and the soothing fountain and the sea just a few yards from her bedroom window. And she was enjoying her job as receptionist even though the work was very demanding.

Each morning at six thirty her alarm clock woke her. It was still dark. Emma made her way down to the deserted beach and had a swim while she watched the dawn light up the sky with a beautiful pattern of pinks and blues. Then she returned to the Casa and had a breakfast of coffee and bread rolls and fruit. At eight o'clock, she was behind her desk in the little front hall, ready to tackle the problems of the day.

And there were plenty of problems to be sorted. It soon became apparent that the management of the operation was in very bad shape. Her first indication of how bad things were came on the fourth day when a group of holidaymakers arrived at her desk around lunchtime to find their accommodation was gone. Somebody had double-booked.

Emma tried not to show her panic. But how was she going to deal with this? She asked old Paco to organise some refreshments for the new arrivals while she tried to sort out the mess. Her first call was to the owner, Señora Alvarez.

"*Madre de Dios!*" she exclaimed when she was told. "This is the fault of Señora Lopez. What a silly woman. I would fire her if she hadn't already resigned."

"But what am I going to do?" Emma pleaded. "The guests are here and they are looking for their rooms."

"Ring Señor Gonzalez at the Hotel Bonito and ask if he can take them. If he has no room, ask him who else might help. We must find them somewhere to sleep. We can't have them wandering the streets. It is bad for business."

What about the effect on my mental health, Emma thought as she thanked Señora Alvarez and began the search for Señor Gonzalez' phone number.

She was in luck. He was able to accommodate the guests but he made such a big fuss about it that he made Emma feel he was doing her an enormous favour. Next, she had to explain the situation to the disgruntled arrivals and apologise for the inconvenience and arrange a couple of taxis to ferry them to their new hotel. Thankfully, none of them threatened to sue.

When they had finally gone, Emma was drenched in

perspiration. She went straight to her room, stripped off her clothes and stood under a cold shower for ten minutes. Then she put on fresh clothes, brushed her hair, arranged her makeup and went back downstairs to her post looking so cool and efficient that no one would have guessed the trauma she had just been through. But the experience taught her a lesson and she determined it would never happen again.

She set about devising a system of double-entry bookkeeping whereby every reservation was entered into a ledger and also filed on the computer. This meant that if someone requested a room, the person on reception could tell immediately if accommodation was available. Since the phone could ring at any time and be answered by whoever happened to be passing, she instructed all the staff to check the computer and make sure to get a phone number so that the booking could later be confirmed. It wasn't foolproof but it was a vast improvement on the haphazard system that had existed till now.

But overbooking was only one of the difficulties she faced. Another was the issue of breakfast. With its limited kitchen facilities, it was the only meal that Casa Clara was able to provide and it was a simple affair of coffee and rolls and a buffet of eggs and cheese and ham and fruit. It was meant to be served in the courtyard from seven o'clock till half nine or indoors if the weather was bad. But Emma had noticed that often some of these items would be missing. One day there would be no ham, another day, no cheese. Worse, the breakfast was frequently late and often guests arrived to find nothing prepared. This was important because people had trips planned or coaches to board. If breakfast wasn't available it naturally led to complaints.

She set about finding out what was causing the problem. She decided to approach Tomàs. He was a cheerful young man of twenty-six with jet-black hair and dark good looks. He was employed as a general handyman who could do most jobs from fixing a leaking water-tap to pruning the roses. Emma had always found him pleasant and intelligent. At the first opportunity, she asked Tomàs why the breakfasts were late.

He laughed as if he was enjoying a private joke.

"They argue over who should take the responsibility."

"I see. So whose job is it?"

"Rosa's."

Emma thought of the plump housekeeper whose main function was to supervise the cleaning staff and organise the laundry and the linen. It sounded ludicrous to ask her to take charge of breakfast on top of her other tasks.

"Rosa?"

"Yes. But she gave the job to Teresa but Teresa says she is only hired to clean and not to organise the breakfast."

Emma could appreciate Teresa's position. But she could also see that Rosa had her hands full with her main responsibilities. And she did a good job. Casa Clara was always sparklingly clean. Whoever had asked her to organise the breakfast as well hadn't been thinking straight.

"Tell me what is involved," she asked.

Tomàs shrugged. "Not a lot. Paco and I set out the tables and the plates. Then there is the coffee to make in the urns. The bread is delivered every morning at six o'clock by Francisco the baker. The ham and the cheese are taken from the big freezer in the kitchen along with the fruit. And there are also the eggs to cook. It is not too difficult."

"But someone must make sure that the food is ordered and invoiced?"

"Of course, but that is a simple matter."

Emma had a flash of inspiration. "Do you think you could do it?"

"Me, *Señorita*?"

"Yes. Why not? It doesn't have to be a woman's job."

He laughed again to reveal a mouthful of beautiful white teeth. "Certainly, it is nothing."

"All right. From now on, you will be in charge of breakfast. But do nothing till I speak to you again."

Emma sensed that she would have to proceed carefully. While Rosa and Teresa might resent the breakfast task, they might also take offence if it was suddenly removed from them. In a small place like this, a person's job defined their status.

She used the next few days to take each of the women aside and tell them how pleased she was with their work and how well they coped with their onerous responsibilities. As part of a reorganisation, she was going to lighten their burden by relieving them of responsibility for breakfast. They were delighted. The following Monday morning, Tomàs took over. The breakfast was never late again.

* * *

Slowly, she began to lick the place into shape. Señora Alvarez, who had made a point of coming in every afternoon to check on her work, began to relax. Her visits became less frequent till she was only coming to the Casa once a week. Emma took this to be a vote of confidence. One Sunday afternoon, she made a surprise visit to the reception desk and invited Emma to have an *aperitivo* with her at Bar Lorenzo across the street.

She seemed in fine mood as she led them to a table outside and snapped her fingers to get the waiter's attention. She was wearing a brightly coloured dress that hugged her ample figure and had a lacquered comb stuck in her shining black hair. In her hand she carried an ornate fan which she flicked open as soon as they sat down. Emma thought she looked quite sultry.

"I have just come from the bull ring," she announced, smiling. "I go there sometimes with my friends and today I had a success. I made a bet and won. So I am very happy."

"Do you often bet on the bullfights?" Emma asked.

Señora Alvarez continued to smile. "It is not something you

can bet on. Not like the horse races at the Hippodroma. You see, always the bull loses."

"Of course."

"But my friend, Señor Montilla, made a bet with me today on a magnificent *toro* from the ranch of Buenavista and the *toro* was spared. So I won my bet." She lowered her voice and gave Emma a sly look. "I think Señor Montilla wanted me to win."

"I see."

Señora Alvarez laughed gaily. "Anyway, I have been meaning to have a little talk with you. You are happy with your work?"

"Very happy," Emma replied.

"I also am happy, Señorita Frazer. You have been most efficient. Señora Lopez was not very capable. She made a lot of mistakes. You require a certain temperament for this work. Would you agree?"

"Definitely," Emma said, wondering where this conversation was leading.

"Without the temperament, everything becomes confusion," Señora Alvarez went on. "You must keep the cold head, isn't that so?"

"Cool head," Emma gently corrected her.

"Pardon me, my English is not very good."

"Oh, no, it's excellent," Emma rushed to reassure her. "You speak English very well."

This seemed to please Señora Alvarez who beamed with pleasure. "As a mark of my satisfaction, I have decided to increase your wages."

This was an unexpected surprise and Emma was thrilled. "Thank you!" she said.

"No, no, it is nothing. You have earned it. I feel confident when you are in charge. I can relax. It means I do not have to be worrying all the time about the business of Casa Clara because I know it is in brave hands."

"Safe hands."

Señora Alvarez smiled again. "Exactly. We must talk more often. This way I will improve my English. It is a very difficult language but very important. My friend, Señor Montilla, is most anxious to learn. He is already taking lessons."

"I would be happy to help you with your English any time I am free," Emma volunteered.

"You are very kind," said Señora Alvarez. "I am most fortunate to have found you. And to show my appreciation, I have decided to give you another hundred euros a week."

It was Emma's turn to smile with pleasure. One hundred euros a week would be most welcome. It would go straight into her bank account since she had very few expenses.

"This is very generous, Señora."

Señora Alvarez smiled and gently waved her hand. "Please."

And then another thought struck Emma. She thought of the years she had spent in the Department of Social Affairs complaining about the lack of motivation. Here was an opportunity to put some of her observations into effect.

"Would you mind if I made a small suggestion? I couldn't have carried out my work without the support of the other staff, people like Tomàs and Rosa and Teresa. If I accepted an increase of €50 instead of €100, do you think it would be possible to give them all a small bonus? I know they would be very grateful."

Señora Alvarez looked surprised. "This is most unusual. Are you sure?"

"I'm perfectly sure. Even a small sum would make a difference. It would let them know that their work is appreciated."

Señora Alvarez thought for a moment. "You are right. What is the proper English word for this?"

"Reward?"

"Exactly. This will be a reward for them."

"They deserve it," Emma said. "They work very hard. And they are extremely loyal to you and to Casa Clara."

A knowing smile spread across the face of Señora Alvarez.

"Now I understand why you are so good at your job, Señorita Frazer."

She snapped her fan shut and stood up.

"It will be done. I am glad we had this little talk. Now when is the best time for us to begin our English lessons?"

* * *

The following week, the staff were delighted to find a bonus of €100 in their wage packets along with a note from Señora Alvarez to say it was in appreciation of their loyalty to Casa Clara. Emma was amazed at the effect the money had on their morale. Nothing like this had ever happened before. And even though the note and the bonus came from Señora Alvarez, everyone seemed to know that Emma was behind it.

Quickly, the atmosphere around the Casa was transformed. The confusion that had existed when she arrived was replaced with smooth efficiency. Now if she asked someone to work late or to double up for a colleague who had gone sick, it was done with a good will. The staff had a cheerful smile on their faces as they went about their tasks.

Very soon, the business was ticking over smoothly. Guests were satisfied and told their friends so bookings increased. Emma began to relax a little and persuaded Señora Alvarez to hire Cristina, a young hotel trainee from Seville, as her assistant. It meant that at last she was able to claim each Saturday as her day off.

It was ironic that shortly afterwards Señora Alvarez decided that Saturday morning at eleven o'clock would be the perfect time for their English conversation lessons.

Chapter 22

But not everything was sweetness and light around Casa Clara. If the staff were now working smoothly together as an efficient team, there were two long-term residents who didn't get along with each other at all. The first was an elderly Irish lady called Mrs Moriarty who had been staying at the Casa for six years, practically since the first day Miguel Ramos had opened his doors for business. She was a widow who had originally come to Fuengirola to get over the death of her husband and had liked the place so much she decided to stay. Now she occupied the highest room in the hotel which also commanded the best view over the tops of the palm trees to the ocean beyond.

Mrs Moriarty was a very private person who kept largely to herself. She was a small, frail-looking woman who appeared every morning for breakfast and then disappeared again back to her room. During the day, she would occasionally leave the Casa and be gone for hours and in the evening when the heat had passed, she liked to go out for a stroll along the beach with the aid of a polished blackthorn stick which she used for support.

Nobody knew where she ate her meals but it was assumed that she called into one of the local restaurants on her excursions where it was possible to eat well for seven or eight euros. And, occasionally, the cleaners would report scraps of stale bread or fruit in her room.

Mrs Moriarty was in her late sixties but she hadn't always been reclusive. When she first turned up in Fuengirola she had led quite a busy social life, throwing herself into the local drama society and the bridge club and a host of other activities that kept her extremely occupied. She told people that she needed to keep busy so that she wouldn't brood too much over her poor dead husband, Brendan, who had been a successful businessman till he died suddenly from a heart attack. More cynical observers said she was on the lookout for a replacement.

But she was an argumentative little woman who held strong opinions and gradually she fell out with her friends. Bit by bit, she gave up her social life and retreated to her room where she spent her days reading and watching old movies on television and conducting her vendetta against Major Sykes.

He was a thin bachelor in his early seventies who liked to wear tweed jackets and pullovers, even in the heat of summer. He had a bristling military moustache and an erect bearing and kept himself fit by a rigorous exercise regime involving dumbbells and a brisk swim in the sea every afternoon. He spoke with an English public-school accent and tended to look down on anybody who wasn't British. He had been known to refer disparagingly to members of the staff as "Johnny Foreigner" on those occasions when they did something to displease him.

He had come to the Casa a couple of months after Mrs Moriarty to live out his days on a military pension and occupied the room directly beneath her. This was a cause of friction between them. Major Sykes complained about the sound from her television which, he claimed, was played at maximum volume deliberately to annoy him. He said he had heard the soundtrack of *Gone with the Wind* so often that he could play the part of Rhett Butler without a script.

For her part, Mrs Moriarty claimed that the Major was plotting to get her room from her because it had the best view. She also said he kept her awake at night with his dumbbells, grunting and panting so much from the exercise that it was like living above an abattoir. When she was particularly upset, she described him as "the Black and Tan murderer", referring to the 1920s police unit notorious for their violent reprisals against the civilian population in Ireland – an insult which caused Major Sykes bitter resentment, particularly since he had never set foot in Ireland in his entire career.

Nobody knew exactly what had caused the rift between them. Some of the older members of staff could even remember a time when they were on quite good terms: when the Major would take Mrs Moriarty out for afternoon tea and scones to the Union Jack tearooms on the Paseo Maretimo and she would invite him to her room for cocktails before dinner. Indeed, some observers believed they could see a romance beginning to blossom before the pair had their falling out. It was even suggested that this was the cause of the enmity between them; that she had rejected him or he had rejected her. Nobody was quite sure.

Old Paco who had become Emma's confidant, said he knew the real cause of the dispute. He claimed to have witnessed it and said it had begun over the simple matter of a boiled egg. Mrs Moriarty liked to have an egg with her breakfast every morning. But the day arrived when she came down late to the buffet table to find the Major happily munching on the last one and clearly enjoying it. She immediately stormed over to where he was sitting in the shade of a palm tree and denounced him as a scoundrel and a blackguard.

"How dare you?" she roared.

"What?" exclaimed the startled Major.

"Take the last piece of food from the mouth of a poor widow

who has shown you nothing but civility since the first day I set eyes on your miserable carcase!"

Major Sykes opened his mouth to reply but she immediately silenced him.

"But then it's only what your forefathers did when they left the poor Irish peasants to starve by the roadside during the Great Famine, so you're well used to it, I dare say."

"I beg your pardon, Madam," the Major finally managed to respond.

"You may beg all you like but you'll get no pardon from me. You are no gentleman to treat a lady so disgracefully. As for being an officer, it's well seen that you couldn't command a platoon of the Boys' Brigade!"

Paco immediately tried to calm matters by offering to boil another egg for Mrs Moriarty but it was too late. The damage had been done. The red-faced Major stood up and stormed off to his room. The pair never spoke to each other again except to hurl insults at each other.

Emma hadn't been long at the Casa when she made the acquaintance of Mrs Moriarty. She was checking bookings on the computer at the reception desk one morning, when she looked up to see a pair of milky blue eyes staring intently at her.

The eyes were set in a thin, wrinkled face whose skin was the texture of old newspapers that had been left out too long in the sun and the whole lot was topped with a head of snow-white hair held in place with a comb. Emma gave a start for she hadn't heard Mrs Moriarty approach.

"Good morning," she said, when she had gathered her wits.

"You're the new girl, are you?" Mrs Moriarty said.

It was quite a while since Emma had been addressed as a girl but she put on her best face and smiled pleasantly.

"I'm the new receptionist. My name is Emma Frazer."

"Well, I hope you'll be better than the last one. It shouldn't be too difficult. She was a total disaster. She couldn't even speak

English properly." Mrs Moriarty sniffed and looked Emma up and down with a disdainful air.

"What can I do for you?" Emma asked.

"You can get my light bulb fixed. It's gone out and I need it to read."

"Of course, I'll get Tomàs to go up and take a look at it."

"Where is he?"

"He's around somewhere. The last time I saw him he was in the garden."

Emma craned her neck to see if she could catch sight of the handyman but he was nowhere to be seen. At that moment, Teresa came past with a bucket and mop.

"*Hola*, Teresa. Have you seen Tomàs anywhere?"

Teresa shrugged. "No, *Señorita*."

"I want it fixed now," Mrs Moriarty demanded, drilling her tiny fingers on the desktop. "I'm paying good money and the least I can expect is that the damned light bulbs should work."

"It's probably worn out," Emma said.

"Then I want it replaced."

Emma spoke again to Teresa. "Would you mind fetching a light bulb from the store cupboard and bringing it up to Mrs Moriarty's room?"

"*Sí, Señorita*."

Emma turned once more to the old lady.

"Now, if you would like to lead the way, we'll see what we can do."

Mrs Moriarty blinked in astonishment.

"You're going to fix it yourself?"

"Why not? It's not exactly heart surgery."

The old lady looked surprised but she began to ascend the stairs with remarkable agility. Emma followed behind.

"It's about time they got a lift installed," Mrs Moriarty grumbled. "I'm getting too old to be trekking up and down these stairs."

"I'll speak to Señora Alvarez," Emma said, sweetly, "and let her know of your concerns."

"And the place could do with a fresh coat of paint. You can tell her that as well. It's so dark it's beginning to look like a morgue."

Emma listened patiently to Mrs Moriarty's complaints. She was determined not to allow the old woman to rile her. The last thing she wanted was to make an enemy of her. They reached her room and Mrs Moriarty opened the door. It was a large double room and Mrs Moriarty had made it very much her own. It was dominated by a big television set which sat in a corner away from the window. There was a comfortable sofa with cushions and an easy chair. Out on the terrace, Emma could see pots of flowering geraniums. Around the walls were pictures of Irish country scenes: the Lakes of Killarney, Galway Bay, the Halfpenny Bridge in Dublin.

"You've made it very comfortable," she commented. "It looks nice and homely."

For the first time since they had met, Mrs Moriarty managed something approximating to a smile.

"Do you like my pictures?"

"I was just admiring them," Emma replied.

"I brought them with me when I came out here to remind me of home. For all their talk about Spain, their scenery isn't a patch on ours." She squinted closely at Emma. "You're Irish too, aren't you?"

"Yes."

"I recognised your accent. Where are you from?"

"Dublin."

"The same as myself. What part?"

"I live in Blackrock," Emma said.

"That's a lovely place, right on Dublin Bay with the sea beside you. I was born and reared in Fairview and then I married my poor husband and we moved out to Sutton. We had a lovely house with a great big garden. I do miss Dublin sometimes. Although the weather here suits me better. I've got arthritis, did I tell you that?"

"No," Emma replied. "But I'm sorry to hear about it."

Mrs Moriarty shrugged.

"You know, they won't allow me to keep a cat," she announced, suddenly changing direction.

"No, I didn't. Why is that?"

She screwed her face up into a scowl and pointed to the floor.

"Him," she said, the word dripping with venom.

"Major Sykes?"

"That's right."

"But what has it got to do with Major Sykes?"

"Exactly!" Mrs Moriarty said, jubilant that she appeared to have found an ally in Emma.

"The ould devil has complained that a cat would keep him awake at night. Did you ever hear the like? Of course, he only did it to spite me."

"So you like animals?" Emma inquired, hoping to distract Mrs Moriarty from the subject of the Major.

"I love cats. And if only I was allowed to keep one, my life would be content. I'd have a little companion. And that's not all he's done."

She launched into a recital of the Major's perceived crimes but at that moment there was a polite knock on the door and Teresa entered with a new bulb.

Emma gratefully took it and thanked her, then spoke again to Mrs Moriarty.

"Now where is the problem?"

The old lady pointed to a lamp beside the sofa.

Emma quickly unscrewed the bulb and replaced it with the new one, then flicked the switch and the light came on.

"There you are," she announced. "I was right. It was worn out. You'll be able to read again."

"Thank you very much," Mrs Moriarty said. "I'm glad there's someone around this place who knows what they're doing."

"*De nada*," Emma said and speedily took her leave to escape to the sanctuary of the reception desk.

* * *

But now that she had made Mrs Moriarty's acquaintance, it wasn't so easy to shake her off. Two days later, Emma put down the phone after accepting a reservation, to find her wizened face staring across the desk at her once more.

"Why, Mrs Moriarty," she said, "how nice to see you! You're looking very well today."

"I'm not feeling well. My arthritis is playing me up. But I'm sure you don't want to listen to my complaints."

"Oh, dear," Emma replied. "What can I do for you?"

"Here," the old lady said, taking a package out of a plastic bag and thrusting it across the desk.

"What is it?" Emma asked in surprise.

"It's a present; for taking care of me the other day."

"A present? What a lovely thought. May I look?"

"Of course you can look. It's for you, isn't it?"

Emma tore open the package to find a hardback copy of *Tara Road* by Maeve Binchy.

"Why, that's lovely," she said. "But you really shouldn't have bothered. All I did was change a light bulb."

"But you did it willingly and with a smile on your face. That makes a big difference." She sniffed. "I think you'll enjoy it. She's a very good writer. I've read all her books."

"Thank you very much," Emma said. "I love reading."

"There's no need to thank me. Just be up at my room tomorrow at three o'clock for afternoon tea. I'll be expecting you."

Emma felt her heart sink a little. She'd suspected there would be a catch.

"That's very kind," she said. "I'll look forward to it."

Chapter 23

The following afternoon at five minutes to three, Emma asked Cristina to take charge of the reception desk while she went to visit Mrs Moriarty. It was normally a quiet period, if any part of her busy day could truly be called quiet. But at least those guests who were leaving had checked out by midday and settled their bills, the rooms had been cleaned, the linen changed and the accounts brought up to date. She also calculated that leaving her assistant in charge would provide the perfect excuse for an early get-away after what she judged to be a reasonable time spent in Mrs Moriarty's company. This was not a visit she was looking forward to.

"You know where to find me if there's an emergency," she told Cristina who was quickly turning out to be a reliable and hardworking employee. Her English was improving by the day and she was eager to take on responsibility as a way to develop her experience. So Emma had no worries about leaving the affairs of the Casa in her capable hands for half an hour.

"Everything is in order," her assistant replied. "Take as long as you like."

"I should only be gone for a short while. Mrs Moriarty has invited me to drink tea with her."

Cristina pulled a face which seemed to say "rather you than me". "Enjoy it," she said with a slight hint of sarcasm and bent her head to some paperwork.

Emma climbed the narrow stairs, past her own room and up another couple of flights till she reached the top of the house. Mrs Moriarty's room had a splendid view of the courtyard and the ocean. She could understand why Major Sykes might covet the room although she wasn't convinced that he really wanted to take it from her at all.

When she arrived outside her door, she paused for a second to straighten her blouse and smooth back her dark hair before knocking.

"Come in," a thin voice squeaked.

Emma pushed open the door and entered Mrs Moriarty's lair. She found her sitting on the terrace with a huge parasol shading her from the sun. She had dressed for the occasion. She wore a white muslin dress and on her breast she had pinned a large silver brooch. She had combed her hair into a large bun which was held in place with a decorated comb. And she had even applied a little lipstick. Altogether, the effect was to make her look like somebody's favourite grandmother.

The table had also been given some attention. It was laid on the terrace with a white linen tablecloth and beautiful china tea set. Starched white napkins had been neatly folded at the two places that had been set. Emma was pleasantly surprised. Mrs Moriarty had obviously gone to some trouble to prepare for their meeting.

"Sit down and make yourself comfortable," the old lady commanded in her cracked voice.

Emma immediately did as she was told and took her seat.

"This won't take a minute," Mrs Moriarty said, getting up and fussing with a kettle.

"You shouldn't have gone to all this trouble," Emma protested.

"What trouble? Sure all I did was lay out the table."

Emma watched as she poured hot water into the teapot, swirled it around and poured it out again into a basin. Then she added three teaspoons of tea and poured in the remainder of the hot water.

"People have forgotten how to make tea," the old lady said. "You've got to warm the teapot and add a spoon for each person and another spoon for the pot. That's the way my mother made tea and her mother before her. And that's the way I make it."

She covered the pot with a knitted cosy and placed it on a little silver stand in the middle of the table.

"Now you have to let it draw for a couple of minutes."

She disappeared into the room again and returned with a cream walnut cake. She proceeded to cut two large slices and place them on plates, one of which she handed to Emma.

"If you would like to do the honours," she said. "I think the tea should be ready now."

A rich amber liquid poured from the pot. Emma watched as Mrs Moriarty added milk from a little jug and passed the sugar bowl across the table.

"I don't take sugar," she said quickly, waving the bowl away.

"Well, that's something we can agree on. I don't like it either. It spoils the flavour. And I only take a spot of milk. Now eat your cake like a good girl."

Emma forked up a piece of cake. It was confectionery heaven. She savoured the soft moist texture and the flavour of walnut bursting in her mouth.

"Mmmm," she said. "This is gorgeous."

"It *is* nice, isn't it?" Mrs Moriarty said, clearly pleased.

"Where did you get it?"

The old lady tapped her nose to indicate this was a secret.

"A little *pastelería* I've discovered. I might tell you some day, if you're good."

"It's the most beautiful cake I've tasted for a very long time," Emma said, taking a sip of tea. "My goodness!" she exclaimed. "I'd forgotten how good tea could taste."

Mrs Moriarty's face lit up with pleasure.

"That's what happens if you live here long enough. The Spanish are coffee drinkers. They haven't got a clue about tea. They make it with hot milk and a tea bag. Did you ever hear the like?"

"Well, *you* certainly know how to make it. This is absolutely divine," Emma said.

"The key is to use real tea leaves and proper water. I get my tea from a little shop in Los Boliches. You'll never make a proper cup of tea with these new-fangled tea bags."

She raised the cup to her mouth and observed Emma across the table.

"Are you thinking of staying here long?" she asked.

"I haven't decided. I like the Spanish lifestyle and the weather, of course. And I enjoy my work."

"That's obvious," Mrs Moriarty said. "You can see it in your face. You're always smiling."

"Thank you."

"You've turned this place around in the short time you've been here. It was going to the dogs before you came along. That Señora Alvarez isn't interested. All she wants is the money it makes. But she isn't prepared to put in the work, unlike her poor dead husband."

Emma didn't want to be drawn into criticising her employer so she said: "It's not just me. Everybody has played a part. It's a team effort."

"Ah, but every team needs a captain. That's what was missing till you came along. I could see it. There was no leadership. The staff didn't know who was in charge. Casa Clara was drifting along like a rudderless ship. Señora Alvarez should be grateful to you."

"Oh, I think she is," Emma said quickly. "And she lets me get on with my work. She doesn't interfere."

"Why should she when everything is humming along so well? She'd be a fool to interfere. And whatever else she might be, Señora Alvarez is no fool."

Emma finished her cake and Mrs Moriarty cut another slice.

"Here," she commanded. "Eat it."

"I couldn't," Emma protested. "I'm full already."

"Worried about your figure, are you? You shouldn't have any concerns in that department. You're as slim as a greyhound." She gave Emma an appreciative look. "It will only go to waste," she coaxed. "Cakes don't keep in this hot weather."

Reluctantly, Emma accepted another slice.

"Do you have tea every afternoon?" she asked.

"I used to when I first came out. Now I only do it on special occasions when I have someone interesting to talk to."

"That's a very nice thing to say."

"Well, you're a nice person. You've got what we used to call character. You have standards of behaviour. Young people nowadays don't know how to behave. I blame it on the schools. I don't know what they teach children but it's not good manners."

"Do you ever go back to Dublin?" Emma asked.

Mrs Moriarty shook her head. "I don't get along with my family."

"Oh, I'm sorry to hear that."

The old lady lowered her eyes. "It's the people closest to you who hurt you the most. You expect more from them than you do from strangers."

Her lip quivered and Emma thought she was about to stop. But suddenly, she rushed on as if she wanted to unburden herself.

"It all started when my husband died. He wasn't a wealthy man but he was thrifty and he had a good bit of money put by. He used to say it was our little nest-egg for when he retired. But

I often think it would have been better if he had left nothing. You wouldn't believe the trouble it caused. All my children turned against me *and* each other. There were constant rows over his estate, each one accusing the other of getting more than they were entitled to. It got so bad in the end that I couldn't stand it any longer. I sold the house and came out here to live. And the sad thing is, the money didn't make them happy. It caused them nothing but misery."

She paused as if she had said enough. Her milky blue eyes stared across the table at Emma.

"You never told me why *you* came here."

Emma didn't know how to respond. "I needed a break," she said. "I was fed up looking at the wind and the rain."

"That's not the real reason," Mrs Moriarty said.

Emma felt rattled. "It *is* the real reason."

"Perhaps," the old lady continued. "People come here for all sorts of reasons. But a lot of them are running away from something. They think if they change locations, it will sort out their problems. But it doesn't work. Sometimes the cause of their unhappiness is inside them."

Emma felt a spooky feeling run along her spine. It was as if Mrs Moriarty could see into her heart.

But suddenly the old woman's attitude seemed to change and her face broke into a gentle smile. She reached out and patted Emma's knee.

"But that doesn't apply to you, my dear. You're much too happy and contented. And if you *were* running away from something, you seem to have escaped."

Emma stayed drinking tea much longer than she had intended. An hour had quickly passed before she happened to glance at her watch and realised how long she had been away from her desk. Mrs Moriarty had turned out to be fascinating company. She seemed to have a wealth of human experience contained in her old white head.

And contrary to Emma's expectations, she hadn't used the occasion to complain about Major Sykes. In fact, she didn't mention him once in the time they spent together drinking tea on the terrace in the bright afternoon sun.

At last she tore herself away. Mrs Moriarty insisted on wrapping up the remains of the cake and giving it to her along with a packet of tea.

"I've enjoyed talking to you," she said as she fussed around. "I'll have you back again soon. And thank you for bringing a bit of lightness and joy to this place."

As Emma went down the stairs, she could hear Mrs Moriarty humming "When Irish Eyes Are Smiling". She wasn't a bad person after all. Emma had misjudged her. She was just a lonely old woman with her own disappointments and pain who was starved of human company.

* * *

About a week later, Emma made the acquaintance of Major Sykes. Of course, she knew him by sight because he made a point of being early for breakfast each morning but they had only exchanged polite pleasantries until the evening when she encountered him on the stairs as she was going up to her room after finishing work.

"Excuse me, Miss Frazer," he said, in a curt military voice that sounded more like a command than a request.

She stopped at once.

"Yes, Major?"

"Do you mind if I ask you? Do you dance?"

"*Dance?*" Emma replied, slightly taken aback.

"Yes, dance."

"I don't understand."

Major Sykes fidgeted with his moustache. Emma could see that he was uncomfortable with this conversation.

"You see it's the annual dinner dance of the Old Comrades

Association next week. Highlight of our year actually and I'm rather stuck for a partner. Normally Mrs Arbuthnot accompanies me but unfortunately she has had to go back to London. Some family business, that's cropped up. So, you see, I was looking around for a lady and well . . ." He coughed to cover his confusion. "I thought, perhaps you might care to join me?"

She was completely bowled over. If Major Sykes had asked her to go paragliding with him she couldn't have been more surprised.

"I . . . I . . . don't really know."

"I realise it's all rather short notice. But Mrs Arbuthnot was called away urgently. And it really is a very good evening – slap-up meal and wonderful entertainment. Of course, I would cover all expenses so you wouldn't be out of pocket in the least."

He peered at her like an expectant supplicant, his hands held tightly together while he waited for her response.

"Which evening is it?" Emma asked.

"Tuesday," Major Sykes replied, brightening up a little. "I would expect to pick you up at seven o'clock. We have a sherry reception at half seven and then dinner at eight."

"Let me think about it," she said. "I'll see if I'm free and let you know tomorrow."

"I do hope you can come," the Major said. "I think you'd enjoy it."

Emma proceeded to her room. Her initial reaction was to say no. She couldn't envisage spending an evening with a bunch of retired military men and their ladies while they discussed their war exploits. And she had the perfect excuse. She could easily tell him she had another engagement or that she had work to complete at the Casa.

But then she remembered the look of hope and expectancy on his face. It had probably taken a lot of courage for him to ask her. If she turned him down he might not find a replacement and knowing the Major's reputation he would probably not go without a partner. And it was the highlight of his year. Would it really bother her so much, if it made the old man happy?

The first thing was to check if she was free. Now that she had Cristina to rely on, Emma was usually able to finish work around six o'clock. The free time had allowed her to expand her social activities. A quick check of her diary confirmed that she would indeed be available. She made up her mind. When she saw him in the morning, she would accept the invitation. She took a leisurely shower and set off to have dinner at a pretty little restaurant she had discovered near the Castillo.

* * *

Major Sykes was down promptly for breakfast the next morning. As he approached the reception desk, Emma couldn't escape the look of hope and expectation that shone from his face. Well, she was about to make one old soldier happy. She greeted him with a cheery smile.

"*Buenos días*, Major."

"Good morning, Miss Frazer."

"About that business we discussed yesterday."

"Yes?" he said, eagerly.

"I've checked my diary and I'm pleased to say I'll be free on Tuesday. So I'll be delighted to accompany you."

All at once, his face lit up like a Christmas tree. "Oh, that is very good news. I'm so pleased."

"The pleasure is all mine," Emma said gallantly.

Major Sykes sailed off to the breakfast buffet with renewed vigour in his step.

Cristina, who had observed the encounter, lowered her voice to ask: "What was that about?"

"I'm going dancing with the Major next Tuesday."

Cristina's mouth fell open. She gave Emma a look that suggested she had finally taken leave of her senses.

Chapter 24

Only later did it occur to Emma that the dinner might be a formal occasion. She had completely forgotten to inquire. And if it was, she was faced with an immediate problem. She had nothing to wear.

She decided to find out fast, so that afternoon she climbed the stairs and knocked on the Major's door. She heard movement inside and then the door opened to reveal the Major wearing a faded grey woollen pullover although the temperature was 25 degrees in the shade. He had a frown on his face but brightened up at once when he saw who it was.

"Ah, Miss Frazer. Good afternoon."

"Good afternoon, Major. I hope I'm not disturbing you."

"Not at all. Delighted to see you. Won't you come in?"

Emma entered the room. The first thing she saw was a large portrait of the queen in her coronation robes which adorned the far wall. Beside it was a framed citation decorated with regimental insignia. A smaller photograph showed a younger version of the Major in military uniform looking stern and smart with moustache bristling.

The room itself was sparsely furnished but rigorously tidy. In one corner, the Major's single bed was made up in neat military fashion. Beside the window, a small square dining table and a couple of chairs looked out on the terrace. A quick glance revealed a faded carpet on the floor and an old-fashioned easy chair beside a shelf that held a handful of books, a couple of bottles and glasses and a small radio. The Major moved at once to switch it off.

"Just listening to the news," he explained. "BBC. Like to stay in touch with the old country."

"You keep your room very tidy," Emma remarked.

The Major appeared pleased at the compliment. "Can't stand clutter. Never could abide it. Can I offer you something to drink? Gin and tonic? Spot of whisky?"

"No thank you," Emma replied. "I'm still at work."

"Ah yes, I see."

"I've really come to ask about the dinner dance."

At once, a cloud passed over the Major's face as if he feared she was about to change her mind.

"I was wondering if it is black-tie?"

"Oh yes," he exclaimed with some relief. "Always black tie. Didn't I say?"

"No," Emma replied and forced herself to smile, despite the tightening feeling in her stomach.

"It's our main bash of the year. Believe in doing things properly. Put on a bit of a show."

"Of course, I just wanted to be sure."

"Black tie. Sherry at seven thirty. Dinner at eight o'clock. Roast beef and Yorkshire pudding. Address by Colonel Tibby Saunders. Then the dancing. You'll thoroughly enjoy it. Mrs Arbuthnot always does."

"I've no doubt I will," Emma said, edging towards the door. "Well, now that matter is cleared up, I'd better get back to my desk."

Major Sykes looked disappointed that the visit had been so brief.

"Pick you up at seven o'clock sharp," he said, politely opening the door for her and twisting his moustache in a playful manner. "Did I mention we have spot prizes? And a special presentation for the best-dressed lady?"

Now Emma was presented with a dilemma. She had left Dublin in a hurry, packing only what she regarded as basic essentials. A ball gown did not feature on her list. She was sorry that she hadn't asked about it earlier; it might have given her a genuine excuse to turn down the invitation. But she had accepted and the Major was clearly relying on her. There was no question of backing out now.

What was she going to wear? She had nothing in her wardrobe that was even remotely suitable. She returned to the reception desk with a worried look on her face. She could always go out and buy a dress. She had no doubt she could find a shop in Malaga or Marbella that sold them. But did she have time? And would the expense be justified for one single occasion that was unlikely to be repeated? She turned these questions over in her mind as she made her way back down the stairs.

"You look worried," Cristina said as she rejoined her at the desk.

"I've got a problem," Emma confessed.

"Is it something I can help you with?"

"I don't think so. This dance I'm attending with the Major next Tuesday . . ."

The assistant made a face. She regarded the whole idea as preposterous.

"I've just discovered it's formal."

"Formal?" Cristina asked, challenged by the new word.

"Yes. It means the guests have to dress up. The men have to wear dress suits and the ladies must wear ball gowns."

"Ah, I see."

"Well, my problem is, I don't have a ball gown."

"So it's not possible for you to attend in a little cocktail dress? Something like that?"

"No way," Emma said. "The other guests would be outraged and poor Major Sykes would die of embarrassment."

"Well, now you must tell him that you can't go. He must find someone else, perhaps a lady of his own age? For myself, I think it would be more suitable."

"I can't do that," Emma said. "I've already promised him. He would be bitterly disappointed."

"Well, if you are determined to go, you must wear the proper clothes." She thought for a moment and Emma saw her examining her with a critical eye.

"I wonder," she said, stroking her chin. "You are about the same height as me and also the same build. I have a dress that might fit you."

"Really?"

"Yes. You could borrow it, if you like."

"That might be a solution," Emma said hopefully. "Where is it?"

"In my room. Would you like to see it?"

"Of course."

At that moment, Tomàs came strolling in from the garden. Emma immediately asked him to cover for them at the reception desk.

"It's only for a few minutes," she explained. "Just answer the phone, that's all." She turned to her assistant. "Let's go and look at this dress."

Cristina's room was on the ground floor near the kitchen. She led the way. Once inside, she walked to the wardrobe and flung it open to reveal a whole rack of dresses. She searched among them till at last she found the one she was looking for. Emma felt her heart sink. The garment Cristina had chosen was a gaudy red and blue flamenco dress with a pattern of flowering bougainvillea and five or six flounces at the hem.

"I bought it a few months ago for the *feria*," Cristina explained.

The *feria* was the local carnival and it was a tradition for the women to wear elaborate flamenco dresses. Emma was busily shaking her head.

"I'm sorry," she said. "It's a beautiful dress but I really don't think it would be suitable for Major Sykes' dance."

"Why?"

"It's far too colourful. I expect this dance will be a very staid affair."

"Staid?"

"Yes. It means dull. If I turn up in that dress, everyone will stare at me."

"But isn't that the whole idea?"

"Not for this kind of dance," Emma explained. "It's not the Carnaval."

Cristina looked disappointed.

"Why don't you try it on?" she urged.

Emma hesitated for a moment, then quickly slipped out of her skirt and blouse and pulled on the dress. It fitted her exactly as if it had been made for her. She glanced in the wardrobe mirror and saw the way the fabric clung to her hips and emphasised her breasts.

"I can lend you these as well," Cristina said, producing a pair of black high-heeled shoes.

Emma put them on. They were the perfect complement to the dress, showing the shape of her calves to extremely good effect.

"I think it suits you very well," Cristina said. "And look, I also have this." She produced a large paper rose and pinned it into Emma's hair. "Now you look like a real *Señorita*. I think you will cause a storm."

Yes, but will it be a storm of abuse and ridicule, Emma thought as she studied herself in the mirror. There was no doubt that she cut a dashing figure in the flamenco dress. And the rose in her long, dark hair was the perfect touch. She looked like an authentic Andalucian beauty. But how would the other guests react? Would they regard it as just too outrageous?

However, Cristina's next remark helped to make up her mind.

"I don't think Major Sykes can object," she said. "After all, you are doing him a favour. If you don't go to the dance, he will have no partner."

Emma glanced once more in the mirror. With some scarlet lipstick and her dark hair pulled into a knot, she would look fabulous.

"You're right," she said. "I think I'll wear it."

*　　*　　*

But when Tuesday arrived, her confidence had begun to ebb. The attendance at the dinner would be mostly elderly military types and their wives. She expected they would all be dressed conservatively in dull dinner jackets and boring gowns. She was bound to stick out like a nun in a massage parlour.

But by now it was too late. Even if she had a mind to, she didn't have time to go shopping for something else. It would have to be the flamenco dress or nothing. And they could like it or lump it. At six o'clock, she finished work at the reception desk and handed the affairs of Casa Clara over to Cristina then went up to her room to get ready.

First, she poured a glass of good Rioja which she had picked up in the supermarket for a couple of euros. Fortified by the wine, she ran the shower while she considered the evening that lay ahead. It was bound to be an ordeal. She expected a night of speeches extolling the war exploits of the old soldiers followed by a dreary meal of roast beef and then a couple of hours of being hauled around the dance floor by Major Sykes. Why on earth had she let herself get roped into it? Wouldn't it have been kinder to all concerned simply to have refused?

At last she got out of the shower, dried herself and began to get dressed. At least she didn't have to agonise over her wardrobe as was often the case. The bright flamenco dress hung on a coat hanger near her bed, beside the shoes and the paper rose and a black lace stole that Cristina had also loaned her. She struggled into the dress. It was tight in all the right places. Then she sat down at the dressing-table to apply her make-up, using mascara to highlight her eyes and bright red lipstick to emphasise the sensuous curve of her lips. She brushed her hair into a bun and held it in place with a comb, then pinned on the rose just above her right ear.

The image that stared back from the mirror was of a dark, sultry Spanish siren. She half expected Major Sykes to have a coronary attack the moment he saw her.

It was now a couple of minutes to seven. Emma locked the door and with some difficulty, began the descent of the stairs. The flamenco dress might hug her figure but it also restricted her movement. At last, she reached the hall where she found the Major waiting for her at the reception desk, looking quite smart in a black dinner jacket and cummerbund and a row of campaign medals pinned to his breast. But it was the look on his face when he saw her enter the vestibule that affected her most. First he blinked. Then he rubbed his eyes as if he was witnessing an apparition. Finally his mouth fell open in utter amazement.

"My dear Miss Frazer," he managed to say.

"Yes, Major?"

"Pardon me if I use the wrong expression. But I think you look . . ."

Emma braced herself for the worst. "Yes?"

"Absolutely swishing!"

Major Sykes had ordered a cab which now waited on the street outside. He gallantly took her arm and led her out, then held open the door of the taxi while Emma settled as best she could on the back seat. Thankfully, the journey would not be long. The dinner was being held in the Majestic Hotel which was only about five minutes away. The Major gave their destination to the driver and the cab sped off.

She heaved a small sigh of relief. She had passed the first hurdle. Major Sykes hadn't passed out from shock at the sight of her. Indeed, he seemed genuinely pleased and was now sneaking admiring glances in her direction. But she knew that the real test was yet to come. How were his friends and colleagues going to react; particularly the women?

She decided that the best approach was to appear casual as if she always turned up at dinner dances wearing a flamenco dress. There was nothing to be gained by being defensive. Meanwhile, beside her, the Major was keeping up a steady stream of conversation. It was obvious that whatever about Emma, he was certainly looking forward to the evening.

"Tibby Saunders always gives a jolly good rant."

"Remind me again who Tibby Saunders is," Emma said.

"He's the Colonel. He always gives the after-dinner address. He lets them have it, I can tell you. Good, stirring, patriotic stuff. Makes you proud to be British."

Emma was about to remind him that she was Irish but thought better of it.

"Do you expect many guests?"

"Several hundred, I should say. Monty Carruthers and his Blue Note Boys are providing the music and they're always a big draw. You're in for a proper treat, Miss Frazer, trust me."

Emma had been turning something over in her mind. Now she said it.

"If we're going to spend the evening together, perhaps you should call me Emma."

Major Sykes turned to her with a look of surprise. "Are you perfectly sure?"

"I think so. Miss Frazer sounds a bit too formal. And we do know each other already."

"Well, in that case, you must call me Clive."

"What a nice name!"

Major Sykes beamed. "Yes, I think it is rather distinguished. I was named after the conqueror of India," he said proudly as the taxi pulled into the forecourt of the hotel.

There was a crowd milling about in the lobby. Now for the moment of truth, she thought as she waited for the Major to pay the taxi-driver. She took a deep breath as he held her arm and she hobbled through the revolving doors into the hotel.

At once, several heads turned in their direction. There were a few audible gasps which Emma did her best to ignore. She and the Major were directed towards the receiving line. Here a plump man with a red face introduced the guests to another plump man in a tuxedo who had a moustache identical to the Major's. With him was a small sparrow-like woman in a pink satin evening dress. As they joined the line, more faces turned to stare.

"Who are these people?" she whispered as they drew closer.

"Tibby Saunders and his good lady. Name of Marjorie. I forgot to mention, but Tibby's the Hon Sec. He's the top dog."

This news didn't do anything for Emma's peace of mind. Oh well, she thought, best to get the worst bit over first. They had now reached the top of the line. The plump man who was making the introductions bent forward and whispered in the Major's ear. The Major whispered back.

"Major Clive Algernon Sykes and Miss Emma Frazer!" the man announced in a booming voice as he passed them over to Colonel Saunders and moved to the next couple in the line.

Tibby Saunders took one look at Emma and his jaw fell down to his chest. He blinked and swallowed hard. His moustache quivered as he turned his fierce gaze on the Major. Emma could feel her heart knocking against her ribs. Colonel Saunders was about to speak when a thin, reed-like voice beat him to it.

"I think you look absolutely stunning, my dear." It was Marjorie. "That dress is a knock-out. It's the nicest dress I've seen at the annual dinner for aeons. It really livens things up. Isn't that so, Tibby?" She nudged her husband in the ribs and he immediately stood to attention.

"Oh, yes," he agreed. "Ratherrrrr."

As if on cue, a group of onlookers burst into a polite round of applause. Major Sykes couldn't have looked more proud if he had just been awarded the Victoria Cross by Lord Kitchener himself.

"I think I could do with a snifter," he said to Emma once they were safely out of range among the general body of the guests. "What would you say to a gin and tonic?"

"I'd say: make it a large one," Emma replied.

From then on, it was plain sailing. Having been given the seal of approval by no less an authority than Marjorie Saunders, there was no one in the room who would dare criticise Emma's dress. Indeed the glances and comments she heard were now warm and admiring. People smiled their appreciation or leaned forward to say "Jolly good show," as Emma made the round of the company to be introduced to the Major's friends and comrades.

At eight o'clock sharp, a bell sounded and they all trooped into the large dining room where the tables had been laid out in long rows facing a stage. As they found their seats, Emma heard the stirring drone of the bagpipes. Tibby and Mrs Saunders, accompanied by several other dignitaries and preceded by a piper, made their way to the stage where they were able to look down on the rest of the guests. The plump man who had made the introductions now said grace and the dinner was served.

It was a pleasant meal: celery soup, roast beef and Yorkshire pudding with roast potatoes, carrots, peas and gravy, followed by treacle pudding and coffee. It was good solid British fare and the guests wolfed it down. Afterwards, brandy was served and a hush descended on the room as Colonel Tibby Saunders rose to speak.

213

He was an imposing-looking man with a row of medals even grander than the Major's. He gave an impassioned speech about upholding British standards of fair play and always maintaining an iron fist inside the velvet glove. As he spoke he glared fiercely at his audience. Emma couldn't help wondering what it must have been like to have served under him. But the audience loved it, breaking into applause at frequent intervals and giving him a standing ovation at the end.

Then it was time for dancing. The tables were cleared away and four elderly men in faded dinner jackets and clarinets came onto the stage. Emma assumed this must be the famed Monty Carruthers and his Blue Note Boys who the Major had mentioned earlier. As they struck up "In the Mood" the Major politely offered his arm and said: "May I?" and the next moment she was being led out onto the floor to join the other dancers.

The Major was a sprightly figure despite his age and a remarkably good dancer, and Emma felt they must look quite dashing, even if she found it difficult to manoeuvre in her flounced dress. When the set had ended another elderly soldier politely approached and led her back onto the floor for a waltz.

And so the evening went on till it was time for the prize-giving. The dancers stood along the sides of the room while Colonel Saunders once more took the microphone to announce the winners. There were prizes for best foxtrot, best cha-cha, best rumba, best slow waltz. As each winner went to the stage to receive their prize, the audience gave a polite round of applause.

Next was the prize for Best Dressed Lady. Tibby Saunders withdrew a piece of paper from his pocket and stared over his glasses.

"And the winner is . . ."

A hush had descended over the assembled guests.

"Miss Emma Frazer!"

At once, the room erupted in a round of applause.

Emma blushed with embarrassment as she found herself

propelled towards the stage where the Colonel was waiting to present her with her prize. He beamed down at her.

"Congratulations, my dear. Unanimous winner. Absolutely spiffing."

He handed her a silver alarm clock and a bottle of champagne. As she muttered her thanks, someone stepped out of the crowd and a flash bulb popped. Emma returned to the Major with the applause still ringing in her ears.

It was after one o'clock when they got back to Casa Clara. By now, she was feeling exhausted. But she had certainly enjoyed herself. Despite her earlier misgivings, the evening had been a brilliant success.

Outside her room, the Major paused to thank her once more for accompanying him to the dinner.

"I thoroughly enjoyed it," she replied. "Thank you for inviting me."

"I'm so pleased. Good night, Emma." A roguish look had entered his eye.

"Good night, Clive," Emma said and politely shook his outstretched hand.

She went into her room, got undressed and slipped under the sheets. Her head had hardly touched the pillow before she was fast asleep.

Chapter 25

However, her decision to accompany Major Sykes to the dinner dance was to have unforeseen consequences. A few days later, she became aware of a distinct coolness on the part of Mrs Moriarty. Emma's cheerful greetings went unanswered and her smiles were met with cold indifference. Indeed, once or twice, she caught the old lady glaring at her quite menacingly. Something had obviously happened to poison the relationship between them. Emma decided to investigate.

One afternoon, she asked Cristina to take over the reception desk and climbed the stairs to Mrs Moriarty's room at the top of the house. With her, she brought a gift – a rich fruit cake that she had picked up in a little bakery near the market. After a few moments, she heard the sound of locks being withdrawn and the door opened. Mrs Moriarty seemed surprised to see her.

"Oh, it's you," she said, with obvious disdain in her voice. "What do *you* want?"

"I thought I'd pay you a little visit," Emma replied cheerily.

"Well, I'm in no mood for visitors today," Mrs Moriarty said. "Goodbye."

CASA *Clara*

She went to close the door but Emma quickly extended the bag containing the cake.

"I brought this for you."

Mrs Moriarty looked at the bag suspiciously as if it might contain a dead rat. "What is it?"

"A fruit cake. I thought you might enjoy it with your afternoon tea."

"I don't accept gifts from traitors."

"What?" Emma said, suppressing a smile. "You're calling me a traitor?"

"Well, you've gone over to the enemy, haven't you? Isn't that what traitors do?"

"The enemy?" Emma responded. "I've no idea what you're talking about." She was determined not to allow Mrs Moriarty to provoke her.

"Oh, haven't you?"

She opened the door wide and picked up a newspaper that lay on her dining table. It was one of the free English language papers that circulated in the resort. It was folded neatly to show a photograph on top. Mrs Moriarty thrust it into Emma's hands.

"What do you say to that?"

Emma took the paper and examined it. The photograph had been taken at the Old Comrades dinner dance. It showed her holding the alarm clock which was the Best Dressed Lady prize. Beside her stood a beaming Major Sykes his moustache bristling with pride.

"I can explain this," Emma said.

"Oh, you can? And look at the get-up of you, dressed for the can-can and that old goat grinning all over his ugly puss like he was Rudolf Valentino."

"It's a flamenco dress, Mrs Moriarty. A can-can dress is entirely different, as I'm sure you know quite well. Now if you were to allow me to come in and make you a nice cup of tea, I'm sure you and I could work this out between us. What do you say?"

217

The old lady hesitated.

"That fruit cake is very tasty," Emma added with a smile. "And I know how to make a proper cup of tea. After all, you showed me yourself."

Mrs Moriarty relented. She stood back and opened the door wide.

"Come in," she said and moved at once to turn off the television set. "I was watching *Rebecca*," she explained.

"I love that film," Emma replied. "Laurence Olivier and Joan Fontaine. It's one of my favourites."

"I've seen it twenty-four times," Mrs Moriarty said with an air of triumph.

"Did you ever read the book?"

"I don't think I have."

"You should, you know. You'd enjoy it. Now, why don't you just sit down and make yourself comfortable? Where is your kettle?"

The old woman pointed to a cupboard. "You'll find the teapot in there too – and the tea and milk. The milk is fresh. It's long-life."

Emma filled the kettle from a large container of spring water and plugged it in. She took a plate from the cupboard and placed the cake on it and then took out a few smaller plates, cups and saucers and a couple of knives. She placed the whole lot on the dining table.

When everything was in order, she set the teapot in its knitted cosy on its silver stand in the centre of the table, along with the milk jug and sugar bowl.

"Now," she said, "this time you can pour. I've made the tea exactly the way you like it."

Mrs Moriarty proceeded to pour two cups of tea and cut two slices of cake. She added milk and raised the cup daintily to her lips.

Emma waited for her response. "Well? What do you think?"

"Mmmmm. Not bad."

"Oh c'mon," Emma coaxed. "You can do better than that."

"All right," Mrs Moriarty said. "It's very good."

"So it should be. I followed your instructions to the letter."

She gave a gentle smile. "Now tell me what you think of the cake." Mrs Moriarty took a bite and expressed her satisfaction with that too.

"Nice and moist," she said. "That's the secret. Some of those bakers shouldn't be let loose on the public. Their cakes taste like concrete. You'd break your teeth on them. If you had teeth," she added with a small grin.

Emma was pleased to see that she was loosening up. She was hoping that Mrs Moriarty would be glad of some human company. But now the difficult bit was coming up. She paused while she took a sip of tea.

"I'd like to apologise if I upset you."

The old lady scowled but Emma immediately held up her hand.

"Allow me to tell you what happened. Major Sykes was stuck for a partner to accompany him to his dinner dance."

"I'm not surprised," Mrs Moriarty muttered. "You'd have to be crazy to have anything to do with an old reprobate like him."

"He came and asked me if I would go with him. And I agreed. I see it as part of my duties at Casa Clara to keep all our guests happy, particularly our long-term residents who we hold in special regard." She paused and glanced meaningfully at Mrs Moriarty to let her know that she was also included in this elite little band.

"You're lucky you didn't get food poisoning!" Mrs Moriarty spat.

But Emma ignored the remark and continued. "My decision had nothing to do with your disagreements with the Major. I wasn't taking his side against you. In fact, if you had asked me to do something similar, I would have been happy to oblige you, too."

"You're too soft-hearted. That's your problem. He was just taking advantage of your kind nature."

"I don't think that's true," Emma continued. "Major Sykes is a gentleman. He's got the most charming manners. And he knows exactly how to treat a lady. In fact, I came to the conclusion that he is really a little bit lonely."

The old woman was watching her carefully now, trying to figure out what she was getting at.

"He's a wonderful dancer. And he likes to enjoy himself. He's also quite generous I believe. I just felt a little bit sorry for him not having anyone to accompany him to the dance, that's all." She glanced at Mrs Moriarty again. "Somebody told me that you and he were once good friends."

The old lady's face darkened. "Whoever told you that is a liar."

"Oh?" Emma said.

Mrs Moriarty lowered her eyes. "I *will* admit I was civil to him. But then I try to be civil to everyone. Live and let live, that's my motto. I even had him up here for cocktails a couple of times. But that was before I discovered what he was really like. That was before he tried to steal the very food out of my mouth. Did you know he robbed the last boiled egg on me? And what's more, he did it deliberately just to spite me. And after everything I did for him."

So it was true what she had heard. The feud really did begin over a boiled egg.

Mrs Moriarty was now working herself into a storm of indignation.

"Did you know he's after my room?" she said, her milky blue eyes now aflame with anger.

Emma shook her head.

"That's his real intention. He can't stand the fact that I have a better room than him. He even went behind my back to Señora Alvarez and offered her more money if she'd evict me and let him have my room. Now what sort of low-down rattlesnake would do a thing like that?"

"I'm sure there's been some mistake."

"Oh, no, there hasn't. I've got chapter and verse. And then he started this keep-fit nonsense, grunting and panting like a mad dog all night long so that I can't get a wink of sleep. It's part of a campaign to drive me out. But he's picked the wrong pigeon, I can assure you. The Moriartys are made of sterner stuff than that. If he thinks he can intimidate me, he's got another think coming."

Emma sat patiently and allowed her to get all the resentment off her chest. There was no point intervening to say that Major Sykes had a similar list of grievances about her. This would only agitate her more. But a plan was beginning to form in Emma's head.

At last, Mrs Moriarty had exhausted herself. "So now you can see," she said. "The way I've been put upon and persecuted. And me a poor widow woman with nobody in the world to defend me!"

Emma half-expected her to burst into tears.

Instead Mrs Moriarty said: "I'm going to have a brandy. Will you join me?"

"Just a small one, I have to get back to work."

The old lady opened another cupboard and took out a large bottle and two glasses. She poured and passed one to Emma.

"Get that inside you," she said. "It will do you good."

Emma wasn't so sure. The brandy looked strong and it was a large measure. Besides, brandy wasn't really her drink. But she could see that Mrs Moriarty was in a sensitive mood and she didn't want to offend her. So she took a few tentative sips and then put the glass down.

"Well, I'm glad we managed to clear up that matter like two sensible adults, Mrs Moriarty. I knew you were a reasonable woman."

The old lady sniffed. "You have a difficult job to do. And you do it well. It's just a pity some people have to make life difficult for everybody else by their selfishness."

At last, Emma stood up.

"I'd better get back to the desk. But I've been thinking. Maybe you'd like to come down to my room and have tea with me some afternoon?"

"I'm sure that would be very nice," Mrs Moriarty said.

Emma patted her sleeve. "I've enjoyed the tea and our little chat. Now, just leave everything to me. I'll get back to you when I'm ready."

* * *

A few days later, having made sure that Mrs Moriarty was safely out of the way on her evening walk, Emma made her way up the stairs again, this time to Major Sykes' room. Under her arm, she carried a parcel wrapped in brown paper.

"Come in!" he cried in answer to her knock.

Emma pushed open the door and found him seated at the window reading a copy of *The Times*.

"Ah, Miss Frazer, what a pleasant surprise," he said. "How good to see you. Won't you sit down?" He gallantly stood up and pulled out a chair for her.

"I just thought I'd stop by to see how you were recovering from the dance," Emma said.

The Major's eyes twinkled. "Jolly good show, wasn't it? By the way, your photograph appeared in the paper. Did you know? Tibby Saunders is absolutely delighted. Damned good publicity, you see. Pretty young woman like you."

"Yes, I did know," Emma replied, recalling Mrs Moriarty's reaction. "I brought you a little present to thank you." She handed over the brown-paper parcel.

The Major looked surprised. "Absolutely no need, I assure you. My pleasure entirely."

"Nevertheless I wanted to get you something."

"Very kind of you, I'm sure. May I open it?"

"Of course, go right ahead."

He tore off the wrapping and withdrew a copy of *Great Battles of the British Army*, which Emma had bought earlier in a bookshop in the town.

His face showed absolute delight. He looked at the book and then at Emma.

"My dear Miss Frazer," he managed to say.

"I thought we had agreed that you would call me Emma?" she teased.

He blushed. "I was about to say that I am totally overwhelmed. This is a perfect present. I enjoy nothing better than a good volume of military history. I shall treasure this."

"Well, I'm glad you like it," Emma said.

"Oh, I certainly do. I'm afraid I'm right out of sherry. May I offer you a spot of whisky?"

Emma shook her head.

"Don't mind if I have a snifter?"

"Not at all, go right ahead."

The Major proceeded to pour himself a tumblerful from a bottle on a sideboard.

"I was thinking of asking you for a small favour," Emma continued.

"Of course, anything I can do."

"I was planning to invite you to have afternoon tea with me some day."

Major Sykes glowed with pleasure. "I'd be honoured."

Emma smiled.

"It will probably be some day next week."

The Major waved his hand. "Whenever suits. I'm entirely at your disposal."

"Well, that's good. Now before we get down to details, may I ask you a question?"

"Certainly."

"What is your opinion of cats?"

* * *

Emma settled on the following Wednesday for her tea party. In the meantime, she had been busy. From the kitchen, she had managed to get hold of a tea set containing pot, hot-water jug, cups, saucers, spoons, knives, plates, sugar bowl and milk jug. She had also borrowed a kettle and a tablecloth from Rosa.

She had spent the previous afternoon at the market and came back with a large bunch of flowers and a mysterious-looking box which she placed underneath the bed in her room. On her way back, she had called into the bakery and bought a cream walnut cake decorated with icing.

When everything was in order, she stood back to admire her handiwork. She had covered her writing desk with the tablecloth and had borrowed two more chairs from Paco who was happy to oblige. She had also acquired a little side table where she had set the cutlery and the kettle. On top of the chest of drawers, she had placed a vase with the flowers. It was a little bit cramped but it looked homely. She took a deep breath. This was a risky strategy. She prayed that everything would go off all right.

She had told Mrs Moriarty that tea would be served at three o'clock. At half past two she nipped up to the Major's room with the mystery box and gave him strict instructions to turn up at her place at ten past three. Then she hurried back to her own room where she had a quick shower, dressed in a plain blue dress and sandals and checked that everything was in order. At three o'clock on the button she heard Mrs Moriarty's knock.

She opened the door and the old lady stood smiling on the doorstep with a bottle of wine.

"I know this is a tea party," she said, thrusting the bottle into Emma's hands. "But a nice bottle of wine will never go astray. I'm sure you can make use of it from time to time."

"That's very thoughtful of you," Emma replied, examining the bottle. It was an expensive vintage.

Meanwhile, Mrs Moriarty was glancing inquisitively around the room.

"You keep it very nice," she said. "Those flowers are lovely."

"Thank you. Now, if you would like to sit at the window, I'll just put on the kettle."

Mrs Moriarty noticed that the table had been set for three. "Expecting someone else?" she asked, doubtfully.

"Just one more," Emma said.

At that moment there was a sharp tap at the door. Mrs Moriarty immediately looked up.

Now for the moment of truth, Emma thought as she pulled it open to reveal Major Sykes standing there with the box under his arm.

He stared at Mrs Moriarty in fear and trepidation. She stared back, her face the colour of chalk. For a moment no one spoke.

Then the Major stepped forward smartly and thrust the box into Mrs Moriarty's startled hands.

She looked at it in horror as if she half expected a giant spider to jump out and take a bite out of her. For once, she had been struck dumb.

"With my compliments, dear lady," the Major managed to mutter, though the words sounded as if they were choking him. He shot an unhappy glance at Emma as if he suspected this was all a plot to have him murdered in his bed.

"Whhhat is it?" Mrs Moriarty managed to say at last.

"Why don't you open it and see?" Emma suggested.

"I certainly will not. It could be a bomb for all I know."

"I think you'll find it's something you will appreciate."

From inside the box there could be heard the sound of scratching and then a soft mewing noise.

Mrs Moriarty let out a shriek and was about to throw the box on the ground when the Major gallantly stepped forward again and took it from her.

"Allow me, dear lady."

He opened the lid and slowly withdrew a little furry ball. It immediately began to purr and nuzzled its head against the Major's arm.

"A kitten?" Mrs Moriarty said in total disbelief.

"Yes," Emma said. "I got it for you and the Major has very kindly agreed to present it to you."

"To *me*?"

"Yes. You always wanted a cat, didn't you? And now you have one. She's a lovely little tabby and she's been seen by the vet and has all her injections. And she's just dying to see her new home."

Mrs Moriarty's face had undergone a transformation. She couldn't conceal her delight and joy. She took the kitten from Major Sykes and began to stroke it. The purring sound intensified.

"You mean I can keep it?"

"Of course."

"And nobody is going to object?"

"Not in the least. She's all yours. Now you have your little companion. You can get her a basket and a litter tray and keep her in your room. And when she gets bigger you can buy her a leash and take her for walks around the garden."

Mrs Moriarty's eyes filled up with tears. "I don't know what to say. Everybody has been so kind."

The Major looked uncertainly at Emma, then pulled out a large white handkerchief and offered it to Mrs Moriarty. She used it to wipe her eyes.

"Thank you, Major," she said.

Emma clapped her hands.

"Now, why don't we all sit down and have our tea before it gets cold. Major Sykes, would you do the honours and pour?"

* * *

Mrs Moriarty was now a changed woman. No longer did she go around Casa Clara scowling as if she was about to bite the head off everyone. Now she was pleasant and cheerful, complimenting the staff on their work and admiring Rosa's hairstyle or the necklace that Teresa happened to be wearing.

The Major, too, had a renewed spring in his step. He came down to breakfast each morning dressed impeccably in a grey lounge suit and regimental tie with a cheery "Good morning!" for the guests and staff.

One morning, Emma was delighted to see the pair of them sitting together at a table under a palm tree happily enjoying their boiled eggs. A few days later, she looked up from her computer to see Major Sykes with Mrs Moriarty on his arm heading through the hall towards the front door.

"Going out?" she inquired.

The Major looked slightly embarrassed, as did Mrs Moriarty.

"Mrs Moriarty has kindly consented to accompany me to the Union Jack tearooms. They do a beautiful afternoon spread – Devon scones and clotted cream with jam."

"And they also know how to make a proper cup of tea," Mrs Moriarty added.

"Make sure to enjoy it," Emma said, as she smiled to herself and bent once more to her computer.

Chapter 26

Shortly after she arrived at Casa Clara, Emma had begun to notice that there was something going on between Tomàs, the young handyman, and Teresa, the beautiful dark-haired cleaning girl. Whenever she was nearby, Tomàs liked to demonstrate how strong and manly he was. He would insist on taking on heavy jobs such as shifting furniture, tasks which he performed with a warm, boyish grin. And he went out of his way to be gallant and chivalrous. He would carry Teresa's mops and brooms and her bucket and cloths. When she was struggling under the weight of a heavy load of bed linen, Tomàs would gently take it from her and toss it onto his shoulder as if it weighed no more than a feather.

For her part, Teresa was shy and coy. She would flash little smiles at Tomàs and roll her eyes in admiration at his skill and physical strength. Whenever he made little jokes, she would lower her face and smile provocatively at him from under her dark, curling lashes. Emma had seen courtship rituals played out before and she had no reason to believe that they were any different here in southern Spain.

So, she was a little perturbed when Tomàs's natural good humour suddenly underwent a dramatic change. He was a bright, intelligent young man and very willing to help out in whatever tasks needed to be performed around the Casa. Emma had grown very fond of him. But now he became withdrawn and moody and the ready smile vanished from his lips. He seemed like a man who had suffered some serious disappointment.

Teresa too, had become less cheerful and more listless. Once or twice, Emma overheard Rosa, the plump housekeeper scolding her because some job had not been carried out to her satisfaction. Emma realised that something had gone wrong between the pair. She wondered if she should make a few discreet inquiries.

She decided to begin with old Paco. He worked closely with Tomàs and might have some idea what was bothering him. So one morning she asked Paco to have coffee with her at Bar Lorenzo across the road where she conducted her English conversation lessons with Señora Alvarez.

"Would you like a little brandy with that?" she asked once they were comfortably seated under the shade of a parasol. Brandy with the coffee was a special treat and Paco eagerly nodded his appreciation.

"I wanted to ask you about Tomàs," she said once the waiter had returned with the brandy and was safely out of earshot. "I'm a little worried about him. Recently he doesn't seem to be his usual cheerful self."

Old Paco slapped his forehead and muttered. "*Locamente enamorado.*" Mad with love. It was a nice way of putting it.

Paco shook his head in pity, the way you might respond to a dog with distemper.

"Is it Teresa?"

"*Sí, sí,*" the old man replied. "Teresa is the one."

"I thought so," Emma said. "But I understood she liked him too. They always seemed to be so happy together."

"She *does* like him," old Paco emphasised. "But something

229

has gone wrong. Now he avoids her. And of course, being a woman, she avoids him too. Who can blame her? This is a game. You must play by the rules."

Emma understood perfectly. Teresa didn't want to appear to be chasing after Tomàs. It would make her look foolish. She had to maintain her dignity.

"What has happened between them?" Emma asked.

Paco shrugged. "Who knows these things?"

"Does he ever talk about it?"

The elderly concierge smiled at the naïvety of the question.

"A man must never complain about such matters. In questions of love, he must be brave like the *toro*."

"I see," Emma replied. "Like the bull. But the bull always ends up in the abattoir."

"*Sí*. That is right."

"And now, poor Tomàs is unhappy."

Old Paco shrugged. "Of course, that is the nature of the game." He finished his coffee and smacked his lips. A knowing grin had crept into his face.

"Sometimes I think I am lucky that I am old. Now I don't have to worry about the game of love."

* * *

A few days later, Emma managed to get Rosa, the housekeeper, on her own. Emma brought her into the little office behind the reception desk and invited her to sit down.

Rosa sat nervously, her face wrinkled as she tried to figure out what this interview might be about.

"I wanted to talk to you privately. Just you and me, you understand?" Emma began.

The housekeeper nodded her agreement and watched Emma cautiously.

"It's about Teresa," Emma went on.

At the mention of the name, Rosa threw up her hands in

exasperation. "Ah, that girl! She is like the calf that is sick. Even the simplest job she does wrong." She bounced her fingers off her head. Then fearing she might have said too much, the plump housekeeper immediately began to defend Teresa. "But she is a good girl, you must understand, Señorita. Usually, she works very hard. She is very obedient. It is just that recently her mind is somewhere else."

"You don't need to worry," Emma rushed to assure her. "I'm not going to discipline her."

Immediately, Rosa looked relieved.

"I think it is something between herself and Tomàs," Emma continued. "They used to be so friendly but not any more."

"*Sí*, that is right. I too have noticed this."

"Do you know what has happened?"

"No," Rosa said and shook her head. "She never speaks about it."

"Has she any other young men?"

"Oh, yes. She has plenty of men who admire her. She is a very beautiful young woman and always they have admirers. But for her it is only Tomàs. He is the only one. Indeed, I thought he was going to marry her."

Ah, Emma thought. Now we are getting close to the problem. "Perhaps she turned him down?"

But Rosa was shaking her plump head. "I don't think so. I think if he had asked she would have accepted him at once."

"Then maybe he didn't ask? Maybe he has found another *Señorita*?"

Rosa shrugged. "Maybe. These matters can be very complicated. In affairs of the heart, things are rarely simple."

* * *

For the next few days, Emma observed the conduct between the pair. A definite coolness had descended. Where before everything had been smiles and little gestures of affection, now whenever

Tomàs encountered Teresa, he nodded stiffly while she turned her head away and didn't respond. But she could see that Teresa was hurt and Tomàs, while he tried to hide his feelings under his manly exterior, was clearly also upset.

She wondered if she should intervene. It was really none of her business. But she was very fond of the young couple and would like to see them happy again. And besides, it was beginning to affect their work and create tension around the peaceful little haven of Casa Clara. If there was anything she could do to smooth matters, Emma was prepared to help. But first she had to discover exactly what the problem was. There was only one way to find out and that was to confront one of them directly.

She decided she would be more likely to succeed with Tomàs, so one morning while he was passing her desk on his way to do some gardening work, Emma detained him.

"Can you spare a moment, Tomàs? I'd like to talk to you."

"Of course, *Señorita*."

Emma signalled for Cristina to cover for her while she led him across the road to Bar Lorenzo. It would be more private and they would be less likely to be disturbed.

Once they were seated with two café leches before them, she began. She knew she had to be diplomatic. She would only get one chance at this so she had to be skilful.

"How long have you been working at Casa Clara, Tomàs?" she asked.

"For six years now, *Señorita*."

"That's a long time. You were here from the beginning?"

"Yes. Señor Alvarez hired me himself. At first it was just to help with the garden. Then gradually, I got more jobs to do."

"Well, I must say that you do your work very efficiently. Sometimes I wonder how we could manage without you."

Tomàs smiled modestly to acknowledge the compliment. "*Gracias, Señorita*."

"Do you like your work?"

"*Sí,* I like it very much. I like to fix things that are broken. And always I am learning new things, so the job is interesting. Never am I bored."

Emma glanced at the young man. He was very handsome, with his dark, good looks and jet-black hair and his easy, charming manner. No wonder Teresa had fallen for him.

"Recently, I have noticed that you seem to be unhappy."

"Unhappy?" Tomàs said with a hollow laugh. "Oh, no, you are mistaken, *Señorita*. I am not unhappy."

"You know that we all care about you, Tomàs? Everyone at the Casa thinks very highly of you."

"*Gracias, Señorita*."

"I would like you to know that you can talk to me at any time if you have a problem."

"*Sí*."

"And if it is possible I will help you."

"*Sí, Señorita*."

"And I give you my word it will be in confidence. No one else will know. You can trust me, Tomàs."

The young man was now beginning to look uncomfortable.

"Is there anything I can help you with?" Emma asked.

Tomàs shook his head. "No, *Señorita*."

Emma took a sip of coffee. "You are friendly with Teresa."

At the mention of her name, Tomàs's face clouded over. Nevertheless, Emma decided to press on.

"She is very beautiful, is she not?"

"Oh, yes, *Señorita*."

"And she has a kind nature. She is graceful and well mannered and a very good worker. I think she will make some man very happy if he marries her."

Tomàs was now staring at the ground. "You are right. I think so too, *Señorita*."

"And you know, Tomàs, I think she cares for you. I have noticed the way she admires you. I have noticed how she always smiles when she sees you. There are many little things that a woman may notice and a man may not."

At these words, Tomàs immediately raised his face again and looked at Emma.

"If you love her, why don't you ask her to marry you, Tomàs?"

He hesitated for a moment. "I did ask her, *Señorita*."

The young man was now biting his lip and there were tears welling in his eyes.

"Oh! And what did she say?"

"She said yes."

"So what happened?"

Tomàs was looking at the ground again. Emma could see that he was struggling with his emotions.

"Her father forbade it."

Emma was shocked. "Her father?"

"*Si, Señorita*."

"But why would he do such a thing? If you and Teresa wanted to get married, why should he forbid it?"

"Because he doesn't think I am worthy of her. He says I am just a *technico* at the Casa. It is not a good enough position for his family. He says it would bring disgrace. Teresa would be throwing herself away if she would marry me."

"And what does Teresa think?"

"She wants to marry me. But she must obey her father. It would cause so much trouble. Everyone would be unhappy. It would just make us all miserable."

He turned his large brown eyes to Emma.

"So, you see, it is hopeless, *Señorita*. There is nothing can be done." He sniffed and tried to hide his face.

Emma reached out and gently touched his shoulder. "Thank you for telling me, Tomàs. No one will know what you have said. It will remain a secret between us."

"Thank you, *Señorita*."

"Now go back to work and leave this matter with me."

Tomàs stood up and tried to look brave. "*Buenos días, Señorita.*"

"*Buenos días, Tomàs.*"

* * *

Emma mulled over the problem. It seemed an outrageous situation but she had no wish to interfere in Teresa's family affairs. However, it was a shame to forbid the marriage on such trivial grounds, particularly since the young couple were so obviously in love with each other. So, on Saturday, when she had her weekly conversation lesson with Señora Alvarez, she politely said: "I have something to ask you, *Señora.*"

Señora Alvarez was dressed in her finery with a revealing low-cut dress and a string of pearls around her beautiful neck. After the lesson, her friend Señor Montilla was taking her to the races at the Hippodroma. Her richly embroidered fan was working like a small windmill to keep her cool.

"*Sí?*"

"I was thinking of making a small rearrangement of the staff at the Casa and I wanted to ask your permission."

"*Sí, sí.* What is it?" Señora Alvarez replied, somewhat brusquely. She was impatient to get on with the lesson. She wanted to learn some new horse-racing terms to impress Señor Montilla.

"Tomàs is a very good worker. I think very highly of him. He is extremely efficient and always willing. There is nothing that he cannot fix."

"Yes, yes. I already know that. My dear departed husband hired him himself. And he always had an excellent eye for good staff."

"You are right, as usual, *Señora.* Tomàs has been with the Casa for six years."

"Indeed."

"Well, I was thinking that perhaps the time has come to give him a promotion."

235

Señora Alvarez immediately stopped fanning herself.

"A promotion? Did he ask for it?"

"No. Tomàs is very modest. He would never seek something like this for himself. It was I decided it."

"But why, Señorita Frazer, if he is not unhappy?"

"Because I am afraid he might be tempted to go elsewhere. You know that good technical staff are very difficult to find. Just last week, Señor Gonzalez at Hotel Bonito rang to ask if Tomàs would go over there and fix a burst boiler for him."

At this news, Señora Alvarez's face went livid. "That Gonzalez is a rattlesnake. He is worse. He is a *cucaracha*!"

"So you see, *Señora*. It would be in our interest to make sure that Tomàs doesn't get lured away from Casa Clara by someone like Señor Gonzalez who might offer him more money. I want him to feel happy at the Casa so he will stay with us."

Señora Alvarez's face was now fixed in a tight scowl of determination.

"You are right, *Señorita*, and so clever of you to make this observation. What do you propose to do?"

"I would like to promote him to Senior Technical Manager."

"I like the sound of that," Señora Alvarez said as she rolled the syllables round her tongue. "Do it. Do it at once."

"It would also involve a slight adjustment to his salary."

"How much?"

"An extra sixty euros a week. But we can afford it. Our bookings are practically full right up to September."

"Certainly," Señora Alvarez agreed. "You have my permission. The nerve of that Gonzalez! What a piece of work he is. Now back to our discussion. What is the correct way to say '*first past the stick*'?"

"The *post*," Emma said with a smile. "The phrase is: *first past the post*."

* * *

The announcement of Tomàs's promotion was made a few days later. After that, events moved very rapidly. The following week, a radiant Teresa appeared at the Casa sporting a beautiful engagement ring which she proudly showed off to the staff who crowded round to see. Tomàs went about with the look of a young man who has accomplished a difficult task but is well satisfied with his prize.

The wedding was planned for three months' time and already the young couple had paid a deposit on a new house that was being built down the coast in the little resort of Carvahal. Señora Alvarez, who had suddenly wakened up to the importance of Tomàs's role in the smooth running of Casa Clara, gave a small engagement reception in the young couple's honour. As they all raised their glasses of *cava* in a toast, Emma felt the eyes of old Paco upon her. She glanced up and saw him give her a knowing look.

Emma returned it with a modest smile.

Chapter 27

By now, almost three months had passed and it was high summer. The weather which had been warm and pleasant when Emma arrived had grown progressively hot and sultry till it was almost unbearable. Each night, she prayed for wind or even rain, anything which would counteract the oppressive heat which sapped her energy and left her perspiring and gasping for breath.

How she wished she could swap places with the holidaymakers who thronged to Casa Clara and headed off each morning after breakfast to spend the day on the beach, where at least there was a breeze, and if that wasn't sufficient to cool them down they could always take to the sea for a bathe. Emma, stuck at reception, had to make do with a large electric fan which hummed and whirred as it ruffled the papers on her desk. But the staff had assured her that after August, the temperature would begin to drop again and life would become more tolerable.

She told herself she must talk to Señora Alvarez about installing an air-conditioning system. It was one of the chief improvements that were required at Casa Clara. Another was a lift which would benefit the older guests like Mrs Moriarty and save Paco the trouble of pulling heavy suitcases up the narrow stairs. And the whole place could do with a makeover. It looked as if it hadn't been touched since the day it opened for business and in several places Emma noticed that the paint had started to peel. But getting her employer interested in such matters was difficult. As long as the Casa was ticking over smoothly, she was content. Señora Alvarez's mind was elsewhere.

Each Saturday morning, the proprietor turned up promptly for her English conversation lesson with Emma and the pair of them spent a pleasant hour drinking coffee at Bar Lorenzo while Emma patiently corrected her employer's pronunciation and diction and explained the proper meaning of words.

In return, she picked up little nuggets of gossip which she stored away for further reference. Señora Alvarez was a bright woman and she learned quickly. As a result, her English had come on by leaps and bounds and she was very pleased. Now, her friend Señor Montilla was anxious to receive English lessons from Emma. She wondered where she was going to find the time.

As the months had passed, Emma's love for Casa Clara had grown. She enjoyed her work and felt a close affinity with the staff. They trusted her and looked to her as their leader and not simply their boss. And she got a quiet satisfaction in seeing her efforts bear fruit and the Casa run smoothly and efficiently. Occasionally, she would think back to the Department of Social Affairs and consider how things might have worked out differently if someone in authority had listened to her and introduced some simple changes.

On her days off, she would take the train to Malaga and spend the time exploring the old city or she would travel up the coast to Marbella and do some shopping in the glitzy stores. Occasionally, she would journey further, up into the mountains to visit the ancient town of Ronda with its little whitewashed

houses and eat lunch in a local restaurant before returning by
bus.

In the evenings after her work was finished, she would sit in the
courtyard of the Casa beside the tinkling fountain and the flowers
and watch the shadows lengthen as the sun went down. She felt so
happy here and safe in the little hotel. It had proved to be a sanctuary
for her. Dublin seemed so far away and the problems which had
forced her to flee were quickly fading into memory. By now, Colin
Enright would have surely given up and Trish would have calmed
down. But she would still be angry with her, if only because Emma
had demonstrated her independence and escaped from under her
power. She decided it was safe to make contact again.

One evening after work, she returned to the internet café in
the old town to check her emails. So much would have happened
in the time she had been away and she was anxious to catch up
with the news. But she was in for a shock. She found dozens of
messages waiting for her. Most of them were junk and she
quickly deleted them till she narrowed the field to those sent by
Trish, Colin, Jackie and her supervisor Dolly O'Brien.

She began by opening the most recent message from her sister.
It was written in a restrained tone but underneath, Emma could
detect a note of menace.

Dear Emma,

*You don't know the relief I felt to receive your mail and learn
you are safe and well. You gave everyone a terrible fright when
you disappeared. But now you must come home. At least you
will be among friends and not strangers.*

*No one will put you under any pressure. But at a time like
this, you need support. People here are very concerned,
especially myself, Colin and Smitty. I had a phone call from your
supervisor at work. They think you might be suffering from a
nervous breakdown. I told her I would do my best to convince
you to return.*

I have to warn you that your job is in jeopardy. Your supervisor was very considerate but she pointed out that there are regulations that must be followed. You can't just disappear like this, Emma. It's not fair to other people.

Please contact me again in confidence. If you need anything, please let me know. Colin and Smitty are prepared to go and assist you at any time. Would you please phone me? Writing emails like this are no substitute for the human voice. Even a short call would be much appreciated.

Your loving sister, Trish.

She stared at the computer screen. She should have known better. Trish had not given up. She read the message again, slowly this time. It was couched in conciliatory language but underneath the smooth surface she could sense her sister's determination.

She quickly opened the message from Colin. It was similar in tone to Trish's, saying how sorry he was if he had upset her, pledging his undying love and begging her to ring and make contact. She had been wrong about him too. Time had not made him change his mind. He still wanted her back. The message from Dolly O'Brien was cold and formal and quite unlike her usual style. It informed her that since she had absented herself from her duties without permission and in contravention of a verbal warning, she had now been suspended without pay pending the outcome of a disciplinary charge. A letter to this effect had been sent to her address.

This came as a shock. A few weeks after she arrived at Casa Clara she had contacted her bank in Dublin and confirmed that her monthly salary cheque had been lodged to her account. She had decided that Dolly O'Brien had relented and found some way to grant her the special leave she had sought. But Emma had been wrong. The rules were being applied rigorously and her pay cheques had been stopped.

But by far the most worrying news was from Trish and Colin. She had been mistaken to believe she was out of danger. She could read between the lines. Trish and Colin were not going to give up without a fight. They were still in league together and determined to get her back. And from Trish's email, she could sense the direction they would take. They would say she was ill. That she had lost her mind and didn't know what she was doing. Colin and Smitty were even threatening to come and get her. Emma suddenly felt very apprehensive.

It was with relief that she finally opened the message from Jackie. Unlike the others, it was genuinely warm and supportive and she felt the gratitude well up inside her.

Hi Em,

Great to hear from you and to know you are safe and well. I hope wherever you are it is nice and warm. It has been pissing rain here in Dublin ever since you left.

The merde has hit the fan in a major way. Trish has rung me several times wanting to know if I've heard from you or can tell her where you are. She sounds manic. Of course I denied everything. My lips are sealed.

Liam sends his regards,
Love, kisses and cuddlies,
Your very best friend,
Jackie

At least Jackie was standing by her, as she knew she would. Suddenly Emma felt an urge to talk to her friend and hear her voice again. Despite her misgivings, she lifted the phone and rang Dublin. She listened to the ringing tone and then Jackie was on the line.

"Hi, it's me," Emma said.

"Emma!"

She could hear the delight in Jackie's voice.

"It's great to hear you. Are you okay?"

"I'm fine, Jackie. Listen, I'm sorry I didn't contact you sooner. Everything was done in a hurry and I was worried about the phone lines being tapped or something. I know that sounds paranoid but you've no idea how insecure I felt."

"No, it's not paranoid at all. I would have done the same. But at least you're safe. Now where the hell are you?"

"Promise you won't tell anyone? This is serious, Jackie. I don't want Trish or Colin Enright finding out."

"Don't worry. I'll deny that I even know you."

"I'm in Spain."

She heard a gasp.

"Spain? You lucky cow! Trish thought you had gone to Tenerife."

"That's where I was planning to go. But I couldn't get a flight. So I came here instead."

"What part of Spain?"

"The Costa del Sol."

"Well, I must say, I envy you. You know we're having the worst weather since records began. It hasn't stopped raining for months. I'm thinking of taking up swimming lessons."

Emma could hear her friend laughing on the phone and realised how much she missed her cheerful company.

"Are you coming back? Everybody misses you, Emma. I'm dying to see you again."

"Not for a while, Jackie. I couldn't face it. Colin Enright has ganged up with Trish. They're trying to railroad me into marrying him. You've no idea of the terrible pressure I was under."

"Just tell him to hump off. This is the twenty-first century. Ever hear of female emancipation?"

Emma found herself smiling. "I love it here, Jackie. You'd love it too. The people are so nice and the lifestyle is so easy."

"What are you living on?"

"I've got a job."

"Really? What sort of job?"

"I'm working in a beautiful little hotel called Casa Clara. It's right on the beach and it's got the most gorgeous courtyard with a fountain and flowers."

"Don't make me jealous," Jackie said. "What exactly do you do?"

"I'm the receptionist. In fact, I'm really running the place. So I have hardly any expenses. And I've got this lovely girl called Cristina who is my assistant. It can be hard work but I'm enjoying every minute."

She heard Jackie sigh.

"I envy you. I really do. I'd give my left leg to see a bit of sunshine."

"It's very hot here right now. You might not like it."

"Don't fool yourself, I'd love it. Anything would be better than the weather we're getting here. So you're really okay and you're happy?"

"I'm delirious."

"I told you Trish has been pestering me for information. She said she was worried that you weren't well and something could happen to you."

"I'm perfectly well, Jackie. In fact I haven't felt better for a long time. You mustn't tell her anything. You mustn't even tell her that we spoke."

"No, of course not."

"I'm relying on you. The last thing I want is for Trish and Colin Enright to turn up here and start pressurising me again."

"Relax," Jackie said. "No one is going to know."

"I have to go now, Jackie. It's been great hearing your voice again. Say hello to Liam for me."

"Will do."

"I'll give you another call next week. Take care of yourself. Goodbye."

"Goodbye," Jackie said, sadly. "And Emma . . ."

"Yes?"

"Good luck."

She put down the phone with an enormous feeling of relief. It had been great to hear Jackie's voice again and listen to her laughter. And the knowledge that she had one friend she could rely on served to strengthen her resolve. At least, she wasn't alone. But before she left the internet café, she had one further job to do. She opened Trish's email and typed a quick response.

Dear Trish,

Thanks for your message. I repeat that I am safe and well. In fact I have never felt better. So stop worrying about me. As for work, I will write to my supervisor so you don't have to concern yourself on that front either. I am enjoying this break and have no immediate plans to return to Dublin.

Regards to Smitty,

Emma

She pressed the SEND key and watched the message disappear. It might keep her sister at bay for another while and give her more time to consider her next move. As for Dolly O'Brien, she felt sorry that she had placed her supervisor in such an awkward situation because Dolly had always been kind to her. But she had no option. She realised that she had probably burned her bridges as far as the Civil Service was concerned. The disciplinary charge would proceed without her and would probably go against her. It was unlikely that she would ever work for them again.

She paid her bill and left the café. By now the worst of the heat had passed and already the air was beginning to cool. People sat about at pavement tables chatting and drinking beer.

She was glad that she had checked her mails and phoned

Jackie. It was with a lighter heart that she made her way back along the beach to Casa Clara.

* * *

When she returned, she found the little hotel humming smoothly under Cristina's watchful eye. She went up to her room, got undressed and stood under the cold shower. Then she poured a glass of wine and went back down to the courtyard. She chose a bench beside the fountain and stretched her face to the dying sun. She felt a restful calm come over her.

She thought back to her visit to the internet café and the emails she had received. Perhaps she should bring matters to a head and resign her job. They were going to fire her anyway and, besides, why continue in a career she disliked? She would miss some of her colleagues but that was all. She wouldn't miss the drudgery and the boredom. And now that she had experienced life at Casa Clara, she could appreciate the challenges and the excitement and the satisfaction of other work.

And then another thought entered her mind. She had planned to stay here for a few months and then return. But why did she have to go back to Dublin at all? Why could she not stay here indefinitely? She had come to Spain to escape. Perhaps it was time to stop running? Perhaps her future lay here, at Casa Clara?

Chapter 28

A few days later, a chance remark from Señora Alvarez gave her further food for thought. It happened at their weekly conversation lesson. Señora Alvarez was in particularly sparkling form this Saturday morning. She was wearing a tight dress with a plunging neckline which reminded Emma of the flamenco dress she had worn to the Major's dance. Her dark hair was coiffed and combed and gleamed in the bright morning sun. Her lips were a bright shade of fire-engine red. Pendants glittered at her ears and a string of pearls adorned her slender neck. She looked superb.

"How is my English, Señorita Frazer? Do you think I am making progress?"

"Very good progress," Emma replied. "You are an excellent student and you pick up the pronunciation very quickly."

Señora Alvarez was pleased. A big smile engulfed her pretty face. "You are also a very good teacher."

"Thank you."

The Señora flicked her fan and invited Emma to move closer

so she could share a confidence. "I have some news." Her dark eyes gleamed.

"Yes?"

"I think my friend Señor Montilla will soon ask me to marry him."

"Really?" Emma replied. "Congratulations. That is *very* good news. From what you have told me, he is a handsome gentleman and so charming."

"And also wealthy," Señora Alvarez reminded her. "You know that he owns several hotels?"

"No," Emma replied. "I didn't know that."

"Oh, yes. He owns the Ambassador in Marbella and the Alhambra in Malaga. And he is already planning to buy another one. Señor Montilla is a very clever businessman. He knows how to make the good investments."

"Well, I am very pleased for you," Emma said. "I am sure you will be very happy together."

"Of course nothing is announced yet," Señora Alvarez hastened to add. "But I expect it soon. A woman learns to pick up the little signs. Is it not so?"

"Indeed."

"So I must be patient. I must wait my time. If I appear too eager, then Señor Montilla will not think so much of me. I must play the game of tough to catch."

"Hard to get," Emma corrected her.

The Señora smiled. "That is right, hard to get. But I am excited. I need not tell you that since my poor Miguel died so suddenly, I have been a broken woman. I have barely recovered yet from my terrible grief."

You could have fooled me, Emma thought mischievously.

"But Señor Montilla is such a kind man. He knows how to bring the joy back into my heart. And he is so generous. Did I tell you that he owns a large *finca* above Mijas?"

"No."

"Oh yes, very large. The house alone has six bedrooms. And then there are the gardens. And Señor Montilla is very fond of giving parties. He likes to entertain his friends and his business associates. When . . ." She paused and a modest little smile crossed her face. "*If*, I marry him, I expect I will be very busy running his house. There will be so much work to do, so many staff to command. Already, I think he hires a dozen people."

"So many?" Emma asked, surprised.

"Of course, for the gardens alone there are five."

"I can certainly see you will be busy," Emma said. "May I ask when you expect the announcement?"

"Soon, very soon. But you must say nothing." She drew her finger across her lips. "Everything must be a secret. Señor Montilla is a proud man and easily offended. I am only telling you because I trust you. And of course there may be a slip between the cup and the mouth." She raised her eyebrows and looked knowingly at Emma.

"The cup and the lip, *Señora*."

"Of course, the lip. It is so easy to mix them up. But I am lucky. I always have you to correct me when I go wrong." She flapped out her fan and vigorously began to cool herself. "Now there is something I must ask you. Whenever I agree to marry Señor Montilla, what is that called in English?"

"The engagement," Emma said.

"Ah yes, the engagement. It has a nice business sound to it, don't you think?"

The conversation set Emma thinking. If Señora Alvarez married Señor Montilla as she expected, what impact would this have on Casa Clara? She had grown used to the easy relationship she had with her employer who largely left her alone and let her get on with the job of managing the hotel.

And the system worked extremely well. She didn't have anyone interfering or peering over her shoulder or countermanding her decisions. If she had an issue about staff or a serious problem, she naturally took it to Señora Alvarez but, by and large, she was her own boss. And this suited her well.

But if the *Señora* married Señor Montilla, that relationship could change. For one thing, she would have his busy house to run and even less time to devote to the Casa. It would mean that more of the management of the hotel would fall onto Emma's shoulders. This was a development she would welcome. It might mean that she would be able to turn over the reception desk to Cristina and concentrate full-time on managing Casa Clara.

The conversation revived the thought that had been growing in her mind since the day she visited the internet café. She was happy here, she loved her work. She felt safe. And it wasn't simply the job. She had fallen in love with Spain, with the climate and the food and the scenery and the people. She loved the lifestyle, the sun in the morning when she woke up, the cool breeze blowing in from the sea, the scent of the flowers in the evening.

Why not stay? Her Spanish had improved out of recognition in the short time she had been in Fuengirola. She had a work permit secured for her by Señora Alvarez. She was earning a good salary and had money in her bank in Dublin if she needed more. She could rent out her apartment and that would provide another source of income. What was stopping her?

The more she considered the idea, the more attractive it became. It would be like starting a new life all over again in a place she loved and enjoyed. She would never again have to worry about Trish and Colin Enright. She would be free of them forever. The thought of these wonderful new possibilities made her head spin. She was so excited that she went back at once to Casa Clara and changed into a little top and shorts and walking shoes. She set out on a long stroll along the beach towards the Castillo while her mind soared off in a delightful flight of fancy.

* * *

But it wasn't very long before she was brought back down to

earth. Just after breakfast on Sunday, she received an urgent phone call from Señora Alvarez. She sounded in a panic. "*Emergencia*" was the first word Emma recognised from the stream of rapid Spanish that came pouring out of the receiver.

"An emergency?" Emma said.

"*Sí, sí. Emergencia.* The health inspectors are coming."

"When are they coming?" Emma asked, trying to remain calm despite Señora Alvarez's rising hysteria.

"Tomorrow morning. They are devils. They are trying to catch me but a friend has tipped me off."

"What do you want me to do, *Señora*?"

"The whole place must be cleaned from top to bottom at once, especially the kitchen. They always pay attention to it ever since that rat, Señor Gonzalez, had an outbreak of food poisoning at Hotel Bonito. He had to install a whole new kitchen at enormous expense. I will come in at once and oversee it."

"There is no need," Emma assured her. "Leave the matter with me."

Señora Alvarez hesitated. "Are you sure you are able for it? This is very important. They could close me down."

"Yes, I am sure. If I have a difficulty, I will ring you at once."

She heard Señora Alvarez begin to relax.

"You are so capable, Señorita Frazer. It is just that I was hoping to go sailing this afternoon with Señor Montilla. Of course, I will be there myself tomorrow when these damned inspectors arrive."

"Enjoy your afternoon with the *Señor* and don't worry."

"Thank you so much. You take the weight off my head."

"Your mind," Emma said. "The weight off your mind."

She heard Señora Alvarez give a nervous laugh.

"Always you are correcting me, *Señorita*. I like that."

Emma put down the phone. She was glad that Señora Alvarez had another engagement. If she was here she would simply spread the panic and get in the way. Emma was pretty sure that the premises were already in a good state of hygiene but, to be certain, she called Rosa and explained the situation to her. The plump housekeeper took enormous pride in the cleanliness of Casa Clara and she was determined that no fault should be found when the inspectors arrived to do their work. She suggested that she bring in some casual cleaners that she used from time to time. Of course, they would have to be paid double time because it was Sunday. But Emma agreed immediately.

Half an hour later, six women arrived in a van armed with buckets, mops, vacuum cleaners and detergents. Under Rosa's eagle-eyed direction, they started at the top of the building and worked their way down to the ground floor. They scrubbed, cleaned, changed linen, vacuumed and swept till the place shone like a new pin.

Then they started on the kitchen. Every surface was polished till it gleamed; every pot, pan and cooking utensil was scrubbed till it sparkled. It was after 10 p.m. when they finished but Emma was now confident that the hotel would pass any inspection, however rigorous.

She paid the cleaners and watched them drive off in their van. Then she poured herself a glass of white wine and went out to the courtyard and sat on a bench. It was a beautiful night and the sky was a blanket of stars. From the nearby shore, she could hear the gentle rise and fall of the tide upon the beach. It merged with the soft tinkling sound of the water from the fountain. She closed her eyes and laid her head back on the bench and felt peace descend on her like a gentle balm.

So far, so good. She had survived Señora Alvarez's *emergencia*. Tomorrow she would know if her efforts were enough to convince the inspectors. She would sleep well tonight and hopefully, she would dream sweet dreams.

* * *

The following morning, she was up early to find the sun coming up like a huge ball of fire. It was going to be another scorching day. She put on her swimsuit and went down to the beach, feeling the cool water refresh her. Then she had a shower and got dressed, ate a breakfast of coffee and fruit and at eight o'clock was on duty behind the reception desk.

By now, all the staff had been warned to be on their best behaviour because the inspectors were coming, although they had been told to act surprised. Under no circumstances must the inspectors get wind that the hotel had been tipped off about their visit.

At half past eight, Señora Alvarez arrived, dressed impeccably in a smart business suit and expertly made up so that her dark eyes flashed seductively beneath their coat of mascara. Señora Alvarez had been through this ordeal before and knew the value of feminine charm when dealing with people like health inspectors. She asked Emma to accompany her at once on a tour of the Casa.

Cristina took over the desk while the two women went around the premises. Señora Alvarez ran a practised finger along window ledges, peered behind curtains, examined skirting boards and held up forks to ensure that not a speck of dirt or grime remained that could earn them the displeasure of the inspectors. By ten o'clock, just as breakfast was finishing, they arrived back at the reception desk.

"I am most impressed, Señorita Frazer. The place is so clean I could eat my dinner off the floor. If these damned inspectors find anything to complain about, I will personally cut their throats with a carving knife."

"Let's hope that won't be necessary," Emma replied with a smile.

"Once the breakfast is cleared away, I want Rosa and Teresa to give the kitchen one final cleaning. It is always the kitchen they concentrate on."

Emma undertook to have her instructions carried out and Señora Alvarez went into the little office and began to make phone calls while they waited tensely for the arrival of the inspectors.

They came at eleven o'clock: two men in dark suits, one tall and thin and the other plump and squat. They carried clipboards and pens and had that air of small-time authority beloved by petty bureaucrats. *Señora* Alvarez, looking suitably surprised, immediately offered them coffee which they declined. They appeared impatient to start at once, so ushering them politely before her, the *Señora* led them off on their tour of inspection.

They took a long time. It was half past twelve when Emma finally saw them emerge from the kitchen. Señora Alvarez was smiling and making little jokes but beneath the veneer, Emma could see that she was strained and worried. An adverse report from this pair could cost her dearly. They arrived at last at the reception desk where they stopped. Señora Alvarez looked expectantly from one face to the other but neither man was giving anything away.

The plump one, who appeared to be in charge, cleared his throat and prepared to speak. Señora Alvarez stiffened in anticipation.

"I noticed a dripping tap in the kitchen sink," the man announced.

"Oh!" Señora Alvarez looked shocked.

"Get it fixed."

"Of course, I will see to it at once. Anything else?" she asked, nervously.

"No. Nothing else to report," the man said with what sounded like disappointment. "We can give you a clean certificate. Your premises have passed our inspection."

Señora Alvarez's face lit up like a rising sun. "I am most gratified, *Señor*. Perhaps, after your exertions, I might offer you a glass of Malaga wine?"

The two men exchanged a glance.

"That is most kind, *Señora*," the plump man said. "I think a small glass would be refreshing."

Señora Alvarez immediately waved a hand towards Teresa and blithely led the inspectors out to the courtyard. It was two o'clock before they left.

"Dripping tap," she muttered to Emma as she passed the reception desk. "I should have held his stupid head under it."

Emma was relieved and Señora Alvarez was delighted that she had got the damned inspectors off her back for another year. She thanked Emma and told her to make sure that the staff were suitably rewarded, then disappeared to get ready for a party that Señor Montilla was giving that evening.

By three o'clock Emma was beginning to feel tired and hungry and she still had a pile of paperwork to get through before she handed over to Cristina. She would have liked nothing better than a cold shower and a nap. So she was startled when she heard a soft voice at her shoulder inquire if they had a room available.

She glanced up to find a tall man standing before her. He had come in quietly and caught her unawares. She stared as if she was witnessing an apparition. It was several years since she had seen him but she recognised him at once.

Tim Devlin was gazing at her with a look of astonishment on his face.

Chapter 29

For a moment, they stared at each other. He was exactly as she remembered him: the same tall, manly frame, the same broad shoulders, the same black hair and intense brown eyes. It wasn't a mirage. He was standing in front of her. But what on earth was he doing in Fuengirola?

It was Tim who broke the silence and spoke first.

"Emma? Is it really you?"

"Yes," she said, trying to recover from the shock.

He laughed and shook his head. "My God, I don't believe it. How are you?"

"I'm very well, thanks. And you?"

"I'm amazed. You are the very last person I expected to find here."

"I could say the same thing about you," she said, trying desperately to cover her embarrassment as her heart thumped loudly in her breast.

"But what are you doing?" he asked, making no effort to hide his surprise.

"I work here. I'm the receptionist."

"Have you left your job in the department?"

"Not quite."

"I don't understand."

"It's rather complicated," she said, brushing a stray lock of hair from her face. "I took a break."

"A break?"

"Yes. Something came up and I had to get away. Technically, I'm still employed in the dear old department."

A playful smile played around Tim Devlin's lips. "So nothing has changed there?"

"No," she said. "Nothing has changed."

He shrugged. "Well, it's great to see you again. You look so good. The change of scenery is obviously agreeing with you."

"Thank you. And what has brought *you* to Fuengirola?"

"Same thing as you, I needed a break. And that takes me neatly to the point of my business. Is there any possible chance you might have a spare room?"

"Let me check," Emma said. "You're looking for a double?"

"No, a single will do. I'll take anything you've got. In fact, I'm so desperate, I'd be happy to sleep in the broom cupboard."

She glanced at the solitary grip bag that appeared to be his only luggage. "Are you travelling alone?"

"Yes."

She was all a-jitter as she tried to concentrate on the computer screen. Seeing him again had completely thrown her. Her fingers trembled as she touched the keyboard.

"How long do you want it for?"

"A week, if that's possible. I know I should have booked but this trip was a last-minute decision."

"Well, let's see what we can do," Emma managed to say. "We can't have you sleeping in the broom cupboard."

She trawled through the reservations list, her mind now totally confused by the man who waited at the desk. By good fortune, a single room had come free that morning. She checked the ledger, just to be certain.

"You're in luck," she said.

"Well, thank God for that. This is the fourth place I've tried and they were all booked out. I didn't expect the resort to be so busy."

"It's the height of the season," she explained. "Everybody heads for the sun."

"Of course, I should have realised."

"Room 15. I'll ask the concierge to show you up."

She took his credit card and passport and completed the formalities, then asked him to sign the register before giving him his key.

"You're a star," he said, as he turned to go. "Imagine meeting you here. Perhaps we could have a drink some time when you're free? You can tell me where I should go and what I should see."

"I'd be happy to do that," Emma replied. "You know where to find me."

"*Buenas tardes*," he said with a grin, as he lifted his single bag and prepared to follow Paco up the narrow stairs to his room.

She watched him go. She was still in shock. She couldn't believe that Tim Devlin of all people had turned up here at Casa Clara.

When Cristina came at six o'clock to take over, Emma's mind was still in turmoil. It had been a very eventful day and now she felt exhausted. She went up to her room, stripped off her clothes and lay down on the bed. From the open window, a gentle breeze cooled her. Her mind filled once more with thoughts of Tim.

It was three years since she had last seen him and she could still remember the occasion as if it was only yesterday. They had been to lunch in the Shelbourne Hotel, an event that had begun with such high expectations and ended with her fighting back the tears. How foolish she had been back then, so naïve to believe that he might be interested in her. And her hopes had been dashed when he told her he was married.

He had given her a present – a collection of the poetry of WB Yeats. She had it with her now. It was one of the few personal things she had brought with her when she had fled from Dublin. She got up from the bed and opened a drawer in the writing desk and took out the book. She flicked to the flyleaf and read the inscription: *For Emma with fond thoughts, from Tim.*

She felt a gentle tugging at her heart as she read those words, a stirring of the old feelings she had nourished since her schooldays. She thought once more of his handsome face and his soft lilting voice and those deep brown eyes burning with passionate intensity. And now their paths had crossed again, here in Fuengirola of all places. It was amazing. What was he doing here? Why was he travelling alone? Where was his wife? And his family, assuming that he had children?

A dozen questions came flashing into Emma's mind as she sat in her room and watched the shadows lengthen across the little courtyard outside her window. Perhaps she would find out in the days that lay ahead. Tim Devlin was staying at Casa Clara for a week. It would be impossible to avoid each other.

But some deep survival instinct urged her to be cautious. Twice before, she had been hurt because she had allowed her imagination to overrule her good sense. But she was older now and she had more experience. She would not make those mistakes again. She would not allow herself to be carried away by Tim Devlin's charm and his handsome looks. Besides, Tim was a married man and that ruled him strictly out of bounds.

She felt the stirrings of hunger. It was time to get dressed and find somewhere to eat. She had a shower and put on a light muslin dress she had bought at one of the local markets and a white vest top and brushed out her long dark hair. She slipped on her sandals and left the room.

On her way down the stairs, she met Major Sykes coming up.

He was in jolly form and smiled warmly as he stood aside to let her to pass.

"Good evening, Emma," he bellowed. "If I might be permitted to say so, you look quite lovely tonight."

"Thank you, Major. And may I say that you are also looking extremely debonair."

His face glowed with pleasure. "Mrs Moriarty and myself are having a little dinner tonight."

"That sounds very cosy," Emma teased.

The major blushed. "It's nothing grand, you understand. But one gets tired of dining alone. I find a little female company quite entertaining from time to time."

"Indeed. I hope Mrs Moriarty's kitten isn't disturbing you?"

"Oh, not in the least. She has trained it perfectly. Tell you the truth you wouldn't even know it was there."

"Enjoy your dinner and give Mrs Moriarty my best regards," Emma said as she made her way downstairs to the street.

The heat of the day had passed and a gentle breeze stirred the air. Inside the old town, the streets were pulsating with life as people emerged for their evening *paseo*, whole families linking arms with aged relatives as they strolled past the crowded restaurants and cafés. From every corner came the sound of throbbing guitar music. The scent of flowers filled the air. This was the time that Emma loved the most when people had finished work for the day and were bent on relaxation; this, and the early morning when the sun had just come up and another day was beginning.

She found a little place near the church and ordered a plate of grilled fish and salad and a cool glass of wine. As she ate her meal, she thought of what Major Sykes had said about dining alone. She had been doing a lot of that recently. Indeed, she now ate most of her meals by herself. She enjoyed her own company and it gave her the chance to unwind after a hectic day at the Casa.

But it would be nice to have someone to share her thoughts with from time to time, a reliable companion like Jackie who she could confide in. Indeed, she would appreciate her friend's company right now as she struggled to make sense of the eventful changes that were rapidly taking place in her life.

Eventually she finished her dinner, paid the waiter and made her way back along the seafront. The restaurants were still packed with holidaymakers and tourists, loud laughter spilling out into the cool night air. It was almost ten o'clock when she arrived back at Casa Clara and by now she was tired. So instead of lingering for a while in the courtyard, she climbed the stairs to her room and began to prepare for bed. The poetry book was still sitting where she had left it on the bedside table. She turned the pages till she came to "The Lake Isle of Innisfree".

As she read, she could hear again the soft Northern lilt of Tim Devlin's voice. Her mind travelled back to the first time she had met him, as a student in St Benedict's school. She felt a lump rise in her throat. She had been so young and innocent then and the world had seemed such a golden place filled with bright promise. It was sad but many of those expectations had come to nothing. Emma closed the book and set it aside. Ten minutes later, she was fast asleep.

* * *

She woke at seven o'clock with thoughts of Tim still fresh in her mind. She drew back the curtains and saw the dawn creeping across the sky. She felt refreshed and energised after her long night's sleep. She slipped into her robe and made her way down to the beach for her morning swim. On her way back, she came across Tomàs setting out the tables for breakfast.

"*Hola, Señorita,*" he said with a cheerful smile. "Did you enjoy your swim?"

"Yes, Tomàs."

"Every day you swim. You must be a very fit lady from all the exercise."

She laughed. "It's only for twenty minutes. It's not so much."

He shrugged. "I admire you. What would you like for breakfast?"

"I'll just have coffee and a croissant, please."

Tomàs poured the coffee while she smeared a croissant with marmalade. While she ate, she kept up her conversation.

"How is your wedding coming along, Tomàs?"

"The wedding has been delayed," he said.

"Oh, I'm sorry to hear that," Emma replied, hoping some new obstacle had not emerged.

"It is the house. It will not be ready on time. We will have to wait for another six months."

"Six months is not so long," Emma commiserated. "I'm sure you can manage that, Tomàs."

"Yes. But Teresa doesn't like to wait. Now we have to go back and arrange everything again."

"You could always get married and rent an apartment till your house is finished."

But Tomàs was shaking his head. "No. Teresa wants everything to be perfect. She wants the house to be ready whenever we marry." He rolled his eyes as if to say "the problems this marriage business brings!"

"Well then, there is nothing you can do," Emma said. "You will just have to wait."

Once in her room, she began to get dressed. By now, the sun was climbing higher in the sky. It was going to be another hot day. Already, the air felt clammy. She would have to approach Señora Alvarez soon about investing in that air-conditioning system. In fact she would do it at their next conversation lesson. They couldn't endure another summer like this one.

She took extra care getting ready, applying a little eyeliner and lip-gloss and even a hint of perfume. She chose a crisp white blouse and a narrow skirt whose hemline stopped an inch or so above her knee. She decided to wear a pair of silver earrings, something she didn't normally do at work around the Casa.

When she was finished, she studied herself in the mirror. She looked good with her dark hair cascading around her shoulders and her bright hazel eyes.

By eight o'clock, she was at her post at reception. This was usually a busy time with breakfast being served in the courtyard and guests checking out and paying their final bills. This morning five guests were leaving. Emma prepared their accounts and alerted the efficient Rosa that the rooms would need to be cleaned and the linen changed. Then she began to tackle the post. By ten o'clock, she had completed her tasks and also dealt with a number of phone inquiries about accommodation.

By now, breakfast was over and the last of the guests were leaving the courtyard. She realised that Tim Devlin had not appeared. She tried to remember if she had told him about breakfast. Perhaps in her confusion she had forgotten but, in any case, there was a card behind the door in each room informing guests. She concluded that he was tired and had decided to skip breakfast and sleep on.

However, as the day progressed without any sight of him, she began to grow curious. At two o'clock, she decided to ring his room but there was no reply. Taking the house keys from their hook on the wall beside her, she asked Tomàs to watch the desk. Then she began the ascent of the stairs to Tim's room.

It was on the third floor and he had been lucky enough to secure a view over the courtyard. Emma knocked sharply on the door but heard no response. She called his name and no one answered. By now, she was growing concerned. She inserted the key in the lock and entered the room.

The first thing she saw was the bed. It was tidily made up in the efficient way she had come to expect from Teresa and the other housemaids.

In fact, it was pristine. But there was no sign of Tim.

Chapter 30

She strode to the wardrobe and flung it open. Some clothes hung neatly from the rail. But Tim's bag was gone, which was odd. She wondered what could have happened. Perhaps he had taken off on a trip somewhere. Guests did that from time to time although, by rights, they were supposed to inform reception in case there was an urgent phone call from a relative or friend.

Still, she was not unduly concerned. She went back down to reception, confident that he would show up sooner or later. But as the day went on, she felt the anxiety return. She found herself watching each time someone entered the hotel, hoping to see Tim arrive back. But she watched in vain through lunchtime and into the afternoon without any sighting of him.

Now she was beginning to get alarmed. What if something had happened to him? What if he had got into trouble? Should she inform the police? She told herself this was ridiculous. Tim was not the sort of man that bad things happened to.

She busied herself with paperwork in an attempt to keep her mind occupied. She checked lists and accounts. She went over the reservations schedule for another time. But it was impossible to rid her mind of thoughts of Tim Devlin. She decided if he hadn't turned up by tonight she would have to take action.

And then, at a quarter to six, just as she was preparing to go off duty and hand over to Cristina, she saw him come striding through the main door and into the hall. He was wearing chinos and a mustard-coloured linen jacket and had his black luggage bag slung carelessly across his shoulder.

She felt a wave of relief sweep over her.

"*Buenas tardes*," he said with a boyish grin.

"Where have you been?" she asked.

He looked sheepish. "I went to Ronda and missed the bus back. I had to stay over."

"You should have told us. We were beginning to get worried about you."

He laughed. "There was nothing to worry about. I found a little guest house. It was cheap and cheerful but not a patch on Casa Clara. I'm sorry if I alarmed you."

Emma nodded. It was hard to get upset with a man like Tim. "Just inform us the next time you're planning a trip," she said with a smile.

"I'll certainly do that."

He turned to go but suddenly stopped and came back again to the desk.

"When do you finish work?"

"In fifteen minutes' time."

"Well then, let me make it up to you. Why don't you have dinner with me tonight?"

The invitation caught her by surprise.

"Unless you have other plans?" he said.

"No, I'm free. I'd be quite pleased."

"So I'll see you here at seven o'clock," he said giving her a warm, affectionate smile that set her pulse racing.

She could barely contain her delight. It was with a light mood that she handed over to Cristina and skipped upstairs to her room. Once inside, she locked the door and flung herself down on the bed and closed her eyes. It was so incredible she couldn't believe it was happening. She was having dinner with Tim Devlin. If someone had told her a few days before that this was possible, she would have said they were mad. But it was really true and she couldn't wait.

There was so much she wanted to talk about. She was dying to know what he was doing now and why he was here in Fuengirola. And on his own! But mainly she just wanted to see him again and spend time in his company. She had a shower and began to get dressed.

Since the panic over Major Sykes' dance, she had managed to acquire a couple of nice little dresses. She took them out and examined them. One was a short white off-the-shoulder dress that showed off her figure to very good effect and would emphasise her tan. But would it look too provocative? Would it send out the wrong signals? After all, Tim was a married man and she didn't want any confusion. She took out another dress and held it up to the light.

This one was lilac. It was a pretty dress but more demure with its oval neckline and gently swirling knee-length skirt. Emma examined each one in turn while she tried to decide. Finally, she laid the lilac dress on the bed and sat down at the dressing-table to apply her make-up.

By now, it was a quarter to seven. She opened her cosmetic bag and quickly set to work. When she had finished, she sat back from the mirror and examined her face. The mascara and brown shadow highlighted her hazel eyes and the blusher emphasised her cheekbones. Her long black hair had been brushed till it shone and nestled in gentle folds around her bare shoulders. She was pleased with the effect. She took out her silver earrings then added a simple necklace to her slender throat. She stood up and straightened out her dress.

Why am I doing this, she thought? Tim Devlin is not available. He has a wife. I have been down this road before and the result was not good. But even if he *was* married, Tim was still the man she admired and respected more than any other man she had known. Why shouldn't she want to look her best? Why wouldn't she want to impress him? What normal woman wouldn't do exactly what she was doing now?

He was waiting in the hall. He had shaved and changed into the lightweight suit he had worn the night he arrived. The moment he saw her, his eyes brightened. Cristina, who was sitting behind the reception desk, saw her too and smiled in appreciation.

"You look marvellous," Tim said, as he approached and kissed her politely on the cheek.

"Thank you," she smiled. "Have you decided where you want to eat?"

"No," he admitted. "I thought I would leave that to you. You know the town much better than I do."

"What sort of food do you like?"

"Right now, I'd eat anything. I'm ravenous."

She thought for a moment. "I know just the place."

"Lead the way," he replied as he offered his arm and they stepped out into the bright evening sunlight.

The restaurant she chose was a cosy little place called El Molino. It sat in a corner of Calle Valencia, one of the streets of the old town. It had pavement tables with crisp white tablecloths and pots with trailing flowers. A taxi took them there in fifteen minutes. They arrived to find the restaurant empty except for a couple of tourists.

"No one here?" Tim said, glancing around.

"We're early. The Spanish don't eat till later."

"That should mean the service will be sharper."

He buried his head in the menu while Emma stole a glance at him. He had hardly aged at all. He was still as handsome as he was when she'd first met him all those years before.

Indeed he was *more* handsome. The years had given him a maturity and the hot Andalucian sun had brought a healthy glow to his face.

He looked up when the waiter brought glasses of sherry.

"I think I'll have grilled steak," he announced. "What about you?"

Emma, who had scarcely glanced at the menu, asked the waiter what the special was tonight.

"Sole, *Señorita*, freshly landed today."

"I'll have it," she said. "And some salad, please."

Tim ordered sirloin and a carafe of red wine then sat back in his chair and let out a contented sigh.

"This is so peaceful," he said. "How did you find this place?"

"I eat here quite often."

"And why are you in Fuengirola? Why are you working at Casa Clara and not back home in the department?"

Emma wondered how much she should tell him. "It's a long story. I came here for a holiday with a gang of school friends after our Leaving exams so I'm fond of the place."

"But why did you come back? You haven't explained what you're doing here."

"I ran away," she said with a mischievous gleam in her eye. "And this is where I ended up."

He looked astonished, not quite sure if she was teasing him. "Ran away? You mean you chucked in your job?"

"Not quite, although I am thinking of it."

"How long have you been here?"

"Three months."

"I'm baffled," he said, as the waiter appeared at his side with the wine.

"Let's say I took leave of absence," Emma continued.

"And they gave it to you? That's most unusual."

"I didn't say they gave it to me. I said I *took* it."

"You mean you just upped and left?"

"That's right. I absconded."

He was shaking his head in disbelief. "I bet that shocked them rigid. They aren't used to headstrong women taking the law into their own hands. How did they react?"

"As you might expect," Emma said. "I've been placed on a disciplinary charge. I suppose I'll be fired."

"You are entitled to appeal," he said, quickly.

"I know. But that would mean returning to Dublin and I don't want to do that."

"There are ways around it."

"You mean deception? Make up some cock and bull story?"

"White lies," he said. "Lots of people do it."

"Not me. The truth is I don't think I want to go back to the department. I'm quite happy here."

He poured two glasses of wine from the carafe that the waiter had left down and passed one to Emma.

"Stop beating around the bush," he said. "Why don't you tell me what really happened?"

She smiled in surprise. Could Tim Devlin read her mind? "If you must know, I had a bad experience with a man," she said.

"Go on."

"He was a man I was living with. I was being pressurised to marry him. But I didn't love him."

Over the next few minutes, she told him the story of Colin Enright and Trish and the unbearable pressure that had compelled her to pack in her job and flee to Spain. When she had finished, he gave a soft whistle.

"That sounds pretty scary. I can't say I blame you. If I had been in your position, I would probably have done the same."

"So you can see why I don't want to go back," she said.

"You're an adult, Emma. No one can force you to do anything against your will."

"I know that. But I don't want to face all that hassle again. Besides, I love it here. This is where I want to stay."

"What are you going to do? Do you plan to spend the rest of your life working at Casa Clara?"

"I don't know. But for the time being, I'm contented here. It's so peaceful. I've got some wonderful colleagues. And I really enjoy my work although it can get a bit hectic at times. But most of all I don't have to endure the relentless pressure from my sister."

At that moment, the waiter arrived with their meal and they started to eat. Tim fell on his steak like a man who hadn't seen food for a week.

"So what are *you* doing here?" Emma finally asked.

He wiped his lips. "Much the same as you. I packed in my job and decided to take a break."

"But I thought you enjoyed your work?"

"I got disillusioned. Then a few months ago something happened to bring matters to a head."

"What?"

She saw a shadow flit across his face.

"My wife died."

Chapter 31

Emma was lost for words, unable to know how to respond. The possibility that Tim's wife was dead had never once crossed her mind.

"I'm terribly sorry," she managed to say. "What happened?"

He sighed. "She got breast cancer."

"That's awful. How old was she?"

"Just thirty-three. She had a mastectomy but it wasn't successful. The cancer spread very quickly."

"Have you any children?"

He shook his head. "No. If we had children, I'm not sure how I would have managed. It was terrible to watch her die. She was so young and talented. She was a painter. Her career was on the verge of taking off when she got ill."

He stopped eating for a moment and looked across the table at Emma.

"When she died, it forced me to make a decision. I was becoming increasingly unhappy with my job. Her death made me look at what I was doing and where my life was going. I picked up the courage to do something I had always wanted to do."

He reached out and placed his hand on hers.

"Remember that lunch we had in the Shelbourne Hotel? I talked to you about my ambitions. I told you not everyone had the courage to do what they really wanted to in their hearts. Well, Sarah's death gave me that courage. I made up my mind to resign my job and become a full-time writer."

"You must miss her terribly."

He lowered his eyes. "I do. But not the way you think."

"Oh?"

"I won't pretend, Emma. The marriage was not a great success. In fact, it was very unhappy. We fought a lot. Sarah was very temperamental and she blamed me for holding back her career."

"Why?"

He took a sip of wine. "Her friends were mainly artistic people, designers and art dealers and people like that. I didn't like them. I thought they were shallow and insincere. But Sarah was convinced she had to cultivate them if she wanted to get her work noticed. Some of them were important figures in the art world and could arrange exhibitions and secure grants and stuff like that. I just didn't fit in with them and it caused friction. We were on the verge of separating when she got ill."

"But you must have loved her?"

"I did in the beginning. But you can grow out of love."

"How long were you married?"

"Seven years. Some people introduced us at a party. Sarah had just graduated from Art College. It was her idea to get married. All her friends were getting married and she decided it was the thing to do."

Emma sat silently trying to come to terms with the dramatic story that was unfolding. She had mixed emotions. She was sorry for him that his wife had died. Even if he didn't love her, they had been married for seven years and that must surely count for something. But his wife's death had also freed him to begin his life again.

"I don't think we should have got married," he continued. "At least, we shouldn't have rushed into it the way we did. We weren't really compatible. It would have been better if we had waited to see if we were suited."

"Don't blame yourself," she said. "How many people can honestly say they have never made a mistake?"

He sighed. "You're right, of course. Anyway, here I am. I have no job. But just like you, I'm really happy. I'm doing what I always wanted. I'm writing."

"So what do you live on?"

"I've got some savings. When that runs out, I'll look around for something."

"And what you are writing?"

"I've started a novel. It's coming along quite well. You know how fond I am of Yeats? This book is going to be about his early life, Maud Gonne and the Irish literary renaissance. It was a very remarkable period and he mixed with some extremely interesting people."

"It sounds fascinating," Emma said. "I'll look forward to reading it."

He smiled. "I've got to finish it first and then I have to persuade someone to publish it."

"I have faith in you," she said. "I know how passionate you are about Yeats. I've no doubt you'll succeed." She paused to sip her wine, then added, "Forgive me if I've been prying into your affairs."

"No, it's been good to talk. You can't keep these things bottled up. Life has to go on."

They finished their meal and the waiter came and took away their plates.

"Would you like some dessert?" he asked.

She shook her head. Her appetite had gone. "Let's go back," she said.

They strolled back along the beach. It was silent apart from the gentle sighing of the sea as it fell upon the shore. The air was still and warm. Above them, the sky was sprinkled with stars.

When they arrived at Casa Clara, Tim excused himself saying he was going to Cordoba the following day and wanted to get an early night. He said goodnight then kissed her gently on the cheek and climbed the stairs to his room.

But Emma's heart was racing. She knew she wouldn't sleep. She had heard so much tonight and now she had to digest it all. She went through the hall and out to the little courtyard. At once, she could smell the sweet scent of the flowers. She sat down on a bench beneath a palm tree and listened to the sound of the cicadas, chirping in the leaves above her head.

It was difficult to take in all she had been told. Her overwhelming emotion was sympathy for Tim. His problems were far greater than hers. He had lost his wife. There were times in the restaurant when she had to restrain the urge to comfort him. She could feel the affection which had never left her come surging back.

She leaned her head on the bench and stared at the vast sky. The heavens stared down at her, pockmarked by stars. As she sat in the deserted courtyard, listening to the gentle sound of the water tinkling in the fountain, she couldn't help reflecting how Fate had brought them together again. What were the odds against meeting Tim Devlin like this in Fuengirola, so far from Dublin? It had to mean something. Was it an omen, a sign of what might be coming?

At last, she heard a far-off church bell toll midnight. She had been sitting here for over an hour. She had another busy day tomorrow. It was time to get to bed. As she passed through the hall, Cristina came out of the little office beside the reception desk.

"So you are back. Did you have a nice dinner?"

"Very nice," Emma replied. "We went to El Molino."

"Oh, the food there is always good. You look very beautiful tonight."

"Thank you."

"And Señor Devlin, did he like it too?"

"Yes. He's a friend, Cristina, someone I knew in Dublin."

"Did he come to see you?"

"No, he came here by accident."

"He is very handsome, I think."

"Your judgment is good, Cristina. Señor Devlin is extremely handsome."

Cristina smiled and bent her head to some papers on her desk. "Goodnight, *Señorita*."

"Goodnight, Cristina."

She climbed the stairs to her room. Her heart felt light again. She got undressed in the moonlight and slipped between the cool white sheets.

* * *

By the time she came down the following morning, Tim had left for Cordoba. Emma had her regular swim and by eight o'clock was busy at the reception desk as the guests arrived for breakfast. She had a hectic morning. A tour group was arriving at lunchtime and she had to arrange the cleaning and prepare the paperwork. In the middle of it all, she had a phone call from Señor Gonzalez at Hotel Bonito to ask if she could help him out with two guests who had been double booked. As usual, the staff were on top of everything and the operation went off smoothly.

Around midday, she looked up to see Mrs Moriarty's milky blue eyes staring at her from the other side of the desk.

"Oh," Emma said, catching her breath. "You gave me a start."

"Don't tell me I've reached the stage where I go around frightening people?" the old lady said.

"That's not what I meant. I just didn't hear you coming."

"That's because you were so engrossed in your work. Still, I suppose it's a sign that you take your job seriously. That makes a welcome change around here."

"Thank you," Emma said, not sure if the remark was entirely a compliment.

"Can you be free tomorrow?" Mrs Moriarty demanded.

"I'm not sure. Why do you ask?"

"I'm inviting you to tea."

"In that case, I'll make sure to be free."

"I've enjoyed the last couple of occasions we had tea together. And Clive is coming too."

So it's Clive now, Emma thought. Matters are certainly coming along very well. It's not so long since he was being called a Black and Tan murderer.

"You bring a breath of fresh air to these occasions. We find it invigorating." There was an ironic smile now playing around the old woman's lips.

"What time?" Emma asked.

"Three o'clock?"

"I'd be delighted to accept."

"Good," Mrs Moriarty said. "We'll be expecting you." She leaned closer. "I see we've got another Irish person staying with us," she said, in a conspiratorial voice. "Quite a fetching young buck too, if I might say so."

So she had spotted Tim, Emma thought. Was there nothing that escaped her eagle gaze?

"Yes," she replied. "Mr Devlin. He's on the third floor."

"I've met him," Mrs Moriarty said triumphantly. "He's a very well-mannered young man. And he's travelling alone."

She fixed Emma with her beady eye.

"I wonder if I should invite him too?"

"He tends to go out a lot," Emma said quickly, aware that tea with Mrs Moriarty and the Major might not be exactly what Tim would regard as a jolly afternoon.

"Well, we'll see. The poor man could be lonely on his own in a foreign land. Anyway, you make sure to be there, young lady. We're depending on you."

Mrs Moriarty hobbled off into the courtyard, swinging her blackthorn stick playfully as she went. Emma watched her go before the sharp ring of the telephone recalled her to her duties.

By two o'clock, something approaching calm had descended on Casa Clara. She decided to go off and get something to eat. She asked Rosa to keep an eye on the reception desk while she was gone and set off into the early afternoon sun.

The resort was throbbing with life. The beaches along the Paseo Maretimo were packed with sunbathers and swimmers and the restaurants were doing a lively trade. But Emma preferred the little bars in the back streets of the old town were the Spanish went to eat. They were cheaper and cosier and she liked to listen to the local gossip spoken in the rapid Andalucian dialect which she was beginning to master. She found a quiet place near the town hall where she ordered a ham omelette, salad and sparkling water and sat under the shade of an umbrella while she ate.

When she had finished her lunch, she decided to drop into the internet café and check her emails. It was close by and when she arrived, she found it deserted. She sat down at a computer and logged on, then quickly navigated into her Hotmail account to find an email from Jackie waiting. She opened it at once.

It was a simple one-line message.

Contact me urgently. I have news for you.

She checked the date. The email had been sent only yesterday.

I wonder what it can be, she thought as she closed down the computer. Maybe Liam has proposed and they're going to get married and she wants to tell me all the details. Maybe she wants to ask me to be her bridesmaid. That could be tricky, she thought as she entered one of the phone booths and began to dial Jackie's number.

Immediately, it was picked up.

"Hi," she announced. "It's me, I got your message."

"Emma?"

"The very same."

But Jackie's response was not the cheery one she was expecting.

"Thank God," she said. "I wanted to warn you."

"Why, what's happened?"

"Trish knows you are in Fuengirola."

Chapter 32

Emma experienced a moment of shock but it quickly passed.

"How did she find out?"

"Don't ask me." Jackie said. "*I* didn't even know. All you told me was that you were on the Costa del Sol and that's a pretty big place."

"So how did *you* get involved?"

"She rang me yesterday," Jackie explained. "She said they knew you were in Fuengirola. She said Colin had managed to track your flight to Malaga. I reckon they put two and two together. Remember the holiday we had down there after the Leaving exams? Maybe that's what put it into their heads."

Yes, Emma thought. That's exactly how they'd figured it out. They put two and two together and came up with the right answer. "Listen, Jackie. This is important. Did she say if she knew for certain or do you think she was fishing?"

"Well, *you* know Trish better than I do. She sounded very confident. On the other hand, she could have been bluffing."

"Did she mention Casa Clara?"

"No. That's why she rang me. She gave me a long spiel about how I was your best friend and had a responsibility towards you and so on. She said you were suffering from a nervous breakdown and needed help."

Emma heard herself give a little gasp. So she had been right about that too. Ever since she read Trish's first email she had suspected this was what they would do. They would make up a story about her being sick in an effort to get her back.

"I'm not having a breakdown, Jackie. I know exactly what I'm doing. In fact I've never felt saner in my entire life."

"You don't have to tell me, Emma. But she sounded very convincing. She said they were worried in case you came to harm. She said I was the person you would confide in and I had a duty to tell her exactly where you were so you could get help."

My God, Emma thought, this is incredible. She felt anger boil up in her. This was the sort of thing that went on in authoritarian regimes. If you stepped out of line they said you were ill and locked you away in a psychiatric hospital.

"What did you tell her?"

"I said I didn't know anything. I told her all I had received was an email and I hadn't a clue where you were. But she was very determined. She really gave me the third degree."

"Did you tell her about our phone conversation?"

"No."

"Did she say anything about coming out here to find me?"

"No. But then she wouldn't, would she? She'd be afraid I'd tip you off."

"You're right. Did she say anything else?"

"No. She wasn't giving anything away. The whole conversation was geared towards getting information out of *me*."

Which means she doesn't know exactly where I am, Emma thought. She's still guessing. But that could change.

"Listen, Jackie, you did the right thing. And I'm very grateful. If she comes back to you again, tell her nothing. And don't believe a word of this nonsense about me being ill. This is just some rubbish they've come up with to excuse their own bullying. That's the real reason I left."

"I know."

"Now, I'm going to give you a number where you can contact me if you need to. Guard it with your life. Have you got a pen handy?"

"Fire away," Jackie said.

Emma gave her the number of the reception desk at Casa Clara.

"I'm usually there in the daytime except Saturday. That's my day off. Ring me immediately if you have any news."

"Does this mean you won't be coming back soon?" Jackie asked. "I really miss you."

"Not for the time being," Emma said. "But maybe when all this fuss has died down, you and Liam could come out here. I'll get you a cheap rate at Casa Clara."

"Oh, could we? That would be brilliant. I'll talk to him this evening. I desperately need a holiday. We both do. You wouldn't believe the awful weather we've been having."

"I've something else to report," Emma said.

"What?"

"Tim Devlin is here."

There was a stunned silence.

"You mean Tim Devlin our old teacher?"

"That's the man."

"Oh my God, I don't believe it. What's he doing there?"

"He's taking a break."

"You mean he just turned up out of the blue?"

"Exactly, he walked in off the street looking for a room. I thought I was seeing things."

"Is he still as hunky as he used to be?"

"Every bit."

"Is he on his own?"

"Yes."

281

"That's amazing," Jackie babbled. "Imagine the chances of that happening. You must be thrilled to bits."

"I'm flabbergasted, just like you."

"I'll bet you are. Do you still fancy him?"

"Before we go there, there's something else you should know. His wife died a few months ago."

"Oh dear," Jackie said. "That's sad. But, Emma . . ."

"Yes?"

"Nothing."

"Go on, speak your mind."

"I was going to say, if you still fancy him, it means the field is wide open for you."

* * *

Emma put down the phone and paid for the call and the use of the internet. She walked out into the bright afternoon sunshine with her head still full of the conversation with Jackie. She sat down at the nearest pavement café and ordered a coffee while she tried to order her thoughts.

One thing was now clear. Any hope that Trish had given up could be forgotten. She was as determined as ever that Emma should be brought back to Dublin and into the arms of Colin Enright. Well, it wasn't going to happen. But she still had the power to make Emma's life uncomfortable and cause her no end of trouble.

She had tracked her to Malaga but the rest was guesswork. If Trish was sure that she was in Fuengirola she wouldn't need to ring Jackie and pump her for information. And even if she had figured out where she was, Fuengirola was still a very big place. Unless she got very lucky, Trish could spend months looking for her in the town and still not find her. So long as she didn't know she was at Casa Clara, Emma was relatively safe.

This thought encouraged her. The passage of time had slowly lessened her sister's hold over her and now she was no longer afraid. Even if Trish managed to find her, she would face her down. She had built a new life at Casa Clara. Wild horses would not drag her back to Dublin and Colin Enright.

She looked at her watch and saw that she had been gone for over an hour. She had better get back to the Casa. It was unfair to leave Rosa in charge for so long.

But when she returned, she found the plump housekeeper comfortably reclining behind the desk, leafing through a celebrity gossip magazine she had found in the room of some departing guest.

"Were there any important calls?" Emma asked as she slipped in beside her.

"Nothing. Some people rang to ask about accommodation and I have written it down for you with the phone numbers as you requested, *Señorita*."

"That's very good. Thank you, Rosa."

"*De nada*." The housekeeper waved her hand.

Emma was beginning to get the impression that Rosa enjoyed these little spells of responsibility when she could sit behind the desk and look down her nose at the rest of the staff.

After Rosa had gone, she contacted the people who had called and set about arranging accommodation for them. Then she spent the remainder of the afternoon dealing with paperwork. At a quarter to six, Cristina turned up for duty dressed smartly in a crisp white blouse and dark skirt, her black hair carefully brushed and held in place by a simple black band.

She was proving more and more efficient. Emma had plans to promote her once she managed to disentangle Señora Alvarez for half an hour from her romantic involvement with Señor Montilla. But right now she was happy to hand over to her assistant after showing her which business was pending and what had still to be done. Then she skipped upstairs to her room. But she barely had time to shower and change into jeans and sweatshirt when she heard a sharp knock on her door.

She opened it to find Tim Devlin standing in the hall.

Emma tried to hide her surprise.

"Hi," he said with a grin. "I've been thinking about you all day."

"Well, that's nice to know," she replied, feeling a rush of pleasure at seeing him again.

"Yes. Even in the solitude of the grand mosque in Cordoba, you were on my mind. I enjoyed our little chat last night and I want to continue. But right now I've got to rush. I'm having dinner with some people I met on the bus. One of them might come in useful." He checked his watch. "What I was wondering was, would you be free for a drink later? Say around nine o'clock?"

She felt a smile break on her face. "I think I might be able to fit you into my busy schedule."

"Brilliant," he said. "That will really round off my day. Why don't I see you at that little bar across the road?"

"Bar Lorenzo?"

"That's it."

"Okay."

"I'll tell you all the biz when I see you later," he said and started down the stairs.

Once he had left, Emma opened her window and gazed out over the courtyard. The sun was going down, sinking like a great red orb into the shining waters of the sea. The scent of magnolia and orange blossom was already filling the evening air. Among the branches of the palm trees, the birds were settling down for the evening.

She closed her eyes and breathed in the night air. So Tim had missed her and wanted to see her again. She felt a familiar stirring in her breast. She could feel her imagination begin to soar. And this time, she didn't rein it in.

* * *

At five past nine she strolled into Bar Lorenzo. She had resisted the temptation to get dressed up and was still wearing her jeans and sweatshirt. But because it was Tim, she had put on a little make-up and sprayed a touch of perfume on her throat.

He was standing at the bar with a glass of beer in his hand. He beamed when he saw her.

"Come and sit down," he said, planting a kiss on her cheek and placing a strong hand across her shoulder as he led her to a table near the door.

"Now what would you like to drink?"

"I'll have a glass of white wine."

"You can have champagne if you prefer," he said. "This is a night for celebration."

"Oh?"

"Yes, indeed." He gave her a mysterious look. "I have good news."

"Champagne it is then," Emma agreed.

He returned with a bottle of *cava* in an ice bucket. He popped the cork and poured till the champagne was running down the sides of their glasses.

"To us!" he said, raising his glass in a toast. "Here's to success and to the future."

He touched his glass against Emma's and raised it to his lips.

"Aren't you going to tell me what we're celebrating?" she asked.

A smile crept across his sunburnt face. "You are looking at a man who may shortly receive a publishing contract."

"*What?*"

He slowly nodded his head. "These people I had dinner with?"

"Yes?"

"One of them works in publishing. We got talking on the bus and one thing led to another. I told him I was a writer and was working on a novel. He said he might be interested and asked to see some chapters. I brought them along tonight. He's going to take them back to London and show them to his boss."

She felt like throwing her arms around him. "Oh, Tim, that's fantastic! I'm so happy for you."

"I will admit I'm very pleased. But I don't want to get my hopes up," he said guardedly. "The editor in London might not like my stuff. But it's a start, Emma. It's a foot in the door. Even if they turn me down, I'll get a professional opinion on my writing. And that alone will be valuable."

"Oh, don't be so modest," she said. "I think its brilliant news. Of course, they'll like your work. Why wouldn't they? You're an English Literature scholar. You know what you're doing. You're not some dilettante who has decided to write a novel because he has nothing better to do."

"Well, thanks for your vote of confidence. But I prefer to wait and see."

"It will all turn out well," she said, taking his hand and giving it a little squeeze. "Think positive. Now tell me about this excursion today. It wasn't too hot in Cordoba, was it?"

"It was sweltering. But it was worth the inconvenience. And we were indoors a lot of the time. Have you ever been there?"

"Sadly not, but it's one of the places I intend to visit whenever I get time."

"You should go. It's a beautiful old city. It was worth it just to see the mosque. So what did you do all day? Tied to the reception desk, I suppose?"

Emma smiled. "More or less but I did manage to speak to my friend back in Dublin. Jackie Flynn. Do you remember her? She was in my class at St Benedict's."

"Was she a small, blonde girl with freckles?"

"That's her. She had some information for me. It turns out my sister has discovered I'm in Fuengirola."

"So? What's the big deal?"

"Hopefully nothing but she's putting about a story that I'm suffering from a nervous breakdown and need help."

"That's ridiculous," he said, putting down his glass.

"But these things have a way of being believed, Tim. And you have to admit, my behaviour *was* very odd. I just packed in my job and took off. It's not the sort of thing people do every day of the week."

"You had a perfectly good reason."

"I know. But what would other people think?"

"What are you worried about?" he asked.

"It crossed my mind that she might ask the Spanish police to find me."

He laughed. "Why on earth would they do that?"

"You don't know her, Tim. She can be very persuasive. I just don't want any more hassle. That's why I came here in the first place."

He waved his hand. "Forget it. The police are busy people. This is the height of the holiday season. There are thousands of tourists in Fuengirola. Why would they come looking for you?"

"If she told them I was mentally ill?"

"No," he said, shaking his head. "She'd need evidence, medical certificates, doctors' reports. The police aren't going to drop everything they're doing just because they get a phone call from Trish."

Hearing him talk so confidently banished any lingering fears.

"Stop worrying," he said. "It isn't going to happen."

It was almost midnight when they left the bar. As they strolled along the beach towards the Casa, Tim took her hand.

"Let me ask you something. What would you do if you could choose anything you wanted?"

"Stay on forever at Casa Clara."

"You have no doubts?"

"None whatsoever," Emma said.

"You would spend the rest of your life here?"

"Yes."

He stopped and turned to her. "You seem very certain."

"I am certain. I have never been so happy, Tim."

The only sound was the gentle sighing of the sea.

"Let me ask you something else."

"Sure."

"Would you mind if I kissed you?" he said.

She looked into his eyes as he drew her closer. They stared back at her with passionate intensity. His soft lips met hers. She felt herself explode with pleasure as he held her in a long, lingering embrace.

At last he released her.

"That was beautiful," he said.

"Yes," she said. "It was beautiful. You don't know this, but I have been waiting for that kiss for a very long time."

Chapter 33

"Now," Mrs Moriarty said, handing Tim a cup of tea. "You don't mind looking after your own requirements, do you? There's milk and sugar on the table. Help yourself."

"Thank you," Tim said as he reached for the milk jug. "I don't take sugar and I only have a little drop of milk."

Mrs Moriarty bathed him in a benevolent smile. "*Exactly* the way tea should be drunk, Mr Devlin. Isn't that right, Clive?"

She turned her attention to Major Sykes who was dressed in cavalry twill trousers, shirt, cravat and grey pullover despite the heat.

"Rather!" the old soldier growled in agreement.

They were seated around the dining table in Mrs Moriarty's room: Emma, Tim, the old lady and the Major. On the table, as well as the tea things was a large chocolate fudge cake which Mrs Moriarty was now cutting expertly into slices. The window to the terrace was open and a cooling breeze wafted around the room.

All morning, Emma had been looking forward to this occasion since Tim had told her that he had also been invited.

She had wakened with memories of the night still fresh in her mind – the stroll along the beach and that wonderful moment when he had taken her in his arms and kissed her.

She could still feel his lips pressing softly on hers. That kiss had sealed all her expectations. It was the kiss she had been longing for since she had first fallen under his spell all those years before. And now here he was, the object of her desire, sitting beside her on a sunny afternoon in Spain while Mrs Moriarty cut up chocolate cake and dispensed advice about making tea.

"You must bring the teapot to the kettle," she said decisively. "That is essential. And you must warm the pot. And of course you must only use real tea leaves. You can't expect to make a proper cup of tea with these new-fangled bags they're going in for nowadays. They're a complete waste of time, if you want my opinion. Isn't that so, Clive?"

Major Sykes shifted the little tabby bundle that was purring contently in his lap and added his assent.

"Well, this tea is wonderful," Tim agreed. "I haven't tasted anything like it since I was a boy. It's like the tea my mother used to make."

"Your mother must have been a very discerning woman," Mrs Moriarty said, placing a slice of cake onto a plate and handing it to him. "She obviously knew a thing or two."

Next, she turned her attention to Emma.

"What about you, my dear?"

Emma had only eaten a croissant for breakfast and the cake looked particularly inviting.

"I'll just have a small piece."

"Tsk, tsk, there's no such thing as a small piece. We don't cater for dainty appetites," the old lady declared and proceeded to hack out a giant slice and pass it to Emma.

"I see you've made a little friend," Emma said to Major Sykes, pointing to the kitten curled up in his lap.

"Granuaille," Mrs Moriarty said.

"Is that what you've decided to call her?"

"Yes. I think it's very fitting. She was a warrior queen, you know. Ruled the whole of Connaught and struck terror into any man who gave her any nonsense. She was a credit to her sex and an example to all of us."

Tim smiled across the table at Emma.

"How is she settling in?" Emma asked.

"Perfectly. She has her litter tray on the terrace. And Clive has very kindly constructed a little kennel for her." She beamed at Major Sykes who smiled back adoringly. "And she has her basket under the table and her feeding dish. She couldn't be more content."

"She has never tried to escape?"

"No. Why should she? She's perfectly happy where she is. Aren't you, Granuaille?" Mrs Moriarty said, reaching out and stroking the kitten. It purred with satisfaction and rolled over to have its tummy tickled.

"Well, I'm glad everything has worked out so well," Emma said.

"It couldn't have been better. And in the evenings, Clive has agreed to accompany me while she takes a little exercise around the garden. On a leash of course."

Major Sykes was on the verge of purring himself.

Mrs Moriarty cut more cake and passed a slice to Emma.

"I couldn't possibly eat any more," she protested.

"Nonsense," Mrs Moriarty responded with a sharp click of her tongue. "I know how much you like it. Besides, you need to keep up your energy levels, standing at that reception desk all day long dealing with those lunatics. Now tell me something. When is Tomàs going to marry that poor girl, Teresa? He can't keep her hanging on forever."

"I think there's been a hitch. Their new house isn't ready."

"Oh dear, I hope they get it finished soon. The change that

has come over that girl is incredible. She looks like a new woman, so serene, so confident. I've seen that look before. I know what it means."

"Yes," Emma replied.

Mrs Moriarty studied her closely. "Talking of which, you look particularly radiant yourself today."

Emma felt a blush creep into her cheeks. She sneaked a glance at Tim who smiled sympathetically and took another sip of tea.

The party continued very pleasantly. They sat in Mrs Moriarty's room while outside the window the afternoon drowsed on. Major Sykes talked about life in the army and lamented the way the world had changed for the worse.

"No discipline, you see. Young people today don't know the meaning of the word. When the government scrapped military service, it was the beginning of the end. Things have gone to hell in a handcart ever since."

Mrs Moriarty heartily agreed. She got onto her favourite topic of good manners and how they were no longer taught in schools. Emma and Tim listened patiently and occasionally exchanged amused glances across the table. Before Emma realised, it was a quarter past four and time to return to her desk.

"I've thoroughly enjoyed myself," she said. "But I really must get back to work. Thank you very much, Mrs Moriarty."

"No need to thank me, my dear. We've enjoyed it too. Haven't we, Clive?"

"Damned right," the Major agreed.

Tim stood up and added his thanks. "Best cup of tea I've tasted in years," he said, taking Mrs Moriarty's hand while she beamed with pleasure.

"I hope you're not feeling lost," she said, looking softly at him. "You know you can always drop in here for a chat anytime you're passing my door."

"I'm not lost," Tim laughed.

"No, I suppose not," Mrs Moriarty agreed giving him a final

look-over. "Good-looking fella like you would never be lost in a place like this."

Tim accompanied Emma back downstairs, barely able to conceal his mirth.

"Whatever made her feel I was lost?" he asked when they arrived at reception.

"She was probing," Emma said. "Don't be fooled by her exterior. Mrs Moriarty is as shrewd as they come. There's nothing goes on around here that she doesn't know about."

He left Emma at reception saying he was going for a walk along the beach.

"What have you planned for this evening?" he asked.

"I'm free."

"So why don't we have dinner again?"

"Okay."

"Same time, seven o'clock?"

"Sure."

"Right," Tim said, as he walked confidently towards the door. "I'll see you here at seven."

She watched him stride out into the bright afternoon sunshine. She felt a strange sensation, as if she was floating on air. She had felt it all day. And Mrs Moriarty had noticed it too when she commented about how radiant she looked. She missed nothing. Was it possible that she had guessed about Tim and her?

But Emma didn't care. She felt so happy that she didn't mind who knew. The man she had idolised since she was a young girl had turned up on her doorstep and suddenly all her problems paled into insignificance. Her job, her sister Trish, Colin Enright, none of it mattered any more, now that Tim Devlin was back in her life again.

Rosa was sitting at the reception desk with a grin on her face as she watched Tomàs carry a ladder out to the courtyard to begin trimming the trees.

She certainly looks as if she has been enjoying herself, Emma thought.

"Thank you for standing in, Rosa," she said. "I appreciate it."

"It is nothing, *Señorita*."

"Have you been busy?"

The plump housekeep shrugged nonchalantly and showed Emma the list of phone calls she had logged and the queries she had dealt with in her absence. Those that still required Emma's attention had been set aside.

"Señor Gonzalez called. He wanted to know if we could take a guest with a dog."

"A dog?"

Si, Señorita." Rosa laughed silently as if to say there are a lot of crazy people in the world.

Emma thought of Mrs Moriarty's reaction if someone appeared in the Casa with a dog. There would be skin and hair flying if it should meet up with her cat.

"What did you tell him, Rosa?"

"I told him we were full up."

"You did the right thing. If we took a dog in here, our guests would all be gone by the morning. Honestly, some of the requests we receive!"

The housekeeper took her leave and went off chuckling to herself while Emma got on with her work. She quickly skipped through the chores and left a clean desk for Cristina when she arrived to take over at a quarter to six.

She went up to her room and opened the window. Down below, Tomàs was busy at his work and had been joined by old Paco. The ground around the courtyard was covered in branches and leaves. But by tomorrow all the debris would be cleared away and the light would shine more clearly into the little courtyard.

She lay on the bed and considered the strange feeling that had overtaken her. Was this how love felt, she wondered. Was this what the poets tried to express when they wrote their love songs? It was as if nothing else mattered but the intense emotion she felt for Tim and the knowledge that it was being returned. She lay in this dreamy state till at last she glanced at her watch and saw it was now half past six. Better start getting ready for my dinner date, she thought as she rose and began to get undressed.

She was just stepping out of the shower when she heard a knock at the door. Damn, she thought. All I need right now is a crisis at reception. Pulling a towel around her, she went and opened the door.

Tim was standing in the hall.

"What is it?" she said in surprise. "Is something wrong?"

"I sincerely hope not," he replied, pushing past her into the room and closing the door firmly behind him.

"So what are you doing here?"

"I couldn't wait any more," he whispered as he took her in his arms and his lips caressed her shoulders. "I've been thinking about you all afternoon. I couldn't get you out of my mind."

His mouth closed firmly on hers. Emma felt her heart beat furiously and desire cascade along her spine.

Her arms went round his neck as she returned his kiss. She felt the towel slip away till her naked body was pressed tight against his. Gently, he lowered her onto the bed and she surrendered herself in hurried, panting gasps of pleasure.

Chapter 34

Afterwards, they lay in the tangled sheets, their bodies drenched in sweat. Emma felt sated. Tim Devlin's lovemaking had been everything she could have desired. She glanced at the gorgeous man who lay beside her on the bed, his strong chest covered in a web of glistening hair, his stomach flat and taut as a drum, the rippling muscles along his neck and arms, the brown eyes and black shiny hair that fell in disorder across his brow. He looked like a God.

He stirred and placed a gentle kiss on her forehead. "Thank you," he murmured.

Emma lay still, listening to the steady rhythm of her heart.

"I have wanted you ever since that day we had lunch together in Dublin," he said. "Do you ever think of it?"

"I have never forgotten it," she said.

"I left you outside to go and meet Sarah. But it was with a sense of foreboding. Our marriage was coming apart. It seemed to have descended into constant arguments and long silences. I remember thinking how much I would have preferred to spend the rest of the day with you."

"I wanted you long before that," she said.

"I never knew."

"I was too young," Emma said. "But the longing never left me. No man I have ever met has measured up to you."

He drew her close. "Don't you think it's strange that our paths have crossed once more? It's as if some greater power has arranged things."

"Yes," she said, burying her head in his broad chest.

He ran his fingers through her long dark hair and bent to kiss her once more.

"We have been given a second chance," he said. "We should make the most of it."

Emma closed her eyes. Finally they had made love and now she was lying naked in his arms.

"What are we going to do?" she said. "You'll leave me and return to Dublin."

"No," he said. "I'll stay."

She felt her heart jump. "Are you serious?"

"Yes. There's nothing dragging me back there."

"I would have to check the register. I'll do it right away."

She went to get up but he held her.

"Leave it till the morning. I'm sure you'll manage something." He drew her closer. "I'm determined to be with you, Emma, even if I have to sleep on the beach. And besides, I'm getting good work done on my book. My head is bursting with ideas and this is the perfect place to write."

She snuggled in his arms, her heart beating wildly in her breast. "We'll have to be careful," she said. "The staff are not supposed to fraternise with guests."

"But I'm more than a guest. Now I'm your lover."

She smiled at the sound of the word. It captured the transformation that had taken place in her life. Tim Devlin was no longer some distant object of her desire. Now he had become her lover.

"Nevertheless, I don't want any gossip around the Casa. It's a small place and word travels fast. Mrs Moriarty doesn't miss a thing."

"I'll be careful," he said.

* * *

The following morning, as soon as she got to reception, she eagerly set about the task of rearranging the bookings so that Tim could stay. It wasn't easy. The holiday season was in full swing and the Casa had been booked solid for many months in advance. But Emma was on a mission. This wasn't some casual guest who had happened along looking for a room. This was the man she loved. And now that Tim Devlin had come back into her life, she wasn't going to let him go so easily.

Eventually, with some judicious juggling and some doubling-up, she achieved her objective. He could have his room for three more weeks. She was so pleased that she went immediately to tell him.

She found him seated at a laptop at a little table beside the window where he could look out towards the sea. He was dressed in khaki shorts and T-shirt. A mug of cold coffee sat before him on the table. The moment she entered, he rose and took her in his arms and covered her in kisses.

"Not now," she said, gently pushing him off. "I'm on duty at the desk. I've just come to tell you that I've managed to rearrange the accommodation. You can keep this room for three more weeks."

He looked surprised, as if he had half expected to be disappointed. "Oh, Emma, that's terrific." He took her in his arms again. "You're a princess. I hope I didn't force some poor devil onto the street?"

"No, you didn't. I juggled the bookings. And when the three weeks are up, if you haven't grown tired of me, we'll juggle the bookings again."

"I won't ever grow tired of you, Emma."

He took her in his arms and kissed her again.

She smiled. "Now you can relax and get on with writing your masterpiece."

* * *

Over the next few days, they fell into a routine. Now that he had the possibility of a publishing contract, Tim wanted to concentrate on his novel. He came down for breakfast each morning at eight and then disappeared back to his room where he usually stayed till the afternoon when he went for a long walk on the beach. Emma didn't have much contact with him till the evenings, when they met for dinner and he would tell her how his work was coming along.

One evening, he said to her: "You won't believe this but I wrote over 2000 words today."

"Is that a lot?" she asked. She had no idea how much writers managed to achieve.

"For me, it is. Normally I'm very slow. But since I've been here, the stuff just seems to come pouring out of me. It's so peaceful. I have no distractions, no phones ringing, no people looking for me. This is what I needed, Emma."

"Well, I'm pleased for you," she said. "I want you to be happy."

He put down his wineglass and took her hand. "I'm certainly happy. But it's not just the peace and quiet of the Casa. It's more than that. It's knowing that you are beside me."

She lowered her face.

"Look at me," he said.

She looked into his eyes.

"When a man's in love, he can do amazing things. He can move mountains. Do you hear what I'm saying?"

"I think so."

"I'm telling you that I love you, Emma."

She let the words resonate in her head. This was what she had longed for but so often thought she would never hear.

"I love you too," she said. "I have always loved you."

* * *

As the time slipped by, Emma found herself drifting along on a beautiful wave of contentment. She had never been so happy in her life. She was so wrapped up in Tim that she didn't realise she had heard nothing from Señora Alvarez till the weekend arrived and she didn't turn up for her weekly English lesson. She wondered what was happening. She rang her number and got the housekeeper who assured her that the *Señora* was well and had just gone away for a few days.

"When will she be back?"

"I don't know, *Señorita*. She went on a trip with Señor Montilla."

Ah, Emma thought, that explains everything.

"If you have a problem, I could try to find her," said the housekeeper.

"No," Emma said. "There is no problem. It's all right. I'll speak to her when she returns."

She put down the phone with a smile on her face. The courtship must be coming to a head, she thought. Any day soon, I expect to hear the sound of wedding bells.

She wasn't wrong. A few days later, she lifted the phone to hear the *Señora*'s voice. She sounded in a very cheerful mood.

"*Buenos días*," she chirped. "You have been looking for me, *Señorita*. Is something the matter?"

"No," Emma explained. "Everything is well. You didn't come for your lesson so I called you. It was nothing."

"I apologise. I had to go away at the small notice."

"Short notice," Emma corrected.

"Of course, short notice. Señor Montilla and I have been to Madrid."

300

"That must have been very nice."

"It was wonderful. Have you ever been there, *Señorita*?"

"No. But I intend to go sometime."

"So you should. We stayed in Hotel Sofia. You don't know it but it is a very grand hotel. Everything is in the top form."

"Top class," Emma said.

"Yes, top class. It is a hotel with five stars. Five! You cannot get any more than that. Everything is the very best quality. The floors are marble. They have chandeliers on the ceilings. And the drapes are made from the finest fabrics."

"It sounds beautiful," Emma agreed.

"It *is* beautiful. If only you could have seen it."

"I'm sure you had a very nice time there."

"We had a wonderful time and Señor Montilla had a little surprise for me."

"Yes?"

The *Señora* lowered her voice and now she sounded conspiratorial. "He asked me to marry him."

"I'm so happy for you," Emma said, genuinely pleased. "Congratulations! That is very exciting news."

"Yes. Señor Montilla is a very good man. He will make an excellent husband."

"When is the wedding planned?" Emma asked.

"In two months. Señor Montilla wants to have it soon. It will mean a lot of arrangements in a very short time."

"But I'm sure you will enjoy it. The planning is one of the great pleasures of a wedding."

"Maybe, but there will be so much to do. There is the wedding dress and the guest list and the reception and, of course, the church. I think I will not find a moment to breathe."

Now was the time to ask something that had been on Emma's mind.

"What will happen to Casa Clara?"

Señora Alvarez sighed.

"I will be very busy. I will be managing Señor Montilla's home. It is so big and he has so many staff. It will be a full-time job for me."

Emma held her breath. Did this mean that the *Señora* was going to ask her to assume the full-time management of the hotel?

"Have you decided what you are going to do?"

"Yes," Señora Alvarez said. "I think I will sell it."

Chapter 35

The *Senora*'s reply left Emma reeling. This was a thunderbolt. She said goodbye and put down the phone with a shaking hand and felt a knot of fear tighten in her stomach. It was terrible news. It was the worst news she could have heard. She had always suspected that the *Señora*'s marriage would mean changes around Casa Clara but it had never occurred to her that she would actually sell the hotel.

The awful reality came crashing in on her like a series of blows. There would be new owners and they would have their own ideas about how to run the place. They might even bring in their own management team. This thought sent a shiver down her spine. It would be a disaster. It would mean the end of her idyllic existence. And it could spell trouble too for Teresa and Tomàs and the rest of the staff. Why did this have to happen just when everything was working so well for her?

At that moment, she looked up and saw Tim come striding into the hall from his afternoon walk.

"Something the matter?" he whispered. "You look upset."

"I *am* upset," she said. "I've just come off the phone with Señora Alvarez."

"Oh? Was she annoyed about something?"

"Quite the contrary, she was deliriously happy. She's getting married."

"So, what's the problem?"

"She's talking about selling the Casa. Oh, Tim, this is terrible news. I don't know what's going to happen."

"Right," he said, immediately taking control of the situation. "We need to talk. When can you get away?"

"An hour?"

"See me in my room as soon as you're free."

Emma tried very hard to remain calm as she busied herself with the routine work of the Casa and at six o'clock she handed over to Cristina. She had decided to say nothing to the staff. She knew how quickly bad news could travel and she didn't want to be responsible for any rumours that started to fly. Besides, it was Señora Alvarez's role to break any news about the Casa's future.

But it was with a heavy heart that she climbed the stairs to Tim's room. She found him bent over his laptop. When he saw her, he got up and closed the door. Then he took her in his arms and kissed her.

He pointed to a chair and Emma sat down.

"Now just try to relax. We'll get to the bottom of this. Tell me exactly what Señora Alvarez said."

"It was only a very brief conversation. I asked her what she was going to do with the Casa when she got married and she said she was thinking of selling."

"And you're afraid the new owners will change everything?"

"Worse than that, they could fire us."

"But she didn't say she was *definitely* going to sell?"

"No. But I got the sense that's the way her mind is working. And that's why I'm worried. I have a cosy lifestyle here, Tim. I work hard but Señora Alvarez leaves me alone. You've seen the way we all get on so well together like one big happy family. I'd like it to continue."

"Maybe you're getting a little bit ahead of yourself," he said, trying to cheer her up. "She might not sell. And even if she does, the new owners could decide to leave everything exactly as it is."

But Emma was fast sinking into a depression. "You're wrong," she insisted. "New people *always* make changes. There are so many things that could be done with Casa Clara if there was spare cash available. If Señora Alvarez sells, the place will not remain as it is, believe me."

He thought for a moment. "When is she getting married?"

"In two months' time."

"Well, that gives us a breathing space, I suppose. I can understand why you're worried. But we're not going to solve this problem tonight. Why don't you put it out of your head and we'll talk again tomorrow. In the meantime, let's decide where we're going to eat this evening."

Emma went off to get ready, feeling somewhat relieved. Just talking to Tim seemed to have calmed her down. But despite his best attempts to cheer her up, she didn't enjoy the meal. She couldn't shake off this new worry and she was glad when she finally returned to her room and slipped under the sheets.

* * *

The following morning when she came down to breakfast, she found Tim waiting for her.

"I've been thinking this over and I might have a solution," he said.

Immediately, she felt her spirits lift. "What?"

"I'll tell you later. Now do you think you could slip away from the desk for half an hour?"

"What time?"

"About eleven o'clock? Meet me on the beach and we'll go for a walk. I'll explain it to you then."

At five to eleven, she asked Rosa to cover for her. She had spent the morning wondering what scheme Tim had come up with and whether it would work. But she trusted him. If there was a way out of this dilemma she was sure he would find it.

He was waiting for her at the gate and they set off along the beach. It was practically deserted at this time of the morning except for some sea birds foraging at the edge of the shore. By now, the sun was high in the sky and it was warm.

"Let me ask you something," he began. "Is Casa Clara profitable?"

"It's very profitable," Emma replied. "It's booked up practically all the year round. Staff numbers are small, so overheads are low. And there are ways to make it even more profitable."

"Like what?"

"Well, at present, we only serve breakfast. But if the kitchen was expanded, we could serve lunch and dinner and even open it to the general public. That old courtyard is perfect. Can you imagine having dinner there in the evening? People would pay for the privilege."

"Anything else?"

"If someone was prepared to spend money they could upgrade the premises, give it a general overhaul, put in a lift and air-conditioning. The place badly needs redecoration. I'm not talking about spending vast sums of money. And they would get the return in increased prices."

"So why would Señora Alvarez want to sell?"

"Because she's going to have her hands full as the new mistress of Señor Montilla's mansion and that's a job she'll thoroughly enjoy. Besides, she has never had any real interest in Casa Clara. She inherited it and it gives her a comfortable income but her heart isn't really in it."

"What sort of price would she expect to get?"

She shrugged. "It's difficult to say. I haven't got much idea about property values here in Fuengirola."

"But they're a lot cheaper than at home?"

"Oh, certainly, why do you ask?"

"An idea has occurred to me. You told me your dearest wish would be to stay here at Casa Clara. Well, my dearest wish is to remain with you."

She laid her head on his shoulder.

"So why don't *we* buy it?" he asked.

For a moment she thought she was hearing things.

"Us?"

"Why not?"

"But how could we afford it? What would we use for capital?"

"That depends what price she asks. We both have assets back in Dublin. You have your apartment. I have the house I shared with Sarah. They may have fallen in value since the recession but they would still sell for more than we paid for them. It may not be impossible like you think, Emma." He was getting into his stride. "And you have run the Casa for the past four months. You've learned all there is to know about it. The staff trusts you. You could make Cristina the manager while you concentrated on the overall running of the place. It would be perfect."

"And what would *you* do?"

"I would write of course. I've told you how much I like this place. This is the ideal location for me."

She closed her eyes. To own Casa Clara, to live here for the foreseeable future with the man she loved? It sounded wonderful. But was it feasible?

"Oh, Tim, it would be marvellous. It would be like a dream. But don't you think we're aiming too high?"

"No, we're not. If needs be, we could borrow some money. So what do you think?"

She flung her arms around his neck. "Do you really think it's possible?"

"That depends on Señora Alvarez. We've got to talk to her.

When we get back to the Casa why don't you ring and set up an appointment? The worst thing she can do is turn us down."

*　*　*

Señora Alvarez sounded surprised when Emma rang to say she would like to speak urgently about an important matter that had arisen.

"I have so much to do," she protested. "This afternoon, the dressmaker is coming to take fittings for my wedding dress. And this evening Señor Montilla is taking me to a concert in Marbella. Can this business not wait?"

"No. I must speak with you."

In the end, Señora Alvarez agreed to a meeting at lunchtime the following day. She would see Emma at Bar Lorenzo. She made it sound as if the appointment was causing her enormous inconvenience.

In the meantime, Tim had been busy making his own phone calls and had managed to locate an estate agent who agreed to give them an estimate of property values in the small hotel sector. The man was from Limerick and had been running an estate agency in Fuengirola for the past five years. He said he would see them that afternoon.

Pat Sheehan turned out to be a dapper figure sporting a deep sun tan and a smart suit and tie and exuding an air of optimism that Emma had come to associate with property agents. He met them in his office on the Paseo Maretimo.

"Coffee?" he asked, after his young secretary had shown them into his large air-conditioned office and they were seated across from him at a vast desk.

They both declined.

"So how can I help you?" he asked, checking his shirt cuffs and reclining in a comfortable swivel-chair.

Tim opened the discussion while Emma sat quietly by his side. He explained that they were interested in purchasing a small hotel beside the sea. He described Casa Clara exactly without mentioning it by name.

"So you want to know what you might be expected to pay?"

"Exactly," Tim said.

"Well, there's no big mystery about it. Property here is no different to property anywhere else. The price will be dictated by square footage, state of repair and, crucially, location. I don't need to tell you that a place by the sea will fetch a higher price than something that's miles away from the beach."

Tim and Emma exchanged a glance.

"Can you give us a rough idea?" Tim asked.

"Going on what you've told me, I'd say you could expect to pay upwards of a million euros. Depends how much interest there is and how quickly the vendor wants to sell."

Emma couldn't remain silent any longer.

"A million euros?" she asked, taken aback.

"Possibly more. I'd need to see this place to give you a proper estimate."

"So what should we do?" Tim asked.

"Find out if the owners are interested in selling. Don't appear too keen. Get them to give you a ball-park figure for price. Bear in mind that you'll also have legal fees and property taxes to pay. If you're still interested come back to me and we'll decide the next move."

He stood up and shook hands again. As he showed them out of his office, he paused before a large artist's impression of a new development of houses. It looked spectacular with waving palm trees and lean, sophisticated couples sipping drinks at poolside tables.

"I couldn't interest you in a nice villa in Puerto Banus?" he said with a salesman's confident smile. "It's got three bedrooms and a swimming pool for just €500,000. I'll give you a discount because you're Irish."

"I think we'll pass right now," Tim said with a smile. "But thanks for your time and advice."

Back out on the street, Emma turned to him with a downcast face.

"Where are we going to get a million euros?"

But Tim was much more upbeat. "Don't give up so easily. Let's find out what we can secure for our own properties in Dublin. In fact, I know someone who just might be able to help."

They found a quiet bench beside the beach. Tim took out his mobile phone and dialled a number.

While he talked, Emma stared out at the sea as it gently washed the shore. The idea of owning Casa Clara was a beautiful dream. But she had to be realistic. A million euros was an enormous sum of money. And that was only the beginning. There would be the additional costs that Pat Sheehan had mentioned and they would need even more money to refurbish the kitchen and expand the dining facilities and hire extra staff. The more she thought about it, the more impossible it seemed.

Beside her on the bench, Tim was already deep in conversation. At last, he snapped his phone shut and turned to her.

"That was Barry Moncrief. He's a journalist I know on one of the property supplements back home."

"And?" Emma asked, afraid to allow her hopes to rise.

"I've got good news and bad news. The market in Dublin is going through a very bad patch right now. People are holding on to their money. But Barry says there are still buyers. He reckons with a bit of luck, we could get €800,000 for our two properties."

"Aren't you forgetting something? You still have to pay off your mortgage.?

"I hadn't forgotten. But we're in the ballpark, Emma. And we've got a fighting chance."

* * *

The following morning, Emma woke at seven o'clock. She had a shower and spent a little longer than usual getting dressed and putting on her make-up. Then she had breakfast and took her place once more at the reception desk. She felt the time crawl along but eventually lunchtime arrived and with it the scheduled meeting with her employer. She had already arranged with Cristina to cover for her.

She made her way across the road to the bar where Tim was already waiting. He had spent the morning doing sums and had worked out that if they sold their Dublin properties for the price Barry Moncrief had suggested, they would have about €650,000 to spend after paying off bank debts and setting aside sufficient finance to cover taxes and legal fees.

"It not enough," Emma said, dismally. "And you haven't factored in the renovation costs." She had been thinking of nothing else since yesterday's conversation with Tim and had been struggling to keep her hopes alive.

"Well, we're about to find out," Tim said, as Señora Alvarez's car pulled into the side of the road and she got out.

"I think you should do the talking," he continued. "She knows you. She will certainly trust you more than me."

"Okay."

"But if you need me to come in at any stage, just nod. How do you feel?"

"Nervous."

"Try to relax. If she turns us down, it's not the end of the world."

The Señora approached in a great bustle of complaints and perspiration. She sat down and opened her fan and began to wave it furiously.

"Oh, the pressure I am under! You have no idea. My dressmaker is a fool and the wedding photographer is a crook. I have fired him already. Now I must find another."

She allowed Emma to introduce her to Tim and accepted her invitation to have a cold beer with them.

"Now," she said. "What is the purpose of this meeting?"

311

"It is about Casa Clara," Emma replied, summoning all the courage she could muster.

"You said you might sell it when you marry Señor Montilla."

"That is right. But you do not have to be concerned, *Señorita*. I will recommend you to the new owners. I will tell them what an efficient worker you are. Your job will be safe."

"Have you got a purchaser in mind?"

Señora Alvarez threw her hands in the air, as if to say "Do you think I have the time to worry about Casa Clara when I am marrying someone as important as Señor Montilla?"

"No, *Señorita*. Not yet. Why do you ask?"

"Because we are interested in buying it."

Señora Alvarez looked amazed. But she quickly regained her composure.

"*You* would buy Casa Clara?"

"If the price was right," Emma continued, quickly.

"What would you do with it?"

"I would keep it exactly as it is. I know how much you revere the memory of your poor dead husband Miguel who built it."

This was exactly the right note to strike because Señora Alvarez immediately managed to squeeze a tear from her left eye and sniffed into her handkerchief.

"You are right. Poor Miguel. He would be so disappointed to see the Casa turned upside down by some cheap developer. You know he named it after his mother?"

"Yes," Emma continued.

"If only you could have met him, *Señorita*. He was such a wonderful man. He was the fire of my life."

"Light," Emma said, unconsciously correcting her.

"That is right. And then he died and left me broken-hearted. The grief I feel is almost too much to bear. Except that Señor Montilla is so kind and understanding I would not have survived. I would be with Miguel in the grave." At this, she let out a sob and began fanning herself again.

"You know how devoted I am to the Casa," Emma went on. "If you sold it to me I would continue Miguel's tradition. I would keep it as a monument to his memory for everyone to see. You could come back to visit whenever you liked."

At these words, Señora Alvarez began to weep in earnest. "A monument to Miguel, that is so beautiful! You have the most sympathetic imagination, Señorita Frazer."

"I think it would be fitting," Emma went on. "He was the man with the vision to develop the Casa. It was his brainchild."

Señora Alvarez grabbed Emma's hand and held it tightly. "The child of his brain, that is exactly right. That is what Casa Clara is. That is how I would like him to be remembered. And Señor Montilla would agree also. He is a most understanding gentleman."

"So do you think you might sell to us?" Emma pressed.

Señora Alvarez considered for a moment. "What price would you pay me?" she asked at last.

"We are not wealthy like Señor Montilla," Emma explained. "We have a small budget."

"Six hundred thousand euros," Tim said from across the table.

Señora Alvarez stopped fanning and stared at him. It was as if he had just insulted her.

"No, *Señor*, it is not possible."

"We might be able to go a bit higher," Tim said.

But Señora Alvarez was not in a mood to haggle. Her face had now become hard and businesslike.

"I will sell it to you, *Señor* but only if you give me one million euros. I cannot accept a single peseta less."

Chapter 36

After she had gone, Tim and Emma stared at each other.

"I think we can forget about it," she said, sadly.

Tim's enthusiasm had evaporated. For the first time, he looked every bit as crestfallen as she did.

"It seems an awful pity."

"We have to be realistic. Where are we going to find the extra money?"

"We could try the banks," he suggested.

Emma was busy shaking her head. "It's useless, Tim. Let's face it we're never going to be able to buy Casa Clara. It's impossible."

But Tim wasn't about to give up yet. "No, I think we should try every option. I'm not letting go without a fight."

He settled the bill for the drinks and they made their way back to the Casa under a cloud of despair. When Emma arrived at the reception desk, Cristina looked at her closely and asked if she was all right.

"You look like you had a shock," she said.

Emma tried to smile. "I'm just feeling tired, that's all."

"If you would like to lie down for a while, I can continue to work here. I don't mind." But Emma waved her offer aside. "That's very kind but I will manage. Thank you for helping me out. Now just go off and enjoy the rest of the day. I'll see you at six o'clock."

Cristina slipped away saying she had some shopping to do before the stores closed for siesta and Emma was left to face the rigours of the reception desk on her own. Thankfully, it was busy and the work took her mind off the crushing disappointment she had just suffered. She had been foolish to get her hopes up. Owning Casa Clara was a beautiful dream but that was all. And like most dreams it had evaporated in the harsh light of reality.

But at least Señora Alvarez had given her word to speak to the new owners on her behalf. Hopefully, her job would be safe. But what about the others? What would happen to Paco and Rosa and Tomàs and Teresa and the rest of the staff who had given loyal service to Casa Clara for so long? And what about Cristina who had been so willing and helpful? Where would they go? And would Emma be able to continue working here when all her friends had gone?

* * *

Over the next few days, she forced herself to keep up a cheerful front. But it was a trial. Daytime was not so bad because she had work to distract her but at night when she crept under the sheets she felt the sadness come over her like a dark shroud. She had allowed herself to glimpse a future that held such promise but it had been dashed and now she didn't know what lay in store. Her dream had crumbled into dust.

Tim, meanwhile, refused to let go. Every morning, he shaved and dressed in his best suit and tie and set off to talk to bank managers and financiers in the hope of raising the extra cash. But each evening he came back to the Casa with a long face. It seemed there were so many obstacles. He wasn't Spanish. He didn't have a business record. He had nobody to act as guarantor for him and he had no references. He didn't have a permanent residence in the country. In the end, he had to admit that he had very little hope of borrowing the money in Spain.

"I'm going to see if I can raise the cash in Ireland," he told Emma one evening as they were having dinner in the old town. "At least we speak the same language."

"Can you do that?" she asked. By now, she had given up and decided that the best thing was if Tim gave up too.

"I don't see why not. We're all in the EU together. I'm sure when I explain that I want to borrow the money to buy a thriving little hotel on the Costa del Sol, they'll be only to happy to oblige. Particularly since I only need €350,000 and the hotel is worth a lot more than that."

But his hopes of raising the cash from an Irish institution were no more successful. The banks had been badly burned by property investments in the boom years and were in no rush to do it again. One by one, they turned him down.

Tim was forced to accept that it was impossible. There was no way he was going to raise the extra cash they required to purchase Casa Clara.

"I don't suppose there's any chance of going back to Señora Alvarez and trying to get her to reduce the price?" he said to Emma one evening.

"You heard her yourself," she replied. "She's a businesswoman. Even if she has no interest in the Casa, she's not going to give it away. And remember she's probably got Señor Montilla advising her and he's no fool by the sound of things."

"I suppose you're right," Tim said, reluctantly. "But it's an awful pity. You could have done so much with the place."

"Don't let's talk about it," she said. "It was a good idea but it wasn't to be. I think we should put it behind us and move on.

Whatever happens, we'll work out some way of staying together, Tim."

"It just feels so sad," he said.

* * *

Ten days had passed since their conversation with Señora Alvarez. Now that she was busy with her wedding plans, the Señora had dropped her weekly conversation lesson altogether and Emma rarely heard from her. She was left alone to get on with the business of running the little hotel.

She busied herself bringing the accounts up to date, arranging payment of various bills for laundry and breakfast provisions and organising staff wages. They still got paid in cash which meant a trip to the bank and a phone call in advance to let the manager know she was coming. Normally Tomàs accompanied her in the role of unofficial security guard. But it was still a risky business and Emma was always nervous. It would be much simpler and safer to pay the staff wages by cheque. She made a note to mention it to Señora Alvarez.

She tried to remain upbeat but it wasn't easy. Now that she knew the fate of Casa Clara was hanging in the balance, much of the joy had gone out of her job. Despite Tim's presence and his efforts to keep her cheerful, she often felt low. Tim meanwhile, had resumed work on his novel while he waited for word from the London publishers. He was still in hope of selling the book and getting a contract.

One evening after she had finished work and had gone up to her room to get changed, she heard a soft knock on her door. She put down the glass of wine she had poured and opened it to find Mrs Moriarty standing outside.

"I hope I'm not disturbing you," the old lady said.

"No," Emma replied. "I'm just winding down before dinner."

"I'd like to talk to you. May I come in?"

"Certainly, would you like a glass of wine?"

But Mrs Moriarty shook her head. She sat on the easy chair and Emma closed the window and sat down beside her.

"Now tell me what you have to say," said Emma.

"I hope you don't think I'm an old busybody but I've noticed that you're not your cheerful self lately," Mrs Moriarty began. "Is something bothering you?"

Emma laughed lightly in an effort to brush the remark aside. "I've just been working very hard that's all. You might have heard that Señora Alvarez is getting married?"

"Yes, I did hear. It's all over the Casa. All the staff know about it. I also hear that she's thinking of selling the place."

Emma started. Wherever this news had come from, it wasn't from her. She had been scrupulous in keeping the information to herself.

"I'm afraid I can't comment on that," Emma said.

"Quite right too," the old lady said. "In business you have to learn to keep your mouth shut. But I understand it's true. And I think it would be a terrible pity." She paused and her steely eye fell on Emma's face. "I believe you offered to buy it from her and she turned you down."

Emma's face went pale with shock. Mrs Moriarty was like a newspaper office. She seemed to know everything that was going on. She probably knew about Tim and her too, she thought as she tried to compose herself.

"I . . . I . . ."

"Look," Mrs Moriarty said. "You don't have to deny it. And I know it's none of my business but I'm here to help. Now do you mind if I ask you what she is looking for it?"

"A million euros," Emma heard herself say.

"That's a very fair price. I'd say the Casa is worth a lot more. How much did you offer her?"

"We were prepared to go to six hundred thousand. It was all we could afford."

"You and young Mr Devlin? He's in with you too, isn't he?"

"Yes," Emma admitted.

"So you're €400,000 short?"

"That's right. We tried everything we could but we weren't able to raise the money anywhere."

"Can I ask what you intended to do with the Casa if you had managed to buy it?"

"Keep it as it is. We were going to upgrade it of course and install a lift and air-conditioning and expand the catering facilities and paint the whole place from top to bottom. But, basically, the Casa would have remained the same."

Mrs Moriarty's face broke into a smile. "And that's exactly how it should be. It would be a tragedy if it fell into the hands of some developer and he turned it into one of those soulless hotels. Or worse still, built a whole lot of glitzy apartments. Now I hope you haven't given up?"

"But what choice do we have?"

"More choice than you might think. I could lend you the money."

Chapter 37

For a moment, Emma thought she had misunderstood.

"*You* would lend us €400,000?"

"Lend it, invest it, however you like to describe it. I could be what they call a sleeping partner."

"But where would you get so much money?" Emma asked, incredulous.

"From my portfolio, I told you my poor husband Brendan, had put away a little nest-egg before he died. Well, I made good and sure that my thieving family didn't get their hands on everything. I have money set aside for a rainy day. And now I think it has arrived."

Emma's mouth had fallen open. "I don't know what to say."

"You don't have to say anything. I like what you have done at Casa Clara. I'm getting on and I want to spend the rest of my days here. If someone else bought the place, God knows what they might do with it."

Suddenly, Emma was overcome with emotion. She felt her eyes mist over. The old lady sitting beside her was offering a lifeline.

"I'm very grateful. You don't know how much this means," she said through her tears.

"No, my dear, I think I do. You have a dream and I have faith in you. You obviously love Casa Clara as much as I do and I want to see it remain in good hands. Now when do you need the money?"

"I'll let you know tomorrow," Emma said.

"Good. Now that's taken care of, I think I'll have that glass of wine."

* * *

Tim was dumbstruck when Emma told him.

"That's unbelievable," he said. "Mrs Moriarty is the last person I would have thought of as a white knight. How did she know we wanted to buy it?"

"Search me. But I told you that nothing around here escapes her attention."

"Well, all I can say is, I'm glad it doesn't."

The following morning after breakfast, Emma rang Señora Alvarez again. She came to the phone sounding harassed and distracted.

"What is it, *Señorita*?" she snapped. "I am terribly busy right now."

"We have managed to raise the cash to buy Casa Clara," Emma said. "We can pay you a million euros."

There was a sharp intake of breath.

"You have the money?"

"Yes and we would like to proceed. Are you still prepared to sell?"

There was a brief pause.

"If you have the money then I will accept your offer. I will instruct my *abogado* to draw up a contract. I hope you know you are getting a bargain. Only that I am so busy with my wedding plans, I would ask for more. But I know you will take care of the

Casa, *Señorita*. That is what my poor dead Miguel would want."

"So, when can we expect the contract?" Emma asked, feeling the hope and optimism come surging back again.

"It will take a few days. I will speak to my *abogado* at once. But now I must rush. I have an appointment with the priest at two o'clock. What an awkward man. He is insisting on sacred music at the service and I want a tenor to sing the theme song from *Titanic*. Oh, the problems I am having with this wedding!"

There was a click and the line went dead. Emma punched the air.

"Yes!" she cried.

* * *

"You handled the whole thing brilliantly," Tim said afterwards as they were having a celebratory drink at Bar Lorenzo. "It was a masterstroke to play up her dead husband. Now that she's marrying Señor Montilla, she wants rid of Casa Clara but she still feels guilty about abandoning Miguel's legacy. She's concerned about what people will think. You gave her a perfect way out."

"Well, thank God it worked. So what do we do now?"

"The first thing is to hire our own lawyer to handle the legal side. But I can look after that. The next thing is to put our properties on the market as soon as possible. I'm going to ring Barry Moncreif and ask him to suggest a good estate agent. He'll want to have a look at the properties to get a fix on their value. How does he get into your place?"

"My friend Jackie has a key. I'll ring her and tell her to expect a call."

"Good. Señora Alvarez's lawyer will probably want a deposit. I've got some cash in an account in Dublin. I'll get it transferred across."

"I have some too," Emma said.

"Then you should do the same. I'll contact Moncrief this morning and talk to his estate agent."

"And then what?"

"We just have to wait."

He took her in his arms and hugged her. They stared into each other's eyes. Emma could see the excitement radiating from his face.

"I have a good feeling about this, Emma. This time, I think everything is going to work out just fine."

She left the bar as if she was walking on air. Her wonderful dream had come alive again and they were about to purchase the Casa. Her mind filled with thoughts of all the things she planned to do: renovate the premises and expand the kitchen, repaint the building from top to bottom, open a restaurant in the courtyard. With Mrs Moriarty's support all these things were now possible.

She would put Cristina in charge of the day-to-day running of the hotel while she concentrated on the overall management and looked after the restaurant. When they were finished, Casa Clara would be transformed but it would still remain the same intimate little hotel she had fallen in love with.

There were lots of other changes she would make. She would provide packed lunches for those guests who wanted to spend the day on the beach or go off on an excursion. They didn't have to be elaborate: just some filled rolls and fruit and a half bottle of wine. The guests would snap them up. They would be simple to make and would be a sure money-spinner.

She would hire a security guard to patrol the premises at night. Fortunately, they had escaped any major crime but a guard would reassure guests and act as a deterrent to any opportunistic thief. She might open a small gift shop where guests could buy beach items and books and postcards. She might even get special Casa Clara postcards designed.

With all these thoughts tumbling through her mind, she was in jubilant mood as she lifted the phone to ring Jackie.

"It's me," she said when her friend came on the line.

"Emma! You sound in fine fettle. Don't tell me. You've just come back from a refreshing swim in the sea and you're planning a lazy lunch in some quaint little tapas bar."

Emma laughed. "Not quite. I'm a little bit nervous to tell you the truth. There's something going on here which I can't explain right now. What I'm ringing about is the key to my apartment. Have you still got it?"

"Sure. It's safe, Emma. Don't worry."

"I might need you to give it to someone."

"Oh?"

"He's an estate agent. I want him to look it over for me."

She heard Jackie's shocked response. "You're not thinking of selling it, are you?"

"Possibly."

"Does this mean you're not coming back?"

"That's the way it's looking."

At this announcement, Jackie let out a groan. "Oh, Emma, that makes me feel so sad. If you don't come back, what am I going to do? You're my best buddy."

"You mustn't feel like that, Jackie. I have a plan and, if things turn out right, it will be the best thing that has ever happened to me."

"Now you have me intrigued," Jackie said. "What about Tim Devlin, is he still there?"

"Yes. He's involved in this too."

"My God, you sound like characters in a mystery movie. What on earth are you up to?"

"I'll explain everything in due course. Just trust me on this."

"You're not leaving me much choice, are you?"

"Something else," Emma said, lowering her voice. "Have you heard any more from Trish?"

"Now, there's an interesting thing," Jackie replied. "She's gone all silent. She hasn't called me for over a fortnight. Maybe she's given up on you."

"I wouldn't bet on it. But keep me posted. I need to know if she's planning anything."

"Of course, I will. And, Em, let me know what the hell is going on, won't you? The suspense is killing me."

Emma put down the phone with a feeling of satisfaction. No news was good news as far as Trish was concerned. She had so much going on in her life right now that interference from her domineering sister was the last thing she needed.

She resumed her post at reception but the day went crawling by. Now that the prospect of owning Casa Clara was tantalisingly close, she found the waiting extremely hard. She was afraid to make too many plans until everything was done and dusted which was why she had been so coy with Jackie. But she couldn't resist the feeling of levity that had overtaken her since this morning's conversation with Señora Alvarez.

When Cristina came on duty at six o'clock, she commented on it.

"You look so much better, *Señorita*. You don't look sad any more."

"Thank you. I feel better."

"Well I am so happy. I didn't like you being sad. Now you look like a new woman."

Emma handed over and climbed the stairs to Tim's room. She found him on the phone. He motioned for her to take a seat while he continued his conversation. At last, he switched off his mobile and turned to her with a wide grin on his face.

"I've got some good news," he said.

"Tell me."

"I've hired an *abogado*, a Señor Romero and he has undertaken to handle the legal work on the sale once the contract comes through from Señora Alvarez. He assures me if everything is in order, we could have the whole business wrapped up in six weeks."

"That's brilliant," Emma said.

"I've spoken to Mrs Moriarty and she is ready to release the money whenever we need it."

"That woman is a saint," Emma said.

"You can say that again. I've also been on to my bank in Dublin and asked them to transfer my cash to your bank account here in Fuengirola."

"You've been busy, Tim."

"And I'm not finished yet. I have also spoken to Eddie Kane. He's the estate agent who Barry Moncrief recommended. He's with a big agency in Dublin and he seems to know his stuff. We had a very interesting conversation."

"Go on," Emma urged.

"He reckons he should be able to get us the €800,000 we need for our two properties, maybe more. I've worked it out. With the money that Mrs Moriarty is lending us, we'll have enough to buy Casa Clara *and* pay for the renovations."

They both burst out laughing at the same time.

That evening, they went for dinner to La Rueda, a fish restaurant that Cristina had recommended. By now, Tim was in a very excited mood at the prospect of buying the Casa.

"I've been thinking," he said. "When we come to do the restoration work we should build a penthouse for ourselves. We can't continue to live in two separate rooms. What do you say?"

"I think we should avoid making definite plans till the ink is dry on the contract," Emma replied.

"Nonsense, nothing can go wrong. There's no harm in planning. The penthouse doesn't have to be massive. A couple of bedrooms, bathroom, kitchen, comfortable living room and I'm going to need a study where I can work, preferably with a view of the sea."

"And a terrace," Emma insisted, caught up in his excitement despite herself. "It must have a good big terrace where we can have pots of mint and basil and flaming geraniums."

As the meal progressed, they allowed their imaginations to

take flight. Emma planned her restaurant. It would seat thirty people; any more and it would seem crowded. She would design special tables and chairs that would blend in with the surroundings. There was bound to be someone in Fuengirola who could make them for her. She would provide simple Spanish food: a lot of fish, lamb, fresh vegetables and the quality hams and cheeses that were regional specialities.

She would have to get advice about the wines because this was an area she knew nothing about but she was confident she would find someone to guide her. She would upgrade all the rooms and turn the Casa into a bijoux hotel. And when the work was finished, she would bring out a party of travel writers, arrange a programme for them and hopefully they would go home and write nice things about Casa Clara. Jackie could probably help with her contacts in the media.

She would advertise on the internet, stressing the quiet, relaxing atmosphere and the beautiful location. She would build up a loyal clientele who would come back year after year and tell their friends. Word of mouth was the best form of advertising. And every day her beloved Tim would work in his study turning out the literary masterpieces that would make him an acclaimed writer. What more could she possibly wish for?

They drank a bottle and a half of wine and she was slightly tipsy when the time came to pay the bill.

"Is this really happening?" she said to Tim.

"I think so."

"And nothing can go wrong?"

He took her in his arms and kissed her warmly.

"You're a terrible pessimist, Emma. How many times must I tell you? Nothing can possibly go wrong."

* * *

It was almost midnight when they finally got back to Casa Clara. As they approached the hotel, Tim pulled her close.

"Spend the night with me," he whispered.

Emma was sorely tempted. She would like nothing better then to fall asleep in the arms of her lover. But she was aware of the dangers of gossip around the little hotel and the damaging effect it could have.

"Not now," she said. "There'll be plenty more opportunities."

Tim looked disappointed but he accepted her decision, kissed her goodnight and climbed the stairs to his room. Emma decided to sit for a while in the quiet courtyard. It had been a long day and an exciting night. A few minutes beside the soothing fountain would help her unwind.

But she was soon interrupted by the sound of Cristina's voice.

"I'm sorry to disturb you but there is a phone call for you, *Señorita*."

Oh, Emma thought. I wonder who it can be at this hour. She quickly got up and followed her assistant back to the reception desk. She picked up the phone and held it to her ear.

"Hello," she said. "Emma Frazer speaking."

A voice she hadn't heard for a long time came down the line.

"Hi, Emma, this is Trish. I know where you are and I'm coming to see you."

Chapter 38

Emma let out a gasp. Her first reaction was to slam the phone back down again. But Trish was already babbling away in her smug voice as if everything was normal between them. Emma could feel her earlier euphoria melt away. Her sister had finally tracked her down.

"How did you find me?" she asked.

"We'll get to that in a moment," Trish replied. "First I want to know how you are."

"I'm perfectly fine. At least I was till you rang," Emma said, making no effort to conceal her hostility.

"Now, now, that's entirely the wrong attitude," Trish scolded. "We're coming to help you."

"*We?* Who else is coming?"

"Smitty and Colin. They're both very anxious to see you. Everyone has been distracted. You've no idea the fright you gave us by running away like that."

"If I ran away it was because you had made my life intolerable."

"I'll pretend you didn't make that remark," Trish said.

"How did you find me?" Emma repeated. "Who told you I was here?"

"No one told me. It was a simple piece of detective work. I figured you had gone to Fuengirola and Colin and I have been ringing every hotel and guesthouse in the town for the past week. But this evening we got lucky. A very helpful man called Señor Gonzalez in Hotel Bonito told me where you were. Only for him we would have missed you."

Emma silently cursed Señor Gonzalez for an interfering fool.

"Now before you start getting excited," Trish continued. "We're simply coming to have a little chat with you. There's no reason to get alarmed. We just want to sit down and have a quiet discussion about what you are doing to your life. Who else knows you are there?"

"No one."

"Well, if they do, they are certainly keeping their mouths shut. That little friend of yours, Jackie Flynn, swore blind she hadn't heard from you and I had a gut instinct she was lying through her teeth."

Good for Jackie, Emma thought. At least someone knows when to keep their mouth shut unlike Señor Bloody Gonzalez.

"Colin has been very good about all this even though you treated him disgracefully."

"I beg your pardon," Emma retorted, angrily. "Did you say I treated him disgracefully?"

"Yes, you did. As your sister, I feel obliged to tell you that. The poor man didn't know where to turn. Did you never stop to consider the effect that running away was going to have on your friends? People have been worried sick about you. Incidentally, how have you managed to survive?"

"I've been begging on the streets," Emma snapped. "The tourists are very kind. And there's a restaurant nearby that gives me their left-over scraps."

"Don't be funny. This is no laughing matter."

"Who's laughing?"

"Look," Trish said, in a soothing voice. "Let's not get into an argument. Colin and I have had a talk and he's prepared to take you back."

"Really?" Emma replied. "That's very generous of him."

"He accepts that you were under a lot of stress recently and it tipped you over the edge. He is happy to put it all behind him."

"I'm finished with him, Trish. There's no way I'm ever going back to Colin Enright. So, if you come here with him, you'll simply be wasting your time."

"Don't get excited," Trish went on. "We all accept the pressure you've been under with your job and Mum dying and everything. It's my fault for not spotting it sooner. But you'll get over it."

Emma felt like screaming but Cristina was standing just a few feet away so she forced herself to remain calm.

"There is nothing wrong with me, Trish. I'm not having a nervous breakdown if that's what you're suggesting. I'm perfectly sane, I assure you. And until you rang I was deliriously happy."

"Of course you're sane. Nobody disputes that."

"So why don't you save yourself the journey?"

"I'm just coming to see you, that's all. I'm your sister, your only living relative. Now, let's all be rational. We'll be arriving in Fuengirola the day after tomorrow. We'd come sooner only Smitty has an important house sale to close."

So good old Smitty has his priorities in the right order, Emma thought. No point in letting a deranged relative stand in the way of business.

"We've booked into Hotel Excelsior. When would be a suitable time to meet you?"

"How about the year 2020?" Emma said, caustically.

"You really have a weird sense of humour. Are you staying at this Casa Clara place?"

"Yes."

"Why don't we call and see you around twelve o'clock? Maybe we could all go and have a nice lunch together."

"I can't have lunch," Emma said, firmly. "I've got another engagement."

"Oh." Trish sounded disappointed. "Then why don't we just meet and have a chat? We can have lunch another time."

Emma could see that she wasn't going to escape unless she packed her bags and ran away again. Trish was obviously counting on that. Besides, she was tired of running. The time had come to stand her ground.

"All right," she said, reluctantly. "But this is not a good place to talk. Why don't we meet in the lobby of your hotel?"

"That would be excellent," Trish said, with a small hint of triumph. "We'll see you there at one o'clock and we can have a nice friendly talk."

"Okay," Emma said, wearily.

"And Emma, you know we love you?"

It was with a heavy heart that Emma dragged herself up the stairs to bed. All her earlier excitement had disappeared and now she felt exhausted. Once again, her sister's overbearing interference had cast a pall over her affairs.

She snuggled under the sheets and lay for a long time staring at the moon's reflection on the wall. She could sense that she was approaching a crossroads in her life. Events were coming together in a way that was going to impact on her future happiness. And despite being tired, her mind continued to race and it was a long time before she drifted off to sleep.

* * *

She was wakened next morning before seven by the loud shrilling of the phone. Drowsily, she grappled for it and pressed it to her ear. It was old Paco, the concierge.

"I have the *Señora* wishing to speak with you," he said.

"The *Señora*?"

332

"*Sí.*"

By now, Emma was wide awake and sitting bolt upright in the bed.

"Señora Alvarez," she said.

"*Buenos días*, Señorita. I am coming into town this morning on business. I wish to speak with you again."

"Oh!" Emma said, "Right."

"I will be at Bar Lorenzo at eleven o'clock. Can you be there?"

"Of course."

"And Señor Devlin? Bring him too."

"Certainly, *Señora*, I am looking forward to seeing you again."

"*Adiós*," the Señora said and the line went dead.

Emma immediately jumped out of bed and dived into the shower. Ten minutes later, she was banging frantically on Tim's door.

"Who is it?" a sleepy voice growled.

"It's me, Emma. Open up. I've got news."

There was a pause while she heard the sound of keys being turned in the locks. Then the door swung open and Tim was standing there in his boxer shorts and tousled hair. He yawned and scratched his unshaven chin.

"Sorry to waken you so abruptly," she said, excitedly. "The *Señora* just called."

"Oh," he replied, now fully alert. "You'd better come in."

He pulled her inside the room, closed the door and kissed her hard.

"Only way to start the day," he said with a grin. "By kissing a beautiful lady. Now, is it good news or bad news?"

"I've no idea. She just said she would see us at the bar at eleven o'clock. You don't think she's changed her mind?"

"No," Tim said, dismissively. "She doesn't need a meeting to tell us that. She could have told you on the phone. This is something else."

"Maybe she's looking for more money?"

Tim's face underwent a sudden change. He rubbed his hand along his chin. "That could be it. Perhaps Señor Montilla has told her to raise the price." He looked worried for a moment and then he brightened up again. "No," he said. "She couldn't do that. She accepted our offer. She wouldn't go back on her word."

"Are you sure?" Emma said, uncertainly.

* * *

For this meeting, Emma asked Cristina to switch shifts with her so she would have the morning free and her young assistant was happy to oblige. She grabbed a quick cup of coffee at the breakfast buffet then returned to her room and began to get ready.

She decided to wear a navy business suit and white blouse and a pair of sensible shoes. She brushed her hair and applied some lip-gloss. When she finally went down to the hall, she found Tim waiting for her. He had also used the time to get spruced up and he wore a white cotton jacket and slacks and a pale shirt and tie. The stubble of the morning had been shaved away and now his cheeks looked smooth and clean.

They were at the bar for ten to eleven but Señora Alvarez was there before them. She sat at a little table under the shade of a giant umbrella and cooled herself with her fan. On her lap was a smart leather briefcase.

"Good. You are on time," she said as they approached. "I am a very busy woman."

She clicked her fingers and the waiter came scurrying.

"*Tres cortados, por favor*," she ordered then turned her attention back to Emma and Tim.

"I have an appointment with my dressmaker in half an hour," she explained. "So we must be quick. Already this wedding is taking up all my time, so many things to be organised. I swear I will never do it again. Not even for five Señor Montillas." She sighed. "Now, in the matter of Casa Clara, I have given this business much thought. The price you have offered me is not good. I could get twice as much. You are robbing me. I know it. You know it."

Emma felt her heart begin to sink. Was she about to go back on their deal? But her next words raised her hopes again.

"But the money is not my main concern. I must be sure that the Casa remains as my poor Miguel would have wanted. What was that word you used, *Señorita*?"

"His brainchild?"

Señora Alvarez nodded. "Exactly. I like that word. It is so fitting."

At that moment, the waiter returned with the coffees.

"I have been thinking," Emma put in as soon as he was gone. "As a mark of respect to Miguel, we should erect a plaque beside the fountain."

"A plaque, *Señorita*? What is that?"

"A bronze plate. It would have his head on it. And it would explain how he came to build the Casa."

A great big smile spread over the *Señora*'s face.

"But that is perfect. What a wonderful idea, a plague for Miguel."

"A plaque, *Señora*, not a plague."

"Yes, a plaque. *Una placa*. I like that idea. It has style. But I must be certain. I have discussed this matter with Señor Montilla and he agrees with me. If I sell to you, I must insist that you keep the Casa exactly as it is."

"There would be some alterations, Señora," Tim put in. "We are planning certain renovations."

Señora Alvarez waved her hands. "Of course, I was about to do that myself. That is not what I mean. But I must be sure that you will not sell Casa Clara to a developer to build an ugly apartment block. That would break poor Miguel's heart."

"We can give you a guarantee," Emma said.

"It must go into the contract," Señora Alvarez insisted. "There must be no misunderstanding. It must be legal."

Emma and Tim exchanged a quick glance.

"That will not be a problem," Emma said.

"Good," Señora Alvarez continued. "It is a matter that cannot be negotiated. You understand that?" She opened her briefcase and withdrew a sheaf of papers. "I have the contract here and the clause is inserted. If you agree to this, you can sign it and we will proceed with the sale." She gave the contract to Emma. "It is the memory of poor Miguel I am concerned about. He was the most sympathetic man that ever lived." She produced a white lace handkerchief from her sleeve and dabbed her eye.

"He will be remembered, *Señora*," Emma said. "I give you an undertaking that we will erect that plaque. It will be one of the first things we do."

"So, it is agreed."

Señora Alvarez stood up and formally shook hands.

"Goodbye," she said. "Now I must go. Oh, you have no idea the work involved in getting married."

They watched her get into her car and drive away.

Tim turned to Emma.

"We've got the contract," he said, barely able to contain his excitement. "Now we just have to give it to our lawyer. It's all falling into place, Emma. In a few weeks' time we will own Casa Clara."

But Emma didn't completely share his enthusiasm. There was still one dark cloud on the horizon.

Tomorrow, Trish and Colin Enright were arriving.

Chapter 39

Hotel Excelsior was easily the most prestigious hotel in the town, standing right on the promenade and commanding spectacular views over the sea. Emma might have known that her sister would only choose the very best. It was a fitting location for Trish to reside during her fleeting visit to Fuengirola.

The previous twenty-four hours had seen a hectic flurry of activity as the business of purchasing Casa Clara moved into gear. First thing was to get the contract to their lawyer, Señor Romero, who promised to read it carefully. If everything was in order, they could sign it and return the document to Señora Alvarez. He said he would do it immediately. Meanwhile, Tim had been busy contacting Eddie Kane in Dublin to put their properties up for sale. Kane sounded upbeat.

"I'm confident we can sell," he enthused. "I'll start immediately and arrange to get brochures printed up."

They agreed that Kane would keep in regular contact about developments.

"There is some urgency with this," Tim pointed out. "We've agreed to purchase another property here in Spain."

"Relax," Kane assured him. "I'll give it my full attention."

Next thing on the agenda was to check that the funds were being transferred smoothly from Dublin to Emma's Spanish bank account. Señora Alvarez was going to require a hefty deposit. Finally, Emma had to ring Jackie.

"Emma!" she said when she came on the line. "What a coincidence! Liam and I were just talking about you last night."

"So that explains why my ears were burning."

"It's miserable here," Jackie complained. "The weather is dreadful. Don't tell me the sun is shining where you are."

Emma glanced from the window at the little courtyard bathed in warm sunlight. "I'm sorry to disappoint you," she said. "But it is."

"You lucky cow!" Jackie grumbled.

"Listen, Jackie. I need you to do me a favour. I'm selling my apartment."

"So, you *have* decided to stay? You know how I feel about that."

"I'm only in Spain, Jackie. It's not the planet Mars. We can talk on the phone. We can text each other. And you can come out here to stay any time. It's only a couple of hours away. There are loads of cheap flights."

"It won't be the same. What am I going to do? You've no idea how much I've missed you. Who am I going to confide in with you gone?"

"We'll work something out, don't worry. There's a very good reason for this."

"What?"

"Tim and I are buying Casa Clara."

"Tim Devlin and you?"

"That's right – we're going into partnership."

"My God, Emma, I don't believe it. So that was why you were so mysterious?"

"Yes, I didn't want to tell you till it was all official."

"Well, I must say I'm bowled over. Tim and you? Are you like, an item?"

"Yes. I love him, Jackie. I've always loved him. I want to spend the rest of my life with him."

"Oh, Emma, I'm so pleased for you both. It all sounds so romantic. I know you'll be very happy together."

"Thank you," Emma said.

"I'm thrilled to bits. I can't take it all in."

"There are times I can't take it in myself. It has all happened so quickly. My life has been completely turned around in the last few weeks."

"I always knew something good would happen to you, Emma. And now it has. You deserved a break. Now what is this favour you want?"

"I need you to give the key of my apartment to a man called Eddie Kane. He's an estate agent. I'll give you his address. And would you mind going out there and checking it over for me? Just make sure everything is in order? Hopefully, we can expect a lot of strangers to come tramping through it in the next few weeks."

"Of course, I'd be delighted to help you."

"There's one other piece of news. Trish is here."

Jackie gasped. "Oh my God, so she's found you? How did she do that?"

"It's a long story."

"What's going to happen?"

"I'm meeting her. She's brought Smitty and Colin Enright as well. We're going to have a serious talk."

"Are you nervous?"

Emma paused for a moment. "No," she said. "Not in the least."

* * *

For the meeting with her sister and Colin Enright, Emma was determined to look her best. She wanted to impress them, to demonstrate that she was doing well and making a success of her new life. She was surprised how calm and confident she felt. This was an encounter she had long been dreading but now that it had arrived she found she was able to face it without fear.

She took her time getting ready. First, she showered and brushed out her long dark hair then carefully applied a light touch of make-up to complement the rich tan she had acquired since coming to Spain. Her skin shone with health and vitality. When she was finished, she chose a slim black dress that gave her an elegant look.

She slipped her feet into a pair of sling-back shoes with kitten heels and finally glanced in the mirror. Her reflection told her all she needed to know. She looked smart and in control as befitted her role as manager and soon-to-be owner of Casa Clara. When she was satisfied, she went down to the hall where Cristina had already ordered a taxi to take her on the short journey to Hotel Excelsior.

The moment she entered the enormous lobby, she was immediately struck by its magnificence. She had never been here before. Her eyes took in the gleaming chandeliers, the marble floors, the potted palms and spreading ferns, the uniformed bellboys and waiters who went scurrying about like worker bees. Inside here it was blissfully cool, a blessed refuge from the heat of the afternoon sun.

She looked around and immediately spotted Trish, Smitty and Colin seated in a quiet corner with glasses of drinks before them. Her sister had chosen well. The location was the perfect place for the frank discussion they were about to have.

They saw her at precisely the same moment. Trish stood up at once and waved.

Emma took a deep breath, summoned her courage and marched across the floor to meet them. As she approached, she could see the reaction on their faces. If they were expecting some sad, bedraggled, creature they were disappointed. The Emma who now stood before them radiated poise and confidence.

"Thank God, we've found you at last!" Trish said, wrapping

her arms around her and hugging her tight. "Oh, you've no idea how pleased we are that you are safe and well. We were worried sick."

"There was no need," Emma replied. "I told you I was perfectly fine."

Colin and Smitty had put down their glasses and were now standing up too. Emma nodded to them, smoothed out her dress and took a seat beside them on the plush sofa.

By now, Colin was staring at her as if he couldn't comprehend the startling vision that had appeared.

"Can I get you something to drink?" he asked.

Emma shook her head. She was already outnumbered three to one and she wanted to be entirely clear-headed for what promised to be a difficult meeting.

"So how have you all been keeping?" she asked, turning confidently to them.

Colin appeared furtive, like a man with a guilty conscience. Otherwise, he looked much the same as she remembered him, still handsome in his linen jacket and chinos and an expensive shirt open at the neck. Smitty, meanwhile, was grinning as if he was enjoying this encounter and the opportunity to escape from work for a few days in the sun.

But Trish had changed dramatically. She was dressed in a grey business suit but it couldn't disguise the rolls of flesh that had accumulated around her midriff and hung in loose folds from her chin. She looked as if she had put on at least half a stone in weight in the four months that had passed.

"We are quite well under the circumstances," she replied, focusing a stern, motherly eye on Emma. "You've no idea the worry and stress you've put us through. We didn't know whether you were alive or dead. As for that poor supervisor at work, Ms O'Brien, she is totally convinced that you've gone completely off your rocker."

"You needn't concern yourself about my employers," Emma

replied coolly. "As for my health, I'm perfectly sane I can assure you."

"Well, you haven't behaved like a sane person," Trish retorted. "Just dropping everything and bolting off like that. Did you never pause to think of the pain you were leaving behind?"

"I thought of the pain *I* was suffering and the pressure you were putting me under. Did *you* never pause to think of that? You left me no option but to flee."

Trish looked aghast.

"Don't try passing the blame onto other people. That decision was entirely your own."

"Well, if it was my decision why don't you just accept it? Why are you continuing to harass me? Why can't you simply leave me alone?"

Trish glanced nervously at the others and bit her lip. "Look, we didn't come here to have an argument. The main thing is we have found you again and you seem to be okay." She ran her eye once more over Emma. She was obviously impressed by what she saw. "What exactly are you living on? Did you transfer money from your Irish bank account or something?"

"I have a job at Casa Clara. It's the hotel where you rang me."

"What do you do there? Serve tables?"

"I manage it," Emma said.

Trish could barely conceal her surprise. "You manage it? But you've no experience at that sort of thing."

"I've no experience in lots of things. Since I left school I've led a very sheltered life. But I'm learning quickly."

"Do they pay you well?" she asked, scrutinising Emma's elegant dress and shoes once more.

"They pay me well enough and I have free board."

"Well, at least you haven't been living rough and sleeping on the street like we feared. Now the point is, it's time to come home. You have made your protest and we've taken it on board.

Colin is prepared to forgive you and take you back. Despite everything you have put him through."

"Yes," Colin said, adopting a martyred look.

"And Ms O'Brien says if you write a letter of apology she thinks you might be able to save your job. Everybody is prepared to forget this unfortunate business. We're here to bring you back to Dublin where you belong."

"Isn't there something you are overlooking?" Emma asked, coolly.

"What?"

"I don't want to go."

For a moment, they all looked stunned. Then Smitty giggled and Trish prodded him in the ribs to silence him.

"Don't be silly," Trish said. "You can't stay here. This place is okay for a holiday but you can't live here. What about your apartment in Blackrock?"

"It's going on the market. I'm selling it."

Trish let out a gasp and Colin looked shocked. Smitty stopped smirking and immediately became serious.

"Selling it? It's a beautiful apartment."

"I won't be needing it again," Emma explained. "I've decided to make my home here."

Trish looked aghast. "But what are you going to live on?" she demanded. "You can't run a hotel, for God's sake."

"You don't understand. I'm buying the hotel. I'm going to own it."

For the first time in her life, Emma saw her sister lost for words. She opened her mouth but nothing came out.

"You're buying it?" Colin asked, incredulous. "What are you using for capital?"

"I'm using the proceeds from the sale of my apartment. I've agreed a price with the present owner. I've received a contract and it's now being processed by my lawyer."

Trish and Colin exchanged anguished glances.

"Who's selling it for you? Have you got an agent?" Smitty put in, sensing a business opportunity now that the shock had worn off.

But one look from Trish silenced him.

"This is utterly ridiculous," she said, finding her voice at last. "I've never heard of such a madcap scheme. Now I know you're off your head."

"It's not madcap," Emma said. "It's been carefully thought out and it will work."

But Trish was in no mood to listen. She seemed to have made up her mind.

"You may look sane, but this is just further evidence that you've gone completely bonkers. I'm your sister and I'm not going to stand by and watch you make a total mess of your life. You're coming back to Dublin with us or I'll get a psychiatrist to have you committed."

She made a move to take hold of Emma's arm but at that moment a commanding voice stopped her.

"Leave her alone."

They all turned to see Tim standing behind them. He had come in unobserved. He went to Emma, drew her up and put a protective arm around her shoulder.

"Who the hell are you?" Colin demanded, his face red with anger.

"My name is Tim Devlin. I'm Emma's business partner. I take it you are Colin Enright?"

"That's correct."

Tim turned to Trish who was staring at him in consternation. "And you are Emma's sister?"

"Yes."

"I think we have met before," he said. "At St Benedict's Secondary School."

Trish looked closer till recognition slowly began to dawn on her face. "I remember you. You used to teach us."

"So I did. And I recall you were a very bright student, Trish. That is why I hope you will see some sense and stop this silly persecution of your sister."

They looked at each other. Nobody seemed to know what to say.

"Emma and I are in love," Tim continued. "She's not insane. She's not suffering from a nervous breakdown. In fact, she's saner than any of you. She has taken control of her own life at last. She has found something that will make her happy. We both have. We are buying Casa Clara between us and we're going to make it our home."

He kissed Emma softly on the cheek.

Trish tried to reply but Tim silenced her once more.

"We appreciate your concern and the fact that you have come out here thinking you were going to help her. But she has just told you that she doesn't want to go back to Dublin. She's an adult and she can make up her own mind. And if you persist in harassing her, you will leave us with no option but to report the matter to the police."

At the mention of the police, a worried look immediately came over Colin's face. He glanced quickly at Trish.

Tim turned to Emma. "Is there anything you want to add?"

"No," she said. "I think you've said it all."

His strong arm tightened around her shoulder.

"In that case, if you will kindly excuse us, we have important business to attend to."

Chapter 40

Thankfully, the plane from Dublin was on time. Emma had checked the arrivals board and Jackie had already sent her a text to say they had just spotted the Spanish coastline like a piece of jigsaw puzzle shimmering in the white heat below. In a few minutes' time, they would be touching down at Malaga airport.

Emma turned to Tim who stood beside her at the gate of the arrivals hall.

"I'm so excited," she said. "It's almost a year since I saw them. Oh, Tim, I can't wait!"

He grinned. "Just a few minutes more."

"How are things back at the Casa?"

"Everything is in order. I left Cristina in charge."

"No better woman."

"And Tomàs and Teresa are taking charge of the catering. I think you can relax and welcome your friend. Everything is under control."

Today was the official reopening of Casa Clara. And to mark the occasion, Señora Alvarez, now officially the wife of Señor

Montilla, had consented to unveil a bronze plaque to the memory of her beloved Miguel.

After months of frantic activity, when Emma and Tim sometimes wondered if they would ever see the end of it all, the work had been completed. Eddie Kane had kept his word and the properties in Dublin had been sold while their solicitor, Señor Romero, had made sure that the purchase of the Casa had gone through without a hitch.

But the builders had almost broken their hearts. No threat could intimidate them and no bribe could seduce them. They seemed to work to their own timetable. And to make matters worse, while the renovation was taking place it had been necessary to move Mrs Moriarty and Major Sykes to emergency accommodation in Hotel Bonito. From there, they launched daily broadsides about the inferior standards of Señor Gonzalez.

But finally, after numerous delays, they had got the work finished. Now all the rooms had been redecorated in bright, airy colours, a brand new air-conditioning system had been installed and a glistening silver lift stood in the front hall beside the reception desk to whisk the guests effortlessly to their accommodation.

At the very top of the building, several rooms had been knocked together to make a commodious penthouse apartment with stunning views across the ocean and this was now Emma and Tim's private quarters. To compensate the Major and Mrs Moriarty and to reward her for her support, they had been allocated refurbished rooms on the top floor, next door to each other.

But it was the bright, new kitchens and the spanking restaurant that had caused most excitement. The staff had watched with intense pride as they slowly took shape and now they were ready. Emma had hired a brilliant young chef straight from catering college to work with her and together they had started planning menus. Just yesterday, the rustic furniture she had got specially designed had arrived and now she was itching to get started.

And then, smack in the middle of all the building work, she had received a call from Trish. The months since her disastrous visit had brought about a change of heart.

"I want to apologise," she began. "I was wrong about you. It appears you have finally grown up, Emma."

Emma knew this was a big concession coming from Trish. Her sister didn't apologise easily.

"I accept your apology," she said.

"I've decided you are quite right to strike out on your own with your hotel. That Civil Service job was going nowhere. I admire your initiative."

"Thank you," Emma replied.

"And I think you've done the correct thing about Colin Enright. I was wrong about him too. He's a bit presumptuous. I think you know what I mean."

"What happened to him?"

"The last I heard he had taken up with some old girlfriend. We've sort of lost touch. But you've got a good man there in Tim. And like I've always told you, they're getting thin on the ground. I know you're going to be very happy together."

Emma could feel herself beginning to thaw a little towards her sister.

"Anyway, Smitty and I want to wish you well with the Casa. We're family, Emma. We're all that's left of the Frazers. We should be friends."

"I agree," Emma said.

"I got it wrong. You can't live other people's lives for them. I know that now. But I want you to know that I always had your best interests at heart."

"Let's put it behind us," Emma said. "Do keep in touch."

She was glad of that phone conversation. Her rift with her sister had been preying on her mind. Trish had been capable of great kindness down through the years. But she had gone overboard in her attempts to control Emma's life even if she had meant well. Hopefully, she had genuinely learnt from the experience.

And then, to cap their good fortune, Tim had received a message from his publisher friend to say that they were very excited about his novel and wanted him to come to London to discuss a contract. But that would have to wait till after the official opening and the sudden, unexpected decision by Jackie and Liam to come out and visit. Jackie had hinted on the phone that she had a special piece of news to deliver. Hence Emma's excitement as she waited now in the arrivals lounge for her friends.

She laid her head on Tim's shoulder.

"Thanks for everything," she whispered. "Without you, I'd probably be back in that boring office in Dublin dealing with Mr Angry from Castleknock about his pension payments. That's if they had taken me back."

Tim shrugged. "I played only a very small role. I think you were going to leave anyway."

"But without you, I would never have bought Casa Clara."

He smiled. "Who knows, maybe you might have met some other partner?"

"I don't think so, Tim. You were always the only man for me."

His lips nuzzled her ear and moved closer to her throat.

"Not here, for Heaven's sake," she protested, pushing him away. "You'll get us arrested for indecent behaviour."

Just then, the arrival of the Dublin flight flashed up on the board. Emma felt her excitement grow. The big thing she had missed most in the months she had been living here was the opportunity for a good old natter with Jackie. Emails and phone calls were no substitute for the real thing. But now she was going to have an entire week to catch up on all the gossip.

Ten minutes later, the gates opened and the first passengers began to stream through. Emma craned her neck to look for her friend and then she spotted her, strolling serenely beside Liam who was already sweating from the heat as he struggled with a trolley loaded with three bulging suitcases.

"Let me look at you!" she shrieked, rushing forward to embrace her friend in a great big hug of welcome. "You look fantastic. How was the flight? How is everybody back in Dublin?"

"One question at a time," Jackie laughed, finally freeing herself from Emma's grasp. "I'm feeling fine. The flight was smooth. And everyone in Dublin was okay the last time I checked."

She turned to Tim.

"I remember you," she said, sticking her fists in her waist and assuming an aggressive pose. "You used to give me dreadful grades for my English composition."

He laughed and gave her a hug.

"You didn't read enough books, Jackie. That was your problem."

Emma introduced Liam and Tim helped him to push the groaning trolley outside into the searing heat where a taxi was thankfully at hand.

"Will there be a big crowd for the opening?" Jackie asked, as she squeezed in beside Emma on the back seat.

"We're not expecting the Mayor or a brass band, if that's what you mean," Emma explained. "It's mainly staff and residents and some of our suppliers. But these are our real friends, Jackie. These are the people who stood by us in the last few months when times were tough. And that's why I'm particularly pleased to see you and Liam."

"All I did was send a few emails and try to keep Trish at bay."

"You did more than that. You gave me vital support when I needed it. And I don't forget these things."

"Get away with you," Jackie said. "You'll have me weeping into my fresh make-up."

The Casa was coming into view. The cab pulled up and Tim paid the driver while Emma led the group inside. The foyer had been remodelled with a larger reception desk and a new telephone and computer system and a little shop selling souvenirs and beach ware. Jackie stood for a moment as her eyes took in her surroundings.

"This is marvellous. Exactly as I pictured it from the photos you sent me. Who is that?" she asked, pointing to a large photograph of a friendly, weather-beaten face that smiled down from the wall.

"That's Miguel Ramos, the man who is responsible for Casa Clara. He is the reason we got the Casa so cheap. I made a promise to his widow to dedicate the place to his memory."

"What a lovely thing to do!"

"Shortly we are going to unveil a plaque to him out in the courtyard."

Old Paco appeared to help Liam with the suitcases and Emma used the opportunity to whisper in her friend's ear.

"When am I going to hear this special news?" she asked. "I'm bursting with curiosity."

"When I'm ready," Jackie said, with a wicked grin.

Emma led her friend out to the courtyard. It looked brilliant in the lush afternoon sunlight. Tables and chairs had been laid out and already a small crowd was gathering. The smell of grilling food wafted out from the kitchen and Tomàs and Teresa circulated with trays of drinks.

Jackie let out a cry of approval when she saw it. "It's absolutely beautiful! Just look at that gorgeous fountain and the cobblestones and the lovely flowers."

"This was the first sight I saw when I arrived," Emma explained. "And immediately I fell in love."

"Why wouldn't you? It's fabulous."

By now, more people had arrived. Mrs Moriarty and Major Sykes were already seated at one of the tables sipping glasses of sherry, the Major resplendent in his regimental blazer.

"Jolly good show," he said when he saw Emma. "Place looks absolutely bull's eye."

"And I'm glad those damned pneumatic drills have finally stopped," Mrs Moriarty muttered. "They had the life scared out of poor little Granuaille. She must have thought the Third World War had broken out."

At the mention of another war, the Major immediately sat bolt upright.

But at that moment, there was a flurry of excitement near the door and the crowd parted to allow Señora Alvarez to make her grand entrance. She was wearing a tight-fitting dress and high-heeled shoes. Her hair was combed into a knot and a large rose was pinned above her ear. Her fingers glittered with rings. Trotting in her wake, a plump middle-aged man in a sober suit was taking in the scene with a professional eye. She made straight for Emma.

"Señorita Frazer, let me introduce my husband, Señor Montilla."

"Delighted to make your acquaintance," Señor Montilla said as he took Emma's hand and gently kissed her fingers.

"Have you now settled into your new home?" Emma inquired.

Señora Alvarez threw her flashing eyes to heaven. "You have no idea the work I have to do. Eduardo, he cares only for business. But me, I have so much to do." She gave Señor Montilla a disapproving glance and he blushed with embarrassment. "And the staff they are so lazy."

"No doubt you will soon bring them into line," Emma replied.

Señora Alvarez looked confused.

"Into the line, what does that mean, *Señorita*?"

"It means discipline. You will quickly let them know you are the boss."

"Ah, but of course. Already they know who is the boss. It is me. Isn't that so, Eduardo?"

"*Sí*," Señor Montilla replied, meekly.

She stroked his cheek. "But what do I care? I am so happy. My little Eduardo is so kind to me."

Emma diplomatically changed the subject. She pointed to Tomàs and Teresa who were ferrying the trays of drinks from table to table.

"Did you know they are also getting married in a few weeks? Their house in Carvahal is finally finished."

"I am so happy for them," Señora Alvarez said. "They are such a nice young couple. And I must say you have made a wonderful improvement to the Casa, *Señorita*. Now it is a fitting erection to my poor dead Miguel."

"Monument," Emma quickly corrected her.

"Yes, monument, I am so touched by this gesture. If he was here now, he would weep with joy."

Beside her, Señor Montilla shuffled uneasily.

"I too am pleased," Emma said. "Now I must make a little speech. And then, if you are ready you can unveil the plaque of Miguel."

She tapped a glass with a fork until the babble of conversation died away and everyone fell silent. Then, she cleared her throat.

"Thank you all for coming," she said. "Today we celebrate a very special occasion – the reopening of Casa Clara!"

Tim came and stood beside her. He reached out and took her hand.

"For me, this is a dream come true," Emma went on. "I cannot think of anywhere else where I would be so happy. I want to thank all of you for making it possible. And now I would ask you to charge your glasses and join me in a toast."

Tomàs and Teresa had reappeared with bottles of *cava* and were filling up the glasses.

"To Casa Clara!"

"To Casa Clara!" they responded.

"And now, Señora Alvarez has kindly agreed to unveil a plaque to her late husband, Señor Miguel Ramos, the man who first conceived of Casa Clara."

The *Señora* sniffed and approached the little curtain. She pulled a cord and the curtain parted to reveal a bronze plaque fastened to the wall. The crowd applauded and a flash bulb popped.

Emma gazed out over the sea of happy faces as the sun spread its light over the little courtyard. Everyone seemed to be present; old Paco, Rosa, Cristina, Tomàs, Teresa, Major Sykes and Mrs Moriarty, Señora Alvarez and Señor Montilla, Jackie and Liam. And beside her, the man she loved and would spend her life with – Tim Devlin. She felt an awkward lump rise in her throat.

To cover her emotion, she turned to Jackie. "Now what is this news you've been keeping from me?"

Jackie lowered her head and looked sheepish. "I'm pregnant," she whispered.

Emma gaped in astonishment. "*What?* I don't believe it."

"Yes," Jackie confirmed. "Two months. We're planning to get married in March and you're going to be my bridesmaid. And I've just decided something else. Can we book Casa Clara for the honeymoon?"

THE END

If you enjoyed *Casa Clara*
by Kate McCabe why not try
Forever Friends also published by Poolbeg?
Here's a sneak preview of Chapter One.

Forever

FRIENDS

KATE McCABE

POOLBEG

Prologue

Maddy wished people would simply forget about her birthday and let it slip by unnoticed. Despite all the upbeat talk about fifty being the start of her golden years and an achievement to be celebrated like winning the Nobel Prize for Literature, Maddy knew what it really meant and she didn't want to be reminded of any of that stuff.

She still felt young and energetic. She jogged every morning before breakfast. She ran her property company with considerable success as the rising profit graph continued to confirm. She was an active member of her local Chamber of Commerce and the Rotary, as well as being a keen gardener and past-President of Sutton Ladies' Golf Society. And on top of all this, she still found the time to be a full-time wife and mother. In fact, she had all the energy and enthusiasm she had possessed all those years ago when she was in her twenties and life had stretched before her filled with abundant promise. So why should she want to celebrate growing old? As her fiftieth birthday approached, Maddy fervently hoped there would be no fuss or fanfare. But she reckoned without her daughter, Emma.

Emma was her eldest child. At seventeen, she was already shaping up to be a younger version of her mother. She had Maddy's tall, elegant bearing, her luxuriant black hair and dark flashing eyes. And she had inherited much of her mother's organisational flare and drive. It was Emma who suggested they have a quiet family dinner in the Ambassador Hotel to celebrate the event and Maddy had jumped at the idea. A quiet dinner would be perfect and then she could put the damned birthday behind her and get on with the rest of her life.

The ballroom should have warned her. Whoever heard of a quiet dinner in a ballroom? But it wasn't till she actually walked through the doors that she realised what was happening. There must have been a hundred people there, neighbours and business colleagues and old friends and relations all sitting round these big tables, their faces aglow with anticipation and goodwill.

And the moment she entered, the band started to play and they all stood up and began to sing 'Happy Birthday to You' while Maddy blinked in amazement and her jaw fell open. That was when she had finally understood she had been outwitted. If there hadn't been so many witnesses she would cheerfully have strangled her daughter on the spot.

When they had finished singing, the guests burst into a round of applause and Emma gave her a great big hug and presented her with a bouquet of flowers and her son Jack pushed a giant card into her hands that had been signed by everyone in the room. Next thing she knew, they were popping champagne corks and people were coming up to congratulate her and tell her that life began at fifty and the best was yet to come. Maddy had no option but to smile and try to pretend that she was thoroughly enjoying herself.

But the birthday celebrations weren't about to end with Emma's party. Just this morning she had received a surprise email from her friend Rosie to say that she had organised further festivities – this time in London. The third participant was to be

360

another old friend – Sophie Kennedy. The three women had known each other since their schooldays and all their birthdays fell within a couple of weeks of each other. So Rosie was proposing a joint fiftieth birthday party, just the three of them. *It's going to be a blast,* she had written. *Looking forward to seeing you again and talking over old times.*

Maddy couldn't wait to go. It had been so long since she had seen them – twenty years in the case of Sophie whom Rosie had managed to track down to Paris where she was living with a young painter half her age. Rosie herself had settled with her family in a cottage in Cornwall where she was growing vegetables and raising chickens and making her own wine while her husband held down a senior accountancy job in a nearby town. It would be lovely to meet and talk once more. Indeed, the more she thought about it, the more she realised that this was one birthday celebration she was definitely going to enjoy.

The odd thing was, when she was younger, Maddy had always looked forward to birthday parties, particularly her own. They gave her the opportunity to be the centre of attention and to wear a pretty dress and boss people around for a few hours. She got birthday cards and presents and, as a bonus, her guests had to invite her to their parties in return. But once she turned twenty-one, her interest began to fade. For one thing, the birthdays seemed to roll round an awful lot faster and they just served to remind her that time was rushing by and she was getting older. For another thing, she was beginning to develop the abhorrence of fuss that would stay with her for the rest of her life. She didn't like it when attention was focussed on her or people singled her out. She preferred to remain in the background and let others hog the limelight. And that was where she might have remained had Greg Delaney not entered her life and changed it so dramatically.

Chapter 1

Maddy was twenty-five and Greg was twenty-eight when they met. She was tall and handsome with the type of figure that film critics described as statuesque. She was working for the busy auctioneering firm of Carroll and Shanley whose offices were in Ballsbridge in the heart of Dublin. It was a job she loved even though the hours were long and the pressure was hectic. But there was an adrenalin buzz about her work that compensated for all the drawbacks. Whenever she negotiated a successful property sale, Maddy felt like someone who had just won the jackpot at the roulette tables in Las Vegas.

It was through her job that she first encountered Greg. He was an investment analyst for an up-and-coming stockbroking company and looking to buy his first home. Their initial contact was a simple phone call one Thursday afternoon in May when Greg rang to say he wanted to buy a house and wondered if Carroll and Shanley could help him. Purely by chance, Maddy took the call.

"Do you have anything particular in mind?" she began.

362

"Not really. I'm wide open to suggestions. I thought perhaps you might be able to advise me."

"What sort of price range?" she continued, hoping for some guidance as to affordability.

"I don't mind splashing out," Greg replied, "provided I get the right place."

Maddy hesitated. Most people knew exactly what they wanted but this Greg person sounded as if he hadn't got a clue. She would need to get more information from him before she could proceed.

"Look, why don't you come in and we can sit down and have a chat? That's probably the best thing. When would suit?"

They agreed on Saturday morning and Greg turned up promptly at ten o'clock, driving a smart black BMW sports coupé. Maddy brought him into her office and asked if he would like some coffee. While she poured, she couldn't help noticing what a handsome man Greg was. He was about six feet tall with fine blond hair, broad shoulders and an infectious smile that spread all over his face whenever he got enthusiastic.

"Do you have *any* idea what you're looking for?" she began.

"Well," he said, stretching his long legs and glancing out the window where the morning sun was sparkling off the forecourt, "I'm single so I don't need an absolutely massive place."

Maddy filed this information away like a good spy.

"However," he continued, "I do a lot of work from home and I have loads of files and stuff so I would need a spare bedroom. And I'd like to be close to the city. Our offices are in Dame Street and it would be handy if I lived within driving distance."

"Plus it would be more convenient for socialising at weekends," Maddy added, just to test his reaction.

"That's right. I do quite a bit of socialising." He gave her a friendly grin.

But Maddy was busy taking notes.

"I'd prefer something new," he went on. "And another thing,

I want a property that will hold its value just in case I need to sell it again at short notice."

"That makes very good sense," Maddy replied, "but I think you'll find that property is a rock-solid investment. Let me ask you something." She leaned back and played with her pencil. "Have you ever considered an apartment?"

He stared at her as if she had suddenly sprouted a second head. Apartments were a novelty in Dublin. Most developers were still concentrating on three-and four-bed houses with lawns and garages.

"Er . . . no."

"There are big advantages for someone in your situation," she continued. "You don't have to worry about garden maintenance for one thing. They are mostly owned by single people so you don't have the problem of noisy children. Not that I have anything against families," she hastened to add.

"Nor me. But I hear what you're saying."

"Apartments also tend to be more private. They have guaranteed parking. And they're very secure."

"What if I wanted to sell it again?"

"That wouldn't be a problem. Between ourselves, I think apartment living is the coming thing. And because they are high-rise, many of them have fabulous views." She decided it was time to deliver the *coup de grâce*. "And if you buy now, you would be able to have the pick of the crop."

His eyes brightened immediately and he sat up straight. "So what are we waiting for? Have you anything to show me?"

"I have several," she said, smiling broadly into his face.

The first place was not far from her office. She suggested that she drive and Greg follow in his BMW but he had a better idea.

"Why don't we use my car? No point bringing both."

"Okay," she said, settling into the passenger seat and thinking how nice it must be to own a fancy car like this.

364

The property was a large three-bed apartment on the second floor of a modern building in Monkstown and it boasted underground parking. It was a resale. Greg looked disapprovingly at the heavy, old-fashioned furniture that cluttered the rooms, tapped the walls once or twice, turned on the taps and flushed the cistern in the bathroom to make sure the plumbing was functioning properly.

"I was thinking you could use one of the bedrooms as an office," Maddy suggested. "That would still leave you a spare bedroom if you had guests to stay."

"How old is it?" he wanted to know.

"Only two years."

"So why are they selling?"

She could sense that he wasn't interested. "It was bought by a retired couple and then unfortunately the husband died."

"Oh, dear."

"Yes, it's sad. The widow is going back to live with her daughter."

Greg nodded. "You couldn't persuade her to take the furniture with her?" he said, with just the faintest hint of a smile.

The next apartment was in Ringsend in a large block fronting onto the river. That was its good feature. Its bad feature was that from the outside it looked like a prison, with rows of tiny little windows gazing sadly out on the road.

"This whole area is scheduled for a revamp," she said encouragingly. "It's going to be totally redeveloped. In a few years' time, it will be so chic that everyone will want to live here."

Greg just grunted as she showed him into the master bedroom.

"And it's practically in the city centre," she rattled on. "Yet the postal address is Dublin 4. Best address in the city. Guaranteed to increase in value."

But he didn't seem to care about the address. She could tell by the speed with which he inspected the rooms that he wasn't impressed.

"What else have you got to show me?" he asked, as she followed him out of the flat with a sinking heart.

The final property was a penthouse in Sandymount, down near the sea front. It was in a brand-new gated development called rather grandly The Beeches. When they arrived, the gardeners were busy installing a rose garden in the central courtyard. Maddy opened the front door and took him up in the lift. As soon as they entered, they found themselves in a spacious hallway, the sunlight flooding in from the big wide windows and lighting up the whole apartment.

"Wow," he said and gave a soft whistle of approval.

"Nice, isn't it?" Maddy said.

"It most certainly is."

It was a beautiful apartment – two bedrooms, one en-suite, large lounge, fitted kitchen, pine floors, pastel walls. Everything smelled of fresh paint.

"You could do a lot with this place," she went on. "Put your own stamp on it. With some nice settees, a few cushions, rugs, a couple of striking pictures for the walls, it would look fantastic."

He immediately turned to her. "Do you know about décor?"

"A little," she confessed.

But it was the terrace which took his breath away. It opened off the lounge and was paved with dark red tiles. Greg immediately walked out and peered from the balcony. In one direction, they had spectacular views across Dublin Bay to the gentle slopes of Howth Head. In the other, the teeming city lay stretched out before them, the rooftops gleaming in the bright morning sun.

"Imagine having breakfast out here," Maddy said. "Or a glass of wine in the evening with the sun doing down."

"It's fabulous," Greg said. "It's like something out of a Hollywood movie."

"Apartment living," Maddy replied. "Get the picture?"

They went back inside where Greg examined the appliances in the airy kitchen, inspected the bathroom and went back several times to the bedrooms. He appeared to be making some calculations. Maddy decided it was time to shut up and let the apartment speak for itself. He was clearly impressed. Any further sales talk would run the risk of making him wonder if she was hiding something.

At last, he turned to her. The playful mood was gone and now it was down to serious business.

"How much is it?"

"Eighty-five thousand pounds."

She waited for his reaction. Eighty-five thousand pounds was an awful lot of money to pay for an apartment. But he didn't flinch.

"I assume there are also management fees to pay."

"Yes. Four hundred pounds a year but that takes care of insurance, maintenance and security."

"Have you had any bidders so far?"

"There is one other interested party but no firm offer."

"Hmhhh," he said and ran a hand across his chin. "Let me go away and do my sums."

"Sure. Take your time."

"If you get an offer in the meantime, come straight back to me, okay?"

"Okay, Mr Delaney."

"And one other thing. Stop calling me Mr Delaney. My name is Greg."

By now, Maddy had sufficient experience of the property market to know that Greg was *seriously* interested. Wednesday arrived and she hadn't heard from him. This wasn't unusual. It took time to organise a mortgage and sort out finance. But by the end of the following week when she still hadn't heard, she began to wonder if he had changed his mind. And the other interested party hadn't contacted her either. She began to think that the property might remain on her books for a little while longer.

And then, on the following Monday afternoon, the phone on her desk rang and she heard his voice on the line.

"Hi," he said. "It's me again – Greg Delaney. Sorry it took so long but I had an awkward bank manager to convince."

"Tell me about it," Maddy trilled. "Some of them react as if you were asking for their fingernails."

"Why stop at the nails? This guy sounded as if I wanted his whole hand." He laughed lightly. "Anyway, I'm now in a position to make an offer."

"Be my guest."

"What do you think the developer would say to £79,000?"

"There's only one way to find out," she said. "I'll put it to him right away and get straight back to you."

She put down the phone and smiled to herself. Now the play was about to begin. It was like a game of poker. This was the bit that Maddy really enjoyed although it required skill and steady nerves.

She rang the developer with the offer. She wasn't surprised when he turned it down. The apartment was brand-new and the promotional campaign hadn't even got under way yet. But the developer did give her a base figure that he *would* accept.

Greg sounded disappointed when she called back to tell him.

"I'm on a tight budget," he complained. "You know I've got stamp duty and legal fees to pay on top of the purchase price. And then I've got to furnish it."

"But it's a unique property," she said. "I'll bet my salary it will start appreciating the minute you close the sale."

"All right," he sighed. "Let me see if I can squeeze some more money out of the bank."

He rang again two days later to increase his offer to £82,000.

"You're still £3,000 short of the asking price."

"Yes. But I also have to eat. If I go any higher I'll be living on baked beans for the next few years."

He put the phone down, sounding gruff and annoyed. Maddy could sense that his competitive instinct was now aroused and he wanted to win. But she had a duty to get the best price for her client.

She left Greg to simmer for a few days while she concentrated on other properties in her portfolio. She knew it would increase the pressure on him and it made her feel a little callous. But they were now locked in serious negotiations which left little room for sentiment. On the third day, he rang again. It was a bad mistake. It meant he had blinked first.

"Any news on my offer?" he asked, sounding testy.

"Not good news, I'm afraid."

"You mean they've turned it down again?"

He sounded shocked.

"I'm afraid so."

"Shit," he said, in exasperation. "This developer sounds like he's a real hard bastard."

"Well, he's not St Vincent de Paul."

"Look," Greg said, letting out a long sigh. "Just give it to me straight. What do you think it would take to swing it?"

"Another thousand."

"Are you absolutely sure? I've already invested a lot of time and energy on this venture and I don't like to be given the run-around."

"I'll tell you what," Maddy said. "Make me an offer of £83,000 and I'll personally recommend it."

"It's my final offer," Greg said reluctantly. "If this doesn't work, I'm walking away."

"I understand. Just leave it with me."

She put down the phone and rubbed her hands in triumph. She felt that warm glow that gamblers feel when their bluff has paid off. Half an hour later, she was back on the line to Greg.

"We've got a deal," she purred.

"Well, thank God for that. Now when can we sign the contract?"

She could hear the relief in his voice.

Everybody was pleased with the price Maddy had achieved including the developer and her boss, Tim Lyons, but principally Greg himself who was convinced he'd just pulled off the property coup of the year. But there were a few more weeks to wait while the legal and administrative work was completed. He rang her almost every day to find out how the sale was coming along.

By now all the tension had gone out of their relationship. Whenever they spoke on the phone, the conversation was light and cosy. Maddy began to grow quite fond of Greg and looked forward to the sound of his voice. But she was totally unprepared for the bombshell he dropped in her lap a few weeks later.

It was a bright, sunny afternoon in June. She was getting ready to take some clients to view the apartment in Ringsend which was proving stubbornly difficult to shift, when the phone on her desk began to ring.

"Yes," she said.

"Hi, it's me, Greg."

"Oh, Greg, how are you?"

"On top of the world if you want to know. I've just left my solicitor's office after signing more pieces of paper than I've ever seen in my life before."

"So the sale has finally gone through?"

"Yes and now I'm the proud owner of a prime piece of Dublin real estate!"

He sounded like a little boy with a new train set. She could hear the enthusiasm bubbling down the phone line.

"I'm absolutely delighted for you."

"Not as delighted as I am," he replied. "I'm going out this evening to celebrate. I've booked for dinner at the Chalet d'Or. And since you helped me to buy the apartment, I'd like to invite you to join me."

◆

If you enjoyed this chapter from

Forever Friends by Kate McCabe

why not order the full book online
@ www.poolbeg.com

See page overleaf for details.

◆

Also published by poolbeg.com

THE
Beach
BAR

KATE McCABE

PEDRO'S BAR in Fuengirola on the Costa del Sol is a hotspot for
holidaymakers enjoying sun, sea, sand and fun. For years it has been run
by local woman Maria who rarely sees the Irish owner from one summer
to the next. But things are about to change.

Now Maria has an assistant, Kevin Joyce from Galway. He is escaping the 'trap'
of his family's business in favour of working in the sun, and he's not the only
one. Maria had better get ready because more Irish are about to touch down in
this seaside paradise.

Emma Dunne, a successful businesswoman from Dublin, spent her twenties
running her father's printing company with plenty of hard work but little fun.
Now she has a reason to celebrate as she takes over the ownership of Pedro's
Bar, but has she been given a poisoned chalice? Mark Chambers, a successful
advertising executive, has come to Spain to overcome a personal tragedy and
find a reason to enjoy life again. And Claire Greene who, much to the chagrin
of her mother, passed over a legal career to sell Spanish
property, has some unfinished business to deal with.

Each hopes Fuengirola will give them a new lease of life, but they
soon get more than they bargained for.

ISBN 978-1-84223-263-7

Also published by poolbeg.com

THE *Book* CLUB

KATE McCABE

Looking for a way to pass the cold winter nights — and take her mind off her lying ex — MARIAN HUNT decides to start a book club. And pretty soon, it begins to take off ...

CHRISTY GRIMES thinks the book club will help his beloved wife in her recovery from a stroke, but little does he know the effect it will have on him.

LIZ BRODERICK hopes the book club will distract her from her grief. But a greater distraction than books lies in store.

Caught up in working hard to support his ex-wife, MATT BOLLINGER reckons the book club will be a good way to meet new people. But while romance beckons, sabotage is not far behind.

Disgraced poet NICK BARRY is in search of the perfect story to relaunch his career, and he expects the book club will be the perfect place for some market research. But Nick finds a bigger story than he bargained for.

With sadness, joy, money, sex, betrayal — and a few novels thrown in for good measure — those cold winter nights are about to heat up ...

ISBN 978-1-84223-315-3